M000211743

THE PROSPECTORS

THE PROSPECTORS

A Novel

ARIEL DJANIKIAN

WILLIAM MORROW
An Imprint of HarperCollins*Publishers*

This is a work of fiction. Names, characters, places, and incidents are products of the author's imagination or are used fictitiously and are not to be construed as real. Any resemblance to actual events, locales, organizations, or persons, living or dead, is entirely coincidental.

HarperCollins books may be purchased for educational, business, or sales promotional use. For information, please email the Special Markets Department at SPsales@harpercollins.com.

FIRST EDITION

Designed by Nancy Singer

Map by Virginia Norey
Title page art © Archivist/stock.adobe.com

Library of Congress Cataloging-in-Publication Data has been applied for.

ISBN 978-0-06-328973-4

23 24 25 26 27 LBC 5 4 3 2 1

For Gregory and Alysa, most trusted of guides

Oh, they scratches the earth and it tumbles out,
More than your hands can hold

—"Klondike," Canadian folk song

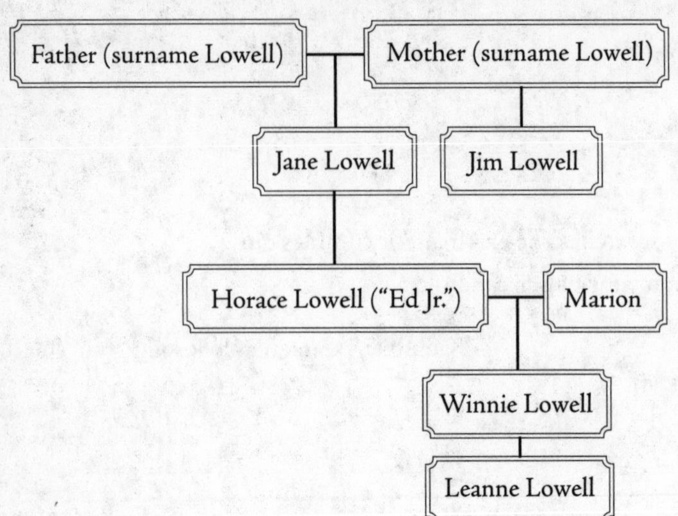

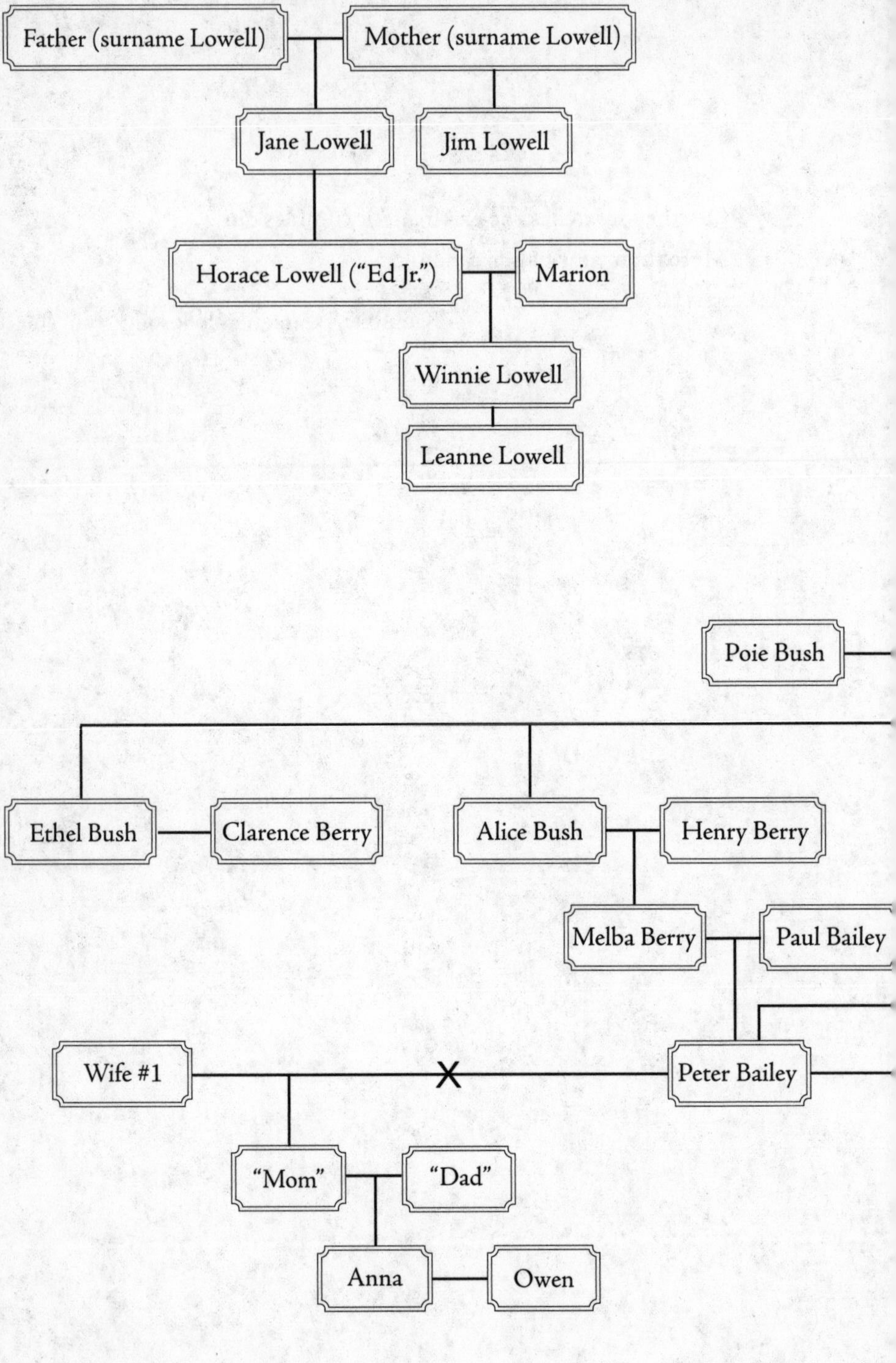

Father (surname Lowell)
Mother (surname Lowell)
Jane Lowell
Jim Lowell
Horace Lowell ("Ed Jr.")
Marion
Winnie Lowell
Leanne Lowell
Poie Bush
Ethel Bush
Clarence Berry
Alice Bush
Henry Berry
Melba Berry
Paul Bailey
Wife #1
Peter Bailey
"Mom"
"Dad"
Anna
Owen

PARTIAL FAMILY TREE OF BUSH, BERRY, AND LOWELL FAMILIES

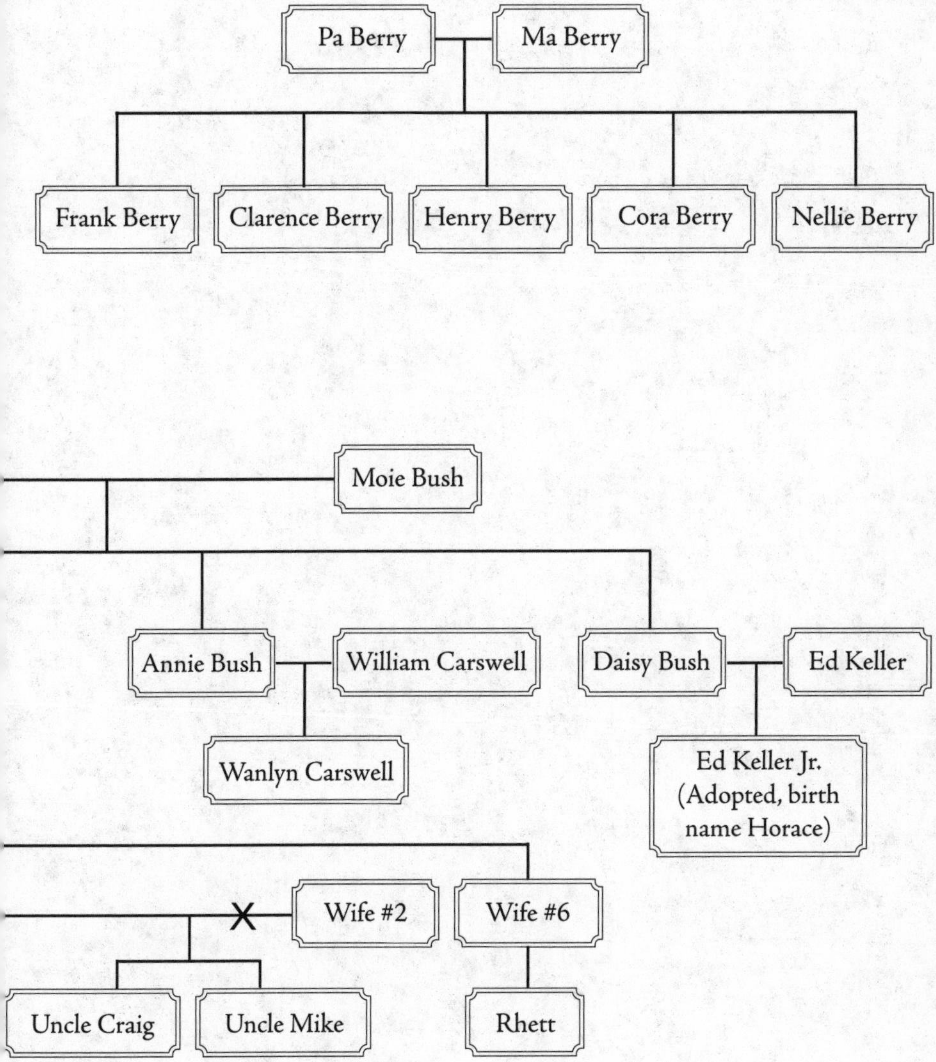

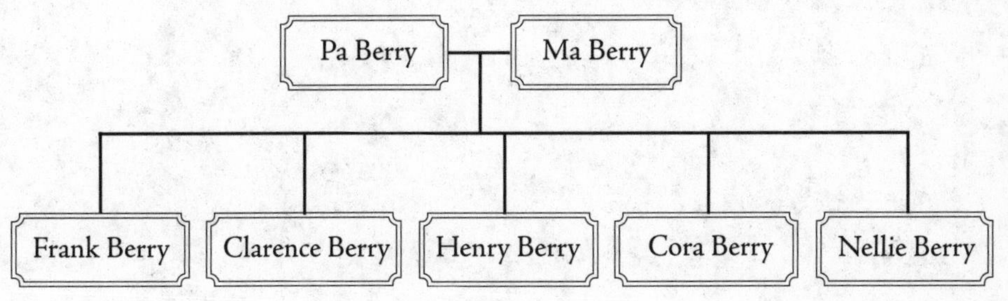

Pa Berry
Ma Berry
Frank Berry
Clarence Berry
Henry Berry
Cora Berry
Nellie Berry
Moie Bush
Annie Bush
William Carswell
Daisy Bush
Ed Keller
Wanlyn Carswell
Ed Keller Jr.
(Adopted, birth
name Horace)
Wife #2
Wife #6
Uncle Craig
Uncle Mike
Rhett

THE PROSPECTORS

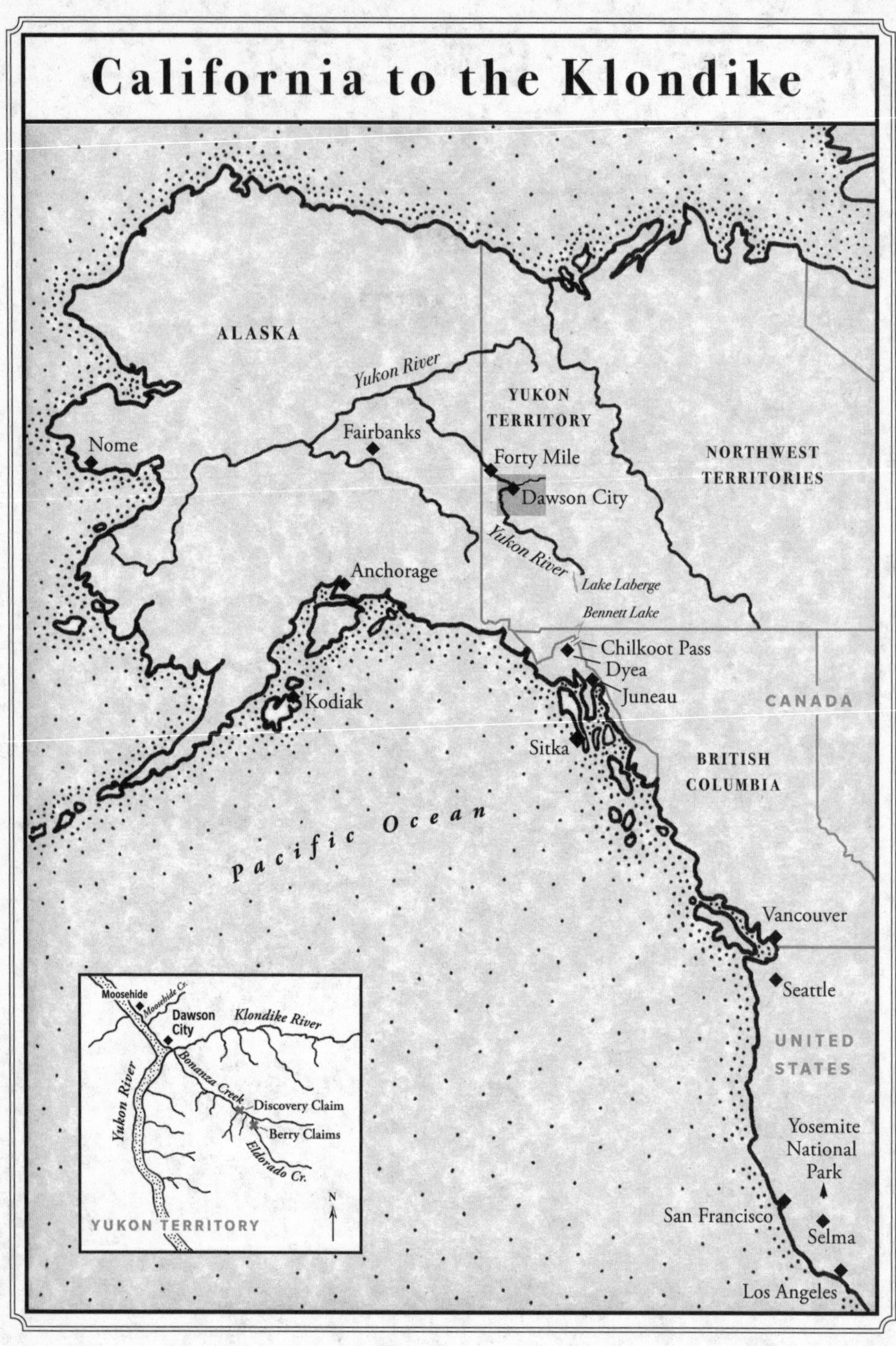
California to the Klondike
ALASKA
Yukon River
YUKON
TERRITORY
Fairbanks
Nome
Forty Mile
NORTHWEST
TERRITORIES
Dawson City
Yukon River
Lake Laberge
Bennett Lake
Anchorage
Chilkoot Pass
Dyea
Juneau
CANADA
Kodiak
Sitka
BRITISH
COLUMBIA
Pacific Ocean
Vancouver
Seattle
UNITED
STATES
Moosehide
Moosehide Cr.
Dawson
City
Klondike River
Bonanza Creek
Yukon River
Discovery Claim
Berry Claims
Eldorado Cr.
N
YUKON TERRITORY
Yosemite
National
Park
San Francisco
Selma
Los Angeles

PROLOGUE

KLONDIKE

1898

In the narrow attic, Alice crouched under a sloping roof, one hand lightly balanced against a rough, burlap bag of gold. The low voices of her sister and brother-in-law wafted below, mixed with the calls of sparrow and wren, until finally sweeping out of the house. She waited, then pushed the rope ladder so that it dropped and struck the lumber floor and descended rung by rung from her perch. The front door had been propped open, and the whole cabin was drenched in white light. No one had slept. Probably no one had gone to bed. The bench and chairs were askew at the table. Last night's bottles stood out, as well as a scatter of small cloudy glasses. The area under the bench was filthy with those mud patties that the boots carried in; and of course, later it would fall to her to clean them. Her head turned slowly toward the empty view of the claim.

What world was this? In the last year, it had kept changing on her. It wouldn't hold still long enough for anyone to answer the question.

She drifted toward the big outside, grabbing a straw hat off the iron peg and pushing it onto her head without pausing. The workers had taken their season's pay and left the pale flapping tents across the creek mostly abandoned. On the bank, in fact dangerously close to the fast-moving water, was a forgotten pan, dull tin and slightly concave, almost exactly the breadth of her hat. A toppled pile of pay dirt sat on a square of canvas next to the sluice. With a farm girl's intolerance for a half-finished job, she dug out a handful of dirt and dropped it into the pan. She scooped in creek water and, in a motion the workers had thought it a lark to teach her, twitched the pan around until the grayish water began to fly off the edge.

A bright spot flashed in the cyclone, then another. She stopped her motions only once the water was gone. With a practiced precision, she touched her fingertip to the largest sliver of gold that was stuck to the base. Pure money transferred itself onto her skin. A thrill. They'd traveled two thousand miles for this, into a treacherous land that was theirs and not theirs, in order to take a piece of metal and, as she was doing now, drop it assuredly into a pocket. Her eyes shot up. Across the creek, Clarence Berry, her brother-in-law, was making his way from his workers' tents. His big round face was clenched and glum, and his thumbs were tucked into the two red lines of his favorite suspenders. Last night he had sprung at her and bullied her into retreat. She'd never felt a hate like that, though it was also proof, she had thought, of his own mounting uncertainties. Joining him now, descending the naked hill, was her sister, Ethel, taking careful steps on the incline. Unlike her husband, Ethel was alert to Alice's presence, and her gaze caught quickly on the hunched figure at the water's edge.

"Alice, come here. We want to talk to you."

But the benefit of the wide land, the whooshing wind, the fast-moving creek, a sister's weak voice: she could neglect to hear what she did not want to hear.

So, with sleeves sopping and heavy and with gravel crunching under her boots, Alice left the pan on the sluice and crossed claims *Three* and *Four* until she'd reached the pit marked *Five*. Ahead, on a bare part of ground and before the ragtag brush, was the low, tilting shed that stored the winter tools. She stopped, then took one more tentative step toward the shed's ill-fitted door. Last night, Clarence had told her, there's a man inside that shed. He'd meant to say, there's a body inside that shed.

A breeze rippled the water and bent the tallest weeds. They could not undo what was already done, though maybe other small cruelties, which were accruing at such a pace that she could hardly make sense of them—perhaps those could be subdued. She stayed very still. Her head and neck were poised in that special way of a mind about to make a decision. I need to stop, she thought. Then, as if in a twinkling: but I don't think I can stop. She could feel in the heat of the sun the growing warmth of a lush and opulent if otherwise hazy future. She thrust a hand into her pocket and, seeking its power, pinched the sliver of gold between finger and thumb.

1

AHWAHNEE HOTEL, YOSEMITE NATIONAL PARK

2015

My grandfather was a wealthy man. For most of his life, he didn't feel guilty about it. Wealth, he believed, was simply something that had happened to him, as bad luck or hardship could have also happened to him. From the outside, it was easy to see how money had formed him into a self-aggrandizing, domineering, and charming if recklessly inconsiderate person. But he wouldn't have viewed it like that. Instead, he'd drifted through life accepting good fortune the way a person might step out the front door, in temperate Southern California, accepting another decade of spectacular weather.

When he called one afternoon in mid-May to ask if my husband and I could pay him a visit, there was something tense and halting in his tone that made me guess there was more he wanted from us, and my first instinct was to answer evasively, even before hearing the details, already on guard.

"We'd love to, Grandpa," I said, saving a biochemistry problem set on my laptop, and speaking over the blare of car music outside. "We're a little busy right now with work and school. But first chance we get. Maybe late June."

At my dodge, though, he was indignant.

"June?" he cried. "How about Friday?"

He had an urgent matter to discuss, he went on to explain. The conversation had to be in person and it could not wait. Really, I didn't want to go anywhere. I was nearing the crucial end-of-semester exams week and already feeling behind. But it wasn't easy to say "no" to my grandfather, not in the least because he happened to be the person footing the bill for the very master's program that was causing my current anxiety. I spun in my desk chair. I raised my eyebrows, looking across the sun-streaked and cluttered apartment at Owen, who met my gaze from over the dreary stacks of high school essays that he was grading.

"Can we do it?" I whispered, holding the phone away.

A hollow sound: Owen's pen tapping the top of his papers.

"It's not convenient," he finally answered, resigning himself. "But for him, I guess we can manage."

I swiveled around again. Outside, a light turned green, and the traffic moved forward.

"All right," I said into the phone, forcing a cheery tone. "Change of plans. We'll drive up this weekend."

From there, though, only more stipulations. My grandfather didn't want to meet us at his ranch near Fresno, where he lived with the irascible woman I thought of only as "Wife Number Six," but rather at the Ahwahnee Hotel in Yosemite Park, the beloved place of his boyhood vacations, and where, he told me next without a hint of bashfulness, he'd already booked a weekend stay for the three of us.

That Friday, on the wings of a prayer that our declining Toyota Corolla could manage the six-hour drive, Owen and I made our way out of Los Angeles through bright landscapes host to almond orchards and strawberry farms, past rows of tall, swinging oil pumps like herds of mythological creatures dipping their heads to take long thirsty sips from the earth. The route brought us along narrowing roads to shadowy hills of firs, sequoias, cypress, juniper, and dogwood. At seven o'clock, we reached the hotel, and stepped into a world that existed on a scale totally different from the human-made, human-sized spaces we usually occupied. We were tired, bleary-eyed, but alive with the simple enthusiasm of young people happy to be somewhere new.

We walked across the pine-needle strewn parking lot and into the lobby of the Ahwahnee, where we were so awed by the majestic architecture, the dark and stately lodge furniture, that we almost missed the sudden appearance of the tall, elegantly mannered, white-haired man, Peter Bailey, my grandfather, who was striding out of the gift shop at just that moment, carting four brown bags overloaded with purchases.

During the drive, I'd been nervous. Even at age ninety-three, my grandfather was a volatile person, and you could never guess what mood he'd be in. But he appeared to us in high spirits, if not boldly amused with himself. He shook Owen's hand, kissed my cheek—"Hello, Anna, good to see you, dear"—then led us to a wide leather couch in the lounge area, where he began to unpack, apparently for our benefit, what must have been two thousand dollars' worth of merchandise.

"Here's a beauty," he said, making a grand show of freeing a glass-and-iron hurricane lantern from its brown paper wrapping. "Tell me how you like this."

In addition to the lantern, he'd bought three decorative baskets, a purse with a braided handle, and a green-and-black Kachina doll, small mouth turned down and arm raised and thrusting a staff. There was also a set of painted bowls, a turquoise bracelet, a pair of wooden serving spoons with bone handles, and a large, stained-glass ornament of an orange sun that you could hang in a window.

To our great surprise, my grandfather announced that these were gifts for us, and began handing them over with an affectation I'd noted in him before: a somewhat off-putting mixture of pomp and self-deprecation.

"These are long overdue," he said, "and I'm sorry for that. Missing your wedding was one thing. But then I completely forgot to send you a present."

It was true that, due to a recent diagnosis of congestive heart failure, he had missed our wedding last fall. The flight cross-country to Philadelphia—the city where Owen and I had met during college, and where most of our friends had stayed on—had been deemed too risky for him. But as I reminded him, delicately, a little afraid of rattling him, he'd already sent us a lovely card and also a check that had covered our honeymoon plane tickets and seven nights at the Hotel Fontana, overlooking the Trevi Fountain in Rome.

"My God, I forgot," he said, slapping his forehead. "I did do that, didn't I? How extremely generous of me." Then, recovering himself, and motioning at the bag I was holding, his eyes merry: "In that case," he teased us, "hand it all back. These presents should go to somebody else."

The hotel had a restaurant, with several available tables. Owen and I were about to bring the brown bags and also our overnight duffel upstairs, when my grandfather intervened and told us to let the bellhop do it instead, as he was hungry now and wanted to eat. I pointed out that Owen and I should probably change into something more suitable than T-shirts and jeans, but my grandfather waved away this idea, and seemed to find it proof of a fussiness that he did not condone.

So on through the lobby and into the dining room, which was even fancier than what I had feared, with its gleaming table settings and high walls and iron-black chandeliers. I wasn't used to places like this. Owen was in his second year of teaching tenth-grade civics at Katella High School in Anaheim. I was in my first year of the master's program in environmental science and ecology at UCLA, a degree that I was hoping to parlay—I couldn't say exactly how—into some bright future work involving carbon capture and storage. It was true that, in Los Angeles, Owen and I couldn't help but live in proximity to extreme wealth, but the experience was more of several economic worlds, all layered on top of each other, with only the rare jump like a quick streak of light crossing between them.

As we sat down at the immaculate table, I felt deeply uncomfortable. I was sure that Owen felt deeply uncomfortable. Though my grandfather, also in blue jeans, did not seem to perceive the faux pas.

Was it possible, I wondered idly, while trying to conceal my legs beneath an oversized napkin, fashioning it into a kind of skirt, to reach a point of feeling so superior that no misstep in the social world can embarrass you?

My grandfather didn't open his menu. Instead, he beckoned the waiter to his side, and said in no hurry:

"Let me ask you something, do you have prime rib back there? Do you have Brussels sprouts?" While the waiter took notes, my grandfather described in detail the meal he expected to see on his plate. He raised one arthritic finger, and said, "Here's what you're going to do . . ."

The waiter left at a clip for the kitchen. Meanwhile, Owen, who had grown up the son of socialist-leaning Macy's salesclerks in Queens, New York, said softly, in a voice that rang with horror: "I've never seen someone order like that."

At this time, I was twenty-seven, recently married, and so—when my grandfather was not immediately forthcoming about his reasons for bringing us here—it felt natural for me to fill in the conversation with anecdotes from that happy event. Though it quickly became clear that my grandfather couldn't have cared less about our wedding, and it wasn't long before he was looking askance, taking a long sip of his scotch, and seemingly ready to broach the matter for which he had summoned us. He cleared his throat into his fist, and said finally, in a voice grave and stentorious:

"Now as you know, I asked you here for more than just the food and the hiking. This isn't easy for me to say, but I've been talking to some of the family about it, and it's time you kids should know too." Owen lowered his glass, and I did the same. We were both in suspense. "The truth is that—" my grandfather's voice cracked as he forced the words through. "The truth is that I'm dying."

I found myself at a complete loss as for how to respond. My grandfather was ninety-three. His heart was failing. Was he expecting this news to be a surprise? I glanced at Owen, who met my eyes only briefly, maybe afraid that a longer look between us would betray something unseemly.

Finally I got a grip on myself. I put my hand to my grandfather's arm. I said, "No, Grandpa. Don't talk like that," as if to admonish him for having said something cruel.

"But I am, I am," he said, brave and resolute. "I'm not thrilled about it. I'd be very happy to live another ten years. Twenty years. Why not? Of course no one in the world agrees with me. They think that when you hit ninety, you should make your exit without complaining. It's all right, dear," he said, patting my hand away. "The end is coming and I've looked it in the face. I've put my things in order. The houses are clean and organized. Your uncle Craig is already taking care of the dogs. I've gone over my will so many times that the lawyers finally wrenched it away from me. They say I'm like a Renaissance painter who can't put down his brush."

He paused. Then wiped his napkin across his chapped, pale lips. His expression narrowed slightly.

"But there's one thing I'm unhappy about," he said. "That damn will involved a lot of compromise, to put it lightly. And the balance didn't end up quite right. It takes care of my wife and her kids"—Wife Number Six, he meant, and her two middle-aged sons—"and it's got a little something in it for my own kids and all you grandchildren"—he had a total of six children from his four middle marriages, fifteen grandchildren, and two great-grandchildren, by my last count—"but there's one person I was forced to exclude," my grandfather continued, "and I'm still pretty damn furious with myself for giving up on this point."

I was pretty sure I knew what was coming. Through multiple channels the gossip had reached me that my grandfather had been in a months-long battle with Wife Number Six over the issue of writing a certain near-stranger into his will: a Tlingit-Hän woman from the Canadian North, whose inclusion—a robust biological progeny was bad enough—would be an insult to her position that Wife Number Six had sworn she could not bear.

"Winifred Lowell," my grandfather said, confirming my guess. "If I have any unfinished business in my life, it's with that woman. We never did right by her and her family. *I* never did. And before they're handing out the poker chips and I'm room temperature, God knows I would like to do right."

Again, although his passion ran fresh, my grandfather's confession did not completely knock me out of my seat. I'd already heard from my relatives about his growing obsession with the Lowells, a family who, in 1898, and very unpropitiously for them, had clashed with my own maternal ancestors, the Bushes and Berrys, during the Klondike Gold Rush. Lately, my grandfather's ruminations (and this gossip was from my relatives too) had folded all the way back to his own great-uncle and benefactor, Clarence Berry, who had left a dried-out fruit farm in the San Joaquin Valley of California to follow the rumor of gold in the North. There, after several years of prospecting, and against million-to-one odds, Clarence had obtained claims on a lucky creek, hit a prosperous vein, and become widely known as the King of the Klondike for all the gold he'd dug up.

"My great-uncle Clarence was a savvy businessman," my grandfather explained to us now, answering our warm requests for clarification—*what did he mean exactly, about never doing right by the Lowells?*—"and I have to credit the man for his nerve. But it's also the case that the whole damn Berry clan and half of California stampeded into the Yukon without a thought for who or what might be harmed in the process. Winnie's grandmother, a Native Canadian by the name of Jane Lowell, worked one summer on the Berry claims, and from what I know of it, the poor woman never recovered from the experience. The details have been lost to time, but her brother died in a horrific accident involving none other than Clarence himself, I'm extremely sorry to say."

"That's terrible," Owen responded. For Owen, it was the first he was hearing of this. For me, given the recent talk of the Lowells, it was actually a bit of family history that had lately passed through my mind, though admittedly not in the many years prior. Probably Owen and I would have said more, but at that moment the waiter arrived with our dinners. It was seafood pasta for me and lemon-caper tilapia for Owen, and prime rib for my grandfather, which he sampled and deemed passable before, not bad-naturedly, waving the waiter away.

"When I was twenty," my grandfather told us, picking up where we'd left off, "I had that same realization. My own grandparents' generation had begun to die off, and my mother inherited the bulk of the family fortune. But what do you know? No sooner were we being flooded with our rightful inheritance than the genius notion started growing in me that the whole thing was unfair. And the more I came to learn about the roots of the money, all the way back to Clarence's big gold discovery, the more I became convinced that we owed this Lowell family some kind of restitution. My parents thought I was nuts, but a couple years later, 1944, right in the thick of the fighting, I was with my LST off the coast of Alaska when I managed to maneuver myself to the Navy base in Sitka. One weekend, I showed up at the house of a Native Canadian fellow named Ed Lowell who was none other than Jane Lowell's grown-up son. My idea was to pay off this fellow's mortgage. Something flashy like that."

"That's nice," I offered, pausing over my meal, "I never knew that." But my grandfather shook his head in response.

"I got about one step into the house before the family figured out who I was and kicked me out, and the wife—Marion, I think her name was—told me in words I won't repeat to mind my own business."

He laughed a small, sad laugh, toward a long row of dark chandeliers.

"They had a daughter though," my grandfather continued, shooting a conspiratorial grin to Owen that Owen did not feel compelled to return. "A spunky, very pretty young woman named Winifred who didn't think I was so bad. After my run-in with her parents, Winnie came to meet me at the Navy base. We went out dancing together two or three nights. Imagine that, proverbial grandson and granddaughter of the gold rush era, spinning and flouncing around. We wrote to each other while I was off in the Pacific. That was the era of love letters, and we were both more than happy to play our parts. We kept in touch, even after we both got involved with other people. I visited her while she was living in Juneau a couple of times. I think the last time I saw her was when she came to LA when we were both about fifty. She was newly divorced then and had her daughter in tow. I remember I offered her a bit of financial help, and she made a joke I found very fresh at the time, about being owed more than a thousand dollars or two, and in response I called her an ingrate or something horrid like that."

"Oh no," Owen said.

"You don't have to tell me." My grandfather leaned over the table and absentmindedly cut several rough bites of steak. For a moment, I sat watching him eat. I hadn't realized the extent of my grandfather's involvement with the Lowells, and with Winnie especially, and I began to wonder what else I was missing. Finally he put down his fork and resumed speaking, now in a deeply serious tone. "We were in and out of touch after that. Honestly, I had enough women in my life to keep me busy. Six wives one after another is a job on its own. Then I got my diagnosis, and it was like the faces of my dead relatives and the whole Lowell family came flooding back into my head. You're too young to understand this, but when you're nearing the end, you're able to see the shape of your life and the people who shared it with you with a new kind of clarity. Unfortunately I'm not sure I like what I see, is what I'm trying to say. I had the chance to set one small thing right with Winnie, and even that I messed up."

He shook his head, and I had the feeling that he was wondering at himself, at his own remarkable instincts.

"Ed and Marion Lowell must be long dead," he said. "I'd like to think that Winnie's alive. She was a few years younger than me. If not, then we can probably track down her daughter. The point is, it's never too late to do the moral thing. Lucky for procrastinators like me. If Sylvia"—Wife Number Six—"really cannot stand for me to write the Lowells into my will, I'll give them the money now."

WITH SURPRISING RAPIDITY, MY GRANDFATHER next unleashed for us the nitty-gritty of, not his feelings, but the details of his brokerage accounts. For the last several months, he'd been moving money around. He had built a secret account from various Morgan Stanley investments, to the tune of three and a half million, that he was ready to transfer to Winnie or her descendants—with the slight complication that he hadn't been in touch with Winnie for decades and had no leads on a current address.

By this time, I was feeling weighed down by the rich dinner, the long day of travel, but even through my fog I was finally starting to understand why my grandfather had invited us here (announcing his imminent death had only been his warm-up) and what he was expecting from us.

A breath later, details began spilling forth, while my thoughts raced, playing catch-up with time. He needed addresses. Signatures. Notarized forms. Then he was discussing the plane tickets he was ready to purchase for a pair of fresh-faced upstarts who might like to help him out on this mission. I was sure that I'd been very specifically targeted. My mother had been his rebel child among a slew of more conservative siblings, and he'd always seemed to view me, not incorrectly, through that particular lens. As for him, he told us now that we were the only people he trusted for the job. We were young, he said, with a good social sense, and boasting the kind of newfangled political leanings he'd guessed would make us look alive at anything involving—what did people call it? he asked—ah, yes, "the redistribution of wealth." He hadn't forgotten, he told us, that ambush last Christmas during our annual family gathering when we'd talked his ears off about higher realized gains taxes, environmental protections, and—I kept expecting him to wince—the need for federally funded, universalized healthcare.

"So, refresh my memory, please," my grandfather said at last, tilting back in his chair. "I sent you lovebirds to Italy, did I?"

"We're so grateful," said Owen, clearing his throat, speaking over the last bites of his ravaged tilapia. "We took a million pictures."

"Well, Rome's a great place," my grandfather said. "And the Trevi Fountain is breathtaking. But I think you'd enjoy a bit of rugged adventure, after all that living in luxury."

OWEN AND I AGREED TO the trip. We did it helplessly, almost against our will. Just like we had agreed to this meeting. We said, yes, we will travel to the Yukon and track down the Lowells. We said, if not in quite so many words, yes, we will help you move money from a place of abundance to a place of probable need, so that when you die, and you soon will die, you can do it with the sense of loose ends tied up, and good deeds finally done.

I heard myself say, "We'd love to go, Grandpa."

I heard Owen say, "I can't think why not."

I heard my grandfather say, giddy, "It's a *relief* to do it. Isn't that funny? Look at me. I couldn't be happier."

By the time the caramel cake and crème brûlée and chocolate mousse were finished, the basic arrangements were settled. A few dates in June had been laid out for our choosing. Questions of passports and money and hotels had been posed and responded to.

The bill for dinner arrived in a thick leather pouch. Owen and I both reached for our wallets, and my grandfather had his biggest laugh of the night.

THEN MY GRANDFATHER STOOD, TESTING his knees, holding the table. Now he wanted a whiskey at the bar, an adjacent room with an impressive six-foot stone fireplace and a roaring, massive fire within. I followed several steps until, thanks to a couple of cues, including his bidding me good night, it dawned on me that my grandfather, who lived according to the social norms of a previous era, expected to have an after-dinner drink with my husband alone. As for me, a young lady, he assumed I should now skip off to bed. Usually I would not acquiesce to such ludicrous sexism. But he was so old, my grandfather. It didn't seem worth it to teach him a lesson. And so, humoring him, standing in for the female ghosts of his youth, I rose on tiptoes, kissed his cheek, spoke a few cheerful words, and, turning quick on a heel, marched off toward the elevator.

An hour later, I was curled in the soft, massive bed, reading my phone, when the door to the hotel room burst open and Owen strode in, still reeling from what had been asked of us.

"My god, Anna, your grandfather is obsessed with that family," Owen said, pulling off his shirt and talking to me from the foot of the bed. "He can't wait to send us up there. He wants to book us the flights over breakfast tomorrow. It's a little unsettling."

"We can back out," I said, sitting up against the headboard and dropping my phone to the bedside table.

My mood, since dinner, had grown subdued. Instead of studying, I'd spent the quiet time alone reading about the Klondike Gold Rush. Though hardly a blip in the story of American history now, it was the phenomenon that had bestowed the words "Klondike" and "Yukon" with the romantic aura that still clung to them today. Historically, it was a summons—and this I did know a bit about—that had brought tens of thousands of prospectors charging into the Canadian North to try their luck in what was, as seems obvious now, a blatant and unrepentant pillaging mission.

Then, in this stately room, with a growing awareness of my moneyed surroundings, of the Kachina doll in a bag on the floor, I'd looked up the Ahwahnee Hotel and come upon information to match my forebodings. These very grounds in fact had once been the home of the Ahwahneechee, a group of Native American survivors who'd retreated deep into the Yosemite Valley during the genocidal violence that accompanied the founding of California. The Ahwahneechee leader, Tenaya, was the namesake of the lake we planned to hike to tomorrow. But—and I'd had no inkling of this, and found both the story and the hiddenness of the story deeply disturbing—it turned out that the lake had been named after him, not in his honor, but as a taunt. A band of newly minted Californians, the Mariposa Battalion, after killing Tenaya's young son and seizing the camp, had promised to call the lake after him to mark the destruction of what the man had tried to preserve.

"I can tell you're having second thoughts," Owen said to me now. He balled up his T-shirt and stuffed it into the side of our duffel bag.

"I am. I feel like my grandfather bullied us into this."

"Do you want to tell him we changed our minds?"

"No. But not for his sake. If he wants to give this family a chunk of his money, I don't want to be the reason it doesn't go through."

"He has you pegged." A loving grin, only slightly pitying. "Do you know what your grandfather called you at the bar? A rigorously ethical, anti-materialistic, heart-of-gold idealist."

"He was probably being sarcastic," I said, while Owen said, before I'd hardly finished speaking, "He was definitely being sarcastic."

"What else did you talk about?"

"He was going on about the Klondike," Owen said with a shrug. "He thinks we'll like it there. He says he wishes he could go and see it himself." Then, dropping onto the mattress beside me and crossing his hands behind his head: "Actually, I'm starting to get excited for this trip. It will be fun to see the gold creeks. All the old buildings in Dawson City. It's this weird, hidden-away corner of the world with a crazy history to match."

"History is an insufficient word for what went on in that place," I answered him flatly. "It was a more brutal interaction than what I think you're imagining."

Really, I was surprised at Owen. I wouldn't have expected him to be taken in by my grandfather's stories: which, as was becoming clear to me—no matter how much my grandfather had sung his regrets over the wrongs done to the Lowells—had lapsed back into the glittering form of a good ol' rags-to-riches tale, with the added dash of a Northern adventure. Now I could tell that Owen was mulling it over, considering other ways of viewing, which, in fact, given his background, was a reorientation that should have been easy for him.

After all, Owen was no novice to the facts of humanity's ugliest moments. He literally taught his students a three-month unit on the horrors of warfare. He hailed from two sets of Jewish grandparents, who'd narrowly escaped death in Germany and Poland. Plus he was married to me, who, on my father's side, was Armenian, a relatively obscure ethnicity (at least in America) that had almost been finished off by ethnic cleansing in Turkey during World War I and its aftermath. It should have been simple work for him, as it was for me, to take my grandfather's stories, and flip them upside down, and turn them in hand, and see the struggle and the bloodshed that ran through them, as their dominant quality.

"My point is," I went on, "no matter how much my grandfather goes on about apologies and reparations, there's still a big part of him that clings to his Klondike stories as this exciting, beautiful history. But the truth is as vicious as it gets. It was all about money."

"Always is," Owen said lightly.

"But in this case, really."

Owen's bright mood faltered. Then, after a thoughtful pause, it returned, and at triple the wattage. He turned to me. His gaze was warm and insistent. I took the two pillows that had fallen into the space between us and dropped them onto the floor.

"It's called a gold rush," he said, sliding over. "Was that your first clue?"

2

SELMA, CALIFORNIA
SEATTLE, WASHINGTON
INSIDE PASSAGE
KLONDIKE TRAIL

1897–1898

1.

The moment the envelope touched into Alice's hand, she began laughing. Not a happy laugh. Not a laugh that invited anyone else to join her. Her filthy, aching fingers grabbed the paper roughly, believing they already knew what was inside. Her chin tipped back. Her face flicked away from the scorched, struggling land that was her family's farm, and away from the post office boy who had jumped off the road and intercepted her as she was coming out of the barn. Her wild eyes saw the open expanse of the San Joaquin Valley and the bright cold sky that was arcing over her head, from mountain to mountain, like the high and polished top of a jar.

She shouldn't be laughing. She was ashamed of herself. But the noises were involuntary: they were the convulsions of a person who has battled for months, for years, and finally receives word that the struggle is over.

The enemy is done with games of hide-and-seek. Done with the merciless hunting. The sword stands at the throat. Soon the metal will touch, and the blood will spill, and she will be relieved of the never-ending drudge of fearing for her life and the lives of her family.

Alice assumed that the letter had come from the bank.

That was the misunderstanding.

It wasn't her fault for thinking so. The whole family had been convinced that the notice of foreclosure would be arriving this week. Before that, they'd had months to prepare, starting last summer, when the letters compiling the list of missed payments had grown long and increasingly stern. Alice's father, her Poie, had been three times to the office in Fresno to plead for extensions. But it hadn't done any good. The missing mortgage payments were the only trouble the bank could see; they blotted out the faces of the people behind them. Helpless, the Bush family had continued to tend the grapes and kitchen garden and peach trees: knowing that, at any odd hour, in a twist of words, all of it might cease to belong to them. Just this morning, Poie had lingered at the parlor window, clutching his teacup, in brutal anticipation of a lone rider approaching in a cloud of trampled-up dust from far down the road.

"I thought they delivered that last notice in person," Alice said now, to this boy who must witness her shame. Her heart beat hard. Her eyes saw the gnarly peach trees, the grape trellises, the bowed barn roof with clarity, like an animal taking a last look at its life.

"Who?" the post office boy replied.

"We heard that when the McCullers got their notice," Alice said, not really speaking to him, but spitting into the air. "A red-haired man from Fresno came out on horseback. We've been watching out for a stranger riding a pinto."

"Oh." The boy sprang alive, his gray cap almost tipping off the back of his head. "But look, Miss Bush. It's not from the bank. This letter comes from your sister."

Alice flipped over the envelope. The direction was not to Poie, but to all the Bush family. The handwriting was unmistakably Ethel's. The letter had come, not from the blank faces in an office in Fresno, but from their darling Ethel, the oldest of the four Bush sisters.

The laugh was gone. Bitterness dispersed into the air like a spray of water eaten up by the sun. Thrill replaced it. No message had come from Ethel in a full eight months. In the Klondike, where Ethel and her husband had been for almost a year hunting for gold, the winters froze even the largest rivers, and the overland routes became an impassible wasteland. Nothing got in or out; no people, and by effect, no mail.

Alice tore open the envelope. The handwriting on the outside proved that Ethel herself was alive. But other than that, inside could be anything. Ethel well or ill. Ethel's husband, Clarence Berry, alive or dead. The underground gold they were hunting still locked inside the chest of the earth. Or else, in reach.

The envelope dropped to the dirt. Alice unfolded a single sheet of blue ink on cream-colored paper.

April 1, 1897, Eldorado Creek

Dear Family,

This is no "April Fools" letter. You are too far away for a joke. We have the opportunity to send a message and though I'll have to write quickly, the chance must not be overlooked. We are doing well here. More than well. The best that can be imagined. By which I mean, we have met our goal. We have staked a claim, many claims, and we have struck it.

At first when we moved our camp to this creek, we didn't find anything, and given our high hopes, we lived in despair. Clarence must have dug twenty pits, and I helped with the washing, and yet none were yielding more than the most meager flecks. But one night, a neighbor appeared out of the dark, by torchlight, to tell us that after digging all the way to bedrock, he'd hit a vein. That got Clarence hopeful, and unable to wait for the sun, he climbed into one of the pits with a shovel.

It was the work of only three hours. He reached deep ground, moved a stone, held up the light, crumbled the wall back some inches, and there was our miracle, a vein sliced through, and fat nuggets tumbling into his bucket. You should have heard him shouting for joy. I'm surprised the noise didn't carry to Selma.

We expect to clear 10,000 dollars this month. But that is Clarence's overcautious prediction. The vein is fat. My hand trembles as I write this. I will need it back soon in order to pinch myself. The news is that good. I will write again when I can.

Until then I am your devoted and
loving, Ethel Berry

The paper stood poised. *She's done it* was the pounding thought in Alice's head. *She's done it, she's done it.* The grape trellises, the California sky, the low peach trees, the dry air in her lungs, the yellow light of afternoon, which an instant ago had been an oppressive and inevitable force, began to lose their grip on her, the stays and claws of her life unhooked from her skin.

The post office boy was talking. He seemed to be asking her questions. He knew that the letter had come from the Klondike, and now he wanted to hear what was inside.

She stared at him. He seemed so distant.

"Go away," she snapped, surprising the boy. "I'm not going to read it to you before I bring it inside to my parents."

She scooped the fallen envelope up from the ground and took off through the yard and the grape trestles along a straight line to the house.

2.

Up the three stone steps, through the open kitchen door, and down the dark hall that gathered the soot of the fires.

She found Moie and Poie in the front room, backlit by their two best windows, with a tray of biscuits and butter already on the table.

"A letter from Ethel!"

The alarmed faces, in shadow before the dusty light, rose to meet hers.

"It's good news," Alice added hastily. "Wait till you see."

Poie's hand reached over his plate and accepted the paper. His lips moved as he read, and his eyes cut across the page. Alice thought he might jump out of his chair. But to her great disbelief, his hunched body stayed low, his expression was steady. He handed the letter to Moie, who followed his lead, and answered Ethel's explosive announcements with only a humble thanks to God that Ethel had survived the Klondike winter.

"But do you see what she says?" Alice cried. They assented. And Alice finally realized that they had read the news about gold without believing it. Now she was derisive. She was actually growing amused. "Are you so used to bad news that you don't know what to do when it's good?"

"Other people have been excited like this," Moie said, a light pain in her voice. "And have been disappointed."

"You think you have a nugget in hand," Poie agreed, "but it's the wrong kind of rock. Or you think you've struck a wealthy vein, but it runs dry before you've covered expenses."

She should have seen this coming, Alice thought of herself, in silent response. Gold, in general, was a fraught issue for Moie and Poie. The trouble had origin in their own childhoods. Nearly fifty years ago, Moie and Poie had each traveled west with their families, with the wagon trains of the 1850s, following the rumor of easy wealth. Moie had crossed Sioux territory at age two, at the head of a train of six Wisconsin families, riding a pony. Poie had journeyed from Texas and arrived in the state at age nine, swinging his own, child-sized axe. But despite the fanfare and expectations, the promise of gold had died with their arrival into the state, and they had found nothing. The two families had both returned to farming, and in a new part of the country where they were compelled to relearn the patterns of sowing, weather, and industry. As Poie had once put it, in one of his rare moments of public reflection, the families had gone from being poor in the east to being poor and lonely in the west. In many ways, it had been the defining experience of Alice's parents' young lives, and it had set them on a path for more disappointments. She could sympathize with her parents' instinct for caution. What she couldn't condone, though, was how they took their experience as proof of a rule.

A thunder of footsteps overhead—Daisy—summoned by what in this house qualified as an uproar. She stomped down the stairs with hairbrush in hand, demanding to know what was happening. She heard the news of Ethel, heard her parents' cautious response, then absorbed for her own reasons Moie's and Poie's disbelief. She read Ethel's letter, smirked at the sincerity, and made a sarcastic comment about Ethel buying her a diamond broach for her birthday.

"She's gotten a bit ahead of herself," Daisy trilled. "All that exercise must have addled her head."

Alice retrieved the letter from those unworthy hands and folded it nicely.

"Of course *you* don't believe it," Alice said, smoothly. She could not scold her parents in any serious way. But she could scold Daisy. "According to *your* thinking, it's impossible that something fantastic could happen to a person who isn't yourself."

Minutes ago, in the yard, during the agonizing moments when she'd thought that Ethel's letter was the note of foreclosure, Alice had been in the grips of a desperate laughter. Now it was an aloof and highly controlled sigh that passed between her teeth. She was nineteen, but her face was thin and tired-looking—she knew it—and her figure was thick but unshapely, thanks to too many meals of plain bread. She was a middle daughter in a family of girls. The youngest sister, Daisy, age sixteen, was the baby and their little dumpling no matter how big she grew. Alice's twin sister, Annie, was the beauty of the family, with her dark seductive eyes and pert chest; the one who, three years ago now, had married a grocer from Illinois, William Carswell, and escaped the chores and farm work she'd disdainfully called "the slog." The oldest sister, Ethel, was a plain-looking young woman of twenty-three. But even long before this miracle letter, Ethel had been the prized child, the hardworking and admirable one, the moral compass, whom no person—and this included Alice—could help but love.

And Alice herself. Who was she? She had no talent. She could not sing. She could not draw. In school, she'd retained her dignity but had never been much of a standout. Their church on Front Street assured her on a weekly basis that her soul mattered in the eyes of God, although—here was the discomfiting part—only precisely as much as everyone else's. Yet here she was. She felt herself blooming with a sense of her own future importance. The letter had brought this hidden feeling out of its latency.

Alice looked around at her family. Poie, with his sloped shoulders, his injured soul. Moie, with her delicate but pinched expression, like that of a rabbit. Daisy, with her pink cheeks and full lips and mind like a spinning display of petty and vainglorious thoughts. Alice loved them. But they were hopeless people.

"Do you not understand?" Alice tried again. "We'll be lifted up, thanks to Ethel and Clarence."

But there was no lighting the fire beneath them. Her parents and her sister were people who did not possess the ability to alter themselves when the moment demanded it, when the summons arrived.

3.

Dear Family, This is no "April Fools" letter.

That was Ethel's first correspondence. The blue-ink miracle letter that Alice carried around in her pocket for weeks. Then, after an almost unbearable silence, as there must have been some delay with the boats, a second letter arrived in Selma mid-May; then three more followed, the first two bundled together in a single delivery, and the next right on their heels.

The mining's going splendidly, Ethel wrote. We cleared out a dig on *Three*. We followed the line and went down near bedrock on our dig on *Four* and there it was. Dust spilling out of the earth like a geyser. We are taking out hundreds of dollars in every wash. After expenses, we expect to come home with a clean twenty thousand.

And in the next: the digs are richer than we'd thought. Clarence brought in a bucket of gravel, and I sit here fat and happy on my stout little stool, pinching out nuggets like plums. To Poie, don't you worry about the mortgage. Clarence will buy out the remainder when we come home. To Daisy and Alice, don't marry too soon. If you wait, I will introduce you to promising young men we've met here.

A cramped postscript ran up the side of the page: I was wrong when I said twenty thousand, I think it will be triple that number.

Their poor parents. Good news kept pouring in. It became a true artwork of pessimism to find new ways to undo it.

This was especially true on June 12, when the red-haired man on a Pinto finally galloped into their yard and delivered into Poie's hand the note of foreclosure. You would have expected Poie to be smug. But no. His confounding response was to announce defeat. "We worked this farm eleven years," he said. "But we ran out of time. I'm sorry, my darlings. I will have to surrender the land." It had taken a full day of Alice's coaxing to get her father to sit down at the table and write an emergency note to the bank, explaining to them that his son-in-law had the money in hand. And even then, he resisted.

"I feel like I'm telling a lie," Poie said.

Alice covered her face in her hands. She called to God, asking for patience.

Finally, at the cusp of summer, Ethel delivered her last provocation. She and Clarence were coming home. They had been in the Klondike a full fifteen months. Clarence had decided they had too much gold to stay another season. It was time they traded a bit in for cash. They had already booked the first passage out of the country.

On July 17, 1897, the SS *Portland* turned its nose to Seattle, with hundreds of spectators lined up on the docks. Who would have guessed—certainly not the Bushes—that Ethel and Clarence's return to the States would not mark only an important family moment, but also a nationwide event? But news of gold in the Klondike had spread. The image of gold locked in a frozen chest in the North had lit again a pioneering spirit that had been at the verge of extinction. The Berrys' ship, for instance, the first to come back to the mainland, arrived with the most extraordinary headlines heralding it into the harbor. STEAMSHIP PORTLAND ARRIVES FROM KLONDIKE CARRYING ONE TON OF GOLD. Too much, people had said, the newspapers must have it wrong. And as it turned out, they did. The actual tonnage was closer to two.

Docks swayed beneath the animal weight of the welcome. Children sat in long rows, smacking on candy. Women openly wept. The mayor stood at the front of the mob, with the eyes of the world floating behind him. Ever since the recession of '93, the economy had been in a low and stagnant state, with the farmers hurting worst of all. But this influx of raw gold might be just the thing to move the markets again; it would at the least shake up the numbers having to do with the rigid gold standard that many claimed had been dragging the country down. New gold had always meant change and upheaval and motion, and people were giddy.

The gangplank fell and the argonauts disembarked. According to the vivid description in the *San Francisco Chronicle*, they were a dirty, ragtag group for heroes. Hair matted and oily and flecked with white filth. The mud of the North still stuck to their clothes. They hauled chunks of gold in rolled-up blankets that took two men to carry because of the weight. They had nuggets inside of emptied tins, in old leather boots topped with a sock. Dust inside of jars covered with writing paper and wound around the neck with twine.

Clarence and Ethel were among the richest. With Anton Stander, Clarence's Austrian business partner, Clarence owned just over a half-share of the claims *Three, Four, Five,* and *Six* on Eldorado, which was proving to be perhaps the richest creek on the earth.

Ethel herself was no slouch. It was widely reported—although she hadn't said a word of this in her letters—that she was coming home with her own little slice of the Klondike. Not a full claim, which were, by law, five hundred feet in length, but rather a portion, what was called a "fraction": which came up when a prospector drove his initial stakes into the land and marked his claim at a distance beyond the five hundred feet that was allowed. In Ethel's case, she was the owner of forty-two feet of land between claims *Five* and *Six* Eldorado, where Clarence and Anton had overmeasured claim *Five* the previous year, and where, in early spring, a Canadian government agent tasked with measuring the claims on the creeks had discovered their error.

The reporters wanted to hear all about it. They asked what she would buy with her diggings. Then ended the interview with some version of the joke of whether or not she would give them a loan. They liked her. They respected her. She was the first white woman to go to the Klondike, and for them she struck the perfect image of a pioneer woman: cheerful, resourceful, and of course, their favorite description: tough-as-nails. None of it was a surprise to Alice. This, after all, was her inimitable sister. Ethel, who once, as a tiny girl, had fainted while washing the floors, because she'd refused to stop for a drink of water until the whole kitchen was done. Ethel, who once, at the tender age of fourteen, had marched herself to bed, closed the door, and insisted that no one do anything for her, then had proceeded to nearly die of the mumps. Now Ethel was not only brave, stoic, and modest but also successful. Soon, it seemed, the world could not talk about the Klondike without a warm mention of her. You could not pick up a newspaper (it was Poie who said this, in quiet awe) without the venerable names of Mr. and Mrs. Clarence Berry leaping up from the type.

4.

Now weeks later, under the glare of a summer sun, Alice experienced, beneath this surface of joy, a disconcerting feeling. Was she really nervous to see them? Ethel, who'd never spoken a harsh word to her in her life. Their longtime neighbor, Clarence Jesse Berry, who, until the age of thirty, had been a nobody, another failed fruit farmer: notorious for losing his eighty acres in Kingsburg when the fruit prices first had dropped.

But today Alice waited with Moie, Poie, and Daisy on the porch, in the earth-splintering heat, watching the carriage holding Clarence and Ethel make its way in a cloud of dust down the last stretch of road, and she felt ill. She couldn't help it. No matter what Clarence and Ethel had been before, their failures no longer counted against them: all their struggles and past indignities seemed like the necessary prelude to the tall, important people they had become.

The couple came into view. Clarence with his round, balding head; the pink crater on one side of the face where he'd suffered from frostbite during his first scouting trip North. His big Irish cheeks were spread wide and plumped into a grin. One gloved hand held the reins high, while the other was madly waving hello.

Beside him sat their darling Ethel. Her lips moved, yelling *hello, hello,* through the haze. Her face was large and pale like Clarence's, and also smiling. As recently as the spring of '96, she'd been the farm girl, Ethel Bush. Now she was Ethel Berry. She had condescended to marry a destitute farmer who'd proposed to her with dirt under his fingernails, now she was his wealthy wife. It seemed that she could hardly wait for Clarence to halt the horses and come around to help her off her seat, before she was flying at them.

"Can you believe it?" she cried, her arms spread wide, meeting them with a rough embrace. "Is it not the gosh darn dandiest thing you've ever heard in your life?"

This was a startling show of exuberance, coming from Ethel. As for the language, *the gosh darn dandiest,* it was among the strongest that had ever been heard from her.

She embraced Moie first, then Poie, then Alice, then Daisy. Then she turned a circle on the porch and embraced Alice a second time.

"Look at you," Ethel whispered into her hair. "Am I dreaming? Here's a secret for you. Alice, I missed you most of all."

A strong, innocent feeling spread over Alice; only Ethel could do that to her. And then, laughing, wiping the tears away, she felt light and happy like everyone else.

Inside the house, the couple had Moie and Poie sit down at the table, then presented them with a pile of bills, crisp from the mint. And more to come, as soon they were joined by a big group from right down the road, Clarence's family: Pa and Ma Berry, the Berry brothers, Frank and Henry, as well as the two Berry sisters, the loud and boorish Nellie, the prim and deeply religious Cora, who was tall, thin, and stiff as a rake.

Clarence's parents, Pa and Ma Berry, received their own stack of crisp cash. Next, the smaller gifts were doled out to the siblings: nuggets the size and texture of raisins, a handful of bear's teeth, jade beads that clinked in your palm, a muskrat pelt that someone might like to nail to a wall.

That evening, in the mild air, with the meat turning on an outdoor spit, the two families carried their chairs and the kitchen table into the yard, a sign like no other in Selma of a true celebration. Habitually a quiet, mild-mannered person, Clarence walked out of the house talking. He turned the meat without attending to what he was doing, and almost toppled the mechanism and lost their dinner into the flames. But no one begrudged his distraction. The man was overcome. His mind was on the faraway people and places. He couldn't believe that this life was his life, that these things that had happened, had happened *to him*.

Poie and Moie sat on one side of the fire, Pa and Ma Berry on the other. Clarence's younger brother, Henry, scuffled near his chair like an eager dog. Daisy, Nellie, and Cora sat in a neat little row, hanging on his every word. Ethel and Alice, by Alice's own design, sat close together by the open back door, attending to the bread and beans inside on the stove.

If there was one person not sharing in the familial joy, it was Clarence's oldest sibling, the strikingly handsome Frank Berry. He had folded his long, narrow body onto a rock a little ways off from the group, and remained there, sulking and smoking his pipe, with all the ominousness of a black spider crouched near its prey. Four years ago, just after Clarence had lost his eighty acres in Kingsburg, it had been in fact big brother Frank who'd suggested that Clarence chase the rumors of gold coming down from the Klondike. When Clarence had actually taken up the idea, Frank had thought it an excellent joke and had told a lot of people about it. He'd mimed Clarence fighting off polar bears and dangling off the side of a cliff. Of course he hadn't meant for Clarence to suffer too much from the trying, not beyond losing a finger or two. But God knows he never would have mentioned the North and all those stupid rumors of gold-laden creeks and of nuggets the size of cherries and ripe for the picking, if he could have foreseen a night like this, or had experienced even the slightest inkling that his brother would come home successful.

Clarence had a chair like everyone else, but he couldn't stay in it. With the great crepuscular sky at his back and the Sierra Nevada stretching behind him, he gesticulated wildly, responding to the questions of his family and in-laws with irrepressible enthusiasm.

"The sea travel was the worst of it," he said, answering Pa Berry first. "I stand by what I told you. That first leg from Seattle up to Alaska, in that tin tub of a boat. Look," he cried joyfully, "my wife's laughing at me, but I was sure we were going to die right out of the gate, before we'd made it free of the harbor. You should have seen me kissing the earth when they spat us out in Dyea. No matter that it was absolutely in the middle of nowhere, with more nowhere ahead."

His sister, Nellie, admonished him: "We already think you're a hero, Clarence. You don't have to convince us you're brave."

From the rock where Frank perched came a scoff of agreement.

But Clarence rebuffed them both.

"Truly, Nell, you'd be aghast to see the place, it's just as wild a country as everyone says. Untouched mountains and virgin forests like don't exist in the States anymore. Plus there are Indians everywhere. It's like traveling fifty years back in time. For instance at the trailhead, we crossed paths with a good Tlingit fellow who called himself Jim. Very quiet. Very hardworking. We were able to put him to work as our packer, and I don't know how we would have managed without him. He hauled our things over the Chilkoot Pass, and I swear to you, without breaking a sweat. Meanwhile, there I was, with only the sugar and meat on my back, ready to weep from exhaustion." He laughed with his gaze to the sky, lost in his memories. "We climbed three thousand feet straight up into the clouds on that day. Ethel climbed it in a skirt and heeled boots. But well worth the agony," he said, full with strong feeling. "Every hard day was worth it. The gold I exchanged at the mint is just the beginning. The real wealth is still in the North, in the deeds that we hold."

He jumped up, eyes to the house, and instructed them all to stay put. When he returned from inside, he was holding that leather folder he'd been walking around with since his return.

He opened the top and retrieved the thick papers inside. At first Alice didn't know what they were. Then she realized. They were the deeds for the claims *Three, Four, Five, Six* on Eldorado Creek. He showed them to his parents, then Moie and Poie, then he put them on the table.

"And bring yours, Ethel. Let's see them all lined up together. The whole of the fortune."

Ethel was embarrassed to do it. But she rose from her chair, and with beatific grace, and without a backward look at Alice, went to join her husband.

She took hold of the chain around her neck and fished from under her dress a small, oil-skin purse. With two fingers, she pinched a piece of paper from the bag, unfolded it, and placed it beside Clarence's four deeds. Her deed for the forty-two feet.

"Here it is," Clarence said, in a voice deeply reverent. "Now I want you to take a good look at this, all of you. This belongs to the Bushes as much as the Berrys. We have every one of us worked ourselves to the bone with farming. But we don't need to live like that anymore. I don't overstate it when I say I put my eyes on these papers and I see our salvation."

When Ethel returned to her chair, her own deed in hand again, she was flushed through with pleasure. It must be something, Alice thought. To make your family proud. To save them. She herself was not on a path for knowing that feeling.

"It took Clarence to get that treasure of yours out in the open," Alice teased quietly, leaning close to her sister. "You didn't say a word in your letters. I had read about it in the newspaper first. I had no idea it was under your dress all this time."

"Oh," said Ethel, flushing still deeper as she tucked the paper away and straightened her collar. "Just to keep it safe."

"As you should. It's your own fortune."

"No, not really." Ethel was embarrassed again. "Don't think of it like that. It was just a formality because Clarence and Anton overmeasured on *Five*. It's a very strict rule. Each claim must measure five hundred feet, along the path of the creek. When the Canadian officials discovered Clarence's mistake, they wouldn't let him put the fraction in his own name, or in Stander's, so the two of them decided to put it in mine. The other option would've been letting a horde of strangers from Dawson rush in with their stakes, and even Stander didn't want that. So you see, I was their best and only option. It's not like I'm going to go off now and start my own business venture."

"I still say you're a grand little thing."

"Please, Alice," said Ethel, laughing and shaking her head. "All right. Let's call it what Clarence does. My prize for trekking North with my husband."

"And is it very rich," Alice asked in a falsely formal tone, "your fraction?"

"It can't help but be, can it?" said Ethel, matching her archness. "On a creek called Eldorado."

"Let me see it up close."

Alice had spoken with a sudden uninhibited passion, and Ethel gave her a rueful look in response. She tugged her little oilskin purse out of her dress again. She pinched out the deed and handed it over. It was nothing, a piece of paper smaller than you'd expect it to be. About the size and thickness of a good sheet of stationery. But the ink was black and bold. The name, *Ethel Bush Berry*, looped unwaveringly across a straight, sure line. The coordinates were written out. The name of the creek. The location of the fraction. It was signed by a Canadian government official by the name of William Ogilvie and stamped in bloodred ink in the lower right corner.

What would it be to own a thing like this? Alice wondered. She couldn't believe it. Her own, lovely sister. She felt a painful longing, touching the deed lightly. A piece of paper. Or not. Its power infused Ethel's being. The deed stood upon the laws of two countries. If you knew how to read it, it read of money. If you knew how to speculate, it could transport you anywhere.

Alice gave it back and as she did, she felt like the air was being sucked out of her. Her ribs felt tight. Her vison blurred. Was her sister real?

She thought: Who would I be, what would I feel, with a fortune like that?

5.

But of course, Alice understood she had no right to be covetous. Not when Clarence and Ethel were so good, so uninhibited in their generosity.

One Monday a week after the joyful return, Clarence and Poie rode into Fresno, and Poie sat down beside his son-in-law at a great mahogany table, looking on while Clarence bought out the loan on the farm in Poie's name. The terrifying future they'd spent so long imagining disappeared, with finality, like dirty water being sucked into the earth. Poie came home from that meeting looking a decade younger, as no one had seen him since their first year in Selma.

Every weekend, Ethel and Clarence went shopping in town. They replenished the stock rooms with salted beef, canned oysters, crackers, pickles, and other wonderful things. They sat in the evenings on the Berrys' porch, talking with visitors. They were always ready to help with picking fruit. Clarence even dug out the Lone Tree canal with his father when a portion collapsed in on itself, though Clarence often reminded both families that this kind of hard work need not continue.

In October, just before the Klondike freeze, Clarence purchased a passage North for his younger brother, Henry. The plan was for Henry to spend the winter on the claims, overseeing the mining work in Clarence's stead, as Clarence felt that his business partner, Anton Stander, had already been left in charge for too long. Henry took leave of them all with his usual charm: telling his mother not to cry for him, it was only a fifty-fifty chance that he'd drown, and sixty-forty he'd take ill during the winter. But the departure, once it was over, proved too much for Frank Berry, and after months of restraint, he finally exploded, unleashing his ugly pride and his jealousy. He told Clarence he should have been the one to go North: firstly, because he was the oldest, secondly, because he had been the originator of all the prospecting talk. He stormed and yelled and cared no more about his own mortification. The result was that, although he'd done nothing since his brother's return but sulk, it ended up that he was promised a passage North in springtime, when Clarence and Ethel planned to return to their claims.

Alice herself hardly had time to feel jealous of Frank before the New Year came around, and it was 1898, and something strange happened. A man named Edward Keller visited the Berrys, occupying Henry's bed in the house. The man was a business acquaintance of Clarence's who'd briefly bought into the partnership with Clarence and Anton Stander on *Five* Eldorado, before deciding that he couldn't abide the mining life. They'd closed the deal amicably, and Clarence had been so pleased with the profit he'd made on the proceedings that he'd invited Ed Keller to come stay at the family home on his way to resettle himself in Los Angeles. Suddenly, Alice was thrust into the center of the family bustle. She was seated beside the man when they went to the Berrys for dinner. She was asked to read from the newspaper for their nighttime amusement: a job that usually would have fallen to Poie. Her minor triumphs at school presentations, not mentioned in years, were remembered warmly one morning that the Bushes hosted a breakfast.

Despite the silent pressure, Alice was not convinced that she should marry Ed Keller, and the torture of indecision kept her up every night. He had money, yes, but he was also conceited and limited in his perceptions to the point of being a fool. His eyes were always jumping around as if on the lookout for slights, and his manners lacked smoothness and grace. Once he'd kissed her hand after winning a game of cards, and a current of revulsion had traveled up the length of her arm. Still, while she was mulling it over, she strove to remain in high spirits, and didn't speak a word of her doubts. Later, she wished that she had. Because then it would have been less humiliating when, after two weeks of this showcasing, Ed Keller announced an interest in Daisy, who was round, pink-cheeked, and fair, and must have seemed, Alice thought, like a soft place to land, after years of camping on boulders. The romance had fleet wings, and they were engaged within the month.

Alice absorbed the hit. She did not crumple. She'd been born a mewling skinny baby, the smaller twin next to Annie, in the wet cold woods of Placer County, where their Poie had been in the logging business, and where they'd almost starved for his lack of good wages. In their childhood, Ethel had made a pet of her, and kept her snug beside her in her bed, because once she'd heard Moie and Poie talk about how little Alice might die. Instead, Alice had lived. She was grateful. She also had been left with the feeling that she could survive whatever came at her. She raised her chin. The man was rich, but only with money from Clarence.

She endeavored to spend more time with Clarence and Ethel. She accompanied them on errands to Fresno. She was their shadow as they walked through the shops. When they were girls, Ethel had doted on her and Alice in turn had clung to Ethel. Now Alice sought to reawaken that closeness. She sat before the outdoor fire with Ethel and Clarence in the evenings while they told stories about the Klondike. They remembered solemnly, for instance, the young Wisconsin man—only nineteen or twenty—who'd likely died of typhoid on the trail, and to whom Ethel had given her scarf and a hot bowl of oats, before the couple had been compelled to leave him and continue on through the trees. They told her how once they'd been sailing along twenty feet behind a scow on the Klondike River when they'd seen it overturn. The two men aboard didn't know how to swim, and though the Berrys had been so tormentingly close to the arms and elbows thrashing above the water, they hadn't been able to stop their own boat in order to grab the drowning men and heave them aboard. They had avoided Skagway, Clarence said, where you could win a game of cards and then be shot standing up in your chair. Even so, Clarence said into the clear, calm night, where there is desperation, there is crime, and one night not far past the Chilkoot, Clarence had been awake to see their tent flaps open and the wan face of a deranged-looking stranger poke through. Clarence had raised his gun, not saying a word, and the man had given one long look and withdrawn. Clarence and Ethel had hurriedly left the area, though for at least a week they'd barely slept, and had feared being followed.

Never was Alice short on questions or expressions of wonderment. When they delved into their "Tales from the Trail" as they called their lighter anecdotes from the journey, she laughed, for instance, at the story of the dog that, during the spring, had stolen the whole stew pot off the fire, then, too smart for its own good, had placed the pot into one of the last of the melting snowbanks to cool. She memorized their route to the Klondike and surprised them by correcting Clarence when he'd once misspoken and said "Lake Bennett" when he'd meant "Lake Laberge."

Clarence replied, speaking from around the side of the outdoor fire, and calling Alice by her family nickname, "Tot," which Ethel was still in the habit of using:

"I sent Henry to the claims. But you're the quicker learn." To Ethel, laughing with the pink frostbitten patch on his cheek wrinkled high: "The person we should have sent is Tot."

6.

Spring came full around again. The passage north opened, and the country went into a fit for gold. In San Francisco, the trolleys stopped running, because the drivers were all preparing to leave for the Klondike. The mayor resigned and announced he was going. Young men took out loans for five hundred dollars, sometimes one thousand dollars, to buy fur robes, mackinaw coats, rubber shoes, hip boots, sacks of oats and flour, pork, evaporated fruits and potatoes, coffee and condensed milk by the pound, mining tools, hatchets, nails, and other supplies. Schoolteachers walked out before the end of term, clapping white chalk from their hands, dreaming of a different sort of dust.

Of everyone, the Bushes and Berrys were best able to anticipate this massive event as, during the winter of '97 into '98, they'd witnessed the bags of letters arriving for Clarence and Ethel from people wanting advice. A man from New York had designed a bicycle for traversing ice and wanted Clarence's opinion. A crew from cannery row was sure they could be indispensable to him, just name a time and place and they'd be happy to join him on his next trip.

Alice laughed as much as anyone. She did not want to align herself with the fools. Though still she felt their compulsion, *I, no, I could really do well, if only fate would deliver me to the foot of that hill.*

As winter faded Clarence and Ethel began to prepare to join the great movement of people, tens of thousands readying themselves to go North, in what was beginning to be known all over the world as a genuine Rush. They would return through the thick spring snow to their claims, resume the mining work, and pry what gold they could from the earth. The trip remained arduous. No matter the crowds planning to travel, or the maps being printed and sold all over the country, the path to the North was a wilderness. Clarence occupied himself with procuring a new team of sled dogs, as the pack from his previous trip had been sold off in the Klondike or given to friends. He devoted mornings to their training, making them haul through the dirt a makeshift sleigh with wooden wheels, which looked exactly as ridiculous as he'd promised it would, when he'd first announced his intentions.

Meanwhile, upstairs in the Berry house, in a little white bedroom—Clarence's childhood bedroom—where Clarence and Ethel had been staying while home, Ethel was darning one of Clarence's sweaters, joy lingering in her broad soft face. Alice was with her, assisting with every decision. She had jumped at the chance to help her sister pack. There was something she'd wanted to say to Ethel for weeks now, and this might be her last opportunity.

Amid a conversation of Henry, who was playfully outraged over the plans to let Frank travel North, Alice put in, as a smooth aside:

"But you know what I'm thinking, dear? In a way, it doesn't seem fair that Clarence will have *two* brothers to help him with the mining this summer, while there you'll be doing the housework alone."

"Oh," Ethel said airily, "I'll be glad for the company. I don't mind the extra cooking and washing."

"Yes, but is it necessary that you should work so hard?" Alice pressed. "I know there'll probably be plenty of hired work for the taking. But wouldn't you rather have a friend? It's been on my mind that I could be a companion for you."

"A companion? How do you mean, Alice?"

She decided to state it bluntly: "I could go with you North."

On Ethel's lovely face, a flicker of pity. The sweater lowered into her lap. Before a word was spoken, Alice's spirits, which had been high with the thrill of finally speaking her mind, began a nauseating descent.

"If I was going to take anyone with me," Ethel said slowly, in true apology, "it would be you. But it's a brutal trek. You've heard all the stories and the close calls we've had. I couldn't ask you to risk your life for me, just to give me help with the cooking and cleaning."

"You had fun, though. You were happy you went."

"That's true," Ethel said carefully.

"I don't mind roughing it," Alice said bracingly, doing her best not to sound desperate, "you know I'm not like Daisy or Annie. I don't get seasick and I can walk for eight hours without getting tired. God knows I do it at least once a week when Mopsey breaks loose from the barn."

But Alice could detect a lost cause. When it came to protecting the well-being of others, Ethel's noble heart would not be persuaded.

"You think it's too dangerous."

"It's one thing to risk my own neck," Ethel answered, her voice full of compassion. "But if something happened to one of my little sisters, to you," a loving touch to Alice with those words, "I could never forgive myself."

7.

Ed Keller's choosing Daisy had been the first humiliation. Now Alice was humiliated a second time by her sister. The third humiliation took place when she was next in Clarence's company, and found him newly gentle with her, and quiet about their "Tales from the Trail," as if he did not want to pain her. Bitter thoughts writhed within her; shame had cracked their shell and let them free. The only relief for Alice was that Clarence and Ethel would soon be gone.

March 2, 1898, Alice stood on the porch with her family and the Berry family, sending the travelers off with a flourish. The couple was radiant, happy to be leaving the crowded farmhouse and returning to their magical place. Meanwhile Frank Berry sat on the carriage bench beside them, looking self-important, his dark eyes on the road ahead, and the reins in his hands. He pretended not to notice his sister, Cora, when she came around the side of the carriage to kiss him goodbye. As for Ethel and Clarence, it was like their wedding in '96, like history repeating itself: exactly two years ago, that other March day, the couple had left home for their honeymoon, yellow streamers swirling from the back of their seat. *Then*, there'd been real worry for the newlyweds. *Now* the pitiable ones were not the couple, but the family members left behind, shouting "Godspeed" from the porch.

The carriage disappeared. The dust on the road settled. A familiar quiet fell over the farm. It was the quiet of petrification. Alice returned to the grape trellises and the blaring sun. She returned to Mopsey's stall, which, gold or no gold, still required a strong arm and a shovel to clean it.

In the evening, the vines drew sharp shadows over the land, so that once Alice caught sight of the black, weblike lines on her hands, and she was startled.

Her sister was rich and happy.

What did that do for her?

She would not starve. Her parents would not lose the farm. But a year had passed. Alice was twenty. New appetites had grown up within her.

8.

The day the message came from Seattle, Alice was languishing in a square of sun in the kitchen, reading the Bible. Their church had announced its competition for best recitation, and she'd put in her name to perform. She'd placed first years ago, during that innocent era when a three-dollar prize could feel like a windfall.

This time Alice never saw the boy. His beseeching eyes. His gray cap. Instead she walked into the front room to find Moie and Poie like a pair of stone sentinels. They had received a telegram, and that was strange, as they never got telegrams. When Poie saw Alice, he lifted the scrap of yellow paper and handed it to her, and said only, "Ethel."

Arrived in Seattle. Boat leaves Tuesday. Bought an extra ticket. Send Tot.

The jolt of surprise. Like last year, only now it was personal. And this time it was Alice who read the message and could not believe it. Her mind worked over the words, plunged into the spaces between them. Weeks ago, as they were packing the suitcases, Alice had made the offer to travel North with the Berrys, and Ethel had rejected that offer. And Ethel was not a fickle person. She was not even a person who was in the habit of changing her mind.

Moie and Poie were mystified. Daisy was outraged. Among Daisy's many pleasures in her engagement to Ed Keller was the chance to leave a wallowing older sister at home. Now she stormed around the kitchen, asking "Tot? Tot? What good is Tot?" as if she'd hit upon a philosophical question that had no possible answer.

It took several minutes for a likely explanation to emerge, and, even then, no one spoke it directly. The suggestion came in the form of a few oblique and worried words from Moie. Clarence and Ethel had been married for a year. There was one shift, one change in Ethel's circumstance, that would abruptly necessitate a female companion. But it was senseless. It would be unthinkable to travel if it were true. The Klondike killed burly men at first touch. It murdered horses in droves. It plucked careful, well-prepared people into the air and dropped them off the sides of towering mountains. And Ethel herself over the winter had told them this very particular story: the tragedy of a pretty, young Fresno wife, not more than eighteen, who'd followed her husband North with their two little babies in arms, bundled in blankets. The poor young woman had underestimated the harsh conditions of the trail and had returned home to Fresno after only two weeks, her face stricken and her arms unburdened.

"Go to Seattle," Moie said, raspy and hushed. "But tell Ethel she has to let Clarence make the trip alone. She needs to come home and stay with us."

"You think I can convince her?" Alice asked. "If she and Clarence have already decided?"

"She's out of her right mind," said Moie. "She went once to the Klondike and back. Now she thinks she's invincible."

"But Moie," pressed Alice, "if she insists?"

Their eyes met, until Moie, losing conviction, shifted her gaze. Insisting was just the sort of thing that Ethel would do, and they both knew it. An understanding passed between mother and daughter. Though it was not pure. Because they both could feel something else. If Alice, not Ethel, had been Moie's favorite daughter, she would have said next, *Do your best to bring Ethel home, but if she insists on traveling North, under no circumstances are you to go with her.* But Moie could not say it. Because if Ethel, as she imagined, was truly with child and needed help on the trail, it was impossible for Moie to take that help away from her, as in, take Alice away from her. Even if it meant putting Alice at risk.

"The Pullman leaves tomorrow morning at eight," Alice said, breaking the silence, relieving her mother of her moral distress. "I could be in Seattle by nightfall. There's no time to waste."

Distantly, Alice heard the uproar of voices—Poie, Moie, and Daisy—but the noise was already falling away, like a shout slowly plummeting into a well. Meanwhile, she gave the room and the people inside it a sweeping, almost malevolent look. Near the back door, visible from down the hall, was her usual chair. Rickety. Spindle-legged. Light pinewood aglow in a square of sun. The chair stuck out exactly as she'd left it, a little askew from the table. For a week she had huddled herself in its lap, with the adventures of Moses flat on her thighs. Now she would miss the competition on Sixth Street, and maybe the next year of her life, as she'd expected the year to unfold. No harm. She was trading up for something better. Her boots were pointed toward the door.

9.

The train bolted North. Past farms. Past rivers and miles of high coarse grass. Then a green expanse fanned out from the windows as the engine drove, on and on, bringing Alice farther than she'd ever traveled from home.

Inside the cars was a raucous crowd. The seats were packed with young men on their way to join the rush. They were on their knees, leaning over the seats, all talking at once. They asked each other questions, then proceeded to spread the same bad information all over the train. No one spoke to Alice. Moie and Poie had worried about Alice amid this rowdy group, and had told her to sit with their neighbors, an elderly couple, who happened to be on the train that day. But the young men did not seem to mark her. At most they said "excuse me" for violently bumping her arm. They assumed that Alice did not belong to their burgeoning world of adventure. It was too bad for them, as after eight months of hearing stories from Clarence and Ethel, she was a human almanac of the ins-and-outs of the trail.

Rain drummed the car roof, leaving long pelleted tails. They stopped in Portland, where the streets were mud and the rain leaked into Alice's boots.

At dusk, their destination leapt out at them, like an ambush from the trees. On the platform, a crowd had gathered. The cloaks of the men and women were drab, with only a few spots of color announcing themselves in the sea of black hats. And yet there was a buzzing warmth here, the heat of hope, which overpowered the drizzly weather.

On the train step, Alice said goodbye to her neighbors, and spotted Clarence and Ethel. A relief—though she'd had no reason for doubt—and proof that Ethel's summons was real.

"Here I am!" Alice cried, running to them and kissing them both. For now, despite the mystery, she was determined to make a spirited entrance.

"I knew you'd miss me too much to leave me at home." She took her sister's shoulder for support and lifted a boot. "And look at this. I'm already filthy. Walking proof of my adventurous spirit."

"Drop those in the next tin can you see," Clarence said. "If they can't hold up in California, they'll be useless in Alaska."

The porter arrived with Alice's bag. Clarence took it and pretended to have injured his shoulder.

"Don't tease her after she's come all this way," Ethel scolded. Then to Alice: "Did you leave everyone well at home?"

The sisters began walking, arms linked, with Clarence behind. Young men from the train now wandered around with big packs on their backs, looking bewildered. A few who'd been in the car with Alice recognized Clarence. They stared, realizing too late that the nobody girl from the aisle seat was in Clarence Berry's party.

"Not everyone's well, I'm sorry to tell you," Alice said, turning attention back to Ethel, as they angled their way through the crowd. "Daisy's sick with jealousy. I'm lucky I made it out of the house before she clawed my eyes out. I'm sorry for Moie and Poie. I'm afraid the only cure for her will be a very expensive wedding."

"I wasn't sure they'd let you come," Ethel answered. "Annie will be furious. You'll miss her visit with Wanlyn this summer."

"I'd forgotten about that," Alice said honestly. Annie, Alice's twin in Illinois. Wanlyn, age three, their little niece. After years of putting off a visit home, Annie had decided, right around the time that Clarence and Ethel had made the national news, that she and Wanlyn might be able to squeeze in a summer trip after all. "Trust me," Alice said, "I'll get over the loss." Then she added, in deference to Moie, "But you should know that Moie would be happier if we were *both* at home to host Annie and Wanlyn. And in a way, I agree with her."

"Is that so?" Ethel was measured, not lifting her eyes. "Why do you say that?"

"You gave us a shock, dear, in sending that telegram. It isn't like you to make a sudden change of plan."

There, Alice thought. See how I cleared a space for you? And now let's hear it: the big explanation.

For a moment Ethel seemed about to speak freely. Then she made an abrupt swerve from the light.

"I'm sorry I worried you. I didn't mean to do that. It was only that your offer to be my travel companion got stuck in my head. Clarence and I happened to walk by the line for boat tickets and, seeing it again, I had this realization. I told Clarence about what you'd offered, and he absolutely seized on the idea. He didn't know why we hadn't planned it that way from the beginning."

Alice stared. She didn't believe it. Though she couldn't understand why Ethel would lie.

"Well, I'm thrilled to go," she said. "You must have guessed I would be."

"Thank you, Tot." A strange collapse with the words. "You can't know how I thank you."

They walked at a hurried pace, down a flight of stairs that was slick from the weather. As they moved out of sight of the station, the street signs, the buildings, the hats dripping with musty rain altered for Alice as if by a three-inch shift; the energy and happiness that painted this jockeying crowd took on a shade that was faintly grotesque.

Alice had greeted her sister and brother-in-law cheerfully, expecting to find nervous, maybe, but basically cheerful people. But even Clarence was deeply subdued, dragging ten steps behind.

Again Alice searched her sister, the navy jacket snug over Ethel's chest, the blouse and skirt where they met at the waist. Nothing showed. Though it could be early. Meanwhile Ethel felt the attention. Her mouth twitched—about to speak?—but no. Her face blazed with unspoken thoughts. She jolted her chin away and marched on.

10.

They turned a corner onto Madison Street, crowded with shoppers, and here Clarence caught up with them. Rows of globe lamps, moons in miniature, swept them down the thoroughfare, where a shimmering early-March drizzle was filling out into snow. Fat sacks of flour barricaded store windows. A sign, freshly painted, read ALASKA OUTFITTERS, and two doors down, inside the Klondike Emporium, tall hats milled around low racks of fur coats.

At a cross street, a shadowy knot of strangers erupted into loud conviviality at the recognition of Clarence. "Hello!" they yelled. "Hold on, now!" Their strides were brisk as they broke apart and closed in around the Berrys. Their fingers squeezed the brims of their hats.

The young men only wanted to know, if Mr. Berry wouldn't mind saying: What, please, was the secret to striking gold in the Klondike? And what route was he planning on? What was the news from Bunker Hill? Was there anything in it? A skinny young fellow joined up on Ethel's free side. He was handsome, and with the wide, overpliant face of an actor. He was wearing one of those ridiculous pins that were all over the country, which read "Yes, I'm Going This Spring." He held it out for Ethel to see, mid-stride, with a bashfulness that she mistook for genuine. When Clarence jiggled his wife free from the stranger's hold, barking, good evening, goodbye, the man dropped off without complaint. Half a minute later he was still on the curb: his hand flopping, his large lower lip thrust forward in a cartoonish pout.

They arrived at their hotel and glided inside the big double doors. A light jingle played in Alice's head as the patrons watched them cross the lobby. *This is what it is to be rich, rich, rich.* Clarence thought they might like to eat in the dining room, where Frank was supposed to be meeting them. But Ethel, cutting him off, said decisively, no. She and Alice would take their meal in their room.

As the sisters passed the dining room, an abundance of sconces, all ablaze, long tables cluttered with chairs, Alice gave it a wistful look.

"I'm sorry," Ethel said, observing her. "I know it would be interesting for you to take supper downstairs. But the crowd has been getting very rough. Yesterday, there was a terrible fight at the bar. A boat ticket was caught in the hand of a thief, just as he was pinching it out of the owner's chest pocket. All of a sudden there were twenty big men pummeling each other, and shifting left and right as if the whole mob was being moved back and forth by a magnet. We heard knives came out at the end."

They began up a narrow flight of stairs, in a dark alcove that held the smells of the kitchen.

"I worry what the trail will be like," Ethel added. "If that kind of barbarity is already cropping up here. I would have expected a fair race to the Klondike. But I suppose that's the female perspective."

"No, Ethel," Alice corrected. "That's your good nature. Many people could learn a lesson from you."

11.

A four-post bed overwhelmed the room: its white cover like a friend of the snow. After a quick glance at the furniture, Alice was drawn to the window, to an elevated view like she'd never experienced, which made her feel like a bird. The fat white snowflakes swirled near the glass. It never snowed in Selma. Alice hadn't seen thick snow like this since she was eight years old, during their last winter in Placer County. She thought of where she was, how far from home, and the feeling of flying persisted, as if traveling north really did mean climbing the globe. It was amazing to think how many strangers there were in the world. All with busy lives. She could hear footsteps over her head, voices wafting past in the hallway; she watched clumps of men making zigzag trails through the snow far below her on the lamplit street. Across the way, the Alaska Outfitters store was still doing business, and at one of the carts by the door, an indecisive buyer lingered, prodding a tall tower of blankets. The man shimmied a dark red quilt from the pile, then spread it wide in his arms and instantly was transformed by it, as if by a massive pair of wings. Alice stared awhile, transfixed, until a light from inside blighted the show.

At the little table, Ethel had lighted the lamp. She put out two napkins and forks and knives that she'd found in a drawer. Then she dropped into the chair. Her hand stretched up, freeing one of the pins from her bun.

Alice made a comment about the dizzying view, to which Ethel responded with a few distracted words of agreement. "I'll have so many things to write in my journal tonight," Alice said, and Ethel made a small noise of acknowledgment. Usually, Ethel's quietness was a nice thing, a peaceful thing. A trait to be valued, especially when you'd grown up in a small house with two other sisters who were perpetually talking. But now Alice was getting impatient. If there was something to say, Ethel would have to put aside her delicate manners and say it. Or did she expect Alice to be at her side, day by day, watching her stomach grow, lending her a hand on the trail, not speaking a word, until some evening, by firelight, in a wind-battered tent in the middle of nowhere, a baby in a river of blood was born into Alice's hands?

"So, tell me," Alice lightly pressed, "have you quarreled with Clarence?"

A pivot. Ethel's moon face in surprise. "Why would you ask that?"

"When I offered to come on this trip, you said no. Then you said you'd had a change of heart, passing the line for tickets. But excuse me for thinking that something more drastic must have happened to bring it on, three days before the boat leaves port."

"Everything's fine between me and Clarence." Ethel's features pinched, as Moie's did, when she was nervous. Alice lifted her bag onto the bedspread and unclasped it.

She nettled: "You understand, though. It got me thinking, if suddenly Ethel wants a companion, does it mean that Clarence—"

"Alice, stop. I said it isn't that."

"I'm upsetting you. I'm sorry."

"It's fine."

She waited. "Then what?"

Ethel inhaled a breath. "All right. I haven't known how to say it."

Alice stayed very still.

"I'm sick."

So Moie's instinct was right. Alice let go of the bag. She met her sister's watery gaze.

"Annie was sick with Wanlyn. Many women get sick."

"No. I knew you'd think that." Ethel was distressed. "Do they think that at home?"

"Maybe," Alice answered, confused. "Moie especially wondered."

"I told Clarence, we should have written, 'Ethel unwell. Needs assistance.' But no, I see, you still would have thought it."

"Unwell, dearest? In what way, unwell?"

Two hairpins, which had been in Ethel's lap, tumbled soundlessly to the floor. The orange flame bent and the metal ring rattled inside of the oil lamp, as the puddle of illumination swept in an unexpected direction. Ethel was moving it, her face aglow.

"I'm sorry to do this," she said. "But I'm going to show you something vile."

Alice stood, moving against a heavy feeling of dread. She followed her sister across the cold, dark room. In the corner near the door was a small barrel with an ill-fitting lid. Ethel lifted it. The light dipped to reveal a heap of crumpled fabric that was stiff with a russet brown substance.

"It's been like this for almost two weeks."

At first, Alice did not understand. Then light touched the upper folds. A gloom oppressed. An outhouse smell. Dank and mineral, like rich soil. Once she had seen bloody debris like this, clumped and wet on rags, and treated with the same kind of solemnity. A bedroom door opened in Alice's memory. And, again, she was in their first home in Placer County, their drafty shack in the woods. The Bushes were the sisters four, but they would have had a little brother, if only that small creature, the year after Daisy was born, had stayed inside their mother to grow.

"Oh, Ethel."

"It's all right."

The top rag was still damp. Lift it, and find, what? A small, scrunched face looking back at you? "Is there a baby in there?"

"No. Thank God."

"Is there one now?" A sweeping look at her sister's waist. "One that hasn't yet—"

"I thought that," said Ethel, voice thick. "But I don't know anymore.

There's only a trickle of blood that won't stop and a screw of pain in my side. Clarence tried to diagnose me with appendicitis. He was so adamant. The doctor came and examined me and, after an hour of Clarence's bullying, he admitted a slight possibility. Thank goodness he wasn't completely persuadable. He drew the line before cutting me open."

"We'll go home." Despite her disappointment, Alice was rallying herself. Suddenly Moie's instructions could not have found a more willing messenger. "You can't hike a trail. You told me once that climbing the Chilkoot Pass was like climbing a ladder forged out of ice. You can't do that if you're sick." Alice gestured at the barrel. "My God, Ethel, imagine *that* in a tent."

But the advice was, surprisingly, unwelcome. Ethel reached behind her head. Unfettered, a thick collection of dark hair tumbled in a wild cascade to her waist.

"Do you think I brought you here to take me home? I could've had my pick of local heroes if all I needed was an escort to Selma."

"Fine. Have Clarence find us a room. We'll stay in Seattle. Tell the family we're waiting for warmer weather before meeting the boys. Many sane people would do just that, healthy or not. Then, in May, June, if you're better, we'll go."

"No."

"You're being stoic. To the point of stupidity."

"It's a dangerous trip," Ethel agreed. A reproof. To whom? "You're right if you decide not to come. I'm mad at myself for doing this to you. I shouldn't."

Their eyes met. Neither spoke.

Then Alice said: "I'm not scared of traveling."

"You should be."

"And you?"

"I can't miss this, Alice. How can I explain it?" Ethel sighed, though it was a sigh that seemed, strangely, to lift her up. At the same time, she seemed to make a decision: at last to tell her sister all. "It may sound silly to you, but I feel that I've found it, the life I was made to live. And I can't give it up. I know the newspapers make me look ridiculous, all 'tough-as-nails' like they say and audacious. But in a lot of ways, they read me right. I do love it." She was in shadow, but her face blazed with the brightness of self-understanding. "For so many years I felt I could do more than what was asked of me. I cared for you little ones when Poie and Moie were down on their luck. I kept house for us all and I wouldn't trade that for anything. But that first time Clarence and I stepped off the boat in Dyea—it was this exhilaration I've never experienced. I felt like four walls around me had cracked and fallen, and I was finally free, I was seeing the world like I'd never been able to see it. Breathing it in, touching its glory. I walked thirty hard miles driving the dogs. I climbed the Chilkoot on my own two legs, grasping at rock with an ice pick in my hand. It was marvelous. Like I really was on the top of the world. I want to breathe that air again. I want to feel like I'm experiencing life to its fullest. Do you understand that? This is *it*, Alice. This is the apex of my life. This is my youth. The last of it. And if I were to stay in this hotel, if I were to go back to Selma, I would miss it, and I would always regret it. I'd never get back to where I am now."

12.

Twenty hours before their ship left port, and amid the swirls of snow and the flurry of packing, Alice was walking a narrow edge. She had sworn to help her sister. She would travel with her and make this trip possible for her. During that intimate night of confessions, she'd felt caught up in Ethel's words, and had said: "You're right, Ethel darling, I think. We cannot miss this." But what had she agreed to? She couldn't stop wondering. Had she killed her sister with her promise to help her travel North—or maybe killed them both? Meanwhile, Clarence was absolutely no use on the subject. He had already determined that his wife would not be persuaded to stay. He'd agreed to have Alice travel with them in order to be a help to Ethel, and, for him, that was the end of it. Alice was mad at him. Though he was almost too pathetic a figure for sustaining her anger. Other worries were subsuming him now. Alice had heard a bit, in Selma, of Clarence's great fear of boat travel. But it was no preparation for watching the man crumple in front of her eyes. He could not be talked to. If he spoke, it was only to tell the story again of the *Nancy G.*, which had sunk. Or the *City of Mexico*, which had sunk. He kept circling back to the tragic fate of the *Aurora*, which had gone the wrong way around an island, near the mouth of the Skeena River, barreled into a reef while under full headway, and—over the course of a painful twelve hours—had sunk. He said, mournfully, I can't get the *Moon Merry* out of my head. That was the rickety old steamer which, as they all knew, had last been spotted tilted sixty degrees and going due west into a squall.

The morning of their departure, Clarence withdrew into himself, and would not touch his breakfast. He stood at the window, his hands clasped behind his back, while his wife and his sister-in-law dug their fingers into the bags. They folded rags for Ethel and counted morphine pills: what Alice couldn't help but feel was a deeply inauspicious start to a journey. A weak early light aged the room. Their coffee, half-finished, sat icily in small white cups.

When Frank Berry strode in, all happy excitement, he was taken aback by the solemnity. He diagnosed the mood as morose without being tragic.

"As if a poor bachelor uncle," Frank said, pinning the feeling down, "whom we didn't know well, has just passed away in the bed."

Finally Ethel gently announced the time, and they were compelled to join the people in the street who were funneling toward the dock. The Berrys were looked at with wonder. Clarence Berry was returning to rich claims that he already owned, while everyone else was going North to stake in a land that was said to be filling up by the day. Alice might have enjoyed the moment, but worry was pulling her down.

Yesterday, Alice had written a telegram to Moie and Poie.

Ethel well enough. As she ever was. We leave on the Bertha.

She hated to think what their thoughts had been upon receiving those enigmatic words. She hardly knew her own state of mind. Just ahead, other passengers might have been going into the water itself, for how they crossed the gangplank: eyes squinting, a jump before you have time to think.

13.

That first night at sea—that blue rush of movement—was too exhilarating to leave space for regret. And Alice thought, prone in her bunk, Ethel was right, despite the danger, we could not have missed this. Then, the second night, the wind blew, the boat rocked. Now Alice thought, in a twist, Clarence was right all along: we will drown.

In the corridor, a man said, "Six inches of horse piss washing the deck. Do you think I'll wear these shoes again?" His companion answered, voice muffled as they moved, "I've got news for you, bub, you're going to die in those boots."

Tap, tap, tap, tap. It was Ethel on the other side of the wall, from her adjacent cabin with Clarence. Alice turned on her side and answered with a double knock. They'd been conversing like this for hours: I'm alive, are you? For now I am, are you?

Then the ship lurched, and Alice covered her mouth. She'd never been sick on rivers, but the motion didn't compare. Now, without knowing what she was doing, she stood and, using the wall for balance, stepped across the room to the door. She opened it, and vomited massively into the hallway, while behind her, her bunkmate, Jeanette, a woman on her way to reunite with her shopkeeper husband in Dyea, was calling: "Where are you going, where are you going?" In the black corridor, the water sloshed and poured over the tops of her boots. She zigzagged down the hallway. She didn't know where she was going until she noticed the open doorway emitting soft light.

Three men. They huddled around a table with a hurricane lantern, attempting a game of cards with a deck that kept slipping from under their hands. A pair of faces angled up, astonished. The man with his back to the door turned all the way around in his chair. There was silence until the shortest, a porter, beckoned her in.

"Here's a girl after our own hearts, ready to meet the fishies with her eyes open. Come sit here, Miss, we don't bite. We'll leave that to the sharks." Then in horror of his own evocation, he shuddered. "Jesus. God forbid."

They pulled over a chair and spoke their names. This was the gentlemen's room. Only slightly larger than the cabins, and humid with the same rotten smell. But the light was nice, as was the reflection of light off the mirror, and Alice decided that she'd rather be here than holding hands with Jeanette. The men with the porter were cook's aides. For now. They confessed they were all three planning to abandon ship in Dyea. They would purchase supplies, build a sled, pack themselves over the Chilkoot, and heigh-ho it for Dawson. It was the same plan everywhere. Though Alice noted that the sailors lacked the boyish enthusiasm of the men on the Pullman train and the Seattle set, as well as her own green excitement for traveling. They spoke about the journey as if it were a path that had unrolled under their feet, and they had no choice but to walk it.

"We'll see if we can find a good pup creek," said a cook's aide. "Maybe even a piece of Bonanza. We heard that Eldorado is staked."

"Fractions come up now and then," Alice said. Her tongue was loose; the rocking boat and fear of death must have freed it. "My sister owns a fraction between *Five* and *Six* Eldorado. Her husband mismeasured the claim by forty-two feet when he put in the stakes. When the error was discovered, he gave the fraction to her."

"Who in God's name is your sister?" they wanted to know.

"Ethel Berry. Her husband is Clarence."

They were amazed. You're rich, they told her, with a brother and sister like that.

"*They're* rich," she corrected, laughing. "I'm Nobody. I'm Little Miss Sister. I wish I could have what they have."

It was a dark confession. She had hardly known the depth of her want—until she heard herself say it. But as these men had no stake in her life, they took it in stride.

The porter wanted to know: "Why'd they bring you?"

She told them Ethel's problem. They flinched. On a ship full of men, she felt sure they wouldn't repeat it. Anyway it seemed wrong to dissemble, when their lives might end here, in this gentlemen's room turned into human aquarium, with only each other's twisting bodies for company.

"If we survive this, those damn Berrys better fill your pockets with gold," said the porter. "The audacity that fellow has, bringing a beautiful girl like you to the Klondike. You should have stayed home."

"Stay home?" Alice cried, as the ocean crashed at the porthole, and the flame tilted into itself and died. "Not for the world."

Now they admired her. They were a little in awe of her. She was the one thing in the room with a hopeful glow. Then the ship swung, and cold water sloshed up her legs. "Oh God," groaned one of the cook's aides, his torso briefly aloft in the seat. They all grasped the edge of the table, which was bolted to the floor. A neat arrangement of fingers appeared in a circle. It looked as if they were preparing a séance. Maybe their own.

Their parting gift to Alice was a tumbler of brandy to take back to her room. Each man had contributed a small amount from his flask. She felt her way down the corridor with her free hand. She hit the wall. The ship righted itself. A brown balloon floated over the top of her boot; a drowned rat. She stomped forward. The water was black with coal dust; the cargo of a previous voyage. She took larger steps, unable to guess what her foot was disappearing into.

Jeanette said, "Your sister's been tapping on that wall for an hour."

"Did you answer?"

"She wasn't tapping for me."

A steady pounding above the bunk. Alice tapped back. Ethel responded. And so on, until day.

14.

Arriving at Dyea, after the ocean's chaos, was like arriving into the open arms of the continent. The narrow inlet caught the boat and carried them in. The bow rose over a hump. It fell, then dove, straight to the heart. Alice walked onto the deck, joining Clarence, Frank, and her sister. She was shaky and bruised but flush with relief at the sight of land. With the wind blowing their hair, she kissed Ethel's soft cheek, slowly, as if she'd never kissed it before. The air stung with invisible barbs of ice. A stack of gray clouds made the sky. The hills were a patchwork of missing timber. A tight collection of buildings—maybe three blocks of shops, inns, and a scatter of private homes and pale tents—huddled together in a low spot, all the doors facing inward, as if taking refuge from their surroundings. Along the outskirts of town were more tents and piles of lumber. In the distance, they could just make out packs of penned-in dogs and wan-looking horses that galloped in short bursts along the side of a low wooden fence.

Anchor dropped. And soon the captain, Captain Mack, who'd been otherwise occupied during the journey, was walking among them, hurrying them off his boat. There was no dock in Dyea. Everything had to go on rafts and skiffs to land. The dogs whined until they were freed, then they turned skittish and stood against the legs of their masters, licking their hands. The horses screamed and stomped and thrashed their heads as they were backed off the ship and made to swim. The deck was warm with their smell, and you had to stay clear of them if you didn't want to be kicked. Clarence said that on a boat last year, the lowest deck had flooded and drowned the smaller animals in five feet of water: the furry corpses of all the dogs found floating at the tops of their crates. This journey had been smooth by comparison. Though Clarence, who knew the country better than most, said gravely, to anyone who cared to hear, "The dogs will make it, but the horses weren't built for this climate. You may count every one of these horses as dead."

After many back-and-forths, they had done it, and all was well. The piles of cargo lined the beach, making a low wall of crates and bags. Alice and Ethel were already starting to talk about dinner: whether they should buy seats at a hotel table or cook. Then a young man, working on arranging his pile, looked down at the ocean splashing his ankles. He shouted, "Christ!"

Realization spread across the crowd. The captain had made a mistake. He had dropped them off at low tide. Now the sea was rising. All the cargo, all the supplies for the trail, piled up at the water's edge, was in danger.

An uproar followed, but there was no time to be mad. Each man had to carry a thousand pounds of grub up the beach, and he had to move fast to beat the incoming waves.

A group of packers—Indians, with a scatter of whites—were advancing in small shuffling steps down the beach, announcing their rates.

Alice, enraptured, was startled to feel the hand on her back: Clarence pushing her and Ethel up the sandy hill, out of the way. "Can't we help?" Alice asked. But even Clarence's liberal attitudes, which had allowed his wife and sister-in-law to travel with him, wouldn't expand to women carrying crates.

Meanwhile, a Greek tragedy played out in the drizzle. A hundred outfits sat at the foot of the champagne beach. Men had spent their life's savings on these or taken loans from their families. The axes, picks, flour, and precious bags of sugar; the salt pork and beans; the fur robes; the canvas for tents. If the tide came in faster than each man could move his cache, he would be done for. Beneath blue glaciers, mortals swirled. In the wind, you could hear the wails of the chorus.

Suddenly Ethel said "Oh!" and grabbed Alice's arm. "Look, there's Jim! I'm so glad Clarence found him. The packers always come to meet the boats, but we didn't know if he'd be among them or not." Jim was the Tlingit man from Clarence and Ethel's "Tales from the Trail," whom they'd met here two years ago, and who had packed them over the Chilkoot during their honeymoon trip. Alice watched him. She was excited to see this person she'd heard about. She observed how, exactly in keeping with her brother-in-law's descriptions, Jim lifted the Berrys' heaviest sack, the flour, as if it were nothing to fuss about.

Soon the mood of their own party changed. It was clear that they were not in danger: not with Clarence, Frank, and Jim hauling supplies. But others were very bad off. The men who'd traveled alone and could not pay a packer were facing their ruin.

There was one frantic-looking youth with blond hair to his shoulders whom Alice could not look away from. He was bent low and rolling a crate up the sand. He looked back and saw where he'd left his sacks. He abandoned the crate. He hurled one sack over his shoulder, doubted himself, and picked up a different one. His boot turned in the soft sand and he fell slowly and comically onto his side. He did not cry out but instead wore the half-smile of a person who is horrified.

From out of the foggy masses, Clarence emerged, throwing down near their feet their rolled canvas tent. Then Jim, with the beans and dried apples. He gave a nod of greeting to Ethel. Frank returned, dropping the ice pick onto the pile. He wiped the sweat from his eyes, then took a second to follow Alice's gaze, which still lingered on the blond-haired man.

"You plan for a year," Frank said. "You line up looking just as smart as the chap on either side of you, then the starting gun shoots a pellet into your ass."

"I feel badly for him," Alice said.

"It's better this way," he answered. "We could help, but it would be giving a man a leg up into a lion's pen. The only thing that man will be losing today is his money and pride."

In two hours' time, it was over. Boxes drifted, dislodged from the ground. A dark hue climbed sacks of grain. A bag of evaporated onions was before their eyes being rehydrated. An axe, lost in the shuffle, was in the process of sinking into the sand.

Thick snow kicked down on a steep diagonal. The packers mingled together, pleased with the day. Jim strode around the beach at a confident clip, talking with everyone.

Then the light was draining from the afternoon, absorbing itself into the spongy earth. The beach began to clear out. The losers slogged toward the same smudge of life as the victors. The town was too new for lampposts, but the window light from the buildings at least combined to a welcoming glow.

The sisters were among the last to leave the beach because Clarence had told them to wait until he'd found them a decent place to stay for the night. Only the *Bertha*'s crew remained, sitting around a bonfire that fed, in part, on the ruins of abandoned crates, which had been smashed open and emptied. Alice and Ethel had just heard Clarence's whistle—their signal to come—when Jim, not noticing them, emerged from between two dark buildings, walking down the beach, a pipe appearing from a narrow pocket of his vest. To Alice's surprise, he was approaching the *Bertha*'s captain, who, in a display of true nerve, had left his ship to take a fireside dinner.

Ethel was already moving up the bank and, reluctantly, Alice took a few hurried steps to catch up.

But then, behind her, came the noise of Jim and the captain exchanging a spirited greeting. She turned. Now Jim was dropping down in the sand at the captain's side. Jim handed over a leather wallet, opening the top as he did. Alice froze. She strained to make out what was happening. Jim never saw her, but the captain did. While accepting the wallet, he shot a long look up the empty beach and noticed her watching. There was something forbidding in his expression that made her spin away and move on. She couldn't imagine what business Clarence's packer had with Captain Mack. And yet, when she dared to look again, they were talking jovially together. The captain, once more relaxed and smoking, made a gesture across the shoreline, at the litter of ruined supplies, and laughed.

15.

Inside the Dyea Hotel, a shack with a grand sign over the door, Alice told Ethel: "You won't believe what I saw." And described the meeting between the captain and Jim.

They weren't alone in the open downstairs. A man head-to-toe in brown fur, in the chair by the hearth, overheard them. He said sourly, "Why do you think the captain let us off at low tide?"

Alice and Ethel did not understand.

"The packers get their payday," he spat. "Thanks to Captain Mack. What you witnessed was the packers giving the captain his cut of the profits."

When Clarence burst indoors with a gust of cold air, Alice said, "Listen to what we're talking about." But Clarence, when she repeated the facts, said it was bull.

The man in brown fur shrugged. He drifted away, to the men's bunkbeds upstairs, as if he didn't care for the trouble of disagreeing with Clarence.

Clarence warmed his stiff, pale hands by the fire, and, after giving him time to thaw, Alice tried the subject again: "Don't you see what they did, Clarence? Wouldn't you call that a conspiracy?"

He grunted.

"Listen though," Alice insisted, growing excited. "I saw the money change hands with my own two eyes."

"Jim and the captain are old acquaintances. I'm sure it was some other business they had together."

Alice wanted to press the subject, though she didn't quite dare to. And in her hesitation, Clarence's anger softened.

"When I lost my farm in Kingsburg," he told her, "the whole world laughed at me. I didn't have the money to eat or change my shirt. I looked a fright. I stunk worse than my dogs. I was a good man. I was a smart man. I was a hardworking man. But no one else could see that. Now I try to do others the favor that wasn't done for me. I judge people by their character. I put no value on surface appearances. Jim might seem very foreign to you. And Captain Mack is not the kind of family man you're used to in Selma. But you can't make inferences about a man's moral character by the polish of his everyday habits."

Clarence looked at her, beneficently. Like the man in brown fur, he was going to teach her a lesson. But Alice muttered, indignant:

"You misjudge me. I'm the same as you. I don't assess people by their surfaces either."

16.

The next dawn, the Berry group hitched their fourteen good dogs to the sleds that Clarence had purchased. They broke through walls of trees and onto the narrow, snowy path, and hacked off the first easy miles that separated them from Dawson City, the hub of the gold fields and a dreamland of two-story cabins and shops.

The dogs were five Malamutes purchased in Dyea, plus the nine that had traveled with them from Selma. The first sled was managed by Jim. The second was managed by Clarence and Frank, with Ethel riding, tucked in with the bags. Ethel would rather be walking. But, still, her face was bright and alive. She liked the snow in her eyes. She held the whip but had to give it back to Clarence as, though she knew how to do it, the work was too much. Alice jogged, skirts heavy, always in danger of falling behind. Other travelers watched them pass with wistful, forlorn expressions. They were well outfitted compared to most: some men wore only one layer of wool and were already freezing.

They stopped for lunch and cooked pork and pancakes on their little sheet-iron stove. They fed dried fish to the dogs, though, poor things, never quite to their fill, as the animals ran faster and obeyed better when hungry.

The next day the trail steepened, and a strong wind wanted to push them back. They passed a horse that looked as if it'd been dragged out of the way, one with its hooves still in the path of the runners. Another seemed dead but wasn't quite, and Clarence spent a bullet doing the job, which was generous of him.

"Still having fun?" Frank yelled in the wind, as he jogged over to take her place by his brother. She'd been trying to help push the sled free from where it had caught on a ridge exposed in the snow. He heaved with Clarence and the sled broke free.

"My sisters and I ran a farm with no brothers," Alice defended herself. "I'm just as used to hard work as anyone here."

But as soon as dinner was done, she fell into her pile of furs. She made note in her travel journal of the distance they'd traveled, the names of people they'd met along the way. Then there was Ethel to deal with. The trickle of blood continued. Alice took the rags, stiff and sullied, and dropped them into a black pot of gently bubbling water. She stirred them with a good stick she'd brought in from outside. When they were still in Seattle, Clarence had said, "Maybe the cold will stop the bleeding up," but so far that wasn't the case.

Ethel's pain was worse at night, so Alice put hot compresses over that wide, indecipherable area of dimpled flesh, under the navel. She fed Ethel a morphine pill when the compresses gave no relief.

"I shouldn't have let you come," Alice said, drawing back from her sister. "There must be a growth, or a wound. I'm beginning to think whatever doctor you saw in Seattle wasn't the best." Then, the question that she held back for the sake of her sister's feelings, "What do you think is causing it?"

A whisper: "You know I don't know."

"I'm sorry." The air in the tent was heavy and damp with the steam from the pot.

"Just help me to the cabin," Ethel murmured. "You'll see once I get there, I'll be able to rest. I'll be fit as a fiddle."

17.

Sixteen days since leaving Seattle, three days since Dyea, the party broke free of the rocky trail. It was April 1, 1898, exactly one year since Ethel had written the fateful letter, announcing that she and Clarence had struck it rich. A low thick storm that had been with them all morning seemed to have its raging, center point here. Without the trees' protection, the wind lashed at their faces and bothered the dogs. Up ahead was the valley called Sheep Camp and towering above the camp—the great divide in the trail—the Chilkoot Pass.

From a distance, through the whirl of snow, they could make out the ropes marking the sharp incline. The Pass looked vertical, and smooth too. It wasn't clear what a person held on to in order to climb.

Snow thumped on their coats. A white stripe appeared down the back of each dog. They had to stop the sleigh to punch away the pyramid of snow that had built itself up on the bags. Clarence lifted his hat straight up, like a waiter lifting a tray. He lowered it to his front, then overturned it, watching, entranced, as the snow cascaded down.

They trudged on into the valley. Hundreds of canvas tents stood in straight lines, making streets like what you'd find in a regular town. Not a soul was out of doors. Then two dark figures came tearing toward them. After a startled moment, the forms solidified: it was a man chasing after a mule.

"No one's been going over the Pass for nearly four weeks," the man yelled in answer to Clarence's question. "You've got to wait for this godforsaken weather to stop, I'm sorry to tell you." He jogged backwards, so as to follow his mule and also finish his thought. "Some fellows tried it, but they were down in an hour. This wind will scrape you off the cliffside and throw you clear into the clouds."

They passed another ghostly figure who told Clarence of a spot recently cleared, the party having given up hope and headed back to Dyea, where they could pitch. They found the bare, flat spot in the howling swirl. First they hammered the pegs into the snow. Then they unfolded the canvas and tented it over the stays. They worked without talking because it was no longer worth the effort to shout. The snow was hitting hard. A man stopped at their tent, begging for food, and was given a pittance. Pine boughs that they'd gathered along the trail went down. Furs went down, as wide as the girth of the bears they had come from. The sheet-iron stove they erected at the center of the tent, with its long nose of fitted-together pipes sticking crookedly through a hole in the canvas. Alice started the fire. Snow thumped over their heads. The wind caused the pipe to rattle. It knocked around in the hole, shaking the walls. The dogs were sprung free of their harnesses and leashed to a pole. Frank left and returned with two hog heads, ears, snouts, and squished little eyes, which the dogs ripped apart with ease, goring the snow with stains of red and small pink tears of flesh, like crepe paper.

The storm blasted on through the dark day, and into the next. The sky was so low it was like living in smoke. Not knowing how long they'd be stuck, Clarence instructed Alice to ration the food; then, upon receiving his meal of beans and bread, he was grumpy.

While Clarence slept, Ethel held her middle. Tears fell from the edge of her eyes straight into the fur. No matter how she rallied herself through the day, she could not hide the pain splintering through the morphine pills.

She told Alice, don't worry, it will pass. But Alice couldn't pretend to agree. She—like Clarence—hadn't thought it possible for Ethel to keep dripping this strange blood for so long.

18.

Palm Sunday, April 3, in a surprise, they woke up to a clear, blue sky.

"Thank God," said Alice, "one more day in this tent, and I was going to scream."

"Think of me," Frank said. He accepted his bowl while pinching his nose, as these were the same beans from last night. "I'm supposed to be off staking claims with Henry. And instead I'm stuck here."

Around them, in the new and brilliant sun, Sheep Camp was dismantling itself. The Chilkoot Pass was finally open, and everyone wanted the front of the line. Alice stacked the cooking things and rolled the furs. She worked quickly. If they could do the climb before noon, Alice thought, that would be better. Already Ethel seemed slow and cautious in her movements. She'd tried telling Clarence this, but Clarence—too overwhelmed with all the changes in plans—had put her off, "I haven't noticed that." Of course he hadn't. He wanted Ethel to be the invincible wife who'd walked the trail with him in '96.

Once the tent was packed, Frank said, "Now all we're missing is our goddamn packer. Maybe he thinks we don't work Sundays."

"Jim knows," answered Clarence.

They waited, smooth snow on either side of them, as their neighbors had packed up and gone. An hour later, Jim made his appearance. Frank tried taking his arm to lead him, but Jim refused his touch.

"He says he won't go!" Frank yelled, slightly amused.

By comparison, Jim was aloof and self-possessed. Of all people, he reminded Alice of Poie, in the way that Poie would disengage his feelings, disengage his mind, when faced with an unworthy aggressor.

Jim found Clarence's eyes. "There's too much snow on the trail. I wouldn't try the Pass today. A hot sun will bring it down pretty quick."

"What are you saying, now?" Clarence asked. "You're saying you don't want to pack?"

"I said two months of snow will come down pretty quick."

Clarence seemed about to make a smart reply, then changed his mind. He turned slowly, shielding his eyes, gazing up at the still, shimmering mountains.

Meanwhile, amid Clarence's prolonged hesitation, his deference to Jim, Alice burned with impatience.

"Be careful, Clarence," she said lowly. "I wouldn't take his advice at face value."

But this was a small nudge, and Clarence ignored it.

Frank, his pack already strapped to his back: "I don't know what you folks are talking about over there. But either we put the tent back up, or we get a new packer."

Alice looked at Jim. She was remembering how he'd laughed with the captain. Jim returned her gaze with plain dislike.

Clarence to Jim, an almost bemused note in his voice: "All right, let's get this straight. You're telling me the sun will loosen the snow? And the snow will come down? We call that an avalanche. Is that what you're saying?"

"The first sunny day after the snow builds up." Jim made a sweep of his hand.

"That does it." Clarence kicked the rolled canvas with the side of his boot. "Put up the tents."

"On his word?" Of all things, it was Clarence's lightheartedness that was making Alice irate. "I told you I saw Jim on the beach in Dyea, giving a wallet of cash to the captain. Captain Mack let us off at low tide, in order to make work for the packers, and Jim paid the captain his share."

It was too much. All attention swung on to her. With no preamble, Clarence flipped into a rage.

"Enough! Who are you to speak of the captain?"

Alice regretted it. A poisonous feeling coursed through her. This was her thanks for trying to help. She hated them all.

"What do you think, Ethel?" Clarence spoke in a modified tone.

"I think," Ethel said, "we should listen to Jim."

For an hour, Ethel kept her distance from Alice. Then she approached with determined steps the younger sister whom she had betrayed. She said, "We've been so careful with the food, what if we cook a big feast for dinner? I'm ready to open those packages of eggs and apricots if you don't think it too hasty." Alice avoided Ethel's thick looks of concern. She readied the pots as if the work demanded all her attention. She had spoken against Clarence and Jim for the good of her sister, for the pride of the Berrys, but her sister and brother-in-law had not wanted or needed her help. A big cloud of steam billowed into her face, as she said:

"Clarence puts his faith in the wrong people. Mark me. There'll be no avalanche."

The sun burned bright. A procession of people moved toward the foothills. They were jolly parties, with bells on their sleighs.

19.

At noon the rumble came from all sides. Alice met Ethel's startled face and, grabbing her sister's waist, together they hurtled out of the tent. Outside, they couldn't tell which way to go. They shielded their eyes to search the luminous cliffs. The dogs were going crazy, straining the tethers, fur bristling. The air trembled. Hats went flying, to be caught in the whirl.

Then silence. Alice and Ethel had run twenty feet in an unstrategic direction. They couldn't find Clarence and Frank.

A young man, still gripping an apple, said, in a tone of wonder, "Avalanche?"

Within minutes, word from the foothills confirmed it. Hundreds of people were buried on the trail. Clarence and Frank showed up and nearly brought down the tent, swinging shovels over their shoulders.

As Frank passed Alice, he said, "Goddamn if that Indian wasn't telling the truth. Doesn't make you look too smart, Miss Bush. Tonight you'll be eating humble pie."

Rescue parties shoveled trenches up the mountain, willy-nilly, as no one could tell anymore where exactly the Pass had been. They dug where heads poked up from the smooth white snow. Like turtle heads sticking up from a surface. They dug, also, where hot breath was burning a pipeline up through the snow. Underfoot were muffled, human cries. One man spotted a lost leather glove; he went to pick it up, then leapt back; inside the glove was a woman's hand. The rest of her body was buried beneath it, like a peg that had been hammered straight into the snow.

Bodies rode down the trail on sleds. No soft corpses, these: frozen arms clawing, knees bent, mouths agape. They were still running. For them, the emergency would always be happening.

Alice saw herself as one of the bodies. It was so close. She had almost walked herself to her own death. If not for Jim's warning.

Two adjoining tents became the makeshift morgue. Alice went in to help, and Ethel insisted on coming with her. The corpses lay on the snow floor. The proprietor of the one market in Sheep Camp had put himself in charge and was asking passersby to come in and attempt identifications. But it was wasted effort, in most cases, as people had perished beside their friends or else had traveled alone. Two more bodies came down on stretchers fashioned from coats and sticks. Next a trio of would-be heroes burst in, pink and baffled and ready to sob. They had dug for two hours around a breath hole in the snow. But when they got through, it was only an ox, chewing its cud in a big hollow it had stomped out for itself under the drift.

The day moved, but the shock was like a brightness across the white expanse that held time still. Everyone was busy. They were afraid to run out of work, because then they'd have to face what had happened. Humiliation pulsed in her. She gazed out the tent flaps at the Pass and had the piercing sensation that the snow had dropped for her, as a reproof.

The count was nearing fifty now. And still more people must be under the snow. Alice looked down at the next body laid flat at her feet. It was a person she knew. The porter from the ship. He looked the same. His beard jumped out from his chin. His flesh was full and damp, like chicken flesh after it's plucked. The memory of that night on the *Bertha* washed over her: his stricken expression and the tilting of the gentleman's room.

The porter had expected to die in the storm. His premonition had come three weeks too soon.

Now Clarence arrived off the slope. His shovel bounced on his shoulder. His cheeks flushed as if the blood were knocking hard against the inner flesh, attempting escape. He spoke private words to Ethel outside, then searched the group until he found her.

"Go back to the tent, Alice."

"I'm helping with the morgue."

She angled a stump of frozen hair off the porter's face.

"Do you know what I'm thinking?"

"You're yelling."

"I'm thinking, we'd all be dead if we'd listened to you."

Terror gripped him. He needed to be angry with someone, or else he would sob. Alice turned slowly to look into the livid face of her brother-in-law. A white fog swirled between them; the freezing breath expelled with his words.

Once they were outside, Clarence shouted, making strangers stare. He said she should have learned her lesson about contradicting him. He said, "You had the gall to do that?" He was a man high in the world. But he feared a mistake that would steal his good life away from him. When he was silent, finally, it was a silence that said, here's a chance for you to say I know best.

When she wouldn't respond, he grabbed her arm and hauled her to the tent.

The moment they were through the flaps, he threw her forward. She tripped and the dark sheet-iron stove filled her vision—it struck her cheek as her hands caught the ground. She looked up. He was surprised that she'd been hurt, but he would not be sorry. She was a fool. That was the funny thing. She agreed with Clarence. She'd almost gotten them killed. But there was also a bitterness flooding her: if Jim had been a better man, she wouldn't have doubted him; if Clarence had been more alert to Ethel's suffering, she wouldn't have had to speak up for her sister.

Alice touched her cheek. The scratch was bleeding. This tender spot would bruise.

"Stay here," said Clarence. His body turning, his boots crunching snow.

A powerful shivering overtook her, and her teeth chattered. The tent, ten hours abandoned, was cold. Crawling on all fours, the weight of this day pressing her close to the ground, she dragged wood from the corner of the tent toward the stove. She had no possible recourse. But maybe one day she would. Her anger blotted out reason. One stick, two stick, three stick, four. In small increments, and with patience, do chilly hands gather fuel.

20.

Four days later, they rolled up the tents, packed all their belongings, and joined the line of people climbing the Chilkoot. The avant-garde was dead in the avalanche. The people who'd been next in line, either because crowding or caution had held them back, now shuffled bashfully, warily, up to the front.

Clarence, Frank, and Jim hauled the food and tools and other supplies. Alice and Ethel needed only to get themselves to the top. The Pass rose sharply before them. A straight white pathway three thousand feet from base to plateau. Alice thought, as she'd thought upon first seeing the incline: we won't be able to do it. But she and Ethel joined the pack with the men.

Then they started up, single file, clutching the guide cable. You could feel the vibrations of the many hands on the line. Ethel's fur coat was the wide brown wilderness in front of Alice's eyes. When they were only twenty feet along, Ethel said that she needed a break, making the line of men stop behind them.

The guide was in fact a double cable: one for going up, one for going down, as the men in their own party had done twice this morning, to retrieve their next bundles. Alice feared that the men would force them to move aside to the down-going cable, as no one had the luxury of waiting around.

"Darling," she said to Ethel, before someone else said it first. "If you need to go back, let's go back."

But Ethel took a breath, and drew upon some reserve within herself, and started again the crouched steps up the incline.

It was nothing like the triumph of '96, when Ethel had carried her own ice pick and kept pace with the boys. Now she cried out as she heaved herself upward—though stoic, always—muffling the noise in the massive sleeve of her coat.

Along the last stretch of the climb, the wind scraped against Alice's face. She could sense their altitude. Snowflakes didn't fall so much as condense directly in front of your eyes, from out of damp air. At the summit, Ethel threw herself over the ledge. And then Alice followed her, gasping.

Here, at the top of the Chilkoot, was the American-Canadian border. The plateau was crowded, not only because of the backup, but also because, before descending to the Canadian side, every group must first pass through Canadian Customs. The country, fearing an influx of unprepared travelers, and the accompanying threat of mass starvation, now required each person who wanted to cross to show proof of a year's worth of food. The Berry tent was pitched next to the customs tent, where red and blue flags beat the air. Jim stood at the flaps. He was puffing a pipe carved into the shape of a leaping fish, with smoke that smelled of sugar and bark.

His second payment, in his hip pocket, was an ample sum. Before the climb, Clarence had paid him far above what packers usually got. And shouldn't he? After Jim had saved their lives?

Ethel joined Clarence, who was kindling the fire, while Alice returned to the snowy crest of the Pass to retrieve Ethel's glove, which they'd thought must have fallen there.

When she returned, Jim was still at the entrance, eyes askance. She considered for a moment saying to him, as she had not said to Clarence, you were right after all. But his look stopped her. Jim was already sneering at her. Why should she humble herself any further? His shoulder bumped against her arm as she passed him. He had taken a half-step and inadvertently blocked her. That was how a man like Clarence might have read the moment. Both Alice and Jim knew it wasn't the case.

She had made an enemy; that hadn't been her intention. And making the situation worse were the questions: Who was lower in the hierarchy? Jim or herself? In California, it would have been Jim. Here, Alice was becoming sharply aware, she was on the bottom.

21.

The flaps dropped closed behind her. Inside the tent was a warm cocoon. The walls dipped comfortably low, and the fire blazed behind the iron teeth of the stove. Ethel lay with her head in Clarence's lap. Her hand resting near the top of his thigh. Since Seattle, they'd had few opportunities for a private talk. Much less other things. Though perhaps, given Ethel's ill health, intimate touches weren't for now. Alice delayed near the entrance, stomping snow from her boots. Clarence whispered into Ethel's hair, then he stood and walked past his sister-in-law. A blast of winter air hit her back. She waited a few seconds, then used a set of clothespins, brought for this purpose, to pinch the flaps closed against the wind.

"Where's Clarence off to?"

"He wanted to check the stays on the other tent." Ethel sat up, reluctantly.

"I don't blame him. One big gust and we'll be swept into the sky." Alice crouched by the fire. Her mood was low. Months stretched before her, marooned on a Northern claim with people who did not welcome her company. She'd left Selma for her big adventure, but what was it worth? She took the spot where Clarence had been, on the rumpled fur. She used the poker to shift the logs. The fire blazed, stinging her eyes. "If I were home right now," Alice said. "I'd be washing dishes with Daisy."

"If you're pining for Daisy, you must feel bad."

Alice laughed.

"Alice," said Ethel. "Tell me how you got that bruise on your face."

"I told you, I bumped into the stove."

"Tell me Clarence isn't responsible."

Alice was silent.

"He was evasive, too, when I asked him." Ethel was grieved. "I'll kill him if he did that to you."

The wind beat against the canvas wall and made it billow and snap. They both looked at it, braced for collapse. But the stays held; these, at least, had been hammered deep.

"Please," Alice said. "Let's just forget that awful day. It's bad enough those people died. But I can't think of that morning without wanting to slap myself. I tried to get Clarence to let us climb. If we had, we would have been buried alive."

"You're not the guide."

"You should have told me that before I made a fool of myself." Alice dropped the poker. She rested her chin on the ledge of skirt, which was tented between her knees. The snow fell on the canvas roof, a granular snow that made a sound from Selma, like a gust of dry dirt hitting a wall. The silence persisted. A hand on her shoulder. Though it roused nothing within her. No gratitude for her sister's sympathy. Not even the feeling of closeness. There was a hot longing pulsing through her that was stronger than tenderness.

"Don't be upset, Alice. I would hate if you're miserable." The hand stroked her braided hair.

I am torturing her, realized Alice. This pain I feel is causing her pain.

Ethel said, "I won't let Clarence treat you badly."

"Forget it. Really, Ethel. Anyway, it's not just Clarence."

The words escaped her. She wasn't even sure what she was doing, but she felt a smoldering warmth. A mysterious part of her mind was awake. Instinct was telling her to push this way, past the world of true feelings, into a world that was fantasy only.

"Then what?" asked Ethel.

"You'll hate me for it." Fantasy, still, yet Alice spoke on.

"Never."

"I feel like the biggest fool in the world. I was trying to hurry us over the Chilkoot because I had the idea that you and Clarence could help me stake my own claim."

A laugh burst from her throat. What was she saying? It wasn't true. The morning of the avalanche, she'd been thinking of her own exhaustion, of Ethel, of her anger at Clarence for not believing her report of Jim's interaction with Captain Mack. But now, without fully seeing through to her own aim, Alice altered the past. Still, it was easy. She took her passing dream of personal wealth, like what she had shared with the porter and cook's aides on the *Bertha,* and shifted the dream to a place where it might thrive.

"Why would you need a claim, darling?" Pity filled the tent. The viscous substance that was Ethel's love. "You know that Clarence and I will take care of you."

"I do know. And I am so grateful. But you have to understand, Ethel, even with your generosity, I'm never going to have a life like yours. You'll have your own house, a family. You'll have your freedom, whatever money can buy. But I might never have things like that."

What was she saying? What was she saying? Alice felt drunk on the moment. The statements were true and not true. But it was the right thing, gauging from Ethel's eyes, which were large, appraising, thoughtful, and, most importantly, filled with the need to help.

"Wait."

Alice wiped her face, then sat motionless, all anticipation.

"I want to give you something," Ethel said. "You're going to like it."

The oilskin pouch emerged, fished, from beneath Ethel's dress. The pouch opened. The deed extracted and unfolded, showing the hot, cursive explosions of ink. The deed for the fraction of land between *Five* and *Six* Eldorado. Alice had not seen it since Selma, when Clarence had made Ethel show it with his, to the Bushes and Berrys, while he told them, rapt: this gold-rich land in the North, here's our salvation.

Ethel: "I want you to have it."

"No!"

"Yes, Alice. I'm no braggart, but I'm a rich woman and I'll give my sister a present if that's what I want to do. Clarence could have given the fraction to one of his brothers. But he gave it to me to thank me for risking my life in coming North. Now I give it to you for the same reason."

"He'll be furious." Then, speaking like a Christian daughter, speaking as one should speak, she added, "If you are going to give this deed away, you should give it to Moie and Poie."

"I'll take care of our parents by other means. As for Clarence." What was that? A flare of unease? If so, it was soon overcome by a wave of stronger feelings. Love for a younger sister. Guilt in summoning her to this perilous place. "I'll tell Clarence about it once we get to our cabin," Ethel said. "When he's sitting pretty with his gold all around him. Now stop asking questions and get me a pen."

Alice did get a pen. And ink. Not too fast. At an appropriate speed.

Ethel crossed out her own name and wrote "Alice Bush" in its place. Then she printed the date and scrawled her own signature across the bottom.

"It takes a Canadian registrar to make it official. They keep a duplicate on file in the office in Dawson. But this is a start."

The paper, light, transferred itself into Alice's hands. She protested with a stream of words that left no opening for a reply. Then it was hers. An exquisite pleasure burst through her. She felt "Alice Bush" expand. She was more than what she'd been a moment ago. She stood, domineeringly, upon a mountain of earth. A riotous joy made waves in the air. Inside her echoed a fit of laughter, like the fit she'd had last year in Selma, when she thought they'd lost the farm—but now in perfect reverse. Instead of loss, an unthinkable gain. It was wonderful. She was, in fact, a little in awe of herself. After all the worry, the embarrassment, the jealousy, she had struck it rich without stepping foot on the creeks.

22.

At Crater Lake, Frank Berry slept with his head outside of his fur robe. In the morning, they called him "Father Christmas," because his beard had crystallized with ice. Though by noon they had amended the name to better fit his nature, and he was "Father Christmas's Evil Twin." One of the dogs stole the thickest slice of pork from the pan. They might have cried except that the contents were fully recovered, and the dog showed further ingenuity with a cunning apology: snout bowed, head lowered, tail curled between its legs.

On Lake Bennett, they passed two partners at the apex of an argument, dividing their cache. One took the tent and the other the sled. Frank yelled, "Perhaps when they're dead, they'll be buried together." The men looked up, red and blinking. Frank had meant to be cruel. But judging by the men's alarm, he'd probably saved their lives.

On Lake Laberge, the whips moved soundlessly through swirls of white, like the ersatz shavings inside a snow globe. Alice was walking with Ethel against her, when, strangely, the front sled with its dogs pulled sharply left with Clarence and Frank heaving it forward. The second sled rushed past and disappeared into the haze.

They ran without knowing why, and it wasn't until they were scampering up the bank on all fours, with three men and fourteen dogs looking on, that they learned that the men had heard the ice cracking under the weight of the sleds.

Spring was here. That night the air exploded with pops and booms, like pistol shots at their backs.

By the morning, the broken, overlapping pieces of ice dazzled where the sun struck the joints, and the water beneath was beginning to soften the edges and sink and digest the ice for its own. Already wide pools had formed. Walk out and a tidy circumference of ice might disappear from under your feet. You'd drop. You'd be underwater, almost able to stand, but no match for the long, clear slab, six inches thick, that was sliding swiftly to make a roof over your head. After breakfast, Frank teased Alice while they were collapsing the tent. "You almost died unmarried." He leered at her, waiting for her reaction. It would have humored Frank to draw her in, then shoo her off. He believed his handsome face was the qualification. But his ideas about himself were his own. She'd never been tempted by mean.

"Forget married," Alice quipped. "I almost died poor."

Not really. Not anymore. Of all the things that might happen to her, poverty was the one thing that had been pushed off the table.

But for Frank, her blithe response had the calculated effect. He was planning to go prospecting with Henry as soon as they reached the gold fields. But other than his mining tools and his big intentions, he had nothing material. He heard her unspoken words, which hit like a slap in the air: *poor like you.*

23.

The break of spring sun had brought the thaw, each shift of daylight excavating a layer of freeze off the pile. The bogs liquefied. The hard-packed snow disappeared, resulting in a four-foot drop in altitude in patches. The mud was treacherous, and one day they passed a man laid up with a twisted leg that was probably broken. After a brief exchange and a small gift of bacon, they'd walked away while the man charted their regress from his immobile spot on a red-and-brown tartan blanket: his body balanced on one elbow, tilted half-upright by the slanting hill.

Once the river was decently clear enough of ice, they built two rafts using the lumber from their sleds and the easiest wood they could cut. They put their supplies on board, dogs and all. And Ethel was able to sit with her legs splayed out in front of her, which eased her discomfort. Alice figured out how to balance their little stove on two irons, a foot above the floor of the boat. They lit a small fire inside the drum, and Alice cooked their bread and beans as they hastened along. There were so many creeks that branched off the river that sometimes they didn't know which way to steer. Clarence would take an empty milk can and drop it into the water; whichever way the current took it was thought to be the deeper, stronger water, so they followed that way. They guessed right most of the time and passed teams who had days ago passed them, and that put everyone in a cheery mood.

When the water began to quicken, it was the sign of the Five Finger Rapids, and Clarence made them steer the rafts onto a low muddy bank and all disembark. They leashed the dogs and carried their things the long way around while a paid man steered their empty rafts through. Frank grumbled about it. But then, from high up the cliff face, they watched the very next boat overturn with its supplies and its passengers, and that shut him up. Later, when the Berry party was back on the rafts, they glided past a little graveyard set upon an elevated spot of burgeoning primrose high over the river. Good citizens would haul out the bodies of those who'd drowned and bury them there. Though at least one of the deaths, Clarence told them solemnly, as they floated away, was suicide. A man named Sam Raymond had run the rapids three times. After the first and second disasters, he'd circled back to Sheep Camp, rebought supplies, and carried on with his plans. After the third loss, he'd said "What will happen to Mae and the babies?" and he'd unholstered his pistol from his belt and shot himself through from one ear to the other.

Finally, May 11, 1898, the Berry party came upon their destination: Dawson City. The rafts turned around the final bend and they received the full, wondrous effect. It seemed like magic: tucked among the great, empty mountains, a city as big as Seattle.

The town was built upon a hot flat cake of earth smack between the hills. And the whole area was swarming with people, with boats on the docks, with the suffuse noise of hammering, sawing, which sent booming, full-bodied echoes bouncing off rock.

As they drifted closer, Clarence grew nervous. And gradually the information came out—new to Alice—that there'd been a tragedy on Clarence's claim over the winter. Two of Clarence's miners had died. Henry had written to Clarence, blood disease, maybe, or some other weakness. Many people had died over the winter and Clarence admitted that he hadn't thought much about it. But now, approaching the place of so many desperate men, all thinned and disheartened by the black days of winter, he was worried. He wondered aloud at Henry's skill as an overseer, and whether people had taken Hen at his word. What if, in his absence, public opinion had turned against the Berrys, and deemed them miserly? A person lucky enough to work for Clarence Berry should not have suffered from hunger or cold.

A couple of young fellows pulled their raft in, and Clarence's expression was one of excruciating suspense.

But then, on the dock, he confirmed the name, "Berry," and no one leapt over to throttle him.

Clarence was relieved. Frank disappointed, as he would have liked to see his brother harassed. But they all enjoyed what followed next: their entrance into the thick of the city. The town was packed, buzzing with men back from the goldfields, as well as with the spring's fresh arrivals. They walked onto Main Street and received warm welcomes from the people who knew Clarence and Ethel from last year. At Turner Co. Auctioneers, they were asked to take their pick of the tables. The Monte Carlo Theater eagerly awaited their business. At Gandolfo Fruit, the proprietor walked out from behind the counter to shake hands with Clarence and then with the women. Alice walked linked with Ethel, smiling at everyone who smiled at them. They didn't see more than a handful of women, and those at a distance, but once they passed an open doorway and could hear a pair of high female voices singing inside.

The Berrys received royal treatment at the Tobacco store, the New York Saloon, the Pacific Hotel, the stand with Waffles and Coffee. There might have been some energetic whispering over Clarence's return, but nothing came close to boiling over.

If anyone was going to hold Clarence responsible for the death of two men, Alice reasoned, it wouldn't be these shopkeepers in Dawson, who wanted his business.

Still. Taking no chances, Clarence made a spectacle of himself—striding across town to the Dawson Cemetery to pay his respects at the graves. Then, in a payment more concrete, he settled the bill for the rented sled that had carried the two bodies from the claim down the frozen creek. The lumber for the coffins. The nails. He found the men who'd dug the graves in increments, lighting fires to thaw the ground, the same as they did when digging for gold, and, in case Henry had neglected to do it, put generous tips into their hands.

When it was done, Clarence was free again. And looking ahead. There were only nineteen miles more of walking until they reached the Eldorado claims.

The next morning, Clarence burst into the sisters' room, where they'd spent the night in the Dawson Hotel, in an actual bed. Alice was disappointed to see him. She'd wanted to sit quietly in this room for as long as she could. She was in a chair. Up off the ground. She'd never been so in love with the invention of furniture. It was the height of luxury just to eat at a table, with a plate before her, and not balanced over the stretched skirts of her lap. Ethel had slept through the night and had woken up in good spirits: she was taking the fact of her rest as further evidence that she only needed a return to normal comforts, and she soon would be on the mend. Their final night in the tent, when Alice and Ethel had boiled the water and stirred in the rags, Ethel had said: "I think the bleeding's less. Maybe whatever it was, I got it all out." Her stomach was still tender and slightly distended. And Alice had wondered—she wouldn't say it yet to Ethel—if perhaps all this time, the symptoms were those of a pregnancy after all, only one that had taken time in mooring itself, and settling in.

"My God," Clarence said, pulling a chair out and joining them, "it feels good to be back. I don't know what I was so afraid of. People like Frank stirring me up. Ever since we got over the Chilkoot, he's been whispering in my ear about the mob that would be lining the streets, wringing their fists, looking to hang me. We're rid of him, by the way. He left early this morning. He told me to bid goodbye to you girls. Last night he met a big group in a bar planning to stake on Quartz Creek, and went crazy, packing his bag, saying this was his chance. After all that whining and worry about Henry not waiting for him to go prospecting, he was the one to give his brother the slip. Henry will be furious. But Henry managed to stake a claim for himself on Bonanza this winter, so I suppose Frank wanted to even the score."

"What about Jim?"

Clarence was surprised. After Sheep Camp, Alice had mostly avoided the name.

"He's visiting his sister in Moosehide. Then he'll join us next week on the claims. He's looking forward to the regular wages that come with mining work. In that way, it's better than packing."

"How much?"

"What do you mean?"

"I was curious to know a worker's salary in this country."

Ethel looked sharply at her, as if Alice had said something obscene. And Alice wondered if she was still nervous about having given the fraction away. Though Clarence, oblivious, only pinched a pork link from Ethel's breakfast. "More than you'd think," he said. "More than I would care to pay him. By the way," he said, pointing to Alice's half-eaten meal. "I hope you're finishing that. Speaking of expensive. That pig scaled mountains to arrive on your plate."

24.

In the arctic air, with their final destination so close, and Dyea an astounding five hundred miles behind them, they were newly vivacious. The yellow sun was a fat nugget for the taking; the ground under their feet might have cracked and revealed long caverns of treasure, like a cave in an old Arabian tale. They were relieved of their supplies. A few men from Dawson, who needed the day work, were a quarter mile behind them with their bags and the dogs. Without Frank and Jim, Clarence seemed more relaxed. Ethel walked without putting all her weight onto Clarence's arm. They seemed happy. They shared a smile. It must be gratifying for them to reach this jewel of a place they'd put claim to all on their own. When they'd married, they'd both been impoverished people. But each had seen the light in the other: the light of a person who liked hard work, who was industrious. They'd each judged the other correctly. They were both thinking it now.

A landmark: the place where Eldorado Creek split off from its mother, Bonanza, and in another fifty paces the Berry cabin came into view. "Look at it," said Ethel, energetic. "It looks just the same." It was a two-story, rough lumber house, plunked solidly onto the earth, with a bare hill behind it. Simple. Sturdy. The kind of thing a child would draw if you instructed "make me a house." On one side, judging from the stovepipe, was the kitchen. Appended to the kitchen was an open-air shack for the dogs.

The pipe in the roof emitted a curling, dark gray thread. From inside, there was a flash of orange. The oven had opened and shut. A large, ruddy face appeared in the glass. Then the front door was flung open. On the threshold stood Henry Berry, grinning and looking as ever like Clarence's twin, except for the fifteen pounds of extra flesh and also the gesture: arms splayed and feet askew and eyes lit by a joyous fire within.

"Welcome to your humble abode! I've eaten your food, stolen your gold out of the earth, fired your best workers and hired my old school chums in their place. I tried to mortgage the property, but I never got good enough at forging your signature, which you so cleverly left on file with the local authorities. Come in then, don't stand there rolling your eyes. I was just checking the meat. My last chance to burn down the house, before the women take over the cooking."

Henry stepped aside, and ushered them in. His duty as caretaker ended this moment, and he seemed glad. His smile made everyone smile. He gave Clarence a crushing hug, lifting him clear off the ground. For Ethel, he had a deferential kiss, a kiss for a queen, except for the smirking.

"The climate suits you, Miss Bush," he said next, taking Alice's hand, making it small in both of his. "Truly you wear your mosquito bites with more class than any lady I've seen."

He held her still a second as they shook hello, and despite his teasing words, his gaze was warm. Finally, he looked past her across the empty claim.

"Don't tell me you lost poor Frank."

"He took off from Dawson with a big group he met at the bar," answered Clarence.

Henry cursed. "That infidel. We were supposed to set off prospecting together. I've been waiting for months. He couldn't wait for one day?"

Clarence stomped past Henry to survey the house. "He says to meet him at Quartz Creek if you care to."

The home was marvelous. Nothing at all like the cabins they had passed on other claims: which were all tiny and one-story and hardly more than huts. Instead, as soon as he'd had the money to do it, Clarence had built a place worthy of his excellent wife. There was a big room with bare, fresh lumber walls, which gave the feeling of being inside of a tree. The principal furniture was a rough, long table with benches on each side. In the corner was Ethel's rocking chair, on an oval blue braided rug. There was a second room, a small bedroom partitioned off at the back of the house; it contained a wide bed that almost entirely filled the space, even pressed flush to the window. A narrow kitchen, which Henry called "the galley," ran along the side of the house to the right.

Alice ducked into the galley just in time to turn the beef. It was a treat. Henry must have purchased the meat in Dawson for them. Against the wall was a large sack of flour and a barrel of crackers. On the shelf were containers for sugar and tea. There was a small bowl of freshly picked bush cherries. The cache, she knew from Ethel, would house all the tins of milk and canned fruit and their other provisions. She checked the sheet-iron oven, which Clarence had put in last year. It was flimsy compared to what she was used to, but better, she'd heard, than what even the hotels had in Dawson. A very lumpy loaf of bread sat baking inside. On a shelf over the lumber counter was a basket for serving, and she used it to scoop up a good portion of crackers.

"You shouldn't have invited that lout," Henry was grumbling, still about Frank, as Alice reentered the main room.

"Wasn't my choice," said Clarence, dropping onto the bench beside Ethel. "Pa was on my case all winter. He takes our poor brother's griping to heart. He worries that Frank can't catch a break in life."

Henry snorted. "How was he to travel with anyway?"

"Like dysentery," Clarence said.

Henry opened his mouth and emitted one of his famous, boisterous laughs. Clarence, with a thin, self-satisfied smile, took from Alice the basket of crackers and ate a big handful.

"On second thought," Henry said, wiping his eyes, "maybe I'll leave the gold to Frank and stay here with you." He winked at Ethel and Alice. "My eyes have seen nothing but filthy, godforsaken men all winter. I'm long overdue for a change."

25.

Dawn emerged as if the sun had the earth on a string and was jerking them back into view. Last night, after they'd eaten the roast down to the bone, Alice had pushed in the bench and unrolled her furs. Now she woke up and felt a rush of relief remembering that she was in the cabin, not on the trail. The Palm Sunday avalanche, trudging through snow, all of it seemed far away. She peered across the bumpy, lumber floor to the bedroom. They'd left the door open, and so she could see Clarence and Ethel under a great heap of blankets: curled together, almost on top of each other, almost indecent. They had not acted that way in the tent. But Ethel was stronger it seemed, her spirits returning. Now, also, they were the Mr. and Mrs. of the house, and perhaps they felt entitled to show it.

A restless body emerged from the opposite side of the main room, from a drape of black bear: Henry. He walked into the galley and pulled the curtain closed. Squinting, Alice could see his shuffling boots in the gap between the curtain and floor. She breathed inconspicuously. Soon there was the sound of boiling water and the crushing of beans and the aroma of coffee.

On Sundays, Henry used to visit their home in Selma, especially during the year when Clarence and Ethel were courting. His favorite thing was to sit down at the organ in their front room and belt out a tune. He would invite a girl to sing with him, then purposefully drown out that superior voice—Annie's, for instance, or one of the Smith sisters from down the road—which was to say, girls who had waited all week for the stage. At first it would seem like a misunderstanding, but gradually he'd fight so hard for preeminence that both performers would reach the point of shouting. Then Henry would collapse in a fit of giggles onto the keys, while the poor girl stood by the bench, blushing.

Once Alice had been alone with Ethel when the boys had come by. Clarence and Ethel had wandered off together, so she and Henry had walked to the ditch and sat beneath the old cypress tree where it was cool. He'd begun talking about himself. His history, his prospects as a farmer.

For one exhilarating moment, Alice had thought he'd been showing an interest in her. She'd seen herself, in a quick flash of light, standing in a pale dress at an altar, about to become the wife of Henry. But then, just when she'd been almost sure, he'd burst out with the confession that he found her twin sister, Annie, to be the loveliest girl in the world, and that he'd been coming here with Clarence with the purpose to see her. He'd declared that he was working hard, saving money, the usual speech. When he'd looked to her for her reply, Alice had been forced to tell him: "I'm sorry, I think Annie likes William Carswell." Henry had nodded and gone on talking, though never again about Annie.

For breakfast Alice served salmon on toast and canned peaches, a wonderful break from the bacon and beans of the trail. Henry sat back in his chair and regarded them all with watery eyes. There'd been long black days in the winter when he thought he'd go crazy, he said, seeing clown faces in the knots on the walls. He was so happy to have people to talk to. He couldn't hear enough about the dangers they'd faced on the journey. "Well look, C.J.," he said, leaning to clap a heavy arm around his brother's shoulders, "I'm not saying I wouldn't have made the most of it, but I'd rather you stay alive and keep your fortune, and I'll assist where I can with the spending." They carried their coffee cups outside. The light brightened the purple hills and made the creek shimmer and dance with white sun. At the table, Alice had been longing to ask, *Where is my fraction? Where is this slice of land, between* Five *and* Six, *for which I have the deed under my dress?* But she didn't dare, not until Ethel explained the arrangement to Clarence.

All around them, pits punctured the land hodgepodge. And these, Henry said, gesturing from the gravel walkway, were the mines. They began about twenty steps from the door, and in such a pattern that you could imagine the frantic work that had sunk them.

"You should stay back," Alice said, when she noticed Ethel coming down the stone step behind her.

But Ethel softly rebuffed the idea. "I came this far. I want to see my claims."

Henry walked them up to the nearest pit, proud to show off his handywork. The hole was narrow, with breadth enough to fit one man, and it dropped a straight eighteen feet down. This pit, like several others, had a wooden windlass built over the top—a little slanted roof that kept the rain out and covered a metal pulley system, with its large bucket and rope coiled tight around a winch. A hill of gravel stood beside the mine, and that was the rich ground, flecked with gold, that had been dug up from deep in the earth. Almost every pit had a little pile like this, most of them covered in canvas and weighted down at the edges with rocks. Now that the creek was running again, the workers would spend the next several months washing the gravel from these mines in order to separate and bag up the gold.

"It looks like child's play," Henry said, bringing them to the next deep pit, then the next. "Digging holes to China. Let me tell you it's anything but. The climate makes mining brutal work. It's nothing like California. Here, the ground is frozen solid for most of the year. You have to light a fire over the spot you've marked for digging. Then, once the wood burns down, you go in with your shovel and work away at the ground as fast as you can. You can get maybe one foot deep until the shovel once again hits frozen dirt. Then you light the next fire, wait till it's burned out, dig another foot, and so on. And all that while," Henry continued, "the wind is bludgeoning your face, and your fingers and ears are dying of cold."

They had a bit of an advantage over the others, however, Henry went on to explain. He walked Alice to a great heap of what looked to her like scrap metal, but was actually Clarence's steam point contraption, his own invention, which this winter they'd begun using in place of wood fires for thawing the earth when they could.

"What you do," Henry said, "is fill this big metal drum up with water, then build a fire beneath it. The water boils and the steam comes down the hose, you point the nozzle right over the place you're planning to dig. It works much better than direct fire for thawing the earth. It's more precise, and it saves the work of hauling the ash and debris. Clever guy, my big brother." Then, dropping his voice, his eyes indicating where Clarence was crouched, tinkering with the valve on the nozzle about ten feet away. "We thought he was a half-wit, when he was a boy. Little did we know that all that sniveling and puttering around were the early signs of genius."

The hired workers emerged from the five tents on the denuded hill, and soon the claim was alive with their movements. Not digging pits. Like Henry had told them, that was winter's work. Summer's work was to wash the gravel and take out the gold. The men gathered around the sluices, which ran parallel to the creek, forty feet long, like log flumes in miniature or wooden water slides for gravel. Men shoveled the dirt to the top of the sluice, then they poured in bucketfuls of creek water to make the gravel run fast down the slide. The useless dirt and rocks ran all the way down with the water, but the heavier pay dirt—the gravel rich with gold—stayed on the slide. Next, the men scooped the sludge from the rough wood with a pan. Then they went to the creek, added in water, and began the final step of washing the pay dirt clean. A few practiced twitches of the arm and the mixture began to swirl. A little cyclone formed. The lightest things flew off the sides of the pan, but the pure, heavy gold stuck.

From along the creek echoed shouts and hoots from their neighbors' claims, where the same work repeated itself. In the sky were the smudges of other fires. Gravel debris floated down current. Soon Clarence emerged from the house and, kissing Ethel's cheek as he passed them, marched away and mixed himself up with his crew. When he did that, Alice noted, he became a man among men: no different from his workers in his movements or build. The only way to pick him out from the horde was by the two red lines of his favorite suspenders.

Henry took Alice and Ethel each on an arm and they toured *Three, Four,* and *Five* Eldorado. Next they came in view of Anton Stander's cabin on *Six,* about a half mile down creek. He was an equal partner with Clarence, and as rich as the Berrys, though you couldn't tell that by his house. The roof was bowed and green with moss and the chimney pipe leaned far to one side. Small bones lay scattered beside the door, as if it were an animal's den.

"I can't count how many dark, winter days I spent alone," Henry whispered with an awed little shake of the head, "when the other option was to spend them in Stander's company. That should tell you all you need to know about the man. Especially coming from me, a person whose requirements for friendship are shamefully low."

They turned back, not wanting a meeting.

The conversation moved to the neighbors and who had or hadn't stayed for the winter. People who were strangers to Alice. They toured more pits on their return and Alice wondered: Is this my own land, under my feet? Deciding it was safe to ask, in general terms, even with Henry present, Alice said:

"Is this the famous fraction? The forty-two feet?"

Henry said, "Ethel's fraction? We walked over it yonder."

Ethel was discomfited. She seemed to have misinterpreted Alice's broaching the subject as a forceful push. Before Alice could stop her, she said:

"The fraction belongs to Alice now. I gave it to her."

"What's that?" Henry cupped his ear. His neck wrinkled with two deep lines as he turned. "Aren't you lucky? I've been here all winter, and I didn't get that."

Alice—stunned by what had just happened—couldn't think what to say. And Ethel, perhaps realizing that she shouldn't have spoken so soon, was reticent too. The dogs lunged as they neared, rocking their pegs. Finally Alice said to Henry, "I thought you had your own claim on Bonanza."

"I do," said Henry. "I took a few days to myself in December and staked *Fifty-Eight* Bonanza. You should see it sometime, it's very impressive. It's slightly more valuable than a cross-section of glacier, next door to the North Pole."

At the cabin, Ethel broke away and doubled back toward the digs. To find Clarence, surely, before Henry spread the news of the fraction all over the claim.

Inside, alone, Alice was hot with embarrassment. She was angry at herself for raising the subject. Then she was angry with Ethel for misunderstanding her and revealing the truth too soon. She was angry with Clarence, for how she imagined he was at this moment taking the news.

She opened her journal then put it away; she got out her stationery, realizing that she needed to announce their arrival, but could not compose so much as a cheerful greeting. She heard Henry's indignant words again in her head, only this time, her own voice retorted: Too bad if you spent the winter here and feel you are owed for it. Too bad if you spent six months as nanny to your brother's gold. Too bad if you believed that scooping gravel out of the earth, swirling it, holding the gold in your palms, in the gray vaulted days of November to March, meant that you owned it. Too bad if you failed to learn this American lesson: it doesn't matter the patch of ground you sleep on, or what your own two hands have wrestled out of the earth. What matters is this piece of paper with English writing. A name, a date, and a signature, like the one I have folded in my oilskin bag.

26.

That afternoon, at the end of a tense, quiet meal, Clarence stood, tipping his chair. "Come with me, Tot. I want to talk to you." Alice tried raising a hint from Ethel, but her sister didn't seem to know what was happening either.

"Come on," barked Clarence. "Before the mosquitos get worse." Then he added, soft though still authoritative, as Ethel moved to accompany Alice, "Ethel, you've done enough walking of late. You stay where you are."

Across *Three* and *Four* to the top of *Five*. The workers' tents made ghost shapes on the hills. The air was misty. The water fast and loud over the rocks. Clarence scooped a wooden peg from the depths of his vest. He indicated a mark on a lonely spruce, then drove the peg down with his foot, into the muck. A length of rope emerged from his pocket.

"Ethel gave you her fraction, did she?" His voice trembled. "Not bad for the kid sister who came along to help with the cooking. I would've suggested a slightly more modest present. Maybe a new pair of gloves and a hat. But no one asked me. Now," he continued, "I brought you here because I thought you'd like to see your land. That's customary, when there's a change of ownership. The stakes move around during the winter. But we can mark it again." He dangled the rope, and said, "This was pre-measured. Forty-two feet."

He tied one end of the rope to the peg, then he walked the loose end carefully over the gravel.

Quick-footed, heart racing, she followed him downstream. When the rope ran out, he drove in the peg. Then he waded across the creek and repeated the task. She stood still, her arms crossed over her chest. He was angry, but that was fine. Anger was to be expected. He'd get used to the strange fact of her owning the land, as the summer went on. He hammered the other two pegs into the earth, across the way. Her eyes swept left and right, surveying the gravel. How much gold was scattered here? What would Moie and Poie think? Would they be happy for her? Or would they think that she should not have accepted the deed?

Clarence splashed across the creek; the water dancing at the tops of his knee-high boots, wetting his trouser thighs. A new expression, she noticed, was emerging from behind his mask. Not just anger, she thought, growing discomfited. More like viciousness. More like rage. The lightness of the morning, its effervescence, was escaping up through the thin air. Seconds later, Clarence splashed up the bank, onto dry land, and crushed the remaining space between them with a look.

"We can borrow a yardstick to correct it down to the inches—but this gives a clear idea of what you've got." He indicated the distance between the two nearest pegs. "Here's what men have killed themselves trying to get. Forty-two feet of the best ground in the Klondike." He glared at her. "What we haven't discussed is the depth." The word was drawn out, hummed like an insect trapped against his teeth. He was up to something but Alice didn't know what. Her gaze skimmed the ground, searching for clues.

"What?" she said. "Go on, say it. You took out the one vein, and now there's no gold? You worked the land empty?"

"There's gold all right. The damn outhouse is sitting on gold. We took out a thousand digging the pit. There's a pay streak here that runs the length of the creek. It would take years to pull it all out. The problem is, how to get it."

She glared at him.

"Two workers died this winter," he said lowly. "On this land. You think it's easy? You think you'll call 'here goldy, goldy,' and watch the dust jump out of the earth?"

"Listen to you. You're as mean as Frank." Briefly, she had interrupted his show. But there was no triumph in the achievement. The crack in his performance allowed for a glimpse of his outrage: how rich and deep that particular well. She clenched her arms again. Chilly, today. Her breath froze white. Beyond that white cloud stood Clarence, beyond Clarence was the cabin. She imagined Ethel inside, fretful and with her face to the glass.

"Probably," said Clarence, endeavoring again for his smooth, businessman's tone, "you could take three thousand dollars a month out of this ground. But the pay streaks lie twenty feet down, which means you'll need several men to work the digging and keep the hole open. You'll need picks, shovels, and one man to haul lumber for the fire. Then sluices to separate the gold out of the pay dirt. I've rented out men and equipment before. I suppose I could do it for you." He pinched into his shirt pocket, then unfolded a piece of Ethel's stationery, which he had destroyed with his writing. "Here's what it will cost you."

He looped his thumbs beneath his suspenders and popped them out, making room for his chest, which was swelling. He had made her an itemized list of the costs. Pickax, ten dollars. Labor, two hundred dollars a week. And so on.

"And the total?" She used a dispassionate tone, the tone she used at the grocer's.

"I'd need a pen." He sneered. "About two thousand dollars just to get going. By the end of the summer you'd owe me—"

"Okay, okay, I understand. I can't afford to mine it."

He was triumphant.

"So I may as well sell it."

He sputtered; his Irish color left his face. "What would your sister say?"

"That I'm overzealous when it comes to making a profit. She must be used to it though. She married you. Next time Henry has an errand in Dawson, I'll walk into town."

"You will not." The mood had changed. The cards spilled and knocked onto a hard surface, bouncing once, into oblivion. The game they'd been playing with numbers and sums had run its course. In a span of seconds, they'd both outgrown it. "You don't realize what I've done for your family. My Christmas present to your mother and father was twelve hundred dollars."

"I wonder what they spent it on. We were still eating eggs for every third supper when I was there."

"Did you hear me? I said, twelve hundred dollars."

She waited.

"They're squirreling the money away, is what I imagine they're doing," Clarence said. "Do you think your father wants to keep running that farm, now that he's past fifty? He and I had a private conference one night, after you girls had gone to bed. I said, 'Mr. Bush, by the end of this year I'll be on my way to half a million dollars, and one thing I would like to do, if you'll indulge me, is put you and Mrs. Bush snug in a pretty white cottage overlooking the seashore.' That wasn't my idea, mind. That's what your parents dream of. I drew it out of him. They want to live near the Pacific and sleep with the windows open, hearing the waves. You should have seen his face. I told him, you give up the farm, whenever you want, and you and Mrs. Bush will have a pension of five hundred dollars a year for the rest of your lives. I promised him. And that's what I'll do."

Alice was silent. She wanted to say, what do you know about Moie and Poie? But she was afraid that she had just heard her answer. In their private exchanges over the course of a decade, her parents would joke about their future retreat, until this year purely imaginary. I'm ready to start packing, they'd say to each other, for our house by the sea.

"Your family," Clarence said, "I consider as dear to me as my own.

Maybe that's why I can't stand to have you treat me as an adversary instead of a brother. That deed was a gift to my wife. She made a mistake in passing it on to you. I believe she understands that now. Show compassion to both of us, and don't capitalize on her error."

Alice could not speak. She couldn't stand to be a person who had taken advantage of Ethel's sweetness, no matter how willingly Ethel had given this gift. She reached toward the fold at her chest with the slowness of a person who knows that these movements will have a lasting effect.

The deed, blood-warmed from its home in her dress, he accepted into a palm.

Gently he said, "Here's the end of it."

The sheath of oilskin dropped—flew into the gray swirl before touching the ground. The deed, with her name, that outrageous defacement, he ripped, combined, and ripped again. No one would know. The record office in Dawson, which held the copy on file, would carry on with its stamping and sorting untroubled; it would not feel the piercing of this familial fight. Alice felt it.

This is how easily, she thought, my big ideas for myself are destroyed.

Clarence marched into the dull gray water, almost to the tops of his boots. He tossed the white pieces so that they sailed and fluttered a short way before sticking fast to the creek's surface and humping along the water's treads. The current was hasty and, in seconds, the bright shards of paper had passed by the cabin and disappeared around the bend to another man's claim.

"I'll tell you what," Clarence said. "I'll give you forty dollars a month for doing the cooking. If you'd like, I can pay you in nuggets, and later you can do as Ethel plans, and have the nuggets soldered onto a chain."

He returned to the shore. He touched the base of her neck with his fingertips. What he seemed to imagine was a comforting gesture.

3

FAIRBANKS, ALASKA
DAWSON CITY, YUKON

2015

At the mirror in the airplane bathroom, I experienced a jolt at the appearance of my own reflection. Not because of how I looked, not because anything in my face had changed. For hours, I'd been reading old letters and entries in a blue, fabric-covered travel journal once belonging to Alice Bush. They were part of a box of historical papers that had been bestowed upon me by my grandfather soon after we'd finalized the arrangements for this trip. Now, immersed in these visions, my thoughts had traveled to the contours of a different landscape, which is to say, a different mind. The result was that, when I'd caught sight of my reflection in the mirror, I'd been so enwrapped in the head of this other person that I'd thought I'd seen, not myself, but the fleeting face of Alice Bush. She was a woman dead for seventy years. But she came alive again, on Alaska Airlines Flight 106, hitching a ride back to the Klondike.

At my seat, I was about to resume my bookmarked place in her letters when Owen, turned to the window, reached for my arm and said, "You've got to see this." At the same time, I realized he wasn't the only one with his attention drawn to something outside the plane. I followed the general gaze to where, far below, a herd of large animals were galloping across a dark green-gray expanse.

"What are they?" I asked. Owen didn't know. But then we overheard other people, amazed like us, say they were caribou.

"Is that the same as reindeer?" Owen asked.

"I think that's right."

Owen, my lifelong city dweller, who'd grown up in Queens, then moved to Philadelphia, then to Los Angeles, had never been much of a naturalist, so I was surprised to hear him say, with deep reverence, "They seem out of a different world."

And really the beasts did seem almost magical, or like creatures that would only show themselves in special moments to human eyes. I didn't get back to reading Alice's letters. I marked my spot in her travel journal and shut the blue fabric cover.

As soon as we lost sight of the caribou herd, Mount McKinley came into view. Its sharp top poked through the soft, gauzy clouds. The mountain had been in the news lately, I told Owen. After nearly a hundred years of debate, the National Park Service was planning in a matter of months to rechristen Mount McKinley to its original First Nations name, Denali.

"Denali means 'the high one,'" I said, as we floated past. "Which I guess is about as appropriate a name as a mountain can ask for."

A soft warning chime came over the speakers, and I repacked the backpack that held not only the historical papers, but also our other, more practical gear: A modern map of the Yukon and Dawson City. A paper copy of our rental car reservation. And last but not least, a crucial piece of information, stored on my phone but also carefully printed on an index card should phones happen to fail: the address in Dawson City for the last two living members of the Lowell family.

BACK AT THE AHWAHNEE, DURING the conversation at the bar that I'd been excluded from, my grandfather had confessed to Owen that he'd tried to track down Winnie Lowell—Tlingit-Hän granddaughter of the Klondike Gold Rush era—several times since their last flurry of correspondence maybe three decades ago. He'd found an address in Whitehorse and written two letters but had never received a response.

Later that night, in our hotel bed, Owen had opened his laptop, determined to check for himself. A tense ten minutes of internet sleuthing, then Owen had muttered something like, got it. "She's dead," I'd said. "Isn't she?" I'd been sure he was about to rotate the screen, to show the obituary. But instead Owen had grinned. "As far as I can tell, she's alive." Winifred Lowell was ninety years old. According to a basic address search, she'd lived in Whitehorse once, though probably not since the mid-1980s. Owen had found her instead linked to an address in Dawson City, a single-family house that was owned by a woman named Leanne Lowell, whom the evidence swiftly proved to be Winnie's now fifty-five-year-old daughter. It took seconds to dig up the daughter's affiliations (the Hän Hwëch'in Cultural Center in Dawson City, her membership in a First Peoples Art Collective) as well as her Facebook profile, with a smiling photo, long shining hair, and the sparkling confluence of the Klondike and Yukon Rivers behind her. There was a recent public post on her page: a picture of a woman we were sure must be Winnie.

I'd written a message to Leanne just before falling asleep, introducing myself, telling her who my grandfather was, and explaining—with rather large omissions—that my husband and I were considering a trip to the Klondike. My tone was hedging. I only said it would be a pleasure to meet them. I wrote that my grandfather had deep regrets about how his ancestors had treated her ancestors, and that it was one of his last wishes to reconnect with her family while he was able.

The next morning, over coffee, I'd opened my computer, not expecting anything yet. But already, the blazing notification of a reply. Yes, Leanne confirmed, she was the daughter of Winifred Lowell, who herself was the granddaughter of Jane Lowell and great-niece of Jim Lowell, both of whom had worked on the Berry claims during the gold rush. She and her mother were both stunned to get my message, but Winnie of course remembered Peter, and she was glad to hear that he was well. "And if you do manage to make the trip," Leanne had written, "My mother and I would be happy to have a visit from you."

That was the first message. Eleven minutes later, she'd sent a second bubble of text. It read to me as a corrective for the exuberance of the first:

> I'm not sure how much of this is new to you, but in case the information got lost through the years, I should tell you that my mother's grandmother, Jane, and Peter's grandmother, Alice, were mortal enemies. During the gold rush, Alice Bush accused Jane of stealing gold from the Berry claim and in the aftermath Jane's brother, Jim, was shot and killed during a fight with Clarence Berry. There must have been some kind of reconciliation between the families, because the Berrys briefly cared for Jane's son (my grandfather, Ed Lowell) when he was a small boy. Though the arrangement apparently ended badly, because when Peter got in touch with the family in 1944, my Grandpa Ed wanted nothing to do with him. Even so, my mother and your grandfather wrote to each other during the war and for some time afterward. I think Peter was always a little in love with my mother. Is this information you are aware of? We would very much like to meet you. But I thought we better first get the facts out in the open.

Despite the misgivings we'd had regarding Leanne's follow-up message, Owen and I had explained to my grandfather the mistake he'd made with the Whitehorse address and, over breakfast, we'd read him Leanne's words.

My grandfather had covered his face, slowly, with his large, age-spotted hand. I'd thought he'd been reacting to the uncomfortable parts of Leanne's message, about his family's mistreatment of her family. But no. He was happy. He was enormously relieved to know Winnie was alive. He was thrilled to learn about Leanne. If he looked distressed to us now, he'd explained, it was only because he knew he should have acted much sooner.

"Think of all the time I lost," he'd mumbled. "I could have been in touch with them thirty years ago."

We'd tried to reassure him. The half-formed thoughts I'd had the previous night, about backing out of the trip, had flown out of my head. My grandfather's anxious excitement and gratitude toward us would have made it impossible.

"My lord. You kids," he'd said next, with a deep wistfulness. "Now tell me how you did all that in one night?"

"Google search," Owen had answered him quietly.

My grandfather had lowered his hand, his eyes shining. "At least I came to the right people, didn't I?"

OWEN AND I LANDED IN Fairbanks several hours past the time we were due. We walked out of the small, empty airport, into the amber glow of a single, flickering floodlight, and were immediately attacked by mosquitos. It was eleven p.m., but at this latitude, during June, the sun was out and hung lazily over the dark, ragged tops of the trees.

We followed the deserted exterior of the building around to the tiny car rental office: a windowed, concrete box, perched at the edge of a parking lot. The man behind the desk jumped when he spotted us coming. When we told him we were going to Dawson City, he was eager to warn us about the driving hazards on the winding Top of the World Highway, which was the road (there were no other options) that would take us there.

"The locals handle it okay," he said. "The outsiders, not so much. I don't want to scare you folks, but there was a minivan of six Danish tourists who went off the road last summer. Missed the turn somehow. Probably took it too fast, or else got distracted. Nobody knows. But take my word for it, it's not a road where you want to be checking your phone."

The man walked us through a desolate parking lot to a tiny red car. He reached past me in order to hand Owen the car keys with a gender discrimination so ingrained that I could hardly take it too personally.

"Good luck," he said, "stay out of trouble."

I happened to look back as we turned out of the airport complex and was surprised to see the man still standing in our empty parking spot, his gaze trailing our car, his hands in his pockets.

THE TRIP FROM FAIRBANKS TO Dawson City would take eight hours. We headed out first thing after breakfast the next day. I drove the first three hours, then switched into the passenger seat. To give my eyes a break from the bright road, the green blur of trees, I opened Alice's journal. Her writing was rushed, slanted; it was an old-fashioned cursive that took concerted work to decipher.

The date on this page was May 16, 1898, and the descriptions were of the Eldorado claims: the deep pits, the bags of gold dust, the rough lumber cabin.

"Would you have joined the gold rush?" I asked Owen. "If you'd been alive then?"

We had just entered the more mountainous region, and I noted that Owen had eyes firmly ahead; two hands gripping the wheel.

"You mean if I were a poor fruit farmer in 1898 California? Probably."

"Seriously? Then you would've been part of settler colonialism. I thought you hated settler colonialism."

"I do. Especially when it's done by people who know exactly what they're up to. But I don't hate individuals who are trying to pull themselves out of poverty. You can't say movements like that are the fault of the people trying to secure for themselves the basics in life."

"And what if it had been your land," I said, continuing this exercise of rotating perspective, a sport among people our age, "that the foreigners were coming to plunder?"

"I would've killed them. What do you think?"

He paused, gripping the wheel harder as the road curved. The dirt was loose. He had taken the turn just a little too fast. The low rock face, where the road cut through a swell in the land, swung close to my window. A moment of tension, then the road straightened and all relaxed to normal again. Was he thinking about the minivan of six Danish tourists? I was.

I looked back at the journal. "Do you think Clarence Berry treated his workers well?"

"I hope so. He could afford to."

"Two men died on his claim that first winter. No one seemed that broken up about it."

"How often do you think about the people who suffered to make your phone?"

"Hmm," I said. "Is that a fair comparison?"

"Keeping underpaid workers in your own backyard and keeping them in a different country isn't much of a moral difference."

"It is though. In one situation you have control, in the other you don't."

"We have control. We can stop buying stuff from corporations that treat people badly."

"Yeah, but who knows where everything comes from," I said. "Every ingredient in the food we eat. Our clothing. Our shoes. This backpack. The parts in this car. Cleaning supplies. It's too much to sort out. The world is too complicated."

"You're right," Owen agreed, though in a way to make me realize that I'd talked myself into a trap. "It *is* too complicated. Which ends up being super convenient for us. The harm we do to other people is so obfuscated by all these layers of economic transactions that it's almost totally hidden. It makes it perfectly rational to give up trying to figure out how our actions affect other people."

"So we're just as bad as Clarence Berry?"

"You could say that about a healthy portion of the American public."

"What about Alice and Ethel? Do they get a pass because they were women?"

"Honestly, I don't know what kind of power women had in that era."

"Anyway," I said. "We were talking about our own mindless consumerism."

"My point was only that we could cut back."

"Last year we had a wedding and traveled to Rome."

Owen was quiet. "Damn. We did do that, didn't we?"

"And that's not the worst of it. Our most valuable assets aren't even material things. You went to an exclusive magnet school. We met at a private college."

"You can't put a price on education," Owen muttered. "You're right. It's the best and worst thing we have. Our first-rate American education. Which I'm still paying off for six more years, by the way, for lack of my own Grandpa Pete."

I closed the journal, returned it to the bag at my feet. Looked at the big sky and deep valley outside the window. The hills upon hills of evergreen trees.

"I'm starting to dread this meeting," I said. "Have you tried to imagine it? Showing up at Winnie and Leanne's house with the papers. Like, here's three million dollars to cover a hundred and fifteen years of racism and disenfranchisement. Whenever I try to walk my way through it, I get stuck. The whole thing gets cringey."

"Would it be better for your grandfather to just keep the money?"

"No. But three million seems exorbitant and stingy at the same time."

"Here's how I'm thinking about it," Owen said. "If you're curious to know how I'm justifying this very questionable trip to myself. You can either do whatever small, good thing is in front of you. Or you can constantly worry about not doing enough and run the risk of ending up paralyzed and of no use to anyone. So you're uncomfortable about taking on the role of a savior, marching into this family's home and handing over your grandfather's money. But you'd also be ethically culpable by *not* doing it. Because then you'd be making the question of *your own* moral purity the front-and-center problem to consider."

"Fantastic," I said, watching a lone signpost rush past the window. "That helps a lot. I feel better already."

THE ROAD HAD BROUGHT US high into the mountains now, and Owen's mood faded to serious. A blind turn. Trees on the driver's side, and out my own window, no guardrails, only a jagged and precipitous drop. I'd gotten off easy taking the first shift in the drive. It wasn't called the Top of the World highway for nothing.

We were thirty minutes from Dawson when the hazy emergency we'd been fearing since early morning reared into life. A dark, hulking mass—a bear—burst out of the dense shadows of trees into the road, fast on its haunches. I cried out. Owen swerved toward the drop-off, and then, overcompensating, toward the inner part of the road. We scraped hard against a tree—the jolt was shocking—before lurching to a rocking stop.

Silence. The world seemed braced. Holding its breath. I was sharply aware of the engine, low and steady, as well as the stillness outside the car. Every detail of past and future burned away, while car, tree, body, burned bright. Owen slowly lowered his forehead to rest on his knuckles, his hands were still holding the wheel.

"Was I imagining things, or was that a bear?"

"It was a bear."

"Remind me what I'm doing here?"

"It will be okay."

A bouquet of colorful wires was visible out his window, and, dangling from them, the driver's side mirror.

Owen squinted at it. "Shit," he said. "This is not good."

"It's fine." My body was still clenched from the impact. "We'll figure it out."

Owen turned off the car. We got out and inspected the blows. In addition to the knocked-off mirror, a large dent in the driver's side door. But there didn't seem to be any danger in driving. That was good, because our phones had no service and, with the notable exception of a pickup we'd passed an hour back, we'd seen no other travelers.

We drove with excruciating slowness down the mountain, until finally we reached the Klondike River. There, a flat, wide boat ferried travelers across. We went up a ramp and waited while strong metal flaps secured the car in place. The operator—a man with a face so sunburned that it matched his red shirt—whistled delightedly at the state of our vehicle. He told us that the guy in Dawson who did car repairs was on a camping trip for this month, so we'd have to fix up that mirror with duct tape for now. He had a lot to say about our accident. How people like us—we'd mentioned we were from Los Angeles—lacked the basic instinct while driving to look out for wildlife.

"Last year," the man said, "there was a minivan of six Danish hikers that went off that road."

"We heard," said Owen. There was a sardonic drop to his voice, though his eyes told another story, shifting nervously back to the mountains.

"You have to keep your attention on your surroundings."

"Yes," Owen agreed, "but it doesn't do much good, does it? When the surroundings jump out at you?"

The ferry docked. We thanked the man, got back into the car, and rolled onto land. Dawson City stood on a flat of earth, at the raging, bubbling confluence of the Yukon and Klondike Rivers. The layout was simple. About fifteen blocks by ten blocks of straight, lumber-made, old-fashioned buildings, with mountains high at its back. The town's economy depended on its influx of intrepid, summer tourists, and, for their benefit, the place had fashioned itself into something like a poor man's Old-Time Western amusement park. In other words, it had preserved the 1890s Old West architecture common at the height of the Klondike Gold Rush: false fronts, wooden boardwalks, dirt streets, buildings that replicated the style and materials of one hundred years prior.

"This is so weird," I said, taking it in as we crept at five miles an hour down the bumpy street. "But good weird. I like it."

The signs were painted in old-fashioned script.

Diamond Tooth Gerties. A gambling hall with dancing shows in the evening.

The Jack London Cabin & Museum. The preserved, ramshackle home where London had lived during his brief foray as a prospector.

We passed a red building that I recognized from my internet searches as the Downtown Hotel, which, as I told Owen, knowing it was a detail he'd relish, was famous for its restaurant, the Sourdough Saloon, where you could order a whiskey poured over a preserved, dehydrated human toe, which the original owner had lost to frostbite. The idea, I explained to Owen, was to take the shot, while letting the mummified toe touch your lips. (No swallowing it, as one rowdy patron had done, or you'd face a large fine.) Complete the challenge, and you'd receive a certificate making you an official member of the Sourtoe Cocktail Club, established 1973.

"Enticing," said Owen. "Definitely my type of thing. But I think I'll pass."

We walked by the Dawson City Museum, which, as I knew from its website, housed a display on Clarence Berry: a giant cardboard cutout of him standing in front of his steam point invention, which had once been used by miners for thawing the frozen ground.

We passed the Hän Hwëch'in Cultural Center, a strikingly modern building with a stark metal and wooden exterior. It was the one exception to the 1898-era architecture of the town—and seemed to suggest, in a reversal, that if the centennial past belonged to the predominantly white miners who'd founded Dawson City, the future belonged to this First Nations group.

We turned onto Fifth Avenue and found the Golden Nugget Inn, our little bed and breakfast. Though as we started to get out of the car, we realized our way to the B&B door was blocked by two men in their fifties or sixties whose heated conversation before our eyes—I almost couldn't believe it—was dissolving into a fistfight. Their movements, the scuff of their sneakers, stirred from the road a fine orange dust. Only finally, with stumbling steps, and as if by a silent agreement, did the two men pull apart from each other. A hot wind blew and, without a glance at us, they scuttled off in opposite ways down the street.

"Was that serious?" Owen asked, sounding demoralized.

"I'm pretty sure that was a real fight."

We crossed the street, dragging the suitcases, as the weak, plastic wheels couldn't get traction on the uneven dirt. Owen's jaw clenched as he took in our ramshackle inn. The wood steps were bowing and rotted. Paint curled from a mustard-yellow exterior. A shadow of mold climbed a large, exposed spot by the door.

"You were excited to come here," I reminded him softly. "You said you wanted to see something different."

"I take it back," he said. "I realize we've been here for less than ten minutes, but I'm beginning to feel that I'm done."

4

KLONDIKE

1898

1.

It happened during a nothing moment, under a big bright sun. Ethel said, I don't feel right. And then, crumpling, grasping her middle, she lowered herself onto the gravel between the cabin and creek. Alice heard her own name. Shot across the claim by Clarence. Not in anger, but in fear. But she was already running to them. She had seen Ethel drop. Clarence was holding Ethel when she'd reached them, one arm crooked under her head. Trying to lift a person who did not consent to be lifted.

The creek was high that day and roared beside them, spraying water. When Ethel's eyes grazed across hers, it caused a jolt of cold understanding. You never want this. A person you love on fetid ground, clear bile coating their clothing. Tears bloated Ethel's face. Tears of pain? They must be, as Ethel allowed for no other. It was the end of May, and their time on the claim had been pleasant and easy. Alice had loved doing the housework and watching the mining any time she could get out of the galley. She had thought that the rest and the fresh air had done Ethel good. But look, the truth was not what she'd thought. Eight weeks had passed since that close, claustrophobic room in Seattle, the cavernous barrel of blood-crusted rags. If there had been a dam, holding the deluge in, allowing only a trickle, now the dam had collapsed. Blood. But not the usual blood. Not cowboy blood. Not scythe-in-a-field blood. This was something else. The dress had ridden up past Ethel's knees. The stockings were sopping, bright red at the thighs. There was a wet stain blooming on the seat of the dress.

Ethel said to Clarence, who was holding her shoulders, "Don't touch me."

Then her eyeballs rolled up in her head. She was dying. There was no one to help them. Alice wrapped herself around her sister's middle, her own knees rutting into the gravel ground, keeping Ethel's head up, because her neck wouldn't do it.

It felt unreal. The white light of day exposed nothing in Alice but stupid surprise. Despite discomfort, Ethel had been carrying on. She'd taken a morphine pill when she'd needed it, yes. But since arriving on the claim, she'd seemed almost herself again. She'd seemed improved. They hadn't known the quiet days had been building to this.

They did not move her. Then, finally, when she did not respond to their touch, Clarence, now with Henry's help, who'd come running back from the well, his front slopped with water, hoisted Ethel up and carried her into the house.

The blood pulsed through the stockings, through the dress. Two hours of it, and Alice had thought, that must be everything. Then Ethel moved, and a big clot, shiny and dense, the size of a grapefruit, passed from between Ethel's legs and onto the bed.

At first Alice could only stare. It was very smooth, like a sphere of jelly. It seemed like a thing with its own life. It didn't seem like a thing that would, even in illness, come out of a person. She lifted the blanket, her hands clumsy, and forced the dark red orb to unstick from the wool and drop into the bucket of water.

What more? And what could they do? The body was announcing itself. It was normal every day, and then it was terrifying and strange without warning; it could come apart in ways you'd never imagine. All Alice could think was to stop it up, crudely, simply, hold Ethel together with the brute pressure of touch, like holding together any earthly thing that was crumbling.

"Bring down those curtains," Alice told Clarence. Alice rolled up the white fabric and placed it firmly between Ethel's legs. She said to Ethel, who was half-awake, "Try not to move. More blood comes out when you move. I'm going to hold you still. And maybe the wound will clot."

What wound though? Nothing was visible. That night, while Ethel tried to sleep, curled up and gasping, Alice lived in torture. Her mind was stuck in Seattle. In the dark hotel room, five stories up, where Ethel had showed her the barrel and said, it's a trickle of blood that won't stop and a pain in my side.

Ethel had said, no, I won't go back to Selma, I won't miss this trip.

In words, Alice had scolded her sister. She'd said, you're being stoic, to the point of stupidity. But in her heart—and her hatred for herself grew with the memory—she'd felt the burn of excitement at Ethel's insistence they go: she hadn't wanted to miss this trip either. She'd said, you're right. We cannot miss this. And with that statement had she swung her sister in the direction of death?

Days passed. Nights passed. They blended together, without the borders of sunset and sunrise to keep them apart. One morning the pillow was dank with sweat, and Alice could feel the heat pumping from Ethel's flesh before her hand had touched her sister's forehead. Henry hiked to Dawson in search of a doctor but came home alone. One doctor was already tending to four bad-off cases of typhoid and would not be induced for any amount of money to come. The other—a man named Moorhead—had taken a break from his work in order to do a bit of prospecting, and no one knew his whereabouts, or when he planned to return.

Alice brought water from the wood pail in the kitchen. She spooned it out in deep ladle scoops that Ethel would sip, a long bone in her neck straining, until that unpredictable moment when she would lean away, revolted by what she was trying to put down her throat.

In the doorway, Clarence lingered, Henry too; they dipped a face into the room, then ducked away, as if Alice had told them, don't come in. Once

Clarence said, strained and remorseful, "She seemed better when we got here. I thought she'd be okay, now that she was on the claims." He said, "In Seattle, I was sure it was her appendix. But she was sure that it wasn't."

He wanted to say more. He wanted to ask, does this have something to do with me? Why not, Alice would have answered, when for eons husbands have killed their wives with pregnancies that didn't go right.

Alice said she needed to write to Moie and Poie to say what was happening. Clarence brought her the paper and pen. But she found she could not put down a word.

"The suspense would be too much for them," she explained to Clarence, returning the blank, cream-colored stationery into his hands. "I'll write to them later, once we know more."

As her sister slept, Alice put her hand around Ethel's hot, soft arm. While her hand was there, it seemed impossible for Ethel to die. The transformation would not dare take place with her watching. It would not give up its mystery. She thought: There is only she and I in this room, sisters who have known each other forever. Nothing can take her while I'm holding on to her. She felt she could hold Ethel to the living world. The trick was never to let go of her arm.

On the fifth day, Ethel woke up asking for strawberries. Alice and Clarence lost themselves in a panic, as they had none. Clarence enlisted Henry and the two of them went up and down Bonanza Creek, knocking on doors, willing to pay. The best they could get was a handful of shriveled blueberries. When Clarence came into the house with them, he held them out to Alice without speaking a word, ready to cry. They fed them to Ethel on a cold spoon. She did not know the difference. She thought they were strawberries and that Clarence had just picked them.

Clarence felt relieved at the trick. He was only glad Ethel had not cried at the failure. But a muscle clenched over Alice's heart. The confusion was worse.

The next night, Alice's chair was angled toward Ethel's head. Her fingers rubbed and pulled at a bit of sewing in her lap. There was a low gray sky, but it had been like that for hours, and not a drop of rain. The bleeding had finally stopped, but not before it seemed to have emptied Ethel of what she needed for life. A fever raged. Her skin looked clammy and cool in its dampness but was hot to touch. Tonight, Alice was afraid, but so far she had refused to say that to Clarence. What she did not put into words, she felt: her sister sinking away from the world, like a swimmer dropping under the surface of rippling water.

Around midnight, the patient stirred. Her chest rose and fell with an uneven beat that you could not look away from. "Ethel, stop," Alice commanded. "Stop it. Calm down." She petted the body; stroked the oily hair; gently, then harder. Ethel's breathing caught on a normal track. Alice sat down. Then there was no breath at all. "Ethel, stop!" She was angry. She stood, she plunged. She put her arm beneath Ethel's shoulders and dragged her up against the pillow. The weight was nothing. Alice could have lifted the bed. Her open palm gripped the back of her sister's head. Her own heart beat and her throat constricted. Who was she fighting? Not Ethel. Not the illness itself, but the force that was here in this room, giving it substance. "Ethel, stop!" Then Ethel did stop, the stillness broke, and her breath resumed a living pace. It was surprising. Not once during all of it had Ethel opened her eyes.

The chair caught her backward fall. It must have. Because Alice was in the chair again without the memory of sitting. Only when Clarence came in did she become aware of herself, sobbing into her sleeve.

"What happened?" Fat-lipped from sleep, he slouched in the doorway. His face was confused. His fist clutched the loose waist of his flannels, holding them bunched at his groin.

"She's worse. Good God. How is it we don't have a doctor?"

"I tried. I sent Henry to town." He defended himself. "Ethel's never been one for doctors."

"She can't tell a blueberry from a strawberry. Don't you think the situation has changed?" His expression in response was wide and innocent. She would have liked to slap it free from his face. "Try again!" she shouted. "Go back to Dawson. Do something!"

He left the room. Now it was several times that Alice had spoken to

Clarence like that. The sharp words flew from her open mouth and for an instant she would expect the world to quake in shock and rise against her; for her mother, at home in Selma, to faint; for indignant faces to appear in the window. But the truth was far stranger than that. Sheep Camp had been the aberration. You behaved like you have the right to shout at people—like you know better than they do—and instead of laughing at you, they believed it. She breathed deeply and clawed around for something to do with her hands. She had no heart for reliving these hours in a journal entry. She settled on an embroidery, for future use on a pillow, "Hitherto Hath the Lord Helped Us," the words alternating in yellow and green. The argument between her husband and sister of all things seemed to have pushed Ethel into a peaceful sleep.

2.

Now the cabin was silent, in a state of suspense. Alice sat at the table, staring into the glass of water she had ready for Ethel. Behind her, Clarence sat in the chair pulled up to the bed. They were listening for the dogs, which would signal the arrival of Dr. Moorhead, the doctor who'd been away prospecting.

The moment they'd heard about his return to Dawson, they'd rallied immediately, and thirteen hours ago, Clarence had walked into the tents of hired miners. He'd found Jim, who could move through the country faster than anyone. He'd sent Jim on the errand to find Dr. Moorhead in Dawson and bring him to the cabin, to Ethel.

We made a mistake in traveling here, Alice thought.

She touched the cool glass with one fingertip, where the candlelight curved and reflected.

We made a mistake in coming here.

The thought poured from her. It filled the dim, brown cabin. She could not think about anything else.

Outside, the dogs barked. It seemed too soon—but a second later, a man's voice, haughty and strange. Alice ran to unfasten the door.

Dr. Moorhead stood against the dim starry night. His eyes happy. His face shone with a patina of sweat, sickly blotches on each of his cheeks. His bulbous nose was pink and the skin cracked over the tip. His hair, when he removed his hat, shot up in stiff white tufts. His legs were wobbly as he strode inside, as if he'd taken the nineteen miles from Dawson at a speed faster than what was good for him.

He bustled past Alice and met Clarence halfway across the floor and shook his hand. "So pleased to finally meet you, Mr. Berry, I only wish the circumstances were different." His tone was energized, obsequious. And the effect on Alice was severe. The hopefulness that had risen in her, when they'd sent for the doctor, dropped in her now, like a delicate thing falling down steps.

The front door had almost swung closed when Dr. Moorhead rushed back and caught it with his fingers. He yelled to the inscrutable person who was walking away from the house:

"Come in, shy fellow. Unless you like the outside. Though I doubt it likes you. I'd say it wants a break from you."

A second later, slinking through the doorway came Jim. He kept his back close to the wall. He breathed evenly, unlike Dr. Moorhead, though you could tell he'd been running by the warm, baking-bread smell off his skin. His expression was calm. Around his torso was a rough, patterned blanket; it briefly dipped off his shoulder, before his darting hand brought it back into place.

"This monster of Adam," the doctor roared, "nabbed a fox with his bare hands and hurled it thirty feet into the bushes. The poor creature had intersected with us quite by accident. But it had the pluck to show its teeth."

Jim moved, as if surprised by this description of himself. By the way he looked at the doctor, he seemed to consider himself betrayed.

"I hope you pay well," Dr. Moorhead said. He was asking for Jim's sake, or so he'd have them believe. "I'm sure he could use a brandy, too, for his trouble. It was a very long way."

"We pay fine," said Clarence. "Wait outside, Jim. I'll be with you in a minute." Then, after the door slammed shut, Clarence explained to the doctor, "You can't serve drinks to Indians. Not even brandy. It's against the law."

Alice stepped forward, before the man could manage an answer.

"May I hang your coat, Dr. Moorhead?"

"Burn it instead. In a public place." He wrestled his arms free and piled the gnarled fur into her arms. "It has two holes in the back I can stick my fist through."

"I'll let my sister know you're here."

"Good. But I'll wet my whistle first."

He glanced hopefully at a couple of bottles Clarence had left on the table.

"Of course." A coolness ran through Alice's voice. Three minutes in this stranger's company, and already she could not hide her antipathy. She poured him a brandy. He requested something salty to go on the side. She brought bread, and he made a show of cracking the crust in his teeth. Was there anything to soften it?

"A bowl of creek water, maybe," Alice said flatly. "The butter's used up. I'm afraid I've been neglecting the kitchen."

Brave words but she was not brave. When she turned away, Clarence's eyes following her, her anger lapsed back into dread. She thought, with clarity: I cannot lose Ethel. My best sister, who has been with me all my life. I cannot lose the person who is the most rational, the most good. To lose Daisy or even Annie would be a family tragedy. It would tear me up in ways I would not recover from. But to lose Ethel would be more. Humanity drops an inch into darkness.

3.

Now Alice hung the doctor's coat—in a breach of orders—on the iron hook by the door. Then went to the bedroom to ready her sister.

"Who's there?" A raspy voice, with insufficient breath to fill it. Ethel's face straining to turn.

"Don't be upset, but we have a doctor here to give you a checkup."

She approached the bed.

"Absolutely not," Ethel said.

"Remember when you nearly died of the mumps because you refused to admit you were suffering? I'm not going to let that happen again."

Ethel was defiant. But Alice was stronger. She lifted the blanket and sent a wave of musty air across the room; then she snapped the blanket again and made it fall flat. She was pert and efficient, she had with her a bowl of warm water, which she used to wash her sister's face, then hands, then thighs. She did this with the same nonembarrassment she used to feel cleaning up the neighbor's feral child whom she used to watch for pay, when the girl had the habit of squatting down in the shade of grape vines and relieving herself into her bloomers.

To Ethel, she said, "A doctor who's delivered three hundred babies. You think you have something he's never seen?"

But the words were unintentionally cruel. Because that was exactly it. Where others had smooth insides that forged the bodies of neat little humans, Ethel's insides had done something else.

During Dr. Moorhead's examination, Alice stood by the bed, holding her sister's hand. It was for this moment—this and the washing of rags, and the washing of thighs—that they had brought her to the Klondike. And she did her job well. Her presence made everything proper. She whispered encouragements to Ethel. When Ethel shifted at the doctor's touch, and gasped, she squeezed her hand harder.

"What do you think?" Clarence said. He rubbed his balding head. Under the dip of the pale canvas adorning the ceiling, the light wrinkled, like the underside of a surface of water. They were at the table, and Ethel now settled again, Alice closed the door of the bedroom behind her and joined them without being asked.

Dr. Moorhead cleared his throat. "How long do you plan to stay on the gold fields? I ask because it's a valley, you know, Dawson included. The damp air settles. Poor air can exacerbate the symptoms."

"We were planning to go before the freeze."

"Good. My concern was that you intended to stay for the winter. If you can set her up in a nice house in a warm climate, I think you'll see an improvement. Though as for the question you mentioned earlier, about your wife's chance of a conception."

He didn't notice, how Clarence's ruddy cheeks turned ruddier. No one looked at Alice: no one marked her horror. What are you doing, she thought, you stupid man? Why would you repeat that? If Clarence asked you in private, why would you answer in front of me?

"I think you'll have to wait another year or two and see. She's twenty-four, still young enough. But I must level with you, my friend. My guess is that the violent flushing out she is experiencing might carry on, and there will continue to be an excess production of fluid. And if that fluid continues, more, if it is sign of an internal injury—the womb will be unable to accept the seed."

A single, sharp bark interrupted the moment. Then a man's voice, answering it. Clarence went to the window. It was Jim, crouched down on the gravel and talking to one of the dogs.

"I forgot," Clarence said, abashed. "I said I'd pay him for the trip. Jesus. Has he been waiting there all this time?"

He was discombobulated. He grabbed the money and thrust it to Alice to take outside. He seemed to deem it irrelevant that, since the debacle at Sheep Camp, Jim and Alice had carefully avoided each other.

She walked into the sunlit night. The stars were gone. After a hesitation, she closed the door behind her. She did not trust Dr. Moorhead to keep his mouth shut while it was opened, and she did not want Jim to overhear whatever else he might say.

Jim gave the dog one more pat, then stood slowly as she approached. It was an awkward moment. They had not met eyes since the terrible morning of the Palm Sunday avalanche, when she'd questioned his integrity, and the snow had killed the men on the Pass in response.

"You were quick," Alice said. "Clarence was right to send you."

"I know the area well. I should be quick."

There was something under the words that Alice chose not to acknowledge. Not now. She put the money into Jim's hands.

"I thought you were from further down. Near the Chilkoot."

"Yes. That's where I'm from. But I know this place too. My mother was both Tlingit and Hän."

"Hän, who are the enemies of the Tlingit? Clarence said that. Or do we have it all wrong?"

"Many of us are beginning to feel we have more in common. Especially since you people came into the country." He smiled.

She was intimidated. He sounded different. She could not immediately find a good way to respond. This quiet touch of his words had set her back.

Now he was looking into his hand, counting the coins with his eyes.

"I hope you think it's enough," she said.

He shrugged again. A heat came into her face.

"Thank you," she said. "And on my sister's behalf. I thank you."

"I hope she recovers."

The tone was light, illegible. He turned away. She could not fasten the door quickly enough.

4.

The doctor stayed on. Each morning he sauntered into the back bedroom and held Ethel's limp wrist to his ear. He gave her no medications. He said her fever was better, then wondered aloud over dinner, dispassionately, if in fact she'd felt hotter than ever.

Still the nursing fell to Alice. Mornings she woke with the sparrow's cries, the warbler's trills, the wren's exaltations. It was a bird's world out there before people marched outside to claim it. She kindled the fire. She put last night's dough into the pan and shoved it into the heat. The dank air of the bedroom she confronted next. She stepped over Clarence, who left Ethel alone in the bed, and slept like a favored dog by the door. She opened the little window in order to make a breeze. When Ethel woke, she gave her a cup of tea while she shook out the blanket. If it happened to be a Monday, then she heaved the patient into a chair, stripped the bed, and forced the sheets into a tub of boiling water, mixing the cloth with a thick branch of spruce, then hung them out on the line. When she washed Ethel's legs, her sister squirmed and made involuntary motions to shove away Alice's hand, as if the cloth and the hand were an insect preying upon her naked legs.

Finally, when Alice could not stand it any longer, she got rid of Moorhead in the easiest way: with bad service. The beans dry; the loaf poorly timed. On the day he left, she went to the cache and found the good food that she'd hidden away; she cooked pork with onions and made a lemon pie for dessert. He was gone and he'd taken his appetite with him. Yet in other ways the man lingered. His diagnosis hung in the air, it settled itself on the walls and furniture and became a part of the cabin. The womb and its washing out, he'd said. He'd told Clarence, wait and see.

One week later, mid-June, with no thanks to anyone, Ethel's fever dropped. The pillow was dry one morning, and Ethel's eyes were open and clear. When Alice saw that, the deep fear lifted, and Alice knew her sister would live. She wrote down the date in her journal and beneath it the words "At last, an improvement." Though it was also true that the weeks of illness had left Ethel—tough-as-nails Ethel—weak and melancholic, and she kept to her bedroom. And some days later a low fever crawled back, then recovery, then days of exhaustion again. Something catastrophic had happened under a soft expanse of flesh. If there had been a chance for children once, it might be the case that it was no longer so.

Clarence sought distraction in work. On the claim, he was a moving pair of suspenders; he was a roving, angled hat. He spent long sessions in a chair pulled up to the front door. He liked best those bright-as-day hours near midnight. He smoked his pipe, looking out at the rushing creek, the fires amid the workers' tents across the creek on the hills.

One evening that week, Clarence startled her: knocking into the house after twelve hours of sluicing the gravel. A misty sun hovered over his shoulder and his expression was inexplicably bright. She could not figure out why he'd be smiling. Then he'd inhaled, dramatically, his chest rising beneath his suspenders. When he did that, she suddenly remembered what she had promised: a pigeon pie from the bird Henry had killed and left for them before leaving for a visit with neighbors. A moment of stillness, followed by a coming-to-terms. Ethel had been fretful today, and the dinner preparations had fallen to the wayside.

The table creaked under Clarence's touch. They sat across from each other, imbibing slow spoonfuls of beans without looking up. Millionaire or not, he was wretched. He ripped the loaf and soaked the broth lacquered to the sides of his bowl; he chewed with his lips open and one arm at his side. The tragic mannerisms of a street urchin.

While she was washing the dishes, he came up behind her and said, threatening and susurrant both, "We need a cook. It's too much for you to do the kitchen work and the nursing. I'm going to hire out. I'll still give you forty dollars a month."

Her face was hot and damp from the steam and she was sweating under her arms. She thought, no, let's not do that. The cabin reeked of femininity. The last thing they needed was a third woman. But she was too exhausted to summon the argument.

"Good," she snapped. "I'm glad to hear it. Go steal a hardworking girl from a cookhouse. I'm like you. I'm starving. I've been up since four, and I haven't stopped moving."

5.

The old Indian fishing camp, at the battleground where the Yukon River met the Klondike River—Dawson as it was today—was a relic that would never return. The Indian graves that Clarence and Ethel had told Alice stories about, those rambling sheds, built on stilts, with giant eyes painted onto the sides, had long since been burned by gold-seekers for fuel. The fords where the Indians used to stand and hunt for salmon had been penned in by docks and boats. A man named Joseph Ladue, who'd officially founded the town in 1896, had for years now been selling lots for many thousands of dollars apiece. He'd moved a sawmill into the town and hummed away building saloons, stores, and providing lumber to visionaries who were doing the same. On Thanksgiving Day, '97, a fire had started in the M&M Establishment when one man had thrown a burning lamp at a rival, and the flames had spread and burned the whole town to the ground. But with every citizen working, it had only taken four months to rebuild, and ever since then, the animals would not go within miles of the place, because of the incessant chopping and hammering and the ever-growing hubbub of disembarking arrivals.

The Hän people had moved the prior year, on Chief Isaac's orders, three miles downriver to a new camp they called Moosehide. No one felt sorry. It was a great big country and there was room enough for everyone. The Hän could keep to themselves if they wished and carry on with their hunting of moose and caribou, their trapping of salmon in great fish nets, no matter if they needed to travel a little farther afield. Near their homes were roots, wild rhubarb, sap from birch trees, and highbush blueberries and cranberries to pick in the fall. Or if they cared to, they could participate in the new gold-based economy. True, they could not register a Discovery claim, which were double the standard size, as that honor was reserved for the prospectors. And true, they never won their cases when they accused a white man of jumping their land. But the fact remained that many were better off in the rush. They could get jobs in Dawson at the lumberyard. They could work on the claims, like Jim was doing. They could lead prospectors into the wild. The women could join the ranks of the women in Dawson—they were certainly just as able, if not more so—and find work doing laundry or cooking.

Clarence must have been thinking along these lines, Alice determined, because he sent a note back to the claims, inside the pocket of one of their neighbors, to say that he'd hired a girl named Jane Lowell. They would arrive in four days to the cabin. He'd offered her thirty-five dollars a month. She was young, he'd written, unmarried. But she was sturdy and competent, with a good Christian sense. She'd grown up among the missionaries and was in possession of a letter from a well-respected priest, vouching for her character.

What was more, Jim had recommended her. Why? Because Jane was Jim's sister.

It was clear, even within this short letter, that Clarence considered the connection a boon. He thought it good business to take a whole family into his hands.

Alice had written an urgent reply. She gave it to Henry—who had an errand in Dawson—to deliver to Clarence. *No. I do not want Jim's sister living with us. Find someone else.*

But Henry, preceding his brother's return, had told her in the most chivalrous tone he could manage, a little embarrassed:

"Clarence says the matter is settled. He says to tell you, make the best of it."

6.

Three days later, Clarence and Jane walked into the cabin. At the sound, Alice dropped the bowl she was washing. It didn't break, just clunked slowly to the dirty water at the base of the sink. Already their coats were off by the time Alice came out of the galley. Jane was a handsome woman, of Alice's breadth and height. Tall, relatively, compared to Jim, though there was a quick, appraising look in the woman's eyes that was identical to what Alice had observed in the brother. A bright expression on her face was in the process of drooping to disappointment. This reaction they'd seen before, in every ilk of visitor. A twitch. A pause, as the cabin interior came into focus. The problem was that people expected wealth to have transcended the basic geographical facts. They expected to open the door and discover a ballroom with a marble floor. A chandelier. A wine cellar built into the rough. Instead there was only a comfortable home with a scattering of the elegant touches that the Klondike could offer: the clean, billowy canvas nailed to the ceiling over the table, the lace curtains at the front windows, a bright quilt draped over the back of a rocking chair, and the coats and hats hung on a row of iron pegs, instead of dumped in a heap on the floor.

Jane recovered, as people do. Clarence said, "Here's my sister-in-law."

Alice took a step forward.

Jane turned.

Their gazes met like two cold things knocking against each other.

Alice wiped her hands on her apron, in preparation to shake, then changed her mind. Jane gave a curt nod. She put down a tasseled satchel, then removed her broad, straw hat, which had encircled her skull like a halo. Her clothes, a white blouse, ironed stiff, and a pleated brown skirt were identical to an outfit that Alice herself had in the bedroom. It didn't seem fair. Because, on Jane, the outfit was a costume, and yet they were more handsome on her. Clarence sat down at the table while Jane remained standing, looking around. Alice thought that she should not serve the cook. But the bread was in the kitchen, under the checkered cloth, and no one else knew. She didn't hurry, in fact her gestures were excruciatingly slow, as she lifted the basket, and chose an appropriate knife. She could hear Jane and Clarence talking while she sliced the loaf at the counter and readied the patty of butter, hesitating twice, three times, over how much to serve. Jane was telling Clarence about the typhus outbreak in Dawson over the winter, and of the putrid mud that had plagued them in March, so deep that the horses could not walk through it for fear of sinking. Clarence told her of the difficulties they had faced on the journey north, of the Palm Sunday avalanche, which, as Jane answered with confidence, everyone knew about now.

A different story was drifting through Alice's mind, that of the early death of her grandfather, her mother's father, who had died when his prized horse bucked him over the edge of a limestone quarry. He had dropped four feet, rolled, dropped another twenty, and landed on his back on a white pillow of stone. Alice's grandmother had said maybe a hundred times at the funeral lunch, "that horse was supposed to be his glorious gift to himself, but the day he brought it home, I knew with a chill in my heart that he wasn't a match for it," and she had gone on to repeat the sentiment on future occasions. Everyone had felt distressed for her, though without believing her.

In the dim galley, Alice thought, they will not believe me either. She thought: now Jim, a person who already hates me, has been given an ally.

How could she explain this idea to her family? That you should be wary of the people you've wronged. But Clarence and Ethel would not understand that they had wronged anyone: because they judged themselves by what was in their hearts.

Yet Alice remembered the smoldering anger that comes with being deprived of what belongs to you. Of being humiliated. Their year of waiting for the red-haired man on the Pinto, for instance. He'd galloped into their yard and put into Poie's hand the note of foreclosure, which, if not for Clarence, would have ripped their own farm and barn and home from their possession. That liquid dread and anger that every night used to flood her heart. What must Jim feel? What must this woman, Jane, feel? What happened inside them every time a dogged go-getter like Clarence barreled into the country and cordoned off a portion of land?

Most crucially: Should not the Berrys sit down and carefully answer those questions before they invited Jane to live in their house?

7.

Jane slept in the galley kitchen on a mat and fur robe on the floor, which in the morning she rolled up and put in the corner. Henry had missed meeting Jane by a matter of hours, as he'd already left for his claim on *Fifty-Eight* Bonanza, another reason for the loss of good cheer in the household. His claim did not have a cabin, so poor Hen had borrowed the canvas tent they'd used on the trail. He'd said he was going to dig around a bit and see what he could see. But once Clarence had surprised him there, and found Henry splayed out on a boulder with a shovel at his side, eyes closed, and enjoying the sun on his face. "I'm still convalescing after that Klondike winter," Henry had grumbled, "don't you laugh at me, Ceej."

During these rearrangements, Alice had moved into the attic. It was stuffy and warm at the top of the cabin. The roof slanted close overhead. But she liked the place for the privacy, for the fact of being spared sleeping beside Jane in the kitchen. The change also granted her—by default—the occupation of guardsman. The attic, accessible through a trapdoor in the ceiling, was Clarence's new hiding spot for the bags of washed gold, now that the spot under the bedroom floor was full. The canvas sacks of pure money lined the wall, their topknots touching the low beam at the eaves. Their paunchy bodies slumped and drooped, like a neat row of stout trolls.

One morning, three days after Jane's arrival, Alice crawled on all fours, got a good grip on the rope ladder, and descended rung by rung into the main room. She dragged back the galley curtain and startled Jane awake. A long face tilted up. Jane yawned without lifting a hand, and she rolled up her mat at an easy pace.

"I'm darting outside," Jane said. "I'll just be a minute."

"You should've lit the stove already. I want my sister to have her tea first thing in the morning."

"What?" said Jane. "And get up even earlier?"

"I did it for weeks. I don't see why you can't."

Jane shrugged, then walked out the door, petting every dog she passed.

At ten o'clock, Henry crossed by the window, hands stuffed into his pockets, whistling songs with the birds. He burst inside, and soon he was at the galley curtain, sticking his head into the kitchen. Alice was happy to see him, and not surprised he'd returned. She'd thought that Henry wouldn't stay away from their cabin for long. "Have you heard my news?" he said. "I'm dying of scurvy. On Clarence's orders you are to feed me orange slices and sugar cookies and rub my feet while I digest." He saw Jane and his eyebrows shot up. He took off his hat in that flippant way of his, which toed the line between respectful and mocking. "Pleased to make your acquaintance."

"Even in such a desperate hour?" Jane's eyes, above her frown, were smiling.

"Yes, indeed. Now I'll have two pretty girls to take care of me."

"Oh, will you?"

"Yes, and saying prayers for me too." He sniffed. "What's cooking?"

"Pies," said Alice. Really he had been asking Jane. But Jane had been slow to answer.

"What kind?"

"Can't you tell?" Alice laughed at him. "Clarence came home with a barrel of apples. They're not close to ripe. We'll be cooking a week before we are rid of them."

"Yum!" Henry patted his stomach and walked out of the room.

"Go say hello to Ethel!" Alice yelled through the doorway. "She's dressed and sitting up today."

Henry turned on his heel and made a salute. Soon they could hear his booming voice from the bedroom, making Ethel laugh. Alice returned to the counter, uneasy. She looked forward to Henry's banter. But she didn't like it as a game for three.

After a quiet, Jane said: "He's teasing me because I'm Catholic. Mr. Berry must have told him. Did you hear? 'And saying prayers for me too.'"

Alice kept her eyes on her work. Is that really how you think of yourself, she wanted to say, as a Catholic? The fire flared. Alice grabbed a towel and opened the oven door. The dough on top was golden brown. She transferred the pie to the counter to set.

Jane's back was to her now. A blue dress with stripes. Calico, only, but the stitching was done by a competent hand.

"Well," said Jane. "I won't take the bait."

"I'm sure you've misunderstood." Alice spoke curtly. "The Berry family has roots in Dublin. You won't find them piling into a pew on Sunday, but their mother adores St. Valentine. They have a big picture of him in his burgundy robes in their sitting room. When you walk into their house, it's the first thing you see." The next batch of apples came to a boil, these for a sauce. "Here," she said. "Before you start mashing those, take Ethel's apron."

"Won't she mind if it's dirty?"

"She won't. In fact you can have it. I speak for her. I give it to you as a gift."

Dubiously, Jane took the apron and slipped it over her head. Alice waited. This was a test. Jane turned. She hummed and bumped the wooden spoon in the pot.

"All right," said Jane. "I'm going to take them out."

Nothing. All afternoon, it had been like that: where you expected thank yous and obsequious words, there was silence.

THE NEXT DAY, HENRY ARRIVED at five o'clock sharp. He'd brought along a poor fellow from Selma named Charlie, whom they'd all gone to school with. Charlie was one of several young men from their hometown who'd made their way North into the country this spring, following in Clarence's footsteps. These boys were hopeful and maybe more than a little bit stupid: because they seemed to believe that being from Selma had been a factor in Clarence's success. It was lucky that Clarence felt some responsibility for them and was inclined to give them jobs on the claims and let them move into the workers' tents, as he'd recently done for Charlie, otherwise they'd have ended up with the heaps of paupers in Dawson.

Now Clarence walked in, streaked with dirt, his fingers stiff and curled, as if he were still gripping a shovel.

"I must've mixed up the days," Clarence said. "Why didn't anyone say it was Christmas?"

A significant look at the company, then at the table: mashed potatoes, gravy, and beef, cooked with two oranges that had cost more than he'd say. Around the edge of the curtain, Alice stopped. Once she was out of view, she no longer felt embarrassed, and she willed her flesh to cool. With Ethel withdrawn from the household, she often allowed herself to forget that the cache belonged to Clarence. She believed herself in Ethel's place, which is to say, the wife's place, and did inappropriate things like this: cook their best food without asking permission.

At the table, Henry was explaining to Charlie: "This is the trouble with firstborn sons. They are absolutely cowed by the very mention of fun. A simple dinner party with one dear old friend and a brother, and they think the indulgence might kill them. I can tell you the root of it too,"

Henry continued. "It goes straight back to childhood. When they were this tall"—Henry thrust out a low hand—"their Pa's told them, 'Work hard and stay the course' or some drivel like that. We younger ones never took it seriously, but the first son has no buffer of siblings and believes every word of it. Twenty years later, you end up with revoltingly stiff and successful people like the specimen seated before us."

Charlie said, "I thought Frank was the oldest."

"He is," said Clarence. "He's older than me by two years."

"Yes," said Henry airily, "but no one counts Frank. Speaking of which." He called toward the kitchen. "Don't tell us you forgot poor Frank!"

The news was that Frank Berry was back from Quartz Creek, destitute, drunk, and rooting around Dawson for some new scheme to support himself.

Alice stepped into the doorway and nearly collided with Jane. They moved around each other without meeting eyes.

"He wrote that he might visit on Monday," said Alice.

"Monday," Henry exclaimed. "Now let me think. Oh yes, that's right. I'm hosting the King and Queen of Spain that evening. Say that I'm terribly sorry to miss him." Then, leaning on elbows, he added in a hushed voice to Charlie, "I had the privilege last week of meeting Frank in town. He complained every minute and didn't offer to pay a cent for our meal. When we went walking along the river, I thought, now's my chance to seize a raft and send good ol' Frank downstream to the Indians."

Clarence wiped his face. "The Indians would have sent him back."

Henry banged his fist on the table and laughed. Alice looked at Jane, who stood at the stove. But there was no reaction, not even a quiver. The spoon continued two clockwise turns. Then Jane tapped the stem on the pot and looked up. "The peas will shrivel if we leave them in longer."

"Then take them out. Here's a bowl."

Jane accepted. These were canned peas, carried all the way from the mainland, first by steamship, then by tug up the river. They should treat the produce more carefully, Alice thought, no matter that Clarence was rich.

"Do you want to bring them in," Jane asked, "or should I?"

"You do it. I'm going to check on my sister."

Alice walked through the main room, wiping her hands on her thighs. She paused and put a finger to her lips. The men went silent. She opened the bedroom door a crack. Ethel was turned away and one could perceive by the slight motions of breathing that she was sleeping. She'd been hot with a bout of fever last night, though it wasn't worth waking her up to check for it now. Gently, Alice pulled the door closed.

"Let's all try to be quiet," she said. She took off her apron and sat down at the table.

Henry said, "Aren't you going to eat with us, Jane?"

Jane was standing near Charlie, delivering into his hands the heavy bowl of peas. "All right. I suppose I will."

She could have pulled the rocking chair up to the table. She could have sat in the spot beside Alice. Instead Jane wiggled onto the bench beside Henry. The show of attention was not lost on him and made him smug and mirthful. Their elbows touched. Their shoulders could not help but meet.

During this dinner, they learned much about Jane. For once you gave Jane the floor, she spoke willingly. Why not? She had stories to tell. She served herself bread and peas and cut her meat. She told them that her father was a mysterious Frenchman, who once had traded at a post not far from here. On one of his trips, he'd encountered a beautiful woman, half-Tlingit, half-Hän, Jane's mother, and he had fallen in love with her on the spot. Though there were so many men in the country who had wanted to marry her, it had taken Jane's father two trips to visit the family, loaded with gifts, before the marriage was allowed to take place.

When she was born, Jane said, it was a big event, and all her distant relatives had come to visit, because the rumor was that there'd never been a prettier baby. All was well and cheerful until she was about eight years old, when her father had gone away for the season as usual, but had never come back. Her mother had thought something bad had happened to him, though recently Jane had come to accept that he'd probably lost interest in her mother, whose health had taken a turn for the worse.

Still, her father's legacy had left its mark. The Catholic Church, her father's church, had heard the tale of a little French girl living among the Indians. It was an opportunity they couldn't resist, and they'd sent out a search party into the area. When the two church men found her, they'd said something to each other in French, and she, Jane, had walked out from the trees and interrupted in French, and the men had just about fallen over in shock.

She didn't remember the conversation, she told them now. Like she said, her mother was ill. It was the coughing sickness, and a serious case, so when the men offered to take Jane away for school, her mother must have felt it would be for the best, though Jane believed she wouldn't have agreed to it had she been well. She, Jane, had not understood she'd be leaving for good. For instance, she remembered thinking about the fishing trips she took with her aunts and uncles and expecting that she'd still be joining them in the spring.

But the men had decided that a Christian child belonged in school. They brought her to the mission, a big wood building with two stories and large glass windows facing the water. The nuns taught her to read and write. One day they'd had a spelling bee, and she'd handily beat all the older children. Then she'd beaten the teacher. Then they'd called in the priest, and she'd beaten him too on, of all things, the word "Diocesan." It wasn't so bad but the problem came when, at the start of summer, she'd said, I want to visit my mother, I'm going, and they'd said no, you aren't allowed to leave. She ran away at night, but the next day she'd badly hurt her ankle and they found her four miles away from the mission and forced her back. She didn't try to leave again until she was fifteen. That time, she was successful, and she found her family's camp near the Porcupine River. But it wasn't the homecoming that Jane had imagined. Her mother was dead. In the meantime, she had brought into the world three young sons, all with her own surname Lowell, as their father had taken no part in raising them. But the boys, her half-siblings (Jim was the middle brother) as enthralled as they'd been by the appearance of an older sister, had also teased her because she couldn't cook a meal over an open flame to save her life, and because she was always mixing up words.

"And Jim?" Alice asked. "Did he tease you?"

"Yes," Jane said, scooping up her last bite of peas and butter, licking the back of the spoon. "Only to keep up with the other two. But it wasn't his nature. Soon he was giving me little gifts instead. He taught me to fish and I taught him English. He was a sweetheart from the beginning."

"Remarkable!" Henry said. "A truly remarkable story. To think that you folks were having these great adventures, while we were chasing horses and pigs through the dust on the same round earth, not knowing there was a different way to live."

Jane smiled, polite.

"And look how the rush bettered the lives of you and your family," Henry continued. "Too often we hear the reverse."

"I don't like *all* the recent changes to the country," Jane amended, gently. "It's been okay for me and Jim, only because of our English. But for others, no."

How similar we are, Alice observed, we keep our true feeling submerged.

When they had wiped the platters of every crumb, Alice began clearing the table. Jane rose to gather the silverware. Charlie stood and insisted on stacking the plates. He said he hadn't eaten so well in a year. Henry, not to be outdone, jumped up and asked for the broom. Clarence, who'd been quiet at dinner, now sat back in his chair. He put his feet up on the table and crossed his ankles and took out his pipe. "Well, isn't this a sight to see. Henry and Charlie doing the chores."

8.

The ground continued to give up its wealth, like a poor thing that didn't know any better. Along the banks, the rich earth was turned inside out, sifted through, then left naked and exposed in the sun. One day a shovel hit bone. A bison skull, perfectly preserved. They shook off the dust and brushed dirt from the crevices. Clarence held it over his head, skulked across the claim, and wore it into the cabin, making Ethel scream. That evening, they looped wire through the eye sockets and hung the head on the wall. They wound black lace around its horns, then sat under the gaze of their hoary god. But they didn't really need the help of a talisman. A division had taken place on the creeks. No longer was Clarence Berry one rich man in a row of fifty others. Instead, thanks to his tireless workers, his fierce management, he was the richest of all. So far, he was adjusting nicely to the change. Once you'd still been able to see the farm boy in him. Now his boyhood self had shrunk to a kernel, tucked deep inside his swelling chest. He'd received letters from Selma announcing that his sister, Cora, had married, and that, as expected, Daisy had married Ed Keller, but you'd never seen anyone do such a bad job pretending to care. He didn't even think of sending wedding gifts, until Ethel, reading over the correspondence in her rocking chair, reminded him.

He did outrageous things. He put out a sign at the edge of the claim, "Help Yourself," and underneath he placed a bucket of nuggets and a bottle of whiskey. Let any lowly prospector following the line of the creek have his fun, he said. Let the others, he did not say, rankle from the taunt. When a group of New York reporters came through—they'd taken the highly expensive all-water route to arrive here, a route only open in summer—Clarence told them to have a go with their hands at the diggings on *Five* and keep what they found. The reporters were polite, but the two youths they'd brought along, each about sixteen years old, went wild. They filled envelopes with gold nuggets and had the best day of their lives. You might have called Clarence Berry generous, but that would have been a mistake. Because he wouldn't have done it if they hadn't been reporters. He wouldn't have put out the bucket and whiskey if he hadn't believed—rightly—that the whole country would soon be telling that story.

AS THE BRIGHT JUNE CAME into its final week, Ethel slowly improved. The fevers stopped flaring; the blood had stopped as mysteriously as it had come. They still had no idea what the root of it was. But Alice's one suspicion—which she wrote down in her journal but was too superstitious to say aloud—was that after Ethel's collapse, there had been an infection, and that by a miracle Ethel had fought it off.

Soon Clarence seemed also to accept the beginnings of a recovery. Because one day, he had an idea. To give his wife something to do, he urged her to resume her hobby from last year and pick up again with her collection of nuggets. Alice was enlisted to help, without any mind paid to all the housework she still needed to do. They got Ethel to the table, and the sisters sat there for hours together. They picked out the pretty nuggets. The odd ones. A nugget like a crescent moon. A nugget in the shape of a heart. There was a brown velvet pouch that Ethel had brought from Selma. They used the pouch for storing their favorite nuggets, and Ethel kept it close at her bedside.

9.

The dogs slept around the cabin now, one at each wall, their new job was guarding the people and the money inside. Several times Clarence awoke purposefully in the dead of night to go outside and catch them in the act. Always, he found them in perfect arrangement. Later he'd say to Alice: "Can you believe these dogs? One time I told them, here, here, here, and here, and that was all the instruction they needed." He stood in the doorway, holding his coffee, shaking his head. When he caught his sister-in-law staring, he added, as if to help her along with the point, "They're the best damn dogs I've ever known."

And what was she, the sister-in-law? Less than a dig. Worse than a dog.

She could have stood beside the gold and whiskey, under the sign "Help Yourself," and been the lowest pick of the three.

There was a bright circle of people who mattered, and she lived outside it. No matter where she traveled, that stayed the case. It was pathetic. She could not even spend three months as the most desirable girl in a house. At home, she'd forever been third to Annie and Ethel; then, once Annie had married, and Daisy grew up, third to Ethel and Daisy. Now Henry and Charlie saw Jane coming, and their talk broke off, their thoughts muddled.

Henry especially was entranced. She overheard him saying to Clarence: "What are you trying to do to us, planting a thing like that in your kitchen? It's not enough to tease us with your gold? You have to torture us with beauty too?"

She knew Henry wouldn't be the first to marry an Indian woman. Look at Jane's Frenchman father. Look at the first wave of gold-seekers into the country, some of whom lived still with their wives, and happily so, by their own reports. George Carmack, the man who'd discovered gold in the country, had a Tagish wife, Kate, whom he toted all over town with their three little children trailing behind them. Ma and Pa Berry would never approve. But their children's money had knocked down their authority. She imagined Jane in a pale dress. She imagined Jane the sister of Ethel. She imagined Jane laughing at Henry's jokes, while she, Alice, stirred pots in the kitchen. What had happened to her great adventure? The past two months had passed by in a flash of never-ending daylight, during most of which she'd been nursing her sister.

She had thought—what had she thought?—that she would make something of herself while she was here. At the very least, she'd expected to go home transformed. But nothing had changed. She herself was poor. She was prospectless. She had left the daughter of a fruit farmer. The only daughter of four still living under her parents' care. And she would return exactly that. She would live in that house without alteration, with gifts from her well-off sisters who had leap-frogged over her head. She would age without experiencing what others experienced. She would age without advancing, like a shriveling child. She would age harboring a potential that never found a chance to uncurl.

10.

"Speak of the devil, and the devil will appear," Henry said.

Alice glanced up, expecting Jane, but the reference was to Frank: his latest letter unfolded next to the poker chips. With July upon them, he was finally on his way—not just to visit—but to live with them on the claims. The note announced his imminent arrival. There was something in the wording that everyone felt was slightly off—Frank seemed to believe they had missed him.

A deep frown on Henry's face. Who knew his mouth could tilt that way? "I'm going to tell you something, Ceej," he said lowly, "which I've been keeping very close to the vest. I don't like saying it, but here goes. I believe that Frank harbors very ill feelings toward you. And I don't mean just his regular whining. He hates that you're rich. More than he even lets on. That week I saw him in town, he took a swipe at you every two minutes, like he was obsessed."

"I'd keep him out of the attic, if I were you," offered Charlie. Then, noticing Clarence's face: "Should I not know there's gold in the attic?"

Henry put his hand over his mouth, his eyes wide and horrified. But it only lasted a second. Then, in a complete reversal, he said, "Oh give it a rest, Ceej. It's only Charlie."

"You have a big mouth, Hen," Clarence grumbled.

"Look," said Henry. "I didn't mean to put you in a sour mood. Really, cheer up. We've managed Frank all our lives, I suppose we can manage him now."

"If you're telling me I can't trust my own family, that's a sorry state to be in."

"Maybe you should move Tot to the galley and sleep in the attic yourself," Charlie said. "And take your gun."

"That's true," Henry said. "That attic might not be safe for our girl here."

He gave Alice a warm look, which was a nice surprise.

"And Charlie makes a good point," Henry continued to his brother. "Your wonderful dogs can't protect you from your own invited guests."

"Well," Alice said, swooping forward to clear the last crumbs from the table, "I like my little perch, but I'll move in with Ethel if needs be." Meaning: don't expect me to sleep in the kitchen with Jane.

Henry, Clarence, and Charlie looked at her, but without understanding. And minutes later it was considerations completely apart from her and Jane that made Clarence decide that Frank would stay in the tents on the hill with Charlie and the other workers. That was life. When two young men disliked each other, the whole town had to know. But when two young women disliked each other, they were expected to do so in private.

And they did.

That week, when the wind screamed over the hills, Jane told Alice: Do you hear that plaintive note in the wind? Those are the cries of a little boy who long ago fell through a crack in the ice. He survived the drop, but couldn't climb out, and all the ropes of the men and women in his party weren't long enough to reach him. His mother wouldn't leave him and sat at the edge weeping, and now when you listen closely—Jane touched her ear as the wind wailed anew—you can still hear mother and son crying and crying.

Was Jane toying with her?

Yes, Alice thought. Then she thought, *no.*

For instance, Jane told her on a different occasion, holding up a bedsheet still bearing a dark stain from the days after Ethel's heaviest bleeding, "When my mother was a girl, women went to a different house during that time. When she had her first blood, she lived in a corner, behind a hanging sheet, and fasted and drank not a sip of water for as long as she could. You see," Jane instructed, "for us, it's different. When the blood is running, a girl can become very powerful. There are stories of girls who've moved mountains, just with their eyes. That's why you have to keep us locked up until that time passes."

It was exhausting to be together all day. Jane had a way of telling a story, then making it twist. For instance, she would talk as if a Christian way of life were superior, and then, when you least expected it, you'd find her stacking her mother's people on top. She said that before the white men came into the country, wives belonged to husbands, and daughters belonged to their families. She said she didn't understand how white people could stand to have it all mixed up. She asked Alice, out of the blue, why there were so many missionaries coming into the Klondike, when it was clear that their lessons must be very much needed at home.

Another time when they were slicing potatoes, Jane said, as if her only aim was to make small conversation: Did you ever hear the story of the first Russian ship to make land in Alaska? The captain sent a skiff to the shore, but the men never returned. Then he sent a second skiff, but those men, too, never returned. At dawn, the captain and the remaining crew got the first view of the native people, yelling war cries from their canoes. The captain was frightened and turned his ship around and went rushing home. He believed his men had been murdered. In fact, his missing sailors had reached the camp and decided to stay. They'd never eaten so well or slept so comfortably or seen such beautiful women. Most importantly, Jane said, pausing the knife and looking up from the counter, they were tired of following their captain's orders. They wanted to live free for once in their lives.

11.

Frank arrived, two days past the date he'd threatened. He came around the bend in the creek, his smirk gleaming in the late summer light. Despite his ratty clothes, the filthy pipe sticking straight out from his lips, he was as good-looking as ever. Clarence and Henry took after their father. But Frank resembled only their Ma. His thick black hair, his string bean body, his elegant strut. At first, you had no choice but to like Frank, because he was charming. He walked into any room with ease. He nudged conversation to provocative political topics when the evening was dull. He could take apart a newspaper and fold it into ten paper hats in a jiffy—though after handing them out, would not sink so low as to wear one himself. He kept a deck of cards on his person and would invite smart-looking strangers into a game. Only gradually, as you got to know him, would your opinion adjust. One day he'd be joking with a fellow, next day he wouldn't want to talk. All the girls in Selma were a little afraid of him. His insinuations had started years ago, when he was still in school, that no hometown farmer's daughter was good enough for him. At parties, he eschewed the dance floor, and instead pulled a chair up to some pretty young matron and worked himself into a deep conversation, which was his way of turning his back on every hopeful unmarried girl in the room.

The evening after he arrived, Alice was alone in the galley when Frank came in. He braced himself on the top shelf and leaned over the spilled-out collection of beans she was sorting.

"That little girl has an awful case on old Hen," he said. "I say we make them both jealous."

"What, both?" Alice asked, without looking up. It was easier to talk to Frank, she'd found, when she pretended she wasn't giving him all her attention. With one finger, she moved a pebble away from the beans to the edge of the counter, "What are you saying?"

"I don't like Jane batting her eyes at my brother," he said, hushed, "so let's you and me whisper together and look at each other mush-like. I'll call you 'honey' whenever they're around and you call Hen 'Cooter' this and 'Cooter' that. Jane will think you've got a claim on Henry and will be checked. And Henry will have his jealousy roused by thinking I have a claim on you." Frank's simper melted into a scowl. "If that doesn't work, I go to plan B, which is to knock my brother upside the head. He's been strutting around here like an overfed rooster, acting like he's a second C.J., and it's making me sick."

"Sure, why not." Alice avoided his eyes. She would have agreed to anything—that was Frank's power. He condescended, though, Alice thought, in allying himself with her, and calling her "honey," even for show. She didn't believe Frank's plan would work. Henry sometimes flirted with her, but she wasn't at all convinced that he'd be provoked if some other man treated her sweetly. Of course she wouldn't admit that to Frank. She was not in the habit of alerting people to her own insignificance. The world did it too often without her help.

The next day, when they were all together, Frank nudged her, and Alice said, in a high and falsely confident voice, "Cooter, will you go to the spring for some fresh water?"

Henry looked around, cautiously. First at her, then at Frank. "Well sure I will, Alice. Just a second while I finish this bite."

Frank, swooping to the table, patting Henry's back: "Don't take a step outside unless Tot goes with you. She's been in the kitchen all day."

Jane thrust out a lower lip. "I've been inside too."

Frank turned his attention on her, languidly, like the slow rotation of a cannon: "You can go with me when they get back. We'll get a second bucket."

The words themselves were friendly, but his expression and tone were chillingly cold.

"Never mind," Jane said briskly. "I'd rather finish these sheets."

Frank winked, and Alice thought, stepping with Henry into the bright afternoon: that was an artful way to put a person down. You pack hatred into a banal suggestion. In such a way that no re-creation of the words alone could give away the truth. Even Henry, standing in the room with them, had missed the push and pull of conversation that had left Jane rocking on her heels. She was quaking from Frank's meanness, though what really was the offense? What had Frank done, out loud, but asked her to go on a walk?

12.

That afternoon, Hen, the brother-in-law, and Alice, the sister-in-law, took only a stroll to the spring and back. But the next evening, emboldened by Frank, Alice suggested they go on a walk after dinner. She was surprised and pleased at her own daring. Jane glowered. Frank hooted with joy.

Alice didn't know what to think. She left the house at Henry's side in a state of confusion. In Selma, Henry had been in love with Annie. When she'd told him that Annie liked William Carswell, the grocer from Illinois, Henry's affections had failed to transfer themselves onto her. But Selma, five years ago, was a different world. And people did change. The radiance of the Klondike, of the Bush-Berry wealth, was perhaps lighting her up. Now she turned her own appraising eye on Hen. And found that he, too, was improved by their surroundings and by the Berrys' new station in life.

Outside the cabin, the claim was noisy and big. In addition to Charlie, Clarence had condescended to hire three other hometown boys from the San Joaquin Valley. Pale and glowing in the sun, they stooped low, with rounded backs, and beat sharp shovel heads into the ground. Jim worked among them, their teacher for the day. He was patient in his instructions.

When he had to fix their work with the sluice, he laughed at them, shaking his head, but in such a way that the new boys could laugh too.

At the creek edge, the more experienced miners swirled their pans. Their hat brims stood out in front of the percolating water like a row of rising suns. Around the sluice, the dance was staccato and fixed, like the inside of a grandfather clock. It was a routine that Alice was accustomed to now. The bucket of pay dirt goes down the sluice. The water goes down. The gold-rich sludge is scooped off the slide and brought to the creek for panning.

Alice and Henry climbed a hill, picking wildflowers to take back to Ethel, enough to fill the little green vase that Clarence had bought her their first Christmas together, in the winter of '96. Henry lumbered to a colorful spot. He dipped, righted himself, and held out a fat fistful of purple blooms. "Well," he said. "How do you like me now?"

A bear paw, flattening butterfly wings; a round boy in a cap and suspenders, crushing a newspaper under his arm.

She accepted the flowers. "I like your help," she said, coyly. "I didn't know you would help in the kitchen, or that you were so handy with the sick."

"I can't do much for Ethel."

"You cheer her up, she always likes seeing you."

"Do you remember that I worked in the hospital in Fresno doing all kinds of jobs? I used to sit with the patients after their surgeries. The nurses said I had a calming effect."

"I'd forgotten. But you've reminded me." She shot him a merry, wicked look. "Didn't your brothers have a story on you?"

"Please, not that."

She grinned. "The doctor told you to give a man a sleeping pill if he required it. And in your report, you said that you had *wakened* the man to give him the pill."

He tipped his hat to cover his face. When he pushed it up again, he was grinning.

They walked along the crest. He asked her opinion of Charlie.

"Oh, he's a nice fellow. We overlapped in school one year when we were both about fourteen. I remember because one day he forgot his lunch and didn't realize until the hour was over, as he'd been busy playing ball with the boys. He whined and complained like a baby over such a small thing. I've never seen anything like it. I believe the teacher sent him home before the end of the afternoon lessons."

"Poor Charlie." Henry was spirited. "I can't blame him. I turn into a monster too, when I miss a meal."

"Trust me, you've never acted like that."

Yellow to red, the sun's weakening light. Lavender hills deepened with long streaks of gray. They reached a little plateau, high on the hill, and faced the large and brilliant west.

Henry said, "When you go home, don't forget who you were with, when you viewed the Alaska sunset."

They stood in silence. Their hands were inches apart, hung at their sides. It would have only taken a small gesture to make the fingers brush. For a minute, Alice was in suspense. But the moment passed and nothing happened. They went down the grade, single file because of the rocks. What was this, exactly? Alice wondered. Was Frank really onto something or not? How did people know when they were liked?

13.

The rope ladder was shaking against the ceiling edge.

"You better come here and see this!" yelled Henry.

The door slammed while Alice was wrestling into her dress. She pushed her journal under her mat. By the time she climbed down, only the two women were left in the cabin: Ethel and Jane each at a window, broad backs to the room, like a pair of stone sentries. Alice joined her sister, pushing the curtain further aside.

Outside, Clarence was yelling and pacing. The men stood in a line before the sluice.

"What on earth—" Alice muttered.

"A sack of pay dirt went missing," Ethel answered, her voice quavering, not moving her eyes away from her husband. "I can hardly believe it, but Clarence is sure."

"What kind of pay dirt?"

"A pile from yesterday. It was washed on the sluice but not yet panned."

In the distance, Clarence was raving, while the stunned collection of workers looked on.

Alice turned her gaze indoors. She didn't want Ethel getting overexcited, and relapsing when she'd been making such progress.

"Are you okay, Ethel? Should I pull up your chair?"

"I'm fine. I'm only worried about this."

The sounds of outrage died in the air. They could only infer from Clarence's movements the tempo of his rant. Alice watched intently, taking it in. No theft had touched the creeks this summer. None, at least, on the millionaire claims. The punishment for theft was hanging. The laws were extremely strict in the Klondike so as to balance the sparse presence of the Mounted Police, whose numbers couldn't keep up with the influx of travelers.

A shuffling in the ragtag row of men. Any minute now, Clarence might pounce.

On whom? Alice wondered. That was the question.

Not Jim. Because Clarence would not hear a word against Jim, ever since he'd saved their lives on the Chilkoot.

Not the hometown boys from the San Joaquin Valley, who seemed to consider themselves an extension of the Berry family.

Among the hirelings, maybe—Handler, Richards, and a dozen others, Alice didn't know all their names—although even that was hard to imagine. Soft, obedient men all, despite having lived in the country for years. They worked on the Berry claim because they'd never drummed up the gumption to set out on their own. They lived for donuts, these men. They relished the loaves of bread that she and Jane dropped off at their tent flaps on Sundays.

Not included in the row, standing at Clarence's back, were Henry, Charlie, and Frank. Charlie was giddy, rubbing his hands together. For a second, she thought, *It's Charlie*. But the thought wouldn't stick. Charlie was in the mold of Henry. Too content with his life to risk an ugly disruption.

And Frank? She wished that Henry would stop eyeing his brother like that, for all the workers to see. Frank could have done it. He was jealous and mean. But another instinct told Alice that it couldn't be Frank. She thought—she didn't know if this was right or not—that he was too proud for this base kind of stealing.

No one slept that night. Not even during the sliver of true dark that July provided them. Lights swept across the attic ceiling, moved forward and aft by shuffling feet. Alice shifted off her mat. Rolled once. Crept along on her stomach, until her fingers closed around the edge of the trapdoor in the ceiling. In a globe of soft illumination, Clarence, Henry, and Charlie convened at the table. Elbows down. Leaning toward the strong, steady flame of the kerosene lamp that looked especially nice tonight, on a lace doily that she had finished that afternoon. Her excuse for drawing a chair into the doorway and keeping her eyes on the claim the whole day.

Charlie said, "Here's what you do. You round up the fellows and take each guy one by one and have him answer a series of questions. Who were you with? What are your debts? And so on. Then you ask the same questions, only of the fellow's tentmates. You pool the information together and look for the inconsistent story."

Henry, kind but dubious: "And the guilty party will out?"

"I'd say so."

Henry shrugged. "What do you say, Ceej? It's as good a plan as any."

A silence. A lumbering coming together of thought. Then Clarence said, "And what if I get in for more than I'm willing to do?"

"Say again, old boy?"

"Once you nab the guy, you don't get to decide what to do with him. The Mounted Police might put the whip in my hand, whether I want it or not. They might hang him and ask me to play some part in stringing him up."

"It's not like it was in the early days," Henry assured. "Now the police take care of the punishment."

"Still." Clarence looked askance. "I'm starting to wonder if it's worth all the trouble."

"Easy for you to say," Henry answered. "I'm happy to stay again this winter. But I'd sleep better knowing the outlaw was caught."

"Plus," Charlie warned, loyal to Henry. "You'll enable crimes against other people if you let this go. Less fortunate people."

"Well, look," Clarence grumbled. "I can't be everything to everybody."

"How kind you are to yourself." Henry laughed to soften his words. Charlie didn't know whether to laugh or not, and his indecision took the form of a grunt. "Honestly though," Henry continued. "What are you scared of? Are you scared it was Frank? Look, I'm the last to defend him. But I'll say he isn't stupid enough to pull a scheme like this."

"You're the one who swore that he'd sabotage me."

"Yes, but I didn't mean in this way. I meant more like he'd hound you for loans until you were broke. But as for these folks." Henry gestured in the direction of the hills that hosted the workers' tents. "You can't expect twenty men to spend every day running their open palms over your money, without one of them closing a fist. It's the law of—what would you call it?—the law of possession."

"You spent ten months on this claim," Clarence said gently. "You mined it and acted as the overseer. You'd never rob me."

"I wouldn't." Henry reclined in his chair. "But I'm the perfect specimen of a human being. You can't judge the others against me."

"Okay, that does it." Clarence stood up from the table. He ignored the gentle protestations. He wasn't angry, only fatigued. "Charlie, get your claws off my sleeve. I'm going to bed. Some of us have to work for a living."

The bedroom door opened on Ethel's voice, then it closed and muffled the conversation. Alice waited a second, then climbed down the ladder. She made as if she'd just woken up, but the boys didn't care one way or the other and reenacted for her the whole conversation.

"He's afraid for his reputation," Henry said, hushed, lacing his large fingers together. "You should have seen the reprimand I got, about the two workers who died in their tents over the winter. All right. I was the acting boss, but I never held back wages, not once. Was it my fault if these guys pissed it away? Was I supposed to be their nanny too, and tell them how much food they'd need for a month? I'll never forget what it feels like to bang a pot outside a man's tent. Joke at him. Call him a few nasty names, then find him stone stiff and blue and glaring up at the tent roof. Now how's that for a Christian way to treat a couple of corpses?"

"Surely that was the first man," Alice ventured. "You wouldn't have done it twice."

Henry rubbed his chin. "Now I only feel worse."

"Poor suckers," Charlie said, sincere.

"Yes. And poor me too. Each grave took a week to dig. I wasn't proud. I took a shovel and worked with the men. It was hell to thaw the ground, but we did it. And it was a striking sight, two big bonfires raging in the Dawson graveyard, right out of the snow. We dug like madmen, the best we could. But we put the coffins in at only four feet. That was on my okay. My opinion was, we'd be dead too, before we got down to six. Then you lot arrived and my brother chewed me out for it. His great fear was people would whisper about the shallow graves and call him disrespectful. Classic C.J. It isn't enough to be the boss, he needs everyone to love him too."

Alice felt the truth in Henry's words. Seemingly haphazard moments arranged into patterns: not the least, Clarence's distance and syrupy politeness toward her ever since he'd ripped up her deed, and his softer manner since Ethel's collapse.

They were quiet awhile. A silence that allowed for a rhythmic snoring to make itself heard from the kitchen. Henry asked if it was Jane or the dogs, and Alice said it was Jane, and Henry tipped back and said, "Goodness."

"Here's what I think," Charlie said, brushing greasy blond locks from his forehead. "Speaking of dogs. First man who runs is guilty. If I were your brother, I'd be up and dressed and listening for the first sign of barking. You can't hide a thousand dollars or two in your boot toe forever."

"What if it's Frank?" Alice ventured.

They stared at her.

Henry pulled up his sleeves. "Then so be it."

"Would you give up your brother to a Canadian jail, just because he's a jerk?"

Henry deliberated, then winked at her. "I like that. You cut right to the chase. No, I don't suppose I would. But let me wait and see how I feel."

14.

Despite the buildup, the next day was sluggish and dull. In the afternoon, Charlie said he was off to Dawson for a little entertainment. He held his hat against the breeze, his hips swinging on the uneven ground; guilty by his own formula, though that fact alone, his blithe forgetfulness, his inability to consider himself inside the pool of suspects, must absolve him.

Jane said, "I hope the theft doesn't affect Henry's plans for the winter."

"Oh?" asked Alice. "Is that your concern?"

"I need the work. That's why I'm thinking about it." Jane smiled into empty space. "Henry has no idea how to cook for himself. He was in here the other day, looking over my shoulder while I poached the eggs. It was like I was performing a miracle."

"He wintered alone on the claim last year and survived it."

"But it was hard on him."

"I wouldn't say so. Not in any big way." Alice poured a cup of tea for herself. "You're going to have to make a little extra for dinner tonight. We have one of the neighbors from down the creek looking in."

"Who's that?"

"Never you mind. Just a man who heard about the theft and would like the full story from Clarence."

Jane didn't answer.

In the next room, Ethel was sitting up, picking at a meal at the table.

"You've done a lot of smiling today," Alice said quietly. "For someone whose boss has just been robbed."

"Like you tell me, it's none of my concern."

Alice sipped the tea. It was scalding.

"And I dare say Clarence will manage fine," Jane continued. "He's taken enough from our little creeks to last him a lifetime." Jane was rolling dough on the counter. She wiped her hands on her thighs. Alice was about to speak when—infuriatingly—Jane put up a hand to stop her words. "Just a second. Hold that thought. I'm off to do some digging. Let's see if we can't put some nuts in this bread."

The cache, she meant, she was going to dig in the cache. When Jane was not in the kitchen, you could find her in there, picking through the shelves of food. She liked to organize it whenever Clarence brought back the shopping from town. She separated out what they must use before it spoiled, or else put aside for a special meal their best delicacies: canned oysters and a wheel of cheese. Sunday morning, even, she was squirreled away. Though previously she'd insisted on sitting on her mat by the stove, muttering prayers to the metal cross she had nailed to the wall.

Alice's face was burning.

A dog pushed inside. Instead of pushing it back out, Alice fed it the scraps of pork from the pot, though half the population in Dawson wouldn't eat that much meat in a week. The pink tongue muscled between her fragrant fingers. Its flank leaned against her thighs. "We're friends now, are we?" she said.

The claim was quiet but for the regular work. The hills abandoned, the creek assured in its forward dash. When a breeze kicked up, little sprays of gravel clicked against the house.

What was Jane doing in there? Fifteen minutes had passed. Maybe twenty. The fire had mellowed. What did they pay her for if she couldn't get a simple lunch onto the table? She herself would not rummage the logs, she wouldn't do Jane's work for her. Perhaps, as the summer went on, Jane assumed her laziness would go unchecked. Perhaps Henry was out there, talking to her.

Discomfited by the urge to fight, Alice threw down the pot and passed behind Ethel and walked around the front of the house. Her skirts swung. A sharp turn, boot toe crushing the gravel, when she intersected with—not Henry—but Clarence.

He was startled. She was startled. His pipe was braced in his teeth. He held up a fistful of crackers.

"Fuel for the fever," he said, meaning gold fever, she supposed, not the real one that his wife had been fighting.

Alice was too stunned to answer. With Ethel right inside, she couldn't have, even if she'd known what to say. Not wanting to follow Clarence into the cabin, she continued toward the cache, her heart pounding. In the dim recesses, a swishing sound, like a cat's tail batting a curtain. She couldn't believe what her senses were telling her: that Jane had been in the cache with Clarence, that circumstances permitted them to have been in there for fifteen, twenty minutes alone. Jane sashayed before the well-packed shelves, buttons gleaming down her back. When she turned to face the intruder, her smug expression, above a tower of tins, spoke the words *I dare you.* Alice almost dared. But the words, tortured and struggling, would not emerge in clear form from her throat. Her motion reversed itself through the open door, across the gravel, and into the house.

15.

Now when Alice woke, it was sudden. No ritual lounging, no rolling about on the points of her shoulders and hips. Her gaze darted. Her heart raced. Her lungs fed upon the frontier air. What had she interrupted, precisely? Maid or not, she would have been happy to have a list of specifics. It did not matter if Clarence was a gentle husband to Ethel. It did not matter, his solicitousness toward his wife. What did the Berrys think of themselves? That they were better than Bushes? That the Bush sisters would endure disrespect? There was no proof. When she wanted to cool herself down, she admitted to that. Only hints. Only guesses. But look up at the stars, and there it is: you connect them, and see the picture.

All my life, thought Alice, I have allowed myself to be carried along, but now I won't. Enough gliding. Enough hoping. Enough making observations for no purpose but to enrich my letters home.

These men, she thought, they will lose a million dollars before they've sat down to breakfast. They will lose a family fortune before they've realized what they've done.

They don't know, Alice thought, how lucky they are to have a person like me in the family. She felt steady. As if, crossing a wild river, her bare feet had finally found the ford.

Later that morning, down in the main room, she was setting the table when Clarence said, "I wonder what the hurry is, here comes Hen."

She followed his gaze through the window and saw the large figure approaching along the creek. She put down the next plate, the next fork, but everything inside her was awake: poised with anticipation.

Seconds later, the door banged open, and there was Henry, empty-handed except for his hat.

"Ho!" shouted Clarence in greeting. "What's wrong with your claim? Aren't you working anymore?"

"I had too good a week last week," Henry said smoothly. "I don't need any more dust for a while."

Clarence laughed at him: called him a liar. He liked conversation that pulled them widely clear of the theft. They were into August now, and he still had done nothing to dig out the culprit. He seemed to want the clock to run out. Finally, Henry let out a laugh too, and waved Clarence off.

"You folks won't be here much longer. What can I tell you?" He found Alice's eyes and winked. "The winter is lonesome. Let me get in my fun."

The appeal worked on his brother, so Henry used the same line during an evening walk with Alice.

"The dark makes me tired," Henry said. "I'm happy to be the overseer for C.J., I'm the only one he trusts, and goodness knows he needs me more than ever. But it's a long winter and the work is grueling. I feel like I never fully wake up. No sun for ninety days, can you imagine? And the solitude is awful. You know me, I like a full table and a song after dinner. It's not easy to eat alone, then spend the evening staring at a crack in the wall." Despite the subject, his own discomfort, he spoke with his usual buoyancy. "What you need in the winter is someone to talk to. Even better if you're still getting to know them."

"Well," Alice answered smoothly. "I suppose you could take in a hobo from Dawson."

He shot her an injured gaze: "I was imagining someone nicer to look at."

"Oh, I see. Then you should know that Jane is hoping to stay on as your cook."

"No," he said, "I didn't mean Jane."

"Why not?" She was pressing him, toying with him. She was beginning to like Henry, and to imagine possibilities that a year ago she wouldn't have dreamed of. But she refused to take a big step forward until she had a better sense of the whole. If there was something between Clarence and Jane, Henry might know it. If there was something between Henry and Jane, God help her, she would like to know that too. "She's a nice girl and she likes you. You don't have to feel embarrassed about it. She's half-French after all. Let's say you married her and brought her home. The worse they'd think is that she spent her younger days running wild outdoors. They'd say, look, there's a young lady who didn't mind her mother and keep her bonnet strings tied."

"That's not nice."

"I suppose it isn't."

"Anyway, it's not her looks. Even Charlie says she's a beauty." They were both silent. Both unhappy. Then Henry said, "You're putting me down, Tot."

"Am I? How so?"

"I'll tell you the real reason one day."

"I'm going home soon, so you better say it now."

"No," he grumbled. "I can't tell you now."

They walked in silence, then Alice said gently: "Remember my first day on the claim? You were annoyed with me then."

"Not so!" He was shocked. "You and Ethel arriving here was like all the world's flowers blooming at once."

"I meant the *next* day. When you found out that Ethel had given her fraction to me."

"Ah. I forgot about that. Maybe I did get a bit grumpy. I wouldn't have objected to C.J. transferring a bit of land to my name. See here though," he continued with force. "If I remember right, it wasn't long before my sense of awe took over. I started asking myself, what kind of remarkable young lady treks two thousand miles from home, cares for her sister, and pockets a fraction of land off my cheap-as-hell brother in the meantime?"

"He took it back."

"I know," Henry said softly. "He can be a real rat, my brother."

"And you can't have wondered too much about me. You've known me since I was ten."

"I'd like to know you better."

A quiet fell. She smiled and looked at her whooshing skirts, the moving pebbled ground.

"Maybe I can give you forty feet of my claim," Henry said, "if you're interested."

"You're always saying it's worthless."

"Who knows? This country is full of surprises."

"You're nice to offer it, Hen," Alice said. "You must think I'm a greedy person. But I'm not, really. I don't have a strong taste for extravagance. But I was poor once, and once is enough."

"Was Selma so bad?"

"I meant before Selma."

"That's right. You all came down from Canyon Creek in Placer County, wasn't that it?" Again, Henry spoke with true sensitivity. "I remember the first time I laid eyes on you girls. You were hardly more than skeletons, and pale as ghosts. We heard you little ones were eating the dirt your last winter there."

"Only once or twice. I didn't know that story had gotten around."

"We never gossiped meanly about you, if that's what you're thinking. Your Poie's a good man. No one took pleasure in his bad luck."

"He wasn't cut out for the logging business. Or for farming, really. It's not that he doesn't work hard. It's more—"

"He doesn't know how to scheme."

Alice looked at Henry, surprised to have been understood. "That's right."

They reached the crest of the hill. From here they could see Anton Stander's cabin and two more claims farther along up the creek. The land stretched around them in peaceful, undulating hills. The creek reflected the sun, the ripples bright as jewels; the creek that had washed the gold from some ancient source through this enclave of country.

"I'd give my whole claim to know what you're thinking," Henry said softly.

A smile. "Only the view."

"Do you want to know what I'm thinking about? How lucky my brother was to find a bride in your sister. You Bush girls are a force to be reckoned with."

"Ethel's better than me. She's not only brave, she's patient and good."

"That's all right. You're the type I like. You're the feisty one."

He laughed. Alice tried not to. But Henry was one of those people whose laughter raised the laughter of everyone near him.

"See?" he said, squeezing her side, abundantly pleased with himself, "I knew you couldn't keep that prim face for long."

That night, Jane insisted that Henry stay for cards. She held his hand in both of hers and pouted. But he condensed his fingers and slipped from her grasp. Alice watched from Ethel's rocking chair, from over her knitting, as they stood together in the kitchen doorway. His eyes roved up the wall. His mind, thanks to a different person, was elsewhere.

16.

The weeks sloped to a single number on the calendar. Their date of departure, September 14, once a purely nebulous thing, had taken weight in the form of boat tickets, and now drew their thoughts toward it. With the coming of fall, Ethel, Clarence, and Alice would soon travel to Dawson. From there, via steamer, to California. Ethel couldn't wait to go. She'd been a good girl. Every morning now, she took her little walk on the creek from *Three* to *Four* and back again, leaning her weight on Alice's shoulder. There was still no more blood, thank God, no more fever, but during the long illness Ethel had lost the strength in her lungs and her legs. She always took the opportunity during these walks to roundly abuse herself. She'd almost died because she had not wanted to miss seeing the Klondike again. Now she longed to be home before anything else could go wrong.

Presumably Jane's departure would coincide with theirs, as she had not secured a hire to stay on as cook for the winter. She was fighting for it, though. She would slip a heap of pancakes under Henry's chin and say, wouldn't this be a cozy meal in November? A significant gaze would follow in the direction of Clarence. As in, isn't that the least you can do for your brother, to keep him plump and healthy under my care?

Then a strange thing happened: one day Ethel walked into the cache to look for crackers while Alice was out, and interrupted some troubling meeting between Jane and Jim, which later she did not want to talk about.

"But *what*?" Alice asked, trying not to show her frustration. "Did they say something about the missing gold?"

"No, no," Ethel protested. "Nothing like that. I'm sorry I mentioned it. I'm putting it out of my mind."

"Just tell me the subject."

Ethel gave her a watery smile.

"Please?"

"Oh, it's stupid. I thought Jane was laughing at me. About how I might never have my own child."

"I'll strangle anyone who does that."

"You see?" said Ethel. "I shouldn't have told you. I heard them say 'baby.' I think Jim was wondering if there was a baby coming—if my trouble had to do with that—and Jane was telling him no. It's not bad of him to be curious. It's my fault if I had my feelings hurt. That's an eavesdropper's punishment."

"This is your house. You're not an eavesdropper. You're allowed to walk where you want."

Still. The event slightly changed things in Alice's mind. She wondered if Jane was less artful, less like herself, than she'd imagined. The facts were: Jane had failed to secure a proposal from Hen. She had failed to receive a winter hire. If Jane had been jeering at Ethel, it was stupid and careless to have done it in the cache, with Ethel right next door and no longer confined to her bed. And Jim. For all of Jim's conspiring with the captain on the beach in Dyea, what had he done in the meantime? He had worked the claim. He had trained the new men who'd come in this summer. What was all that, in the scheme of things? It was practically nothing.

Or not.

Bright afternoon. Clarence's exclamations popped like dynamite bursts. He stood near the sluice. He was flushed and kicking the gravel, like a person with two cursed feet. His face had drained of all qualities save for his pink, Irish rage. The bewildered group of sorry-looking miners had frozen in odd positions, mid-task: balanced on a heap of earth, standing by the long, wooden sluice, tipping a shovelful of wet gravel into a rocker. Clarence grabbed a pick from the nearest man and began overturning debris: splintering lengths of dark, mossy lumber. He hooked the wheelbarrow at its axle and flipped it over, so that it lay helpless like an overturned beetle.

"Hey old boy, what's the problem here?"

Another theft. Unwashed gold. Raw shovelfuls of prized gravel, worth maybe ten thousand dollars, the best of a new pay streak on *Five*.

Hired men stared deeply into the hills, into the ripples of low gray sky. Others looked directly back at Clarence. The goal for all was not to seem guilty, but no one was really sure how to do it.

Until now it had been possible that the culprit was a vagabond from Dawson, picking his way down Eldorado and choosing a claim.

Unfortunately, they couldn't believe that now. The stolen gravel was one precise, very rich pile among twenty less abundant others. A stranger wouldn't have chanced upon it. Now Henry closed ranks with his brother, grasping his shoulder and pulling him gently away. They walked down to the creek, Henry speaking into Clarence's ear.

"They must be plotting a way to banish Frank," Ethel said. "I couldn't believe it at first, but now Clarence is convinced. Clarence saw Frank rutting around in that area three days ago. Then Henry heard from some fellows in town that Frank's in debt over some badly placed bets." A pause.

Alice held her tongue. The only way to get Ethel to speak at length was to stand there not saying a word. "The funny thing is," Ethel said slowly, "that we've already given Frank five thousand dollars, at least. And Clarence was willing to give him more when he asked for it. He's his older brother, after all. But Clarence won't stand for theft."

"Do you want my opinion, Ethel, dear?" Alice said after a pause, her voice shaking slightly. "I don't think Frank took that gold. It's like you said, when Frank wants money, he'll put out his hand and ask for it. He's too proud for that kind of stealing. He's not patient enough for it either. Can you imagine him up on his tippy toes, sneaking around in the dark?"

While they'd been talking, Frank himself had appeared, fifty feet off. He was dragging a short, sapling spruce, almost fully intact, like a hunter coming home with his kill. The topside scraped the dirt, so that it created a wide path at his heels. His expression was one of blatant amusement. His gaze bounced around, he didn't seem to know what was happening.

"If Frank didn't do it, who did?"

Alice raised her eyebrows and tilted her head toward the galley window, which all this time had been opened. The thumping spoon, the spoon that was stirring a broth, ceased its rhythm. For a moment they were all three lifted by an invisible hook at the back of their necks. They held there, an inch off the ground.

"No," said Ethel.

"I don't mean doing the grunt work," Alice whispered. "I mean the person calling the shots."

17.

"What are you saying to Ethel, to give her ideas about Jane?"

She was standing in the creek, rubber boots protecting her calves, her skirt tied in a knot at her knees. The bucket, she skimmed across the rushing surface, then dumped.

"Either you've heard," Clarence said from the bank, "or you're hearing it now. Frank was behind the theft. He came to the Yukon for gold and he was going to get it, by hook or by crook. Don't you realize why I haven't gone to the Mounted Police? Though if it weren't for my mother, I swear I would."

"Some mothers would consider it a favor," Alice said, "to have her other children discipline her prodigal son."

"I don't think so. When a man needs correcting, you women like to do it yourselves."

The water sloshed into the bucket. Then out. It was no good. Too many people working today, too much mud in the creek for clean water. The laundry would have to wait.

"I wonder if Frank isn't the only person you feel bound to protect."

"Go on."

She turned around slowly to face him.

"I remember that day Jane was with you in the cache. I wonder for how long. I'm learning a lot about this country. Henry and Charlie mentioned once that it used to be custom for prospectors to live alongside the native women. Was that how it was in Forty Mile?"

He was surprised. But not too much. He was getting used to her belligerence.

"What I did as a bachelor living in Forty Mile," he said, "was survive the winter and dig in the mud. I'm sorry if Henry or Charlie thought it appropriate to entertain you with general stories of that time. It was a men's camp. Those are stories for men."

"Would you protect Jane if you thought she was the thief? That's my question."

"It's a fine question. But I'm not going to answer it."

He seemed proud of himself, which was outrageous. Meanwhile, her hands were freezing in the creek. That matted blue sky again. That matted sun. As if a layer of wax paper cut mid-level across the atmosphere. In Selma, by comparison, the landscape was often sharp and in conflict with itself.

She, now, was in conflict with herself. She could let this go. A loss of ten thousand, twenty thousand even, would hardly touch her sister. And yet. Who was to say that losing wouldn't become the Berrys' new habit? She couldn't allow Clarence to sink.

"You don't understand the anger in people like Jane and Jim," she said. "You think they don't care that you're rich and they're poor. You think you can pay their wages and have them be grateful. Hasn't it ever occurred to you that they might despise you? That they might say, it's our country, and we deserve a cut of what you have?"

"Like border customs?"

"I was imagining something less civil."

"Okay. I see where this is going."

"Only now?"

"No, don't misunderstand me. I agree with you in a general way. The Indians have their grievances. But Jane and Jim aren't the angry sort, lurking in the woods with an axe. They're English-speaking and they have manners. You see how they benefit from the work we give them. Wages are wages. And I pay them well. They're better off since Americans came into the country. They've both hinted as much."

"Maybe ask them again."

"I'm serious, Tot. Unless you have proof or saw Jane or Jim out in the night. I don't want to hear another word about it. You grew up in a family of girls. You don't know how brothers can be. We'll send Frank home and, watch, that will be the end of it."

His pride bloomed, the tidy solution already playing itself out in his mind.

"It wasn't Frank," she said flatly. "You're a chump if you think so."

She left Clarence and returned up the bank to the cabin. In the cache, she found Jane, alone, imposing order on the cluttered shelves.

"Well, what do you think, Miss Jane? The boys are about to run brother Frank out of the country."

"Oh?"

"Clarence says that Frank stole the pay dirt. Put it God knows where. But apparently that's more than what's needed for an accusation."

No response. But she turned. An expression duller than bread. A light in the eyes no more telling than the flash of afternoon sun off the cans.

"So what do you think about that?"

"An older brother thinks he's the boss of the others," Jane answered carefully. "Isn't that the general way of things? The younger ones can grow up and marry. They can be rich. But the oldest one will still think himself in charge." She continued more boldly, as if pleasantly surprised by her own response. "I'll tell you the truth, I think it's quite strange how Mr. Frank Berry sleeps in a tent with the workers. If there's room for me and you in the house, there's room for him."

"You think Frank was justified. I see what you mean. An older brother should be respected. And if he's not, then he has the right to act out against the family. To rob them."

Jane smiled.

"What? Do you find this funny?"

"I was thinking of something else. I was thinking how you treat your sister's concerns as your own."

"My sister and I are very close." She bristled. "All the Bushes are close with the Berrys. I've known the boys since we were children."

"You don't have to explain yourself to me, Miss Bush. When your brother-in-law hired me, he said, I'll pay you thirty-five dollars a month. It can't be a dollar more because I'm paying my wife's kid sister forty. And if she doesn't have that edge, then my ears will fall off before I hear the end of it." A tower of canned pears stood braced between Jane's hands and chin. She took a small step. "I promised Henry something sweet for dessert. This is the best I can do. It's too late to start on a pie."

Jane went out, circled around to the front of the house, banging the door. In the cache, motes swirled in a broad slanting pathway of sun. People moved around by the creek. They shouted. Gravel rained down the sluice. Alice placed her hand on her heart. That hot, pulsing animal buried within her.

5

DAWSON CITY, YUKON

2015

The morning we were to meet Winnie and Leanne, it occurred to me, as I opened my eyes, that the Lowell family might come to dislike me. Not just find my grandfather's offer alarming, but find something about me, as I delivered the Morgan Stanley papers into their hands, too reminiscent of previous harms. I guess I'd been stupid for not thinking it all the way through. After all, I couldn't pretend to be a messenger with no personal stake in this history. No matter how distantly I was related to them, it had been my grandfather's great-uncle and -aunt, my own great-great-great-uncle and -aunt, who'd cracked through an invisible wall and trespassed into the Klondike region. Clarence and Ethel Berry had grabbed all the gold they could shake from the earth. They'd moved that wealth to Los Angeles, invested it wisely, and, with the growing American infrastructure lifting them up, and with their respective siblings close at their sides, had once again made their own family rich. It seemed long ago. And yet theirs had been the kind of robust affluence that didn't wear away easily. The type of money that logged hours each day in the stock market and brought home its own wages. So much so that, well into the twenty-first century, even my fourteen cousins and I had been guaranteed a combined fifty-years' worth of tuition bills on my grandfather's dime. So much so that, in a desperate moment, anyone boasting a blood relation could shake Peter Bailey down for ten thousand dollars: he enjoyed the pleasure of writing checks like that on the spot. In what way was that not reprehensible? And what person today—certainly not me—could call it fair?

"How am I going to broach the subject?" I asked Owen, swinging the backpack over my shoulder, and jostling the lock on our bedroom door.

"You'll have to just blurt it out. It's going to come off a little greasy no matter what spin you put on it."

"I thought you were in favor of this."

"Yeah, but I never said it wouldn't be awkward. If it was coming from an organization, great. But Peter doing it on his own"—he looked serious—"I don't know how it will seem to Leanne especially. Like—"

"Woke grandpa?" I offered.

"In the worst possible way."

"And us?"

He gave me an appraising look. "Just try not to act like your grandfather's doing something noble. That's my advice."

"Maybe you should do the talking. You've got it all figured out."

"No, you're the smart, well-spoken one." He surprised me while I was clipping the key to my bag, leaning around to kiss my mouth. "In other words, good luck, you're on your own."

We walked toward the looming mountains and down a narrow quiet road, until we arrived at the house. It was a cozy, one-story white bungalow, positioned close to its neighbors. Along the walkway, a scatter of painted rocks. Wind chimes dangled from the lowest branch of a tree, and several more hung in a row from the chipping porch fascia.

We climbed the low, sagging steps, and a couple of Huskies ran barking at us, pushing their noses against the screen panels in the door. Then a woman, who could only be Leanne, threw open the door, while holding the dogs back by their collars. Her long hair brushed into her face, and she tried to shake it back, while yanking at the dogs and also keeping the door open for us with her shoulder.

"Hello!" she called. "Don't worry. They're loud but friendly. Just ignore them and come straight to the back."

We walked through to a cluttered yellow kitchen, with open shelves and cabinets: a bright mismatch of plates and bowls making a cheerful display.

At the end of the table, across the length of a green-and-blue tablecloth, sat a round-faced elderly woman. It was the granddaughter of the gold rush era, granddaughter of Jane, the woman from my grandfather's stories: Winnie Lowell. Again, it took a second for the real person to overtake the mental image I'd constructed of her. She had dark lively eyes and thick gray hair that was pulled tautly back. I knew she was ninety, only three years younger than my grandfather, but there was a kind of glowing healthiness to her that made her appear younger than that.

"This is amazing," I said. I walked forward and shook her hand. "I'm Anna, it's so nice to meet you. I'm so happy to see you in person."

Winnie looked me up and down. She announced, by way of response: "You don't look like Peter."

I laughed. Reflexively, I brushed a hand over my nose, my eyebrows, the thick, dark hair that my ears could barely hold back. I supposed it was true that I looked more like my Armenian side of the family, and less like my tall, Irish-Anglo grandfather. The irony registered. This morning, I'd been worried that Winnie would see me as the reincarnation of the vicious, gold-seeking side of my family—perhaps even the reincarnation of Alice—but apparently that wasn't the first impression I struck.

Meanwhile, Leanne was serving everyone lunch: salmon, rice, a bowl of cold vegetables flavored with lemon and pepper, the zucchini and cucumbers right from their garden out back. She brightened when Owen mentioned that he was a teacher. She herself visited schools in Dawson and Whitehorse, giving presentations based on artifacts from the Hän Hwëch'in Cultural Center, and so, as she put it wryly, slipping back into her seat, had an interest in "the delicate art of connecting to teenagers."

She also wanted to know about my studies, so I did my best to summarize the research in the environmental chemistry lab where I'd been logging my thesis hours.

"We're working on an experiment that involves putting down a layer of reactive rock called 'basalt dust' over nearby agricultural fields," I explained, putting my fork down on my orange plate. "It's really cool, because the basalt reacts with carbon dioxide, essentially pulling it out of the air. And then, once the reaction's taken place, the product you end up with isn't waste at all, but this new, stable carbon-rich topsoil, which is actually really good for the crops."

"So basically you're the opposite of a miner," Leanne said, teasingly, from over her meal. "Spreading a layer of rock over the earth."

I hadn't meant to present myself like that, and I blushed, laughing, agreeing with her. Then, looking for a way to divert attention away from myself, I took out my phone and showed Leanne and Winnie a picture of my grandfather—marked expressly for this purpose.

"Well!" Winnie exclaimed. "Time goes on, doesn't it?"

On behalf of my grandfather, I said next how much he regretted losing touch with her. I said that he was sorry, too, for the long-ago clashes between his family and theirs, which perhaps had also been a wedge between them, and which he understood were unjust.

"He had the same message for us in '44," Winnie said languidly, between small bites of salmon. "He came striding into my family's house in his uniform, with his hat in his hands, ready to make a long speech. The problem was that my parents weren't interested in hearing apologies. I don't think Peter lasted ten minutes before my father kicked him out. No matter that his intentions were good."

"You two went out a few times, didn't you?" I asked.

"Yes. My family didn't live far from the Navy base, so I could sneak out pretty easily. I remember that first night I put on my best dress—about the same bright orange as your plate, if you can believe that—and I had an orange flower in my hair. I still remember there was a big mirror that filled the whole wall near the dance floor, and every time I turned, I looked in the mirror to admire myself, and thought, oh look at me, I'm falling in love." She laughed. "We wrote to each other while he was with the Navy. Every so often, he would send five pages about how he was head-over-heels for me. It was a hard time. I think he did that whenever he got scared he wouldn't make it back home alive. Afterward, we kept writing. But I had my limits. I kept him at arm's length, as they say. And good for me, because the one time I did ask him for help, he deliberated. He liked the idea of justice. But only a bit."

"That was when I was a kid," Leanne put in, "I remember meeting him in LA."

"He told me," I said, "he feels bad about that."

"Anyway," Winnie continued, "like I was saying, we were friends. But it couldn't be more than that. There was far worse that had happened between our families before either of us were born. During the gold rush, my father's uncle, Jim Lowell, was killed by the Berrys. I think Leanne told you that."

"She did," I assented. "And Alice did write about it in her travel journal. Though she didn't really go into the details."

"Jane never had the whole story. An accident. So they say. Clarence Berry's gun went off during a fight."

"We think it was terrible for Jane," Leanne added, "not only to lose a brother, but also to never know for sure exactly what happened to him. She couldn't catch a break, that woman. From birth to death, there were precious few people who treated her decently."

Was this my segue? It wasn't ideal. But before I could second-guess myself, and without even a glance at Owen, my backpack was in my lap, and I was pulling the Morgan Stanley paperwork out of a folder and putting it onto the table.

"I don't know what you're going to think about this," I said, speaking the words I'd been loosely rehearsing inside my head all morning. "But my grandfather feels really, deeply sorry about everything that happened. And maybe it took him too long to get here, but he does understand that the wealth he's had all his life didn't come to him fairly. He's in the process of divvying up the Berry fortune, and—" I was nervous, I was beginning to infer, from Winnie's narrowing expression, from Leanne's piercing gaze, that this information was not information that pleased. I finished, "He feels that a portion of this money is rightfully yours. He's hoping he can do something for you."

Without further explanation, I slid the paperwork to Leanne and Winnie.

"I had a feeling there'd be something like this," Leanne said.

"I'm sorry. I should have mentioned it earlier."

Leanne touched the papers, read them methodically. She showed her mother, who made a noise of condescension, as if this was exactly the kind of antics that she would have expected from the blithe young man she'd first met long ago.

"That's quite a lot of money," Winnie said archly.

"It's long overdue. He's sorry it took him so long." I added, "He's sorry his parents or grandparents never did anything."

"Look, we've had a lot of hard times," Leanne said finally, "haven't we, Mom?" To Owen and me: "My own father was never part of the picture. When I was a child, there were a few years there when a gift like this would have been a small miracle. But not anymore. We're living a stable life here." She glanced at her mother, in silent communication, and I had the strong impression they'd discussed this exact eventuality, though maybe not in ways that had predicted the terms of the account. Then, resolute, Leanne pushed the papers to me. "We don't want his money."

"I completely understand," I said. And I did. So much so that, no matter everything Owen and I had said to each other, I did feel like, in obeying my grandfather's orders, I'd made a misstep.

"But," Leanne said, and something in her voice made me look up sharply. "We do have a counteroffer for him."

"Yes?"

"Like I mentioned earlier, for the last ten years I've been on the executive board at the Cultural Center. We're always looking to increase our endowment. If Peter were willing, we'd gladly accept this money as a donation."

THE HÄN HWËCH'IN CULTURAL CENTER was on the opposite side of town, at the bank overlooking the Yukon River. Owen and I walked there with Leanne, leaving Winnie, who'd decided that she'd had enough excitement for one afternoon. The building, as I'd felt upon first seeing it yesterday, was striking. The modern architecture, its clean, sharp lines, the wooden beams pointing into the sky seemed to flick its fingers at the rest of Dawson City, in fact making its 1890s throwback style seem silly.

"The design is in the spirit of the Hän winter houses," Leanne explained as we approached. "It draws inspiration from drying racks that would have been built for fish."

We walked inside, and Leanne gave us a brief tour of the main, circular gallery. There was the re-creation of a Hän hut, a low, wooden dome covered with furs; a long, narrow canoe that had been carved from the trunk of a birch tree. A pair of snowshoes, with intricate lacing, were pinned to the wall. A life-sized cardboard cutout of Chief Isaac presided over the room. He was the person, Leanne explained, who, in 1897, had moved the Hän from their traditional grounds in the footprint of Dawson City, and founded a new community three miles downriver called Moosehide. He'd been prescient to the danger to his people's traditions, and highly deliberate in preserving dances, songs, stories, ceremonies, many of which were still practiced today.

"First and foremost," Leanne said, leading us through the exhibits, "our goal is to preserve the history of the Hän for our own descendants. I don't have kids myself, but there is a big community of young people who are really involved in the center. They act in the performances, and the older teenagers help run our summer programs. I think of them all as my nieces and nephews. Our second goal," she went on, pausing beside the Chief Isaac cutout, "is to teach the true story of this region to everyone who passes through here. I want people to think of *us*, not just the gold rush, when they think about what happened in this place. We're always fighting to maintain our sovereignty, and the Center is a constant reminder for all of us of what is at stake. It's a small museum, and we're pretty new in the scheme of things, but we're optimistic about how it's going."

I, too, was hopeful. I felt immediately that my grandfather—no matter his intentions to give to the Lowell family directly—couldn't pour his money to a more appropriate spot. We walked outside, Leanne, Owen, and I, into the cool, fresh air, misty here at the bank, and loud with the noise of the two clashing rivers.

"I hope your grandfather will be on board," Leanne said.

"Of course," I said a little breathlessly. "I'm going to call him and tell him everything you said."

But I didn't call my grandfather right away. I was still trying to decide how to present the idea to him, as I was sure he'd be disappointed at the turn of events. That evening, Owen and I went to Diamond Tooth Gerties. It was a tourist trap, complete with cabaret show and ragtime piano. At an old-fashioned slot machine, I won about thirty dollars in quarters, and felt immensely pleased with myself. We found a table, ordered drinks and pasta dinners, and ate while watching the show. The women danced in big, colorful fringed 1890s dresses, flipping them up every few seconds to flash the triangle crotch of a black leotard. It was—very approximately—the kind of cancan dancing that would have been popular in Dawson City during the gold rush. Though, of course, it was a mock rendering of the wild nights that once had been. According to the establishment's own brochure, in 1898, the more riveting acts would have taken place after the performance, around the corner in one of the little shacks that ran along a street called Paradise Alley. There, if a man had between fifty cents and five dollars, depending on the girl and the terms, he could crawl into a small wooden bed, draped with a makeshift canopy for privacy, and have his way with one of the dancers.

After the show, around nine o'clock, we walked the trail that wound along the riverbank. I said to Owen:

"Now it's too late. I'll have to call Grandpa tomorrow." It was bright daylight. The river sparkled with the sun's reflections, making me feel, as I'd felt since our arrival here, like sleep might cease to be necessary. Like sleep depended on the lights turning off.

My phone was in my pocket. I was surprised when it rang.

"Either the meeting didn't happen," my grandfather drawled, "or else you have a cruel streak to you, that enjoys keeping me waiting."

Abashed, I told him, yes, the meeting had happened, Winnie was wonderful and remembered everything about their time together. Leanne even remembered him too. But eventually, after I gave a summary of the conversation, we did arrive at the subject of the Morgan Stanley paperwork, and I was forced to tell him: "The Lowells don't want to accept ownership of the account."

"What?"

"I'm sorry. They say they have no need for that kind of money."

He was upset. Before I could stop him, he began berating himself for not being in touch with Winnie decades ago, when he still might have had the chance to convince her.

"But wait, Grandpa," I finally managed to interrupt. "They have an idea. Leanne is on the board of a museum here. The Hän Hwëch'in Cultural Center. They'd like to know if you'd donate the money to the museum instead."

A brief silence. Then: "They'd like that?"

"Very much, I think."

"That's perfect."

"Is it?"

"Yes. And assuming it's a registered nonprofit, I could even do more. Hell, I might be able to move over five million."

"Sure, wow," I said, stumbling. "I'm sure that'd be great."

Occasionally, hearing news of one of his new houses, or his latest three-month vacation with Wife Number Six, I realized how little I knew about the fortune my grandfather had at his fingertips. Like the terms of his will, he absolutely and somewhat maddeningly insisted on secrecy. Sometimes I thought he wasn't as rich as he made himself seem. In different moments, like this one, I thought the reverse.

"Maybe I better come up there myself," he said.

I was alarmed. "Come to Dawson?"

"Why not?" His voice was suddenly stubborn.

"You can't," I said. "You're not supposed to fly."

"It's not far. I'd like to see them myself. Why should I let you have all the fun?"

"But it *is* far," I insisted. Beside me, Owen, who'd been staring out at the river, turned with a stunned and inquiring look. "It was a seven-hour flight to Fairbanks," I said with barely managed evenness into the phone, "and then an eight-hour drive to Dawson City."

"I could probably charter a flight into Dawson."

"But that's still flying," I said desperately. I returned a long look from Owen, who now was shaking his head, no, no, no. "Remember, Grandpa? The doctor said pressure changes could be dangerous for your heart. That's why you couldn't come to our wedding. That's the whole reason you asked Owen and me to come here."

"All right already," he grumbled. "I suppose you've got a point."

I was relieved. Then I wasn't relieved. I was sad. After all, what was there to lose? He was ninety-three. This might be the last grand, exciting thing in his life that he wanted to do. He was not a child, who, by doing something unsafe, gambles a lifetime. He might die tomorrow, in California, watching syndicated court shows on TV. If there was a chance to meet Winnie and revisit the place that had been the seed of his wealth, then maybe the right attitude was: *let him*.

"So what else did they say about me?" my grandfather asked, changing course. "I imagine they were pretty taken aback when they saw the Morgan Stanley papers. It's not the kind of money they're used to. By the way, did they have any message for me or what? Did you remember to show Winnie my picture?"

His attitude startled me. I almost laughed out loud. For all his little moments of anxiety, he remained purely himself. He was still the golden boy son of his doting parents, Melba and Paul, still the golden boy grandson and nephew of the Bushes and Berrys. In other words, he was a man whose ego, no matter how many swipes you took at it, still bloomed large and bright thanks to ninety-three years of healthy growth in the fertile American soil.

6

KLONDIKE

1898

1.

They were engaged. Two short meetings of the willing parties had done it: had led to the crucial exchange of words. In her attic bed, Alice laughed into her pillow. She felt the heat of her own soft face. Me, she thought. No more the tagalong. No more the kid sister. Me, Alice Bush, soon to be Berry. Her hand traced the arc of her jaw. Then it reached farther. She ran her fingertips across the rough burlap, the bumpy bags of gold, those stout troll bellies, and was stirred by the touch. Why was I ever worried? She lay stomach-down on her mat, flush to the attic floor. Her middle shook. She laughed out loud with relief.

The first meeting had taken place in the cache. Alice had recently staked out Jane's favorite spot for herself. In a landscape that was bright and wide and barren, it was actually a comforting corner, this close, dim, dusty shack with its rough-hewn shelves. There were the cartons of dried fruits, which must every so often be turned over by a hasty scoop to keep from sticking, the gleam of cans, the little envelopes of herbs spicing the stagnant air, and always the white remnants of flour on everything. The cache had, in fact, an amorous quality to it—even for one person alone—even, she imagined, when no one was here to create possibility.

She was there, making herself available for anyone who wished to visit her privately, on a day Henry was having dinner with them, when a little time into restocking the tins she heard Ethel say, from inside the cabin: "Tot's in the cache, if that's who you're looking for."

That's right. Tot's in the cache. Her arm was still. Her breaths counted the seconds. The front door slammed. The gravel crunched, as a big man with a shuffling gait ambled around the outside of the house. Then he was there, momentarily blocking the light.

"I'll help." Henry's voice was soft and tentative. As if he were afraid of disrupting this, the ideal situation for hosting his purpose.

They worked. Condensing half-filled bags of beef jerky. Combining the last of the dehydrated plums. Shifting the sugar into a smaller container. She let her arm brush against his. He seemed to be doing the same. They were standing close when finally Henry reached out and pulled her into a bear hug. Her arms were braced at her sides. He buried his warm face into her neck. Then he let his hot mouth touch her flesh. He said nothing and neither did she. He had a nice, manly scent. And he was of that good, big Irish type that she liked for its solidness. When he released her and left the cache, still without having spoken a word about what they were doing, the pressure lingered on her ribs.

The following evening, Henry came to visit again, and there was a second meeting. Alice said she was off to the hills to pick flowers, and Frank answered, "Wait till I finish my pie, sweetheart, and I'll go with you." The challenge was heard and accepted. Henry stood, pink in the face and pushing his chair so that it made a loud scraping sound on the floor. He said, "Come on, Alice, I'll go with you now."

As they moved around the table together, their fingers brushed. A significant look passed between them. Frank saw it. He was suspicious, then amazed, then stricken. The game he'd invented himself, for the purpose of checking Jane, for the purpose of punishing Henry's pride, had gone too far for his liking. He'd never imagined an actual match.

Poor Frank, Alice thought. As the distance closed between brother Henry and sister Tot, Frank's cheeks were drooping, his lips became slack. Before their eyes, he was growing depressed. Here he'd been so preoccupied with the game of keeping Indian blood out of the family, he'd neglected the danger to himself: an advantage Alice herself had realized largely thanks to Frank's help. Now after all his fine attentions to Ethel—his little flirtations, the flowers and funny-shaped nuggets he brought to her—jolly, bumbling Henry would trump him with this mighty, brutish blow. Henry will have married the sister, and their blood, Henry's and Alice's, should it commingle in the flesh of a child, would be near as possible to the wish of Ethel's heart: the combined blood of Bush and Berry, and as close as Ethel and Clarence might ever get to an heir.

Outside, Alice turned her attention on Henry. His nature, which had always been good, was now beginning to seem to her the obvious complement to her own. A sense of humor, after all, you cannot teach a person; and laughter you can't put a price on. As for the business side of his life, well, perhaps he'd require a nudge or two, but that she could manage. The important thing was that he was a Berry; he stood as close to big money as any bachelor she knew.

On the walkway, Henry offered his arm, and Alice accepted it, and he drew her in very close to his side. Years ago, Annie had courted William Carswell for all of six weeks before consenting to marry him. This spring, Daisy had known Ed Keller for less than that before closing the deal. If something was going to happen, Alice thought, it wasn't a moment too soon.

They climbed up the hill behind the claims. They gathered bunches of purple fireweed, the petals fresh and tough, enough again for that little vase.

"There," Henry said, putting a fistful of flowers into her hand. "Do you like me now?"

"Why do you keep asking me that?" she answered, coy.

"I've never had a straight answer."

"Well, sure I do. You're goodhearted and you're hardworking."

"Oh, is that all?"

They kept getting stuck there, so she tried the same question on him: "Do you like me much?"

"If you weren't so dense," he said, "you wouldn't ask."

Alice sighed. He stopped. "Why don't you say what you're trying to hint at," she said, "and I'll answer you."

His feelings came to a crest. Then, as if he himself, the great vessel that was Henry, could no longer contain them, they broke and traveled every which way.

"Oh Tot," he cried. "Don't you know that I love you?"

She smiled and took his hand in hers. He grinned back at her, his eyes thick with feeling. They walked awhile. Usually they'd take the trail that passed along the workers' tents. But he wouldn't go near it now.

"You must have known I was falling in love with you. I haven't been able to keep my eyes off you."

She was modest. "Maybe I noticed you staring once or twice."

"You aren't scared off?"

"I'm here, aren't I? I haven't made some excuse and hightailed it for home. I haven't crossed myself and started shouting for Ethel."

He laughed with relief.

Tentatively, he offered a plan.

"We could get married in Dawson and stay the winter together."

"I like the idea," she said. "But I don't know if it's possible. I came as Ethel's companion. She might still need me on the way home. Plus, your brother might not allow it. He'll say it's his responsibility to my parents to bring me back to Selma."

"Then I'll come with you. Clarence can find someone else to watch over his claim."

"Please don't. It doesn't help me if you give up your work."

"All right. Have it your way. I'll come home in May and we'll get married in Selma."

He was nervous. He drew her close to him. The creek came into view, a wide bend bringing it inland.

"You never said your answer. Say yes or no right now."

"To what?" she laughed. "You never asked the question."

He stopped and made her turn and face him. He held her still.

"Will you marry me, Alice?"

"Yes."

"That's the best thing I ever heard in my life."

"I'm glad you say so. I'm happy too."

He put a hand on her cheek. She was surprised to observe in herself what that did to her.

"And I promise I'll do right by you. You're a woman with high standards and I swear on my life I'll work to meet them."

"I know you will, Hen." She meant that. She knew how he valued women. She believed he'd find joy in the family life. She felt sure in her choice of Henry Berry. And yet. There was one itch in her side she could not ignore. What she hadn't yet wrapped her mind around were the details of his prior experience. He loved to flirt. He did that in front of everyone. What else did he do when no one was watching? She would like a little time to learn the details, before their engagement, then marriage, closed over his bachelor past. She said, "But listen, I do have one condition."

"Anything."

"I don't want you to say a word about the engagement until I give you leave."

He was rankled. She watched him carefully. This was, perhaps, the last vulnerable moment.

"Fine. But name a date for the wedding. I want to settle it now."

"I'd need some time to think."

He insisted.

"I'm not sure what's best. And maybe you're not either. Then, too, there is Jane."

His expression soured. "What does Jane have to do with it?"

"You tell me. I have two good eyes and I know how to use them. Losing you will be a big disappointment for her. She's been counting on being your cook this winter."

He dropped his elbow, which had been supporting her hand. "If you want to take back what you agreed to, you can." From sour, he moved to injured. Then he was wretched. "You don't need to make excuses for yourself if you don't want me. There's never been anything between me and Jane. I didn't say she could stay for the winter, and I don't plan to say it."

"Good."

When Alice didn't immediately say more, he made to start walking away. But his response had satisfied her, and she didn't sense any secrets lurking behind it. After a couple of steps, she pulled him back.

"Wait. I told you 'yes,' Henry. 'Yes' with all my heart. We're engaged. It's real."

"Then why shouldn't we make the announcement now?" He was suspicious. "I was thinking I could stand up at dinner and toast my fiancée. They'd love it. It would give them a shock."

"I want to tell them too, but it will be even better at the end of the summer." What was she hoping for? She could hardly name it herself, but she wanted to avoid the bright explosion having to do with love dispensed, love unrequited. She could imagine Jane and Henry whispering together, and Jane packing her things. She felt that she didn't want Jane disappearing yet. She felt that she didn't want Jane's disappearance, if it happened, to be reduced to the cause of an injured heart. There was gold missing; why give her an excuse for making a sensible exit?

"Trust me," she said. "I feel strongly on this point. Let me wait till the timing's right."

He didn't like the secrecy, but he agreed. She put a hand to his shoulder and kissed him on the cheek.

"Now hold on," he said, "that won't do." He took her into his large, strong hands and kissed her on the mouth.

2.

The claim was empty, quiet. In an act of feigned generosity, Clarence had given his workers the Saturday and Sunday off. The men had trooped off in a big group for a night on the town. Jane had left too, with her brother her escort, remarking to everyone that it was high time she'd been given a break. The breakfast plates were cleared from the table. A wide stripe of sun fell across the bare cabin floor from the opened doorway. Clarence nodded to Henry. They'd been working up their nerve for a week.

When the two of them got to Frank's tent, they had to wake him in order to drag him out. Then the claim was no longer quiet. They told Frank what they had come for, and Frank was shocked. He laughed at them. Cursed them. From where they watched, Alice and Ethel could hear every word. Henry took the job of restraining his brother, holding his skinny arms at his back, while Clarence disappeared into the tent. A big fur blanket unfurled through the flaps, then three pots came through, a shovel, a winter coat, a sack of flour, and a sack of coffee. Then Clarence himself emerged, stooped and empty-handed, and growing confused.

Frank kicked, the dust rising. He nearly caught Clarence square in the groin. Finally Henry released him and Frank fell forward on his stumbling legs.

"Accuse me of stealing?" Frank spat in Clarence's face. "Accuse me? You pompous little goddamned jerk."

"Now Frank—" started Henry.

"Oh, shut up, Hen. No one wants your opinion." To Clarence, Frank growled, "What the hell is the matter with you? Look at you, Ceej. Your damned money has gone to your head."

"I won't stand for stealing, Frank," Clarence said steadily, though it seemed to be taking his entire force of will to speak those words to his brother. "I've been nothing but good to you. It isn't right."

"Jesus, you're dumber than I thought."

Frank finished the sentiment with repeated kicks at his own tent until the canvas caught on his boot and fell. By the time he had gathered up his possessions, Clarence and Henry were already crossing the creek toward the cabin, wearing expressions that attempted calm resoluteness, when in fact they were both completely unnerved.

Frank's insults lashed at their backs. He gathered the canvas that had been his tent, made it into a bag, and put his meager belongings into the fold. He swung it over his shoulder. Alice and Ethel retreated into the house. Then the two brothers walked inside, ignoring the women. They clomped to the table, sat down. At a distance, they all watched as Frank crossed the claim. He was still yelling curses at them, as if he were drunk—although they knew he wasn't, as he owned no store of liquor and whatever he drank was at Clarence's pleasure, which of late hadn't amounted to much.

Doubt made the air waver, made every utterance thin and inviting of interruption. As soon as Frank was gone from the property, Clarence wafted out the door. Henry and Ethel logged his movements, toward the bend in the creek. They depended on Clarence, those two. They wanted to know that accusing Frank had been the right thing.

Alice put on Ethel's straw hat. She slipped out the door and headed down the bank and past the dirty sluice that the sun had dried out since its last employ. But Clarence was nowhere on the claim. She came back to the cabin and told them so.

3.

Late that night, like a predator, like a spider on swift crooked legs, she glided across the dusty attic, suspended herself down the rope ladder from attic to floor. She passed Henry, fast asleep in the chair. She'd heard the front door some minutes ago, and there, as she'd expected, was Clarence at the table, still in his boots. She crept upon him. He was hunched over, head in his hands, tortured, illuminated by the soft orb of a kerosene lamp.

"So? That's it then? I told you it wasn't Frank. You realized it as you were tearing his tent apart, didn't you? You understand that you made a mistake. You didn't listen to me before, so listen now. Or are you going to just sit there, letting Jane and Jim rob you dollar by dollar? I can't even imagine what they must think of you. They must laugh themselves to sleep."

His shoulders startled an inch then fell. When she came around to his front, he said, "Isn't everyone laughing at me? No one else was robbed this summer. I don't see why two more people laughing at me would make any difference."

Knee-jerk, humble humor, left over from his farming days.

"How much are you worth, Clarence? I'd honestly like to know."

"And I will honestly decline to give you an answer."

"Enough to throw money away. I guess that should tell me enough. What a show you put on today with Frank," Alice crowed softly. "But you couldn't keep it up, could you? You were so horrified by what you'd done, you had to run away."

"Alice," he said, "in one minute, I'm going to be mad."

She withdrew, ebbed as water does, before it rushes back with ten times the height. "Jim's been playing you since Dyea," she said. "His goal was to get to the claim, and you let him. You think I'm being unfair to them, but you're actually the person who treats them unfairly. Yes, you're generous and open with them, but only because you think they're so low that you have noble dominion over them, as if they were children. It's not worth disliking them. You won't even give credit to Jim for being intelligent. I told you I saw him sitting on the beach, laughing with the captain. You didn't think it was possible that Jim could hold the fates of one hundred white men in the palm of his hand. Then you made a big fuss over his warning us off the Chilkoot. You act like it was some magnificent act of loyalty. Don't you see it was in his own best interest to keep us alive? Once you get your claws into a millionaire, you don't let him march off to bury himself in the snow."

"You seem to know a lot about getting your claws into millionaires."

"How dare you?" Her hoarse whisper matched his tone. "You called me your sister once, as good as blood, or don't you remember? Let me help you, then. It was right before you ripped up my deed. My deed. Which my sister had given to me with her full heart. I'm telling you, Jim's been sticking to you so that he could pick your pocket, pick your mines. Simple as that. And wait, let me finish. I've been wondering something. One more question, then I'll go," she spoke quickly, sensing the end. "Did you know Jane before you hired her as our cook, yes or no?"

A red, spotted flush climbed his throat.

Alice shrieked. But that exhilaration was a push too far. The flame shuddered as Clarence's hand rushed down beside it, on its way to violent contact with wood.

"Enough of this. I mean it. Enough!"

4.

The workers returned in the morning, happy for their break and refreshed for this last spurt of labor. No one missed Frank, as he'd been aloof with the workers and only ever got in the way of the sluicing and panning.

The following Saturday came fast. It was September 10, the going-away party that Clarence and Ethel had planned for themselves. They'd done it last year, for all the neighbors, and it had been a big hit. Ethel had been saying for days, against Clarence's protestations, "There's no fever. No pain. I don't have my energy back, but I refuse to give up this party."

She'd made a big display for her husband, getting up one morning and cooking with Alice and Jane the big chicken eggs that Clarence had specially ordered delivered from Dawson. She'd served him a pile of buttered toast. She had announced that she fancied a stroll to pick flowers, and had walked the length of the claims and back, gathering purple fireweed, pink river beauties, white tufted fleabane, arctic lupine, and tall dramatic stalks of green sage.

"You see?" she'd said.

Her round face had shone with calm, as she'd proffered the bright colors of her overflowing bouquet.

And so Clarence had caved, and now Ethel—who wanted to make Clarence happy too—presided over the evening in her own way, allowing Jane and Alice to take over the hosting, and mostly staying in her rocking chair, where guests might gather around her and make conversation.

Henry and Charlie were the first to arrive. Then Anton Stander, Clarence's business partner. Then a pair of Bush cousins, Peggy and Tom, who had just arrived into the country. Their neighbor from *Ten* Eldorado came in, took a bad step on the front-door stone, and almost fell backward. He'd already had a few drinks on his own. The hired miners came in as a group. They had washed their faces and arms. A once-hirsute fellow had shaved, transforming himself. Clarence slapped the man's back and called him a stranger, here to impersonate his scruffy employee and walk off with his pay. He was handing out their last six weeks' wages tonight. Most of the men would be leaving the country in days. Only a few would winter here, to work the claim under Henry's direction. Previously they'd grumbled about Clarence holding the money, but now they seemed at peace with the arrangement, and saw the goodness in the plan.

For Alice, it was a different party. She was caught in a dance with Hen. The agreement stood: to keep their engagement a secret. She'd insisted that she didn't want to disrupt the household at a delicate moment like this. Even so, secrets have a way of nudging against their enclosures and bumping playfully against the walls. Through the crowd, Henry found her eyes and winked. They passed each other in the kitchen doorway—Henry leaving with a glass refreshed, she walking in to check the stove—and he brushed his fingertips across her waist.

Jane, pink-cheeked from the trapped heat in the galley, was looking into the oven. She was fanning herself with a newspaper like it was any old item, and not one of a mere twenty from Dawson that had been procured at a heavy price. "If I were you, I'd take a big slice of that pie," she told Alice. "A neighbor of yours was just in here saying how the boat food's all crawling with bugs. Because of the damp weather, I suppose. I don't know. I'm not one for boats." She produced a tray of cheese biscuits and added, with confidence, "Think how soon you'll be gone. Only Henry in the house and most of the workers dismissed. Jim will be here, though. He's just had it official from Clarence."

"Has he?" Alice was stunned.

"I'm happy for him." Jane looked around. Her eyes were small, from staring into the fire. She asked, disingenuous. "Have you ever talked to my brother?"

"What kind of question is that? I came in with him, didn't I? I've lived here all summer."

"That's right. Then I don't have to tell you what a fine person he is."

Jane scraped the biscuits off the tray, covered the basket with a napkin. In the other room, ten men broke into laughter at once, a baritone that saturated the walls.

"I haven't given up on Hen. I still say I should stay for the winter. No one wants a repeat of last year. If they'd had a cook on the claim, those two workers who died might be here tonight."

"You should wait a bit on talking to Hen. The plans for the winter are still in flux. There's a small chance I'll be staying on with Henry. Which means I'd be doing the cooking myself." Alice took the bowl. "My sister of course will be traveling home."

Now Jane was surprised. Did she understand the implication?

No, thought Alice. Then, yes.

Because Jane's expression, which had tried for impassive, now broke with distress.

"I need winter work."

"You'll have to look elsewhere."

Jane threw off her apron—Ethel's apron. She didn't say a word, but marched out of the galley. She left Alice standing there, with all the party food half-cooked and a second tray of biscuits still in the oven.

Alice stepped into the main room to join the party. Where had Jane gone? She went outside, where she found three separate groupings of men, each deep into a particular story. The air was pungent with pipe smoke. The stars were starting to show. Ah, there. Across the creek, on the wrong side, on the opposite side of the creek from the party, almost invisible in the close-to-midnight gloaming: Jane and Jim walking together, heads bowed in talk, stepping carefully over the stones. What could they be saying? For months there had been nothing on the surface but a temperate sibling relationship. But Ethel had seen through a crack, to a rebellious heat, that day in the cache. And Alice was seeing it now.

5.

A man appeared at Alice's side. Anton Stander. He had bright orange hair and a bristly orange mustache and full beard to match. Earlier in the evening, without an instrument for digging in hand, he'd seemed rather lost. But alcohol had shored up his sense of self and deadened his nerves. A change had come over him. He remembered that he was a millionaire, the discoverer of Eldorado.

"Seen a ghost?" He came close, bringing a cloud of human reek. He had washed his shirt for the party, but not his pants. Alice had followed her family's instructions all summer and kept her distance from Anton. They hadn't exchanged a word until now.

"No ghosts, no." Alice smiled. The cabin door slammed, accidentally, and they plunged into darkness, until the door was propped open again. "It's a bit disappointing," Alice said jauntily, "now that you mention it. After all this talk about Indian graveyards, I was expecting to have a good story to take home to my sisters. A floating head in a dim corner or something like that."

He followed her gaze across the creek, and now he was watching them too: man and woman walking the desolate bank, with the desolate, rocky hill behind them. The creek ran fast. It separated the land like a line drawn by a god. On their side it was a clement, late summer night in 1898; while on the other side it was Adam and Eve, and the bloom of disconcerting human capacities: avarice, conspiracy.

"You'll have other stories though."

"I suppose I will."

"Looks like your brother is going to let those goddamned Indians get away with stealing his gold."

A flash. The fireworks inside her skull were nonexistent to every person on earth, except herself.

She said, with absolute control, "You suspect it was them?"

"Forget suspect. Jim was out of his tent the night the gold went missing. I know that from a worker by the name of Jefferson Handler, who's had an eye on him from the beginning. And because you're so nice I'll tell you another sweet fact. Clarence paid off my one-half share of that pay dirt. Which tells me that he considers himself culpable for the thief going loose."

Her interest—which had climbed to a brilliant apex—now waned.

"He paid your share because he thinks Frank took the gold. That's reasonable. He can spare his brother if he wants, but it wouldn't be right to make you pay for it too."

"Brother. Mistress. Works out to the same behavior."

Her interest swung back. Now to new heights. In the blaze of it, she spoke without thinking:

"I once caught Clarence in the cache with Jane."

"Well 'once' isn't the start or the end of it. You can bet your pretty hat on that."

Reflexively, she touched the brim. It *was* pretty, with a new ribbon and a purple flower peeking around the side. Anton dipped his face and lit his pipe.

"I've always had the impression"—she didn't say how or why—"that it's been a long-standing relationship."

"As far back as '95, which was when I met Clarence. Before all you ladies trampled up here and civilized the place." He looked at her, sizing her up. A new thought germinated, and the effort showed on his face. "Is Mrs. Berry your sister-in-law or your sister?"

Alice was slightly amazed that he hadn't bothered to learn this about her, but she answered calmly, "Sister. Her maiden name is Bush. My name is Bush."

"I reckon your sister doesn't like Jane."

"If she were smart, she wouldn't." She amended herself. "My sister has a tender heart. She sees the good in everyone. She takes Jane to be an innocent girl."

"Innocent? No. I can attest to that myself." A couple of men emerged from the cabin. Not Henry or Clarence, so he kept on. "Last winter she came to my door with her little papoose. I guess she'd gotten nowhere shoving the baby in C.J.'s face, so she thought she'd try me. She said it was mine. She wanted cash and a place to live. I told her to try the next house down the creek. She came back the next day, more insistent, with the little thing tied to her chest and mewling, so that time I gave her a slap. She fell back in the dirt, clutching her bundle. It's not a habit of mine to strike a woman holding a baby. But with thick-skulled hussies like that, you have to go to extremes in order to make a point."

"Maybe it wasn't her papoose," she suggested, feeling him out, though remembering also what Ethel had said about Jane and Jim in the cache, how they'd said the word "baby." Ethel had thought they were speaking of her, but sadness can do that to a person, can produce a kind of self-centeredness. "In Chicago," Alice continued, "or so my twin sister tells me, there are women who collect stray children for an hour or two and make them beg. Or else they tie a bonnet onto a whiskey bottle and tell you they need money for milk."

"No. That was Jane's bastard. I can tell by the look of her. Jane was a steam pipe in Forty Mile. Now she's all top-heavy and plump."

It took Alice a moment to absorb his meaning. Then she said:

"Did Clarence think it was his child?"

Anton laughed. "If he did, he wasn't dumb enough to say so."

"Where is the baby now?"

"How should I know? It ain't none of my business."

His boot soles shuffled the gravel. His jaw hung slightly opened, anesthetized by drink. Across the creek, Jane and Jim had slipped into the overlapping dark hills. The moisture in the air, which during the day had been refreshing, was chilling now, and carried with it the whiff of contagion. Each time you took a breath, there was a bad taste at the back of your throat. A breeze blew across the water, rippling its surface though leaving the depths undisturbed.

"Brrrr," said Anton, holding his elbows. "I think I'm going in."

6.

They could have been in Selma. The party broke up in the same way. The cousins, Peggy and Tom, left first, glancing at the dark sky. Alice didn't know them well, but she'd determined they were the kind of people who'd rather be in front of a stove with a cat in each lap than away from home, brushing shoulders with strangers.

Still, she couldn't think badly of them. They'd spent most of the evening next to Ethel's chair. During their little conference, too, Ethel had opened her velvet pouch of nuggets and displayed, for Peggy especially, one by one, her entire collection. The heart-shaped nugget. The nugget that looked like a turtle's shell. The nugget with a hole through the middle, like a doughnut, which formed it into a natural pendant. And Peggy, the perfect audience member, had oohed and ahhed over each little treasure, and couldn't say for her life which was the best: each was so spectacular in its own right.

Once the couples and married men were gone, it took more to get the single men out. Clarence said, "Take what's left of the whiskey back to your tents," and you'd think that would do it, but instead they all stood around, with two bottles hanging like a pair of geese in Henry Shuttler's muscular hands. They said goodbye to Hen, who was everyone's favorite. Then Clarence patted their shoulders, clung some extra moments to their calloused palms. He wished them all the best "for their health and their wealth," as the year's saying went. As for the few who would stay for the winter, it was: "Work hard, but not too hard." In other words, don't die on me like those two fellows last year.

The door closed.

Alice walked Ethel to bed. Then she returned to the main room.

"I wonder where Jane has gone off to?"

"Oh, cut her a break tonight," answered Hen. "We'll leave the string out, and she can lift the latch and come in when she likes. The boys will be hopping around the tents until morning and making a racket. It's not like she can lose her way in the hills."

The door moved, pushing Henry back.

"Here I am."

"Jesus, you scared me."

Jane muttered something smart out the side of her mouth that Alice didn't quite catch. She walked into the kitchen and pulled the curtain closed on its rail.

Henry raised his brows. "La-di-da."

Clarence shrugged. Hen closed the door again. This time he pulled in the string, so that no one could open the door from outside.

The voices of the men outside disappeared. Clarence yawned. He pushed the bench back toward the table and hung the brown velvet pouch, Ethel's collection of nuggets, on an iron peg by the door. Then he dropped into the rocker and put up his feet, as Ethel had done. He knitted his fingers together then rested them on the highest part of his stomach and closed his eyes.

"Hey," said Henry, gently kicking the side of his brother's boot. "Go sleep in the bedroom. I wanted the chair."

Clarence, eyes willfully shut: "Too bad."

"You can have the attic if you want," Alice said to Henry. "I'll sleep in the bedroom with Ethel."

"That's nice of you." Henry's gaze softened as it fell upon his fiancée. "But no need, on second thought I'll be fine on the floor. I won't be the cause of disturbing Mrs. Berry. Not for the world."

Alice stood near the ladder, not ready to climb it, silently presiding over Clarence and Henry. A turn. A yawn. Settled down for sleep, the brothers were near-identical, as they'd been the first day that Alice had arrived at the claim, when Hen had thrown open the door, and invited them with spread arms into the house. She was in such high spirits then, in love with the whole family. She had felt proud of her sister for getting in with the Berrys, before Clarence was something. Now she'd be a Berry too. If she'd heard that three months ago, she never would have believed it. She would have thought it too good.

Her hands rubbed together, her eyes darted; she couldn't stay still. It was not that she cared, in a general way, what Clarence had done before marriage. She didn't blame him for having once been twenty-seven and attracted to women. No one would have asked him, on his wedding day, whether or not he went into it pure. It was the *now* that mattered. The girls of your youth you did not keep around. But Clarence had actually sought Jane out. He had invited her into their home. If Jane had given birth to Clarence's baby, when his own wife could not conceive a child, it would be horrible. It would kill Ethel. He must understand that. So why hire her? Why, when of course she must badly want to be closer to him? Why indulge that?

You know a lot, he'd said, *about getting your claws into millionaires.*

But she wouldn't let his insults stop her from protecting her sister.

She crept past the sleeping men to the window. The workers had built two bonfires on the hills. They were dancing, maybe. Their bodies crossed and re-crossed the orange outbursts of light, indistinct and far away. A loud, mucus-crackling snore from Hen made her jump. No sound from the bedroom. No sound from the galley. She wondered what Jane was up to, and what her excuse would be for leaving the dishes. No one had told her to take the night off.

She threw back the galley curtain, and the face popped up. Jane squatted on the ground at the far end of the kitchen. In front of her was a steaming bucket, her arms were sopping all the way to the rolled-up sleeves. The plates and cups were on the floor. The stove fire was low in the drum, barely up past the logs, but enough to throw a scalding heat across the legs as you passed it.

"Did I make too much noise?" Jane asked, nettling her. Understanding that Alice had marched in to scold her.

"No." Alice stared, momentarily flustered. Jane was the same person. But everything around her had shifted. Her brother, Jim, had taken Clarence's gold. Perhaps he considered it a retribution for what people like Clarence had taken from him. Though if what Stander had said was true, then the right to Clarence's money was even more specific: it flowed from the deep, natural right of a mother and child. "I came to tell you something," Alice said, gathering herself. "Don't get up." Jane's raised knee, tenting her skirt, returned to the floor. "I know that I was enigmatic before, when I said I might stay for the winter. The reason is that I'm engaged to Henry. Secretly engaged. Even Ethel and Clarence don't know."

A plate dipped into the water, reemerged. "Am I the first one you're telling?"

"I didn't think about it like that. But, yes."

A blank expression as Jane dried her hands on her apron. She wasn't going to lose her cool again. She was a good Catholic girl who knew the art of control. Her expression transformed from blank to haughty.

"Then I'm honored to be the first to wish you joy."

Ah. Alice had expected that. She had prepared for that. Her answer flowed quickly from a well of prior rumination: "We owe it to you, I thought, to tell you early. With the number of people who've been pouring into the country, women especially, it won't be as easy for you to find work. Last time Hen was in Dawson, he had five different ladies approach him, asking to do his laundry. And they were well-dressed, well-spoken ladies too. All from good backgrounds. Every day new groups come in. It's not the place it was when Clarence first hired you."

A silence.

Then Jane said: "You know? That's probably true."

Closer, they moved, almost too close to stop it: little pushes toward the revelation of mutual dislike.

"Anton Stander told me something tonight I never knew. He said you met Clarence in '95. Is that really the case?"

Jane did not speak. She picked up a plate, stuck with little pieces of meat, and placed it carefully into the depths of the bucket. Her look said: your sister is married, you will be married, why should it matter to you, you little tart, whether or not it's the case?

"He told me several things," Alice said. "I don't think I can repeat them."

Disdain palpitating; like heat coming in waves off the skin.

"Though I think I see now," Alice said, "where your sense of entitlement comes from."

Jane shrugged. She turned her head, as if to bring this talk to a close. From next door, a low creaking of wood, someone turning over in sleep.

"Clarence won't put up with this outrageous behavior forever," Alice said, light and whispering. "I hope you understand that. I hope your brother understands that."

No response.

"I swear to God, if I can prove your brother stole that gold, I'll have him hanged."

Jane stopped the washing. She held the rim of the bucket to balance herself and lifted her eyes.

"Thank you for the information about the ladies in Dawson. You're kind to take an interest. You've taken an extraordinary interest in me since the day I arrived."

7.

That same night, only hours later, still steeped in the heat of agitation, Alice woke in her perch to the sound of angry voices. The attic roof dipped. The slouching trolls stood in a row by her mat, her simpering companions, the raw source of too much feeling in too many people. True dark. They were well into September now, and past the summer's flirtations with night. Now the nighttime was substantial. It had heft and weight. It dropped a blanket over the house, as it did in nearly every other place in the world, on every day of the year.

The glow coming from the trapdoor was candlelight. The hushed voices ricocheted back and forth. She couldn't make out a word or even guess who was speaking. Man and woman. Man and man. She placed the voices into familiar heads, tested the fit. Clarence and Ethel, Ethel and Hen, Hen and Jane, Jane and Clarence, Clarence and Hen, maybe. Or Jim. Everyone sounded alike, whispering.

Alice sat up. She slid toward the trapdoor on her stomach, not making a sound.

The front door slammed. She waited. The light turned off. Beneath the bags of gold, the bedroom door opened and shut. Then, nothing. Her eyes adjusted to the change. She was as awake as she'd ever been. She rolled over and looked through the open trapdoor. The fine details of the cabin came hazily into view.

She had an idea. The beginning of an idea. She could go back to her mat now and forget it. But did she dare?

8.

Late the next morning, the stove was cold. The mat rolled and shoved into the corner. No breakfast ready for Ethel. Jane's tasseled bag missing from its spot in the galley. The metal cross gone from the nail.

"We're missing our cook," Alice said sharply, practically singing it, though not loud enough to wake Hen, who was still asleep on the floor.

Clarence of course already knew. He was sitting at the table, sipping from a mug of plain water. His gaze was wide, vulnerable, morose.

"What's the matter? Did you quarrel with Jane?"

The veins in his eyes were standout pink. "Did you hear us last night?"

"I heard talking and it woke me, but I didn't know more than that. I thought it was you and Ethel, so I stayed upstairs. I thought it was none of my business."

"It wasn't Ethel. Jane knocked on our door around three o'clock. She was wearing her coat and she was upset. She told me that she was leaving that minute. She'd packed her things and there was no convincing her. She seems to believe that she was used badly by our family. She thought this was meant to be an enduring position. At the least she expected to work through the winter, which I swear I never promised her. Hen wouldn't agree to it. So she asked to be paid for the month, and I gave her the cash. She's on her way to Dawson to look for new work."

"And to say nasty things about us, I guess," Alice ventured. "But we'll survive."

She opened the grate and lit the flame. A single orange poke of heat, the catch, and then the satisfying crackle and whoosh of fire. How effortlessly he diffused responsibility. Used badly by our family, he'd said. As if he weren't the sole employer. A small pot with water was on the stove. She covered it and returned to the main room.

"Ethel's sleeping?"

"Yes. She never woke up."

"Never woke up?"

"I mean to say, Jane didn't wake her."

"Good. She shouldn't have to trouble herself over Jane."

"I have bad news for her, though. I'm afraid to say it."

"What?"

Before her eyes, the man was crumpling. His unhappiness was breaking him down. His chin low, his arms on the table.

"I think I made a mistake about Frank," Clarence said.

"Frank as in your brother, Frank?"

His nod was minuscule. "I can't find Ethel's collection of nuggets. She had them out last night to show Peggy. Right before I went to sleep, I hung them up on a peg with the hats. This morning I had a bad feeling. I went to look for the pouch, and it was gone."

Alice walked to the hats. She lifted them off their pegs, one by one, and threw them onto the floor.

"You're sure you didn't put them somewhere else? In the bedroom?"

"I'm sure."

The door was shut. Ethel asleep inside. "We can look later."

"Jane took them," Clarence said morosely. "There's no point in looking. No one else has been in the house since I hung them up by the door. And it gets worse. Jim's gone too. The boys came with the news twenty minutes ago. He was supposed to work for us this winter." A heavy sigh, like a horse, except that it had the throat-clearing finish of human grief. "You were right about them."

"You give me too much credit. I never had proof."

"You knew it wasn't Frank who did it."

"I said he was too proud for stealing."

"God. I'm sorry for Ethel. She doesn't deserve that. She's been collecting those nuggets on and off for two years."

"What was the value, if you don't mind my asking?"

"Fifteen hundred. Less than the other gold that went missing. But it was more—"

"A sentimental thing."

"Yes." He looked at the bedroom door.

"Do you want me to tell her?" asked Alice.

"No. That's up to me."

The water was boiling. She returned to the galley and stood out of view. The bubbles climbed the dark insides of the pot. Her hand found its way to her chest. She stood there without making a sound, feeling the strong pounds of her heart.

9.

They missed their boat. Clarence bought tickets for a different steamer, the *Orlantha*, which wouldn't depart until the second week of October. For days, he agonized over the choice. He was superstitious about any change of plans. But he felt also that he couldn't leave his affairs so unsettled. Of course, he was sure he'd killed them all, especially when Henry came by with the news that their original boat, the *Caroline's Pines*, had reached San Francisco ahead of schedule and without any trouble. Terrible, terrible, when you start to imagine too much. Had he traded their safe passage for one that was doomed? He kept asking himself; no one could answer.

Ethel cried over her nuggets. She tried to hold it in, for her husband's sake, but she couldn't. She spoke loudly over her tears, about how stupid she was for blubbering on like this. She was shocked at the revelation of Jane's true self: she hadn't perceived in the woman the capacity for that kind of meanness. But now she only wanted to wipe her hands clean of the cook. The nuggets didn't matter. The value was nothing. She scrubbed her eyes. She laughed at herself, her whole face glistening wet.

Outside, they'd halted the sluices. The mounds of pay dirt that had, in early spring, stood as tall as their heads were now down to ground level. Soon the lumpy trolls that Alice slept beside would be carried down the ladder. Soon she would be parted from them. She pressed her palm to the burlap, feeling the crunch of gold inside. Hers to touch but not hers to possess.

She had never received a straight answer from Clarence to the simple question, How much are you worth? No man in the Klondike would say. A general reticence, she knew, was understandable, as it wasn't just crass to throw your own numbers around, it was bad business practice. The Canadian government took ten percent of each fortune as you crossed the border. The final number, therefore, must remain versatile. Depending on the official you got, it could drop fifty thousand, maybe three hundred thousand, from its actual worth.

"And so what?" she asked Henry while she was adding salmon filets, squash, and green cabbage to sizzling oil, and letting the whole cabin hear. "Does he think I'm going to walk up and down the creek, announcing his secrets? Does he think I'll take a piece of charcoal and write the number across our front door?"

She could have harassed Ethel about it, but she never felt right doing that.

Hen, at least, was too in love with her to leave her wanting. After dinner, while she was clearing the plates, during a moment that they were alone in the main room together, he wrapped a fat arm around her waist and pulled her backward into his lap.

Whispered into her ear: "One million, fourteen thousand, and twelve."

10.

Meanwhile, the insult festered. The days clicked by. The calendar turned on its metal spool, and still Clarence remained in a wretched state of indecision. He didn't know if he should report the three thefts of gold to the Mounted Police or not. Doing so would mean naming Jane and Jim as the suspects—and that worried him. He feared his naming them would be the whole of their trial. It was astounding. Alice pressed. Henry pressed, thanks to Alice's urging. Charlie, almost crossing a line, made a few bold statements about the integrity of American, no, Canadian law. Even Ethel, who hated to disagree with Clarence, did once venture to say, "Will our neighbors be shocked that we made no report?" None could infer, in their gentle confusion, what Alice was able to see: that accusing Frank had come from a place of deep wishful thinking, and that only intense fear, intense guilt, intense love, or some combination, could now be causing Clarence to act so irrationally.

A hint of husky candlelight illuminated the square hole in the attic floor, and Alice was out of her bed. She drifted to the glow like a moth. To the big table and the man there, huddled over a slanting pen.

It was rare to see him writing. According to his sisters, Nellie and Cora, he had gone the entire spring and summer of '95 with exactly two letters home.

"Tell me that's a note to the Mounted Police."

He put down the pen. "I wish you'd drop the subject."

"So you're letting them get away with it, are you? That woman stole from you, she stole from your wife, and here you are too cowardly to report it to the police, like any normal person would do. Jim took ten thousand dollars from under your nose."

"If I'm at peace with it, then why are you still bothering me?"

"Ethel's nuggets, for starters. You said they were worth fifteen hundred just on their own."

"Small change."

"Oh, is it?" She held out her palm. "Then give it to me." He would not mistake it as a playful gesture. His eyes tonight were clear pools. You looked into them and went sinking down.

"You'll need to make it up to poor Frank."

"My Ma will be on my case soon enough. There'll be hell to pay, for falsely accusing her firstborn son. Trust me, she doesn't need your help."

"No word of Jane in Dawson?"

"No."

"Then they've disappeared into an Indian camp. I can just picture them around a fire, with all that gold spread on a blanket for the little children to see. They're laughing at us."

"Don't try to rile me up, Tot. It's not going to work."

Clarence's pen, released, rolled across the uneven table, halted against a knot in the wood. He sat back in his chair, pulled the ends of his coat over his belly.

"They can make my effigy and stuff it with horseshit for all I care. When we disembark in San Francisco, the governor, the mayor, and every pipsqueak with a downtown office will be lined up on the dock to shake my hand. Do you think a couple of Indians will factor into the conversation?"

"I'm sure they will. You'll tell the funny story of the vixen who stole your gold and skipped out the door. That's the kind of raucous tale that gets men like that pink in the face and giggling." She curled her toes on the cold floorboards. Looked away. "Horseshit," she whispered. "That's accuracy if I've ever heard it."

11.

Each time she sparred with Clarence, she grew bolder. Over the next several days, a glow within her intensified. She remembered back to the time on the trail when she would have crumpled under the power of one disapproving glare. He had injured her. He had thrown her across the tent at Sheep Camp. He had torn up her deed. But he had left her to slink away and lick her wounds. And then, when she did, when she lifted her limbs, as the moment demanded, she was pleased to find the injuries shallow. She didn't mind them now. They were the marks of someone who knew how to fight.

The fall season was short in the Klondike. When winter arrived, it did so with a bang. Alice charted each day, each hour. Now they only had thirteen days before their departure from Dawson. Ethel had fallen again into a slow, morose mood, which, before the strange darkness of her ill health this spring, would have seemed impossible for that vigorous and contented soul. Alice couldn't calm down. Her letter to Moie and Poie was short. Her journal entry was shorter. She decided that she didn't like the look of her life when she recorded the salient points.

In front of the stove, Clarence was on his side, on Jane's old mat. It was dark; a little past one o'clock in the morning. Gray embers glowed intensely orange. Round and plump in that way that made you want to open the grate and scoop them up into your palm. Ethel must have been having a restless night, sending Clarence searching for a quieter place, too bad for him, he wasn't going to get quiet. His prayerful hands were tucked under his cheek, like the pose of a child in a nursery book.

"I know you're awake, Clarence. You don't realize it, but we can always tell when you're sleeping because of your snoring."

He rolled over and groaned. Not quite willing to give up the act. An emptied tin of peaches sat near his head, with the spoon still inside.

"Anton Stander told me something at the party."

"Oh?" he muttered.

"I couldn't go to bed, for thinking about it, and I decided you had no right to sleep either."

He opened his eyes. "What do my rights say about boxing your ears?"

"He told me that Jane had a child."

"You're getting your facts from Stander?"

"I wish I could trust you instead."

"Watch it, Tot." He sat up. "You're toeing a line."

"How can I help it?" she whispered. "I'm going in circles, trying to follow your logic with this. You with Jane, if it's true, that's only the start. Bringing her here as a cook. Letting Jim steal from you. It all pushes too far. You're letting Jane get away with taking Ethel's nuggets, as good as a gift. Even if you let the pay dirt go, I thought for sure you'd never condone a wrong against Ethel. Do you know that once Ethel overheard Jane and Jim talking in the cache? She heard them say 'baby.' She assumed they were speaking about her—of her own incapacities. Imagine if she'd heard more."

In the quiet, his anger was building.

"I'm sorry." A skillful swerve—now she was all conciliatory. "But you see how this would destroy Ethel. All she wants is a child. And she might never have one. You never told her Dr. Moorhead's exact words, how pessimistic he was."

"Three years ago," said Clarence, slowly, "on my first prospecting trip, I landed in Dyea with fifty dollars in my pocket. That was all I had in the world and look at me now. So don't tell me a situation can't change on a dime."

"On a dime." She smiled. "There are no puny dimes around here." He seemed about to interrupt, she cut him off. "The problem is, Clarence, a woman's body is not a business plan. It doesn't answer to hard work and persistence."

"For a maid, you seem to know a lot about it."

"You think I'm all touch-me-not, but in fact I'm engaged to your brother."

There, that woke everyone up. He really hadn't known. She'd thought there was a chance that Jane had told him, or that Henry had let it slip; but pure surprise showed on his face.

"Hen?"

"Who do you think?"

"Your Poie and Moie know about this?"

"Not yet. But you know they'll be happy. I'm sure it's more than what they expected of me. Besides, who can object to a Berry?"

A gruff noise in reply.

"Is that all I get for congratulations?" She laughed. "Think of it, Clarence. You and I will be siblings twice over. But please don't tell Ethel. I'm waiting until she has a really good day, and then I'm going to make it a big surprise over dessert." She smiled again. "See? I keep secrets too. Only mine's a nice one."

"Please," he groaned. "Jane and Jim are gone. The matter rests." The straining single eye of his profile fixed on her. Then, in a low voice, with equal parts gloom and irritation, he asked a question that she felt revealed—and admittedly, she did not consistently see it—the streak of intelligence that had brought him this far:

"Just what are you after?"

12.

The boxes nailed shut; the clothing washed and folded; the pots scrubbed; the curtain removed from the galley for airing and bleaching in the sun; the floor swept clean of those patties of dirt that were always sneaking into the house with the boots; the dust evanesced to a sparkling cloud and sent out the open doorway. Her thoughts were drifting some miles down the Pacific, not to Selma, but to a salty cliff and green outcrop, where on a bit of level ground stood a home, a little white cottage, which would one day belong to her parents.

She missed them. She supposed she did. She wondered if her engagement to Henry would please them, or if they'd be sad to lose their last daughter. She kneeled down to polish the chair legs. Not because Henry would notice, but because it was against her conscience to abandon a house and not leave it pristine. It was October 5. As soon as Clarence gave them word, they would hike to Dawson, enjoy a last hurrah in town, then be ready to board the steamer early on the morning of the eleventh. Ethel was dressed. She was perched on the kitchen stool, stirring the beans. The house was filled with that familiar scent: like honeyed bile, that disintegrating mash.

"Well, have you heard?" Henry blustered in. Startled, Alice shouted at him to take off his boots. He complied, then curled each foot to crack his toes on the floor. "Jane's in town. We thought she'd done the polite thing and moved up near Circle City, but she's sauntering up and down the Dawson boardwalk in a silk dress and a big straw hat with a bow. One of our neighbors saw her and happened to mention it to me. Oh, and I forgot to say, a matching fan, in blue silk, with white lace on it too. No one told her that Clarence was still on the creek. That's my guess. You all were supposed to be landed in California last week."

The moment Hen was in the galley, Alice went out the door and hurtled down the bank with her skirts fisted high. She could sense the two winter miners watching her. A caked, dusty face peeking above a shovel handle, another from in-between wheelbarrow poles.

She came upon Clarence. Hammer-handed. Metal-mouthed. He was boarding up their active pits in anticipation of snow. Last year he'd left the job to Stander, and they'd lost two mines when the snow had filled them up, and then with the melt in spring, had pulled the mud walls into collapse.

"Hen says that Jane's in Dawson."

Clarence spit the nails into his hand. "I know. He found me on his way to the house."

"Have they sighted Jim too?"

He paused. Deciding what he could hide from her, probably. "He was on the claim this morning. The boys say he wandered into the tents around dawn, looking for some things he'd left. He thought we were already gone for the winter. Richards and Handler chased him off."

"Did he say anything?"

"He didn't see why he shouldn't be allowed to retrieve his own belongings."

"Of course. Nothing scares him. Why should it?"

That night was marked by shallow talk, nervous, like a bird's timid dips into water. Dawson, Selma, what all the workers, the "boys," planned to do with their wages, the impending trip home. But everyone was ill at ease. They were listening for other noises. They finally understood the danger that Alice had been anticipating for the whole of the summer; now when it was too late to change course.

Then, the dishes washed and dried. The Mr. and Mrs. of the house retired for the evening. In a dim corner, Henry opened his arms. Alice walked into them. He held her, rocked her, as if there was gentle music playing from the eaves. Soon they would be doing this dance without four layers of wool rubbing between them; soon, perhaps, she would have a little gopher of a Berry curled inside her gut. She was ready. She had said of Jane and Jim, nothing scares them. And though she stood by the statement, she understood that the revelation had come easily to her because it also described herself.

13.

A riot of barking echoed off the hills. Darkness, still, and Alice was surprised she had slept at all. Surprised by the black sky out the little round window and the wavering moonlight that made a path across the creek. Shuffling and panicked voices below. She grabbed her socks and got down the ladder quickly. Ethel leaned beside the bedroom door, face waxen and stiff. Clarence was yanking a pair of trousers over his shorts, while Henry, already dressed, scooped on his hat. The dogs around the house were barking. While Alice was descending the ladder, she'd heard Henry say, "What the devil is this about?" Now, at the window, in a steadier tone, he said, "Someone's coming."

Two someones, in fact, the pair of winter workers. Matthew Richards and Jefferson Handler. They entered the cabin with Boomy, their dog, just as Clarence was lifting his gun from the pegs.

"And now he's going to shoot us!" Handler said, as if during the walk he'd been drawing up a litany of grievances against his boss, only to arrive, unexpectedly, face-to-face with the grand finale.

Clarence was baffled.

The dog, Boomy, snapped at Henry, who'd reached down to examine it. A diagonal cut marred the dog's face and blood crusted the fur.

Handler put out the explanation first. Jim had come back to the tents in the night. In his escape, he'd slashed their dog, the very one they'd trained to bark at Indians.

The fuller story came from Richards. The dogs were barking, that's what had tipped them off, although by then Jim was already gone. They'd heard Boomy whining, and that was strange, as the dog wasn't prone to it. And then they'd discovered the dog's bloody face. Richards had thought to check the other tent, where they kept the stash of things that had previously belonged to Jim. His instinct had been right. The tent was ransacked; the furs disarrayed, and several valuables missing: the axe, the beaded spoon, the tin bowl, the tobacco and pipe.

"We heard you never reported the thefts of gold," Handler said. "Three thefts in two months, and the Mounties haven't heard whisper of it."

"We thought it was Frank," Henry said weakly, by way defending his brother.

But Handler said: "We hear you have a soft spot for the Indians."

Clarence was losing confidence. His authority was atrophying by the second in the company of these indignant men. Meanwhile, Handler counted on his fingertips the other things Jim had stolen. Not tonight, mind, but at points over the summer, as was only obvious now. Four potatoes, a pair of suspenders. Handler himself needed to count his bills again, no matter that they'd been secured. He said that Indian bodies weren't built solid like theirs. He'd heard of a Tlingit, he said, who could slip one long finger through a keyhole and unlock the door from the inside. "We interrupted him," Handler said. "But mark my words, he's just getting started."

A wind rocked the glass in the windows. "Jesus," said Henry, then, relieved, fell down in his chair. Ethel stood with her hand lightly covering her mouth.

An argument ensued. Whether or not Jim was still on the claim, or else nearby, biding his time. Clarence said he was not but Handler and Richards believed that he was, and no reassurance could induce them home to their tents.

"Fine," said Clarence. "Bed in the cache. If you promise not to eat your way through it."

They agreed. The cache had no windows and only one thick door that locked from the inside, with a bar dropped into an iron catch, too cumbersome, apparently, for even the touch of magical fingers.

Once they were gone, Alice said, "I wouldn't sleep in there for all your millions, Clarence. If Jim sets fire to the cabin, they might not realize until they're trapped and burning up like a torch."

"What a horrible thought!" Ethel's eyes went large. "Is that what you're expecting?"

"Oh, of course not. I was being flip. Ethel, let Clarence tuck you in now, and I'll put up the tea. A big warm cup in hand will calm us all down."

Beautiful, how they did exactly as she said. Clarence led Ethel into the bedroom. Meanwhile Henry obeyed a tilt of her chin toward the kitchen. They had not noticed her uncertainty. But she was shocked. She hadn't really expected Jim to come back, even to retrieve his own belongings.

"I'm worried about you," Alice whispered to Henry, once they were deep into the galley. "I didn't want to say more in front of my sister, but I'm shocked by this, I'm shaking. What if Jim comes back? He could hurt you and we'd be gone and no one would realize for days."

Henry's pride swelled; her concern was his compliment. "I'm not bothered," he assured. "I always got along fine with Jim."

"Henry, my God, it's bigger than that. Jane and Jim don't believe that we Americans have the right to be here. They don't believe we have a right to a single nugget sucked out of the ground. Those stakes men used to mark the claims. What are those? They're just sticks. Put them in, pull them out. You have to believe in them for them to mean anything. And the Indians don't believe. They have no impetus for believing. It's not that I blame them. In fact, I understand them completely. I wouldn't lie down and give up my country if I were them. I would fight. I would use any art. That's exactly what makes me so scared."

Henry blinked. Her words had poured over him like rain; he seemed to have missed most of it.

"The stakes are the law," he said. "Once you stake and record, it's over."

"Recorded how, though? Think about it. Ledgers in a Dawson office. Books kept by pale little men about the width of Jim's forearm."

Henry grunted, smiled. He had recognized an exaggeration, and now snatched at a bit of levity on his way to being disturbed.

"Jim can lift the same as me. He's no hulking beast born out of a crack in the earth."

"But imagine it's winter. What happens if he comes here while you're sleeping?"

"I'll have the dogs."

"You've seen the great fear he has of dogs."

His eyes roamed, his cheeks slack while his thoughts groped for a definitive statement.

"I'll have the door and windows barred. And I'll take the gun to bed."

"A loaded gun in bed? Is that wise?"

"Leaning against the wall, I mean."

"That's fine if you spend eight months indoors," she pressed. "But let's say one morning you decide to go out. Who's to say he won't be on the claim, waiting for you?"

A nimbus of steam alive from the kettle. Mud to water, water to tea. A California family flung to the arctic. Paupers made into millionaires. The Indian who saved their lives in April kills them in October. Why not? These were easy transformations.

Imagine Hen on the gravel ground, before the cabin door. His body split open down the middle, showing the wet stuff inside. His skin pallid, his hands folded. His mind insentient to the perfect pyramid of yellow nuggets balanced on top of his forehead.

"What can I do?" His question a sigh.

"You have to talk to your brother. Tell him he's putting you in danger by not going to the Mounted Police right away. Soon he'll be snug in a fancy hotel in San Francisco. But what about you? In a week, the whole Klondike will know about the unfortified claims on Eldorado. If we don't go after Jim now, he'll be back with his friends to harass the whole creek. Remind Clarence how Jane stole Ethel's collection of nuggets. They will stop at nothing. Go to your brother and tell him that."

14.

Gray dawn cracked across the land—the hills, the creek—surprising to watch the earth reemerge, exactly as they had left it. And soon, what would it be like? The hills denuded and hollowed out, the banks eroded. After another season, the place would be further altered; three more, and perhaps this wild country would be nothing at all like it had been.

"We're going to Dawson to give a report to the Mounted Police." The way Clarence spoke, you'd think that the idea was his own. He asked, "Do I need to leave Hen to watch over you girls?"

They refused the offer, as it was more important that the boys travel together. Though Alice's confidence faded a bit once the door had closed. She had never been in this big, new country without the protection of Clarence or some of their party nearby. Now she and her sister were—what?—not so much themselves but any two women in history standing behind a barred door. Each thing in the cabin was exactly itself. Four bumpy walls of horizontal trees. A rope ladder connecting the floor to a hole in the ceiling. A stout table with two dogs dozing underneath. Empty iron pegs by the door. A bison skull with black lace ornamenting his horns. Ethel dragged her rocking chair out of the corner and into the dead center of the room. She clutched the dormant ball of yarn that had been in the seat. She folded her body and all its accompanying layers of fabric, as if to protect herself. Why? Alice wondered, watching her sister. Surely not because the idea of the lumber walls engulfed by fire had stuck?

The night dragged. But not forever.

By noon the next day, the men appeared at the edge of the claim. Alice spotted them from the galley window. The party had grown to eleven. It was Clarence, Henry, Charlie, and their two workers, Handler and Richards. Plus two members of the Mounted Police, both in uniform—though Alice could see even from a distance that they were not more than boys. Four of their Eldorado neighbors had also joined the group: it looked like James Renoncourt, Martin Pratt, Samuel Evans, and Herman Whipple.

The group had the aura of purposefulness, and by their confident march, Alice wondered if they already knew the trailhead that would put them on the path to Jim. She hadn't expected them back so soon. Now it would take some fancy maneuvering to get the cold meat and fruit laid out on the table. She rushed out of the galley to the sound of knocking.

"Who's there?" Ethel called, and Alice said, "Shush, Ethel, that *who* is your husband."

She was wrong about lunch. Clarence entered the cabin alone. They'd only stopped to give the women an update. They had word from some miners in Dawson that Jane and Jim were together and moving northwest through the country. There was an Indian camp about thirty miles in that direction. So Jim hadn't been lurking near the claims after all. But there was no question, now that the Mounted Police were involved, about going after them. Like Clarence had predicted, with the theft reported, that decision was out of his hands.

"Do you think it's safe?" With Clarence here, Ethel had eyes only for Clarence.

"Safe for who?" he grumbled. "Eleven men to one. It's safe for us." Strong words but spoken wrong—as if he'd just limped home from a losing fight, instead of being on his way to a good one. "We have Patrick and Larson from the Mounted Police. I asked for horses, but they weren't willing to let their horses so far."

Alice cut in, "You should have told them they must do better than that." When Clarence shook his head, she said, "Tell the boys to come in and have a quick bite." But a lesson had taken place—a lesson in justice—and this new knowledge pulled on Clarence, as much as he despised it, and kept him near the door. He'd already made an urgent appeal to his neighbors, to the police. Now he couldn't slow them down. They were pawing at the dirt to get going.

Four bags of dried beef would have to suffice. She scooped them up. "Here. At the very least, take these with you."

Clarence and Ethel turned in one motion. They regarded her with the same frightened gaze. They understood that she, Alice, spoke for the majority. Then Ethel, balking, took Clarence's arm. She hated this hurriedness.

"Please stay here. Blame it on me. Tell them I'm afraid. You can't leave two women alone with your gold."

He worked over the idea. Likely he could do it. He could say, I must stand guard over a million dollars in dust and also my wife. But before he had the chance to think it over fully, one of the young Mounties shouted that they were starting off. A tough group all of a sudden, Alice observed. Even Hen.

Alice looped her hand through Ethel's arm. "I know you're scared, my love, but we have to let him go. Clarence isn't a monarch. He can't send other men to do his fighting for him."

Again, both looked at Alice with terrified eyes. Then Clarence kissed his wife, clomped out the door. The bar lowered. The curtains lingered open. Once the party had moved around the creek bend, the curtains whisked closed across the rail. If Henry is killed, Alice thought, I will never forgive myself for leading him wrong. If Clarence is killed, she thought further, Ethel will hold me responsible, and she will hate me forever.

15.

There was a thunderous boom. Alice opened her eyes. Darkness still. The men were throwing themselves against the door. They'd been gone for eighteen hours at most, why back so early? She jumped up and went to the door, but their combined weight was pressing the bar flush and unmovable against its catch, and she could not lift it. She shouted at them to stand back. She kicked the dog away. She shouted at Ethel to open the window and tell the men to stand back. But there was no transfer of information from one group to the other, and it was several minutes before they'd paused their assaults long enough for her to lift the bar and bring them inside.

Eleven men had left the claim. Three returned. Not the three Alice would have picked. The dog, Boomy, bounded across the cabin to Handler, Richards, Charlie.

"Where are the others?" Ethel demanded.

But the men breezed past Ethel, checked the windows, checked the lock on the door, readied their guns.

"Charlie," snapped Alice, "answer my sister, please."

"We don't know," Charlie said, without looking away from the window. "We heard Clarence and Henry shouting. I think Jim got free. Hen yelled something to Clarence about holding on to the gun. He was scared. We heard the shots, then nothing."

"Who shot?" Alice could hardly speak. Fear flooded through her. "Clarence? Or did Jim get Clarence's gun?"

Charlie answered, in a voice strange and unlike him, "Lady, that's what we couldn't tell! That's why we ran back here!"

The wind blew. Ethel, ignoring the men's protestations, threw open the door. Beyond the door, the empty claim. Beyond the claim, a scrape of stars. And the dark all around was hollow, like the inside of a drum. So hollow it seemed to reach into the cabin and empty it out and suck the qualities out of them. "Clarence!" Ethel screamed. Charlie grabbed Ethel's arm and pulled her inside. He locked the door again as Ethel, sobbing, fell into a heap behind him. Now, at Alice's back, a fortune in gold and a crying widow collapsed on the rug. She felt something. She felt that the days she had crafted, like cuts into ivory, were tumbling out of her lap, along a horizontal, into oblivion, as if she had done something stupid, stood up too quickly, and lost something unbearably precious to the cause of her own careless mistake.

As Handler put out the lamp on the table, and Richards stood at the wall by the window, and Charlie drank from the open brandy bottle, the facts poured out in a jumble. Jim. A grubby lean-to in the woods. A swift discovery. The gold recovered. They'd sent one of the young Mounties, Larson, to Dawson to find the police commissioner, a fellow named Dells, but there hadn't been time to hear the reply. Clarence and Henry had tied Jim's wrists and had been walking with him, with Renoncourt, Pratt, Evans, Whipple, and the other Mountie, Patrick, backing them up. Jane was gone—flown off like a bird—they'd never even laid eyes on her. They only knew by a scatter of blue beads and a shawl left in the lean-to that a woman had been there. They three—Charlie, Handler, and Richards—had taken the lead in the victory walk down the creek. But they'd pulled too far ahead and hadn't realized how far until they'd heard the shouting, Clarence and Hen. Then the gunshots. Of which they couldn't say how many and certainly couldn't say why.

"It's Clarence," Ethel wailed. "I know it is. He had a bad feeling about this. He didn't want to go. I shouldn't have let him."

Layers of white clothing showed where Ethel's skirts had climbed above her knees. She was sobbing. She almost couldn't inhale. She was doubled over alongside her rocking chair. The men paid no attention. It was odd to see a woman fall and the men in the room do nothing. Alice imagined Henry. She'd had it all arranged. She had already begun to picture herself in a silk dress and holding his hands before their gathered families. She couldn't imagine him gone. He was too big and mirthful, too much a presence. Could the Berrys really slip away into the vast dark of the Klondike, just like that, leaving the Bushes to keep living without them? Beside her, Ethel was curled, head down. The vertebrae pressed the skin in the bare space above the dip of her dress. "You have to wait," she assured Ethel. "I'm sure Clarence and Henry are fine."

But something else was lighting up inside her. She was thinking along a different track: if Clarence is dead, it will be up to me to be the one in charge. Ethel will be too distraught to do it.

Overhead: the slouched, canvas bags of gold. She half-expected them to fall through the ceiling, and land in a cloud of bright dust at her feet.

Charlie yelled from the window: "They're coming! Looks like Clarence and Hen and the others!"

A hot blush spread over Alice.

Ethel scurried up to her feet. She flew to the door and swung it open and bounced awkwardly off the step. She hobbled across a dim stretch of ground and hurled herself at her husband. Alice watched. Then, from around the side of Ethel's hair, peeked Clarence's face. His gaze was violent. The reproof shook Alice where she stood. She almost didn't see Hen coming at her. And when Hen lifted her up in one of his great bear hugs, his suspender buckles pressing into her, she was still so distracted by Clarence that it took her a second to remember to feel relieved.

"Charlie said there were gunshots," Alice said. "Thank God you're okay."

And Clarence said, "We aren't okay. Jim's dead."

16.

Now came the unfolding of the cursed events, which was to say, each spectacular failure. First of all, they'd heard that rumor in Dawson of the couple on the move, northwest with the river. They'd walked five hours then camped when they couldn't walk farther. Today, when they'd come upon a lean-to in the woods near the bank, they weren't even thinking of Jane and Jim. It seemed too soon. They'd figured it was a couple of prospectors, and they'd been calling out pleasantries as they approached. It was hard to say who'd been more surprised. The familiar face, Jim's, had emerged, and a second later, the realization had hit them all. Jim bolted. Eleven pairs of arms ensnared him. There was no Jane. Clarence had spent twenty minutes stomping around the rocks and trees. They felt she was nearby, watching them, even, but it would have been fool's work to search any longer for her. An Indian woman in her own country will bend and curl away from an enemy as evasive as smoke through the leaves. Meanwhile Henry had been in the lean-to rummaging around. "It's here!" he'd cried. The gold, he meant. The pay streak from *Five*. The washed ten thousand. Jim really had taken it. At that point, the situation had changed. Now they had in their possession a guilty person. Patrick had formally announced an arrest. Then the other boy, Larson, had run off for Dawson to find Dells, the police commissioner, and ask what they were supposed to do next. They'd tied Jim's wrists and led him on a leash. Henry had told him he'd be hanged in Dawson by the Mounted Police, which was, in retrospect, Henry said now, a mistake, as it may have been the thing that caused Jim to panic. About a mile later it happened. Jim broke loose from the rope and went for Clarence's gun. In the struggle, the gun had gone off while the barrel was moving along the underside of Jim's chin. A boom that split the air. The man dropped. He fell onto Clarence's feet. He didn't take another breath, and they had only half stopped up the wound before they gave up. He was now outside, on the claim. They had bundled him into a shed on *Five,* not too close, but still in range of the house. They spoke of Jim in the present tense. So much so that once Alice became confused, and wondered if she had misunderstood. She asked, "He needs a doctor, or you're sure the shot killed him?"

"He killed himself," corrected Renoncourt, one of their neighbors, speaking cross-purposes, "going after that gun."

"I put him under arrest" was the addendum from Patrick, the young Mountie. "In the name of the law. I did it. He'd been caught with the gold."

Alice stared at the boy. He seemed to take what had happened as a personal insult, a sign that he'd not been respected. From the boy, she moved her attention to Clarence. When Clarence looked back, she felt her face burn.

"At first," Henry said, "when I saw the body go down, I thought it was C.J."

Now everyone turned to Clarence. But Clarence just stood there, blinking.

Behind him, by the front door, sat the bags of recovered pay dirt. No one seemed to want to touch them. "Where's Ethel's collection of nuggets?" Alice asked next, as if it had just occurred to her. "Did they mix it in with the others?"

At this Clarence finally spoke: "We didn't find the nuggets. They must have stashed the pouch someplace else. Or else they already spent it."

"It doesn't matter, Clarence." This time Ethel's assurance was genuine. She had tucked herself to her husband's side and was rubbing the rough side of his cheek. She cupped his chin and kissed his face.

Outside the light broke over the trees, over the water, over the shed on *Five* with its incredible contents. It was the same sun that had set on Jim, though God willing he would have no corresponding reemergence. Alice looked at Ethel, who remained occupied in preening and patting her silent and petrified trunk of a husband. From a corner of the room emerged a quiet grumbling for food. Alice told her sister to stay where she was; she would do the cooking herself.

In the galley, she fed the drum. It still felt strange to be in the galley alone. She'd gotten so used to cooking with Jane. The dog, Boomy, came in and stood against her legs. It turned up its doleful eyes then greedily licked up the scrap that she fed it.

She put the dough into the oven to bake. But there must have been a break of thought within the group. Just as she was putting butter into a pan, she heard the bench and chairs kicking back from the table. She came back to the room in time to see it emptying out. They had raided the bin of crackers and taken the cheese.

Henry, lingering with Clarence, put on his hat. "I'll walk to Dawson. At least it should be your own brother who makes the report to the commissioner. Better that than a neighbor."

"That's fine."

Henry saw her. "Maybe Tot would like to come with me."

"No," said Clarence. "She needs to stay with her sister."

Henry went out. The door slammed.

Clarence turned to Alice. Now they were alone. Ethel must have gone to change her clothes in the bedroom. He said, "Keep standing there with that insolent look on your face, and I'll split your lip."

The pan would burn. Alice ducked back to the galley. She thought he would go now, perhaps to stand guard over Jim's body, but instead he followed her, clomping into the doorway. She kept her chin low. She couldn't tell how her face seemed to him now: whether it was more provoking or less.

"You're happy about this."

The situation did not lean in her favor. His prey had gone down too soon, and his claws, unretracted, were still searching the air. "Of course not," she said quietly. "A man died. What must you think of me if you think I'd be happy?"

Her body swung, busying itself with taking three plates off a shelf, though she wasn't sure if Clarence wanted to eat, or if she was preparing this breakfast for no one. She gave Clarence one side of her face to look at. As if her attention was divided, as if her senses weren't straining to catch the slightest shift in his mood. She sliced potatoes into a bowl. His anger dropped into his sinkhole eyes, black hollows at the edge of which all things teetered and fell.

"You had it in for Jane."

"No."

"You despised her."

"Maybe I did dislike her." She heard her own voice, its clipped and almost dispassionate tone. "But only as much as would be expected, given who she is and who I am. Think of it from my position, as a woman who very recently became your brother's fiancée. Why would I want a woman like Jane in the house?"

She dumped the potatoes into the pan. She knew she was not saying anything of interest to Clarence, but what could she do but keep talking and talking?

"Ask your sisters if you don't believe me," she said. "Nellie and Cora would tell you the same."

They moved into the main room. She untied her apron and laid it on the back of a chair. She felt safer here, with Ethel just on the other side of the door.

"Go visit Jim," Clarence said. "Lift the blanket and see what's left of his face. Maybe then you'll stop acting so smug."

He broke off, overcome by emotion, beginning to cry. He couldn't believe, yet, what had happened.

"Clarence, listen to me." She was seizing this chance to speak reason to him, in spite of the danger. "You're putting too much on yourself. Jim knew what risks he was taking when he started stealing your gold. He wasn't some young kid. The law could have intervened at any point and the result would have turned out the same. The Mounted Police aren't known for their clemency."

"So he deserved to die?"

She hesitated. "Not for stealing, no. But for going after your gun, yes. He could have shot you. Thank God it isn't you in that shed."

He was silent.

"Or imagine if it was the boy, Patrick. Imagine if it was Hen."

But Clarence was not in the mood to follow her into these fantasy worlds. His feet remained planted. When he spoke next, his voice was seething.

"You wanted to get Jane and Jim off the claim, and you've done it."

Startled, sliced by his anger, she withdrew. The feeling was the only real thing for him now—his anger—and he would throw it at whatever creature was stupid enough to stand in his way. She stepped back. Then again.

"You made a murderer out of me." He said it. And then he was bolstered by it. He had found his accusation. He tried it again. "You made me a murderer!"

"How did I do it? Bought you the powder?" A rapid, desperate whisper now. "Was I at Forty Mile during your bachelor days? Did I bring Jane and Jim on to the claim? Did I shove you into the cache with Jane and slam the door? Where is Jane now? That's what I'd love to know. They say you searched the woods for her for twenty minutes and didn't find her. Or did you? Did you whisper into her ear a place for her to hide? It's a great country, isn't it? No shortage of real estate here."

He lunged at her. She'd been expecting it though, and before he knew what was happening, she was out of his sight. All this time, she'd been moving casually across the cabin. Now she slipped behind the bedroom door, slammed it, dropped the rail.

Ethel: upright in the bed, shoulders straight, hair frizzed and loose of its pins.

"What's happened? I heard you say 'Jane.'"

The thud of a body against the door.

"Alice, your mouth is bleeding."

She touched her lip and her finger came away watery red. The door must have scraped her face while she was closing it.

Ethel, horrified, was trying to get to the lock. Alice stopped her sister with a barricade of an embrace.

"What have you said to Clarence?"

"Please stay, Ethel. Don't! Everyone's in a state, but we'll calm down."

A second thud.

All their lives, Ethel had been the heartier one. Now Alice squeezed her sister around the middle, easily restraining her. Through a plush layer of flesh, the bump of bones. During the worst of her fevers, Alice had consoled herself that Ethel was as round as ever. But it seemed that she'd been wrong to take comfort in that. What if, Alice wondered, through all of this, I have failed to keep her well? A sadness crashed over Alice while at the same time they heard Clarence withdraw, then the front door open and shut. Ethel went limp. She took two steps back and dropped to the bed.

"You treat me like a child, you and Clarence both."

"I don't—"

"No. I can't take it anymore. I hate this place. Poor Jim. I can't stop crying. I know he stole from Clarence, but I don't even care. We haven't made things easy for those poor people. Jim was a good man. He saved our lives on the Chilkoot."

It was bad. The same sadness came over Alice. Briefly, she was, with Ethel, immersed in the horror. But then she fought her way through the mire of feeling.

"No one will blame Clarence for this."

"Clarence should have never gone after Jim. It wasn't worth this."

A fissure of pain ran through Alice's chest, as if a fist were squeezing her heart. "I promise, Ethel, everything will be better. Once we leave the Klondike, the world starts over. Imagine being in Selma with Moie and Poie. The sun shining down on us. You and Clarence will have so much to do. Houses to buy. Friends to visit. You can travel, maybe. England. Italy."

Ethel, grief-stricken: "Stop it, Alice. You know that's not even the future I want."

"All right. Then I'm going to tell you something else. I wasn't planning to tell you yet, but I feel that I should. It's a nice thing. It's lovely. Henry and I are engaged to be married."

"What?" Ethel was shocked, confused. Enough to stop crying. "Truly?"

"Yes, truly, my darling. See? It's not only bad things that happen here. And maybe we'll have children soon, Henry and I, and we'll share them with you. You and I will love them together. Maybe I'll have a big boy you can take off my hands. You were always much better at mothering the neighbors' little brats than I was. You remember when they climbed the hen house and peed off the roof? If I hadn't been wearing a hat—well!" The distraction wore off. Ethel sobbed, a heaving sound almost like laughter. "You remember it, though! I can't stand that sort of wildness. If you hadn't come to their rescue, I would have whipped their skinny bottoms raw."

Outside, they could hear Clarence. It sounded like he was shouting, at Pratt and Evans, maybe. Then they realized he was shouting at no one.

"He's overcome." Alice drew her sister's body to hers. Though Ethel was limp and warm, and it was Alice who was shaking. "He can't believe that Jim's dead. But he'll leave his troubles here. You'll have your old Clarence back soon."

17.

Late morning on the claim. A hawk flew low, its shadow bumping over the land. Alice walked toward the shed. She stopped where the ground was raw and pebbly. The air was cool and damp with vapors roused from the creek. Once Jim had picked up a fox and thrown it violently aside. Or had he? That was the doctor telling a story. Another way to imagine the moment was Jim's arms scooping beneath the velvet animal belly, the gentle toss with no harm done. Light poured down from the bare blue sky. Time was nothing. She could have stood for a minute or an hour and the measure would have come out the same. He seemed still sentient. He seemed not completely gone. But hear the silence. See the lumber. It was dry and splintered and cut in regular lines. Nothing inside that shed could stand up against the force of new days. And those days would be arriving soon, in their own unstoppable rush, and carrying them away from here.

18.

The last days in the North unfolded for Alice like a series of pictures in front of her eyes. Here they were packing their final bags, shutting the cabin door, and walking along the nineteen-mile creek trail. Here was Alice

Bush and Mr. and Mrs. Clarence Berry and Henry Berry arriving to town. The younger brother sporting a bashful smile, burs and thorns caught in his clothing, and a long scratch marking his chin: the results of a shortcut through the backwoods between *Fifty-Eight* on Bonanza and *Four* Eldorado, taken the previous evening, when he was in danger of arriving late to see his family off. Here was Clarence, sober in mood and body both. His cup at Gertie's Saloon held only black coffee and the appearance of cards only made him scowl. He was moping about the death of an Indian, people were saying, who'd done his best to rob him blind; a grief that most found eccentric, available only to those who could afford to harbor such a sensitive soul.

And then there was Mrs. Clarence Berry. Her own sister, even, Alice saw as if from a distance. In '96 Ethel had been the grinning, buxom adventurer. The lady who'd famously climbed the Chilkoot in heeled boots and a skirt. Now she seemed like a different person: as if the Klondike, gold and all, had left her chilled and withered from within.

Accompanying her—and sharply aware of herself, how she was perceived in these strangers' eyes—was the younger sister: Miss Alice Bush. The news was out that Alice Bush was engaged to Henry Berry, which was such an obvious match that it almost wasn't news at all. On sight, the shadow Bush-Berry couple couldn't quite arouse the willing interest of hotel clerks, wives, laundresses, shopkeepers, paupers, or the claim owners they sat with at dinner. Mr. H. Berry and Miss Bush were not wealthy. Or rather, they were not wealthy when detached from their siblings. He was fat and silly. She was quiet and plain. When put together in the mind's eye, they rubbed together like two squares of wet wool, with absolutely no hope of igniting between them the silver sparks that make the union of a pair of young people worth heralding about in the first place.

Alice caught the message in each long look, then tossed it aside. She bought a straw hat trimmed in orange and walked into the sunlight.

On October 11, 1898, Alice, with Ethel and Clarence, boarded an Alaska Commercial Steamer headed for St. Michael. It was one of the last scheduled departures from Dawson, which was to say, one of the last chances out. Henry yelled from the dock and chased the boat several yards down the bank, pretending to have experienced a change of heart, and begging the captain to drop anchor and let him on board. The last thing they saw before the river turned was Henry, his big hands cupped around his mouth, shouting a joyful, "Don't leave me!"

19.

The cabins were all spoken for, and the deck was covered with people rolled into black or brown furs. The gold was stored under a locked trapdoor on the lowest level, with three members of the Mounted Police standing guard. Alice wrote in her journal a sentence or two, pure description, for each day of the plodding, weeklong river voyage. The land was green, amber, brown around them; so different from the muddy and snowy expanses of spring. The steamer stopped every few hours to pick up travelers who frantically waved them down from the banks. They passed camps puffing gray smoke in the sun. Indians in canoes pulled toward the bank. They took hold of overhung branches and vines and rode out the steamer's waves. Then they watched, steadily, until the surface stilled, then they rotated their shoulders, dipped their paddles, and glided on.

The passengers woke in Eagle City, in American waters, and sidled up to a creaking, American dock. The Canadian Mounties changed out for three Midwestern boys, who wore expressions of obliging bewilderment so much a match that one of the porters dubbed them "the triplets." Not exactly the type to strike fear into the hearts of con men and thieves; although, on the flip side, the chance of an inside job felt scant.

At St. Michael, they switched to the *Orlantha*, which would take them to San Francisco. Alice gripped the rail. Her head felt as if a perpetual motion machine had been set off inside it, as if she would never experience stillness again. Sawdust made wispy shapes on the deck. They'd put it there to catch the animal waste and the sickness, but someone had laid it down too soon, before the cargo was loaded, and it was scattered all over the boat.

On the third night, the inevitable wind kicked up. When Alice stood at the end of the boat, facing the stern, the deck was at such an angle that it looked as if she were climbing steps. The seams between the boards widened and closed. A man near her noticed it too, but his companion said, "No, they're supposed to do that, they're built loosely on purpose, so they won't crack."

Sailors were a group more tied to their customs than any she'd known. She kept asking, "Do you think it will storm?" But until they were neck-deep in it, they refused to say the water looked bad. One passenger in a green vest lectured a group of down-and-out miners on the equinoctial squalls, and the deckhands glared at him as if he were summoning the devil by name.

Dark clouds closed in overhead. At the last moment before everything movable, including the people, had to shelter below, Alice walked right up to the rail, to the foaming uproar, and removed Ethel's brown velvet pouch from the secret pocket that was sown into her dress.

She held the pouch a moment. Felt the crunch of nuggets inside. Then, with a strong launch of her arm, she threw it hard into the spray.

A tumbling dark shape through the air, a slip under the water, the roll of a wave. The man in the green vest looked over, his audience dispersing around him.

"What was that," he asked, "something to wish on?"

"No," she said. "Something I didn't want in my grave."

The deck pitched. She joined the people lunging for the stairs. She lost her footing and tumbled down the last five steps and slammed against the corridor wall. Knees loose, she collapsed, but no harm done. She felt fine upon standing, laughing wildly over her fall. Light with relief.

20.

Again, they had bad luck with weather.

A foot of water sloshed into Alice's room, spraying foul droplets when it hit the wall. Haven't I done this already, thought Alice. Isn't one storm at sea enough for a lifetime? When the boat dipped, it was quiet, like dropping into a well, and with no guarantee of returning onto a higher plane.

Hours went on. Her lifetime coalesced to a point. She worried about her parents. In one notice, four children might drop to two. That would be a loss. Ethel especially would be a loss. The Berrys' gold would be a loss.

She thought of Henry, and how he'd be the man whose fiancée had drowned at sea. She could imagine him dragging himself from house to house, sobbing at dinner, telling everyone who'd listen how Alice Bush was the sweetest girl whose little feet had ever tickled this earth, and how he could never replace her.

A version of herself split off from her body and squatted, steely-eyed, in a stiff lace collar, taking her place in the historical record. It was a stuffed, simplified version of what she was. A thing you might keep high on a shelf. But that was life. Or rather, that was what happened to you when you died.

She held her breath. She would keep her lips and nose pinched tight. She would make herself faint before the water filled the room to the ceiling. A bubble of air built in her throat. Her cheeks popped. She huffed and gasped.

21.

True, broad strokes of sky emerged the following morning. She and Ethel sat on the deck, far from the rail. They'd pressed their chairs so close that their arms were flush. They stared at the water, at the dully dressed people milling around them. It was a hushed group. Together they had stumbled to the edge of life and dipped a toe into nonexistence. A hand had grabbed them and pulled them back. But even so, they found themselves chilled. Their tentative faces tilted to the sun. When the *Orlantha* made a mild plunge, everyone flinched.

"You'll have a story for Henry," said Ethel.

"Yes." A long pause. "I think I'll soften it for him, though. I don't want him to balk when it's his turn to come home."

"Does he have a firm date in mind for the wedding? I never asked."

This was a private conversation, but the breeze was strong, so they had to be loud.

"Spring. That's all we've said. It'll depend on when the winter breaks."

"As soon as possible, then."

"That's right. I want to start on some dresses when we get home. That way I'll be ready in case he comes early."

"I'd love to buy your silk."

"You would?"

"In San Francisco. The prices will be better. More choices too."

"The Macintyres will take it personally." The Macintyres were their usual supplier, on Front Street in Selma.

"We'll give them other business." Ethel was quiet. Then a jaunty question forced itself out.

"Have you talked about the next generation?"

She answered Ethel as gently as the wind would allow. "Oh, cart before the horse, you know. I'm usually a planner, but right now I'm afraid to think that far ahead."

"That was quite a storm," Ethel agreed. "Clarence swore to Jesus Christ that if we made it to land, he'd never sail again." Quickly she added, realizing that such a plan affected Henry: "But this morning he was already talking about booking a trip in March, one with several stops. He thinks if you stay in sight of the shore, then at least you have the chance of swimming to land."

"I suppose there's logic in that."

"We talked a lot last night. Some of what we said concerns you."

"Oh?"

"We decided that, if you and Henry have a son, and you name him Clarence Jesse, we might be able to do something for you."

"I'm not sure what you mean."

"What I mean is, we could make that child our heir."

Alice was alert, awake. Four deckhands passed by, carrying loops of rope like a Christmas garland between them. She herself was balanced on a rope, this one taut, strung inches above a floor of shattered glass. The slightest misstep, a heel badly placed, would be heard, would devastate the performance.

"Clarence wants that too?"

"We talked about it last night. He wants this for me. He knows I'm telling you now."

"In that case, I'm sure Henry and I could do that. We could name a child for Clarence."

"It would be Bush and Berry blood. It would be the same as Clarence and me bringing our two families together."

Ethel's eyes were bright and thick with tears, though perhaps only as they'd been all morning, stung by the wind.

"Of course," Alice said, "it might be one girl after another. Look at us four."

"Years ago, I picked out a name for a daughter. Clarence likes it too. Melba."

"That's a lovely name." Their neighbors had once had a dairymaid named Melba Bride, with rotten teeth, but Ethel must have forgotten. She took a risk. "I can just see it. You and me drinking nice, cold teas while a whole gang of little ankle-biters play games in the grass."

"Grass? What grass?"

"A pool, then." She made a quick correction. "A real one. Sunk down. With a layer of sand at the bottom. Not an old tin tub like we had."

Little bare feet; dark heads of hair; the pale, flashing backs of knees; two matrons with vein-marbled hands flying to make a wreath of flowers stand up on a child's crown. A roof of palms, like green flags, rustling in sedate breezes, lending a comfortable, high-end shadow over the yard.

The soft flesh wrinkled, released, tightened over her sister's brow. Meanwhile Alice clasped her fingers over her chest. Her heart throbbed through four layers of wool.

I am ready for a change of weather, she thought. Clarence Jesse. Melba. You may call them whatever you'd like.

7

DAWSON CITY, YUKON

2015

My grandfather flew first-class from Los Angeles to Fairbanks. Then he chartered a four-seat Cessna to take him from Fairbanks to Dawson City.

Owen and I stood on the opposite side of the chain-link fence, sipping hot coffees, watching the sharp-nosed, silver plane make a wide loop over the town and the fir trees.

The runway was gravel, rustic, and, to my unprofessional eyes, forbiddingly short. But the plane soared down gracefully. It tilted its flaps, and with a billow of air, came to rest with forty feet to spare before the thick trunks of the trees.

The engine turned off. A door opened. A pair of long legs appeared. Then, ever so gingerly, my grandfather stepped out of the plane, gripping the handhold. He looked around, his eyes gleaming, soaking in the mountains, the trees, the air that was different from the air he had left.

Then my grandfather noticed us, and his face filled with a prideful defiance; he was like a child who's just climbed to a dangerous height, and can't believe how clever he is, and wants the world to see.

He wore a button-down shirt and blue jeans, and a large, black camera hung around his neck. We opened the gate for him and he hobbled over to where we were standing, taking hold of the fence for support.

"Aren't you ashamed of yourselves," he said, his eyes merry, "dragging an old man on a trip to the Yukon?"

OWEN STEPPED FORWARD TO LEND an arm, or at the least relieve him of the cumbersome camera. But my grandfather refused all assistance. His knees bothered him from sitting so long, but once they loosened up, he was sure he'd be fine.

We took a second to say hello to the pilot, a self-confident, athletic-looking man in his forties.

"I'm happy they put this fence up," the pilot said, shading his face above his blue-tinted sunglasses. "They've had way too many problems with wildlife here. Last year, a moose wandered onto the runway and collided with a little prop during takeoff, and the pilot was killed when the engine caught fire."

It was only then, as Owen launched into the story about our near miss with the bear, and I was looking back at the runway, imagining the collision between plane and moose, the conflagration, that I noticed there was a third person who'd been on the plane.

He was stocky, round-shouldered, about fifty, with dark hair slicked straight back on his skull. He wore a jean jacket and a large silver belt-buckle pressed into his gut.

Co-pilot, I thought.

Then I realized, with a slice of bad feeling, that this was someone I knew.

Rhett. The younger son of Wife Number Six and one of her previous husbands. I had met him on several occasions, at the large, insufferable family parties that my grandfather insisted on throwing at least once a year. Rhett was an MBA who floated among jobs and projects, chasing that elusive position that would catapult him into Steve Jobs–like preeminence. He was, in both small and large ways, a person I disliked. He was small-minded, materialistic, and coarse. He had stuck close to his mother and my grandfather since their marriage, for reasons that everyone was sure had to do with the clandestine loans they were constantly giving him. My two uncles, who also lived in the Fresno area, could not stand to be in the room with Rhett for more than a minute.

Now he was getting his suitcase, checking his phone with one hand, looking uncomfortable, as if the simple issue of when to walk over and how to announce himself was causing him great mental distress.

Was Rhett here of his own volition? I was actually beginning to sense he was not. He would have tagged along with my grandfather on a trip to New York or Vegas, certainly (I believed he'd done both), but not to some run-down old mining town turned tourist spot in the middle of nowhere.

At last, Rhett ambled over.

"You decided to come along for the ride?" I asked.

"Something like that."

"That's nice you can take vacation days on such short notice," I pressed, nettling him, not even knowing why I cared, but guessing that he was between jobs at the moment, and intent to begin with the upper hand.

"Rhett's plasma screen company didn't take off," my grandfather said. He patted Rhett's shoulder. "Some difficulties on the marketing side, wouldn't you say? Oh well. You can't win them all."

Then my grandfather turned his back on his stepson. A gesture that told me, definitively, that Wife Number Six had sent her son here against both his and my grandfather's wishes. Even in normal circumstances, she liked to keep an eye on my grandfather's movements. If he'd announced a sudden trip to the Yukon, and if she'd connected the dots back to Winifred Lowell, I could imagine the arguments and screaming and crying, and the last-ditch ultimatum that her son would go too.

WHEN YOU ARE NINETY-THREE, AND there's something you want to do, you do it. You don't give in to your granddaughter who is currently trying to slow you down, advising against barging in on your hosts. And so, following orders, I messaged Leanne that my grandfather, whose travel plans I'd already shared with her, had arrived in town, and was anxious to see them. The response came one minute later.

Of course, Leanne replied. *Come by at 3.*

When I showed my grandfather, he beamed. "See there! They're just as impatient as I am." Then he strode down the length of Second Avenue, vivacious and pleased with the world. We came upon the red building of the Downtown Hotel, where yesterday my grandfather had booked a couple of rooms. Not the Ahwahnee, by any stretch of the mind, but there was a large lobby with tall windows, and, adjacent, its restaurant, the Sourdough Saloon, the place of the famous "Sourtoe Cocktail," with the mummified, human toe in the glass. We ate a quick lunch there, where the captain's chairs and mirrored bar cluttered with bottles made me feel like I'd entered a different time. Rhett asked our waiter, a pretty woman in her twenties, about the Sourtoe Cocktail, then boasted to her, while she pretended to care, that he'd be back one night soon to give it a try.

At quarter to three, my grandfather went to his hotel room to spruce himself up, then ducked into the general market next door, reemerging with an ostentatious bouquet of pink flowers.

"Now don't go telling your mom I did this," my grandpa told Rhett. "But it would be an affront to my upbringing to arrive at a woman's house empty-handed."

What a strange parade we made, through the streets of Dawson. The same flat ground at the base of the hills, beneath the rock formations of the Midnight Dome, that had once hosted the Hän in the warmer months for the catching of salmon. It was the ground that had supported the drying racks set out along the banks, among the warmth of low, crackling fires. It was the ground that had hosted George Carmack and Anton Stander and Clarence Berry, and the other men who'd first sent out the word of gold in the country. These mud streets, in 1898, had caught the footfalls of the hundred thousand argonauts who'd arrived here, confused, beginning to sense that all was not-quite-right, perhaps as I was feeling now, like people trapped inside of a dream.

We reached the white bungalow, with its overabundance of wind chimes and painted rocks. My grandfather murmured, "Even better than what I imagined."

The door opened, and Winnie was there. Her expression curious, brazen. Her hair loose over her shoulders, her purple dress fluttering down to her ankles.

They had eyes only for one another. Peter and Winnie. Briefly, we were all brought back seventy years, to the springtime when a young woman and an American soldier went dancing in a crowded room near a Navy base in Sitka. To the era of love letters. To the time of a bygone LA that had hosted their last meeting. Then deeper still: we slipped into a subterranean world of dead faces and feelings, Bush, Berry, and Lowell, the people who—though they could not have imagined it—had laid the conditions for this present-day meeting.

My grandfather gave Winnie the bouquet. "I didn't expect to see you again."

She sniffed the flowers, then smiled and said, "I thought you were dead."

"Well, hey," my grandfather answered. "This little adventure was worth staying alive for."

At the edge of the yard, Rhett muttered something incomprehensible and looked at the sky. Leanne beamed. Then, with a gesture that included us all, she asked if we'd like to come in for iced tea.

But Winnie was not interested in this plan. "You go in, sweetheart," she said to Leanne. "I've got to make the most of this. How often do I get visitors? I'll take Peter on my usual walk."

Without waiting for a response, she led my newly obedient grandfather down the stone walkway and toward a trail that, as I'd recently learned, swooped along the bank of the Klondike River. Meanwhile Leanne, watching them go, was in battle with herself. She tugged at her pockets. She craned her neck, charting the slow steps of the couple as they disappeared around the end of the block. She'd just invited us into the house, but it was clear she didn't want to follow through on the offer.

"I think I'll just make sure they get—" she stammered.

"Should we follow them?" Owen asked, at the same time, saying what she did not want to say.

Leanne was relieved. "It's so bad. But I want to. I'm afraid that one of them is going to fall and bring the other down."

"Go," Owen said grinning, "we won't tell."

"Please," I agreed when Leanne glanced over for my opinion. "It would make me feel better too. My grandfather's knees are all out of whack from the plane."

So Leanne hurried off, stealthily, down the trail.

Unfortunately this had the effect of leaving Owen and me alone with Rhett.

"Headed back to the hotel?" Owen asked Rhett politely, as he started away.

"It's okay," Rhett answered. "Peter's not here."

"Excuse me?"

"You can drop the act. I already know about the paperwork you brought up here. Peter's trying to transfer a pretty significant amount of cash to that lady."

Owen raised his eyebrows at me. He seemed as surprised as I felt. First of all by the fact that my grandfather's secret was apparently already out in the open. And second that the anger and accusations were being directed at Owen instead of at me.

But Rhett had eyes only for Owen. "What are you doing? Taking thirty percent for your trouble?"

This time, Owen's surprise lasted only a second, and soon melted, leaving cold understanding. "I've got nothing to do with this. I'm a high school civics teacher. Not a stock guy."

"Well, it's in the blood, isn't it? Handling money?"

It seemed that Owen absorbed Rhett's meaning before I did, because he was quick to reply, now hostile: "Did you really just say that?"

"A joke." Rhett put up his hands. Then, amused by the surprise and antipathy that must have been coming off us in waves, "Jesus Christ, you people are uptight." He walked away, shaking his head, opening the long, dirt road between us.

8

SAN FRANCISCO

1898

1.

As the *Orlantha* turned toward port, Clarence Berry stood at the edge of the deck, holding the rail, the wave of his accomplishments crested at his back. His wool coat was speckled with droplets of ocean. His hat was very upright on his head. A thick, burgundy scarf protected his neck and added to his stern and serious pose. From a distance he was stalwart; valorous, even. But his mouth twitched and his body was rigid in a way that suggested a deep agitation. When he took his hands away—he was missing his gloves, and the rail was sprayed with water and freezing—they found their way into his pockets like two things that didn't know what they were. He seemed to be touching something. Again. And—yes, there it was—the flash of an envelope corner. Alice watched him, not daring to move, only sliding her eyes. Though still, he became aware of her spying, and, with a tap, the white provocation disappeared into the wool.

Earlier, down below, Alice had spotted him several times with that letter he wouldn't let go of. In his cabin. Again in the corridor. The soft paper held close to his lips. If he'd been about to take it out again, he'd thought the better of it. The letter, or whatever it was—like his problems—he would keep to himself. He would keep, for now, his thoughts to himself.

Alice breathed the sharp, freezing air. Jim was dead. Jane had run away. Soon they would be in California. The ocean journey had scraped them clean. They were free of all the bad things that had taken place in the Klondike.

Weren't they free?

But it was up to Clarence to make it so.

Finally Clarence turned his eyes to his sister-in-law, soon to be his sister twice over, and a strong current of feeling drummed the sea air in between them. A damp gust hit at an angle, interrupting the moment, and Alice was grateful for it. The cold swept the nervousness right off her face. Too much had happened between them. She couldn't tell what Clarence thought of her now.

A huddle of filthy miners shuffled by like a multilegged, multiheaded animal. Their long mustaches probed the air between passengers, as they searched the deck for a less crowded spot. Their fur bedrolls were tied to their backs, their fronts were fat with supplies. As soon as they'd moved on, Ethel appeared, which was a relief. The wool shawl Ethel had gone to fetch now covered her shoulders. Her features were clenched in the wind. She spotted San Francisco, the colorful buildings giving life to the land, and said, "Thank God." A surge of freezing water struck the hull and scattered, dousing them with mist. Clarence held one arm aloft. Ethel went to her husband and wrapped herself around his waist. He placed his chin to the top of her hat, in a simple and domestic gesture, the way one might place a cup to a shelf.

In the distance, a little tug broke from the rows of tethered vessels. A wide, arching turn, then it blazed across the flat expanse. In a matter of minutes, two men had come into focus, and into close range with the *Orlantha*, and were soon gaining permission to board.

The brown derby of the reporter bobbed between the crowds on the deck. His face appeared and reappeared, until he had forced himself to Clarence's side. Then his determined expression cracked open with joy.

"I saw your name but I didn't know whether or not to believe it. We'd expected you on the *Caroline's Pines*."

"Last minute business." Clarence accepted the outstretched hand. "One more week and we would've been stranded. Our steamer was the last boat out before the freeze."

"Well, welcome back. I hope the voyage was uneventful."

"In fact we were very nearly drowned."

"Ricky Delaney."

"Which one are you from?"

"Pardon?"

"*Chronicle* or *Call* or what?

"*Chronicle*. For sure. *Chronicle*. The good one." He laughed. "We were hoping you'd stay loyal to us and give us another exclusive."

"What more can you squeeze out of this old lemon? You printed my life story last year."

"We did, but if my colleagues will excuse me, the story had gaping holes."

"What holes?"

"For instance, we never pinned down your place of birth."

"Well," Clarence drawled, "there's an excellent reason for that, Mr. Delaney. You see, it's rather complicated. I washed up a naked infant onto the sandy beaches of Beirut, and no one quite understands where I came from."

The reporter was patting his chest for a pen, his eyes alight, before he saw his mistake, smiled, and blushed.

"You almost had me."

Ethel, speaking around the bulk of her husband, reviving her old jolly self, the self beloved by the press: "He gets that from his mother. Try showing up at her house one day if you're ever in the mood for a challenge. She invites young men like you inside for dinner, then she lights firecrackers under their chairs."

"She teases them?"

"No," said Ethel, laughing. "She hoards what's left over from the Fourth of July. She'll light an actual firecracker under your chair."

They eased a little closer toward land. Clarence gazed at the city. "Okay, youngblood," he said, "what is it you want from me?"

"How about the key to success?" Delaney had recovered from his gaffes. Now he matched the Berrys' jocular tone. "Tens of thousands go into the Klondike, five hundred strike gold, and only thirty return to California with money in tow. What set you apart?"

"Dumb luck."

"I think it's more than that."

"Okay. Dogged persistence."

"I read an interview in which you mentioned early failure as the spur in your side."

"I said that, did I?" Disingenuous, but playfully so. Clarence had said the same around campfires, around the table in the Eldorado cabin, in speeches to strangers. Delaney didn't realize his good timing. Clarence was nervous, which meant, for him, in a talkative mood. Myth, specifically, the myth of himself, was a blanket for Clarence to wrap himself up in. His hunched shoulders, his shivering corpse.

"I could make a story from that," Delaney urged. "If you would give an example."

"What shall I tell him, Ethel?"

She had a way, Ethel Berry, of melting into the spray, then reappearing, bright and clear. "How about your first winter in the Klondike? Those were hard times, if ever there were."

"That's good." To Delaney: "I don't believe your predecessor delved much into my first trip North. You'll like this. It ends with me pulling a boat through the mud with fifty godforsaken Indians."

Clarence laughed. It was a forceful laugh. One that desired to press Jim deeper into his grave.

"This was in '97?"

"No. I arrived in the country in '95. Come on now, Rick." Clarence grabbed Delaney's shoulder and gave him a shake. The young man's derby fell and hit the slick top of the railing, and only a quick response from herself, Miss Alice Bush, the silent sister-in-law, saved it from the abyss. "Clearly you grasp the concept as well as I do. One must arrive ahead of the mob."

2.

They dropped anchor, forced to wait out the gales before heading into the dock. The city of San Francisco, so beautiful, so spectacularly American, climbed the hill, and beckoning them with the open embrace of its colors. Delaney and Clarence put four chairs into a group so they could sit and talk while they waited: Delaney with his pen, Clarence with his smoldering pipe, the gray wisp of smoke no match for the ocean air, and disappearing almost on contact.

Now Clarence Berry started on the story of his success—beginning, in deference to Delaney's chosen journalistic angle, with his low beginnings, his early false starts and nadirs. He was a boy in the nascent San Joaquin Valley, at a time when it was hardly a town, and when the site was still horrifically dry. He'd missed the last years of schooling because he'd been digging irrigation canals from the mountains in order to bring water down to the farms. He'd worked alongside his father and brothers, urging from the soil grapes, oranges, lemons, peaches. The usual struggle. The family set aside enough to buy a threshing machine, and after that the Berry brothers had been put in charge of making extra money that way, taking in grain from their neighbors. At seventeen, Clarence had rebelled against his father's tyranny, and insisted on spending at least half the week working for wages, doing harvest and ranch work. He'd saved everything until he had eighty-six dollars—in that jar he'd store under his bed, he'd never forget it—with which he purchased his first eighty acres of land.

He'd done well for a while. He was on his way to being a successful young farmer. Then, at twenty-two, he'd decided to take a risk. He'd mortgaged his property and tripled his acreage. The timing was so perfectly awful that it seemed like a joke from the heavens. Because, of course, in a matter of months was the panic of '93, the worst recession America had ever seen, when along with every third business folding and the railroad industry going to pieces, all the fruit prices dropped. He could not spend one afternoon in the field with a scythe without it coming out at a loss. One night his orange trees were looted while he hid inside the shed, taking shots at the crooks from the window. He missed the thieves and killed his own dog by accident and thought that life couldn't get any worse. Next fall, five hundred banks collapsed but not the one that held his debt. He got three warnings that foreclosure was coming. He thought they wouldn't dare. He imagined they'd still have faith in him that he could turn it around once the prices bounced back. But one day, two armed riders had come out with the order to repossess his farm. He'd been forced to walk away from his fields and his little cabin, built by his own two hands. He'd thought he was the biggest failure in the world. He'd wanted to die of grief and shame. For several years he'd done day work for wages, but even then, it was still the drought, and though he said "yes" to every job, he still couldn't earn enough to clear.

At twenty-five years old, at what should have been the prime of his life, he, Clarence Jesse Berry, was run-down and completely discouraged. He would come downstairs to dinner in his parents' house, and for the entire meal he'd sit before his plate unable to eat. What could he do? His older brother Frank had been talking about Alaska, about the rumors of ancient gold buried deep in the earth. And so finally, after some time, egged on by Frank (who seemed to think it was funny to dispose of a mopey brother this way), but, more importantly, possessed by a sense of dazzling hopelessness, Clarence had decided to go.

His grubstake was ten dollars from his Pa, plus forty from a stranger who sensed promise in the reports from Forty Mile but would not go so far as to travel North himself. In the spring of 1895, Clarence arrived on the soft shores of Dyea with dried vomit stuck to his shirt and a vow in his heart never to travel by boat again. A group of Indians had just come through the little town, and all the talk was of gold dust and the nuggets in small, swinging pouches that had been pinned to the leather cross-sacks at their breast. Clarence had joined the first group of men that would have him, a motley crew of about thirty novices. They packed over the snow and glacial rocks toward the Chilkoot. When they got there, and saw the white towering precipice, the height of the summit, the party dropped to sixteen, the others having turned back with the thought of waiting for the thaw. But the rest of them, and Clarence included, dug in with picks and boots and climbed over. At first, they were pretty darned pleased with themselves. Though the good feelings ended when, on the Canadian side, on what he now believed was Lake Bennett, the floor fell out from under them and they'd lost a sled carrying half their provisions through a big crack in the ice. All but three turned back, and he, Clarence, split off from those remaining two, two brothers, at a fork in the river.

A month later, almost totally broken, he'd crawled into the mining camp, Forty Mile: he could have slept for a year but there was no time to waste. That season, seventy-three white men used Forty Mile as their base. They would march out every so often on prospecting trips. You couldn't watch three broken men hobble off across the muck and mire without thinking, damn, there's the group that's going to strike it.

Around mid-July, Clarence set off on a journey that would change his life—or at least that would bring him to the absolute bedrock of failure, and, in doing so, would finally halt his years-long drop. He had partnered with a man named Herbert Yates, a sourdough who'd lived three years in the country. They'd come thirty miles up Forty Mile creek, when Clarence, who'd been trailing Yates by about twenty feet, lost traction on a flat river boulder. He fell on his shoulder, down in the stream. For a long time, all he could see was a world of blue, and a wisp of white cloud. He called for Yates. A long delay. He called again. He said, "Goddammit Yates, I know you can hear me!" Neither friends nor even close acquaintances, it was only the thought of his name spit all over the tables of McPhee's saloon that had pulled Yates into a slow turn and down along the bank to where Clarence, dripping, had hauled himself upright. "Broken?" Yates grumbled. No, Clarence had not felt a break. But he had a problem with his left-hand shoulder. In fact the whole damn arm was lame. They built a fire and Clarence bunched close to it, making his clothes steam. But only a few minutes went by before Yates suggested an end to their partnership. He was heedful to observe that Clarence could walk without help, he just couldn't shovel. Fine, said Clarence, and Yates replied, after a pause, "You'll understand once you've been in the country longer, the summer months are precious." Fine, Clarence answered again, I said fine, didn't I? I didn't ask for an explanation.

Warily, Yates had stood, slow and long-limbed, and muttering a stiff goodbye. The two of them were distanced by several thicknesses of trees, the air sliced up by scrawny branches, when Clarence had cupped his good hand to his mouth. With a sudden and furious crack of clear voice, he'd started to sing, "We hate to see you go, we hate to see you go, we don't give a damn if you ever come back but we hate to see you go." Yates had pivoted on a heel, contemplating the man he had left. A flock of moose-birds startled to flight. "We hate to see you go! Ho! We hate to see you go! Ho!" When Yates was gone, Clarence, exhausted, had comforted himself to think: he thinks I'm nuts, he'll cut between a black bear and her cubs before he crosses my path again.

Alone, then, some days later, having made dangerously meager progress toward camp, he was on his back, hat tipped over his eyes, when he heard yelling. He'd decided to investigate, and came upon an interesting sight. There were dozens of them, split along two banks, towing a freight boat through shallow water with two lengths of rope. Their faces were painted with thick black lines to repel the sun. They wore a hodgepodge of Indian shirts, English trousers, Indian boots. Their collective stance was sturdy and simple and unobliging—even despite their predicament. A white man stood at the helm of the boat. He said, in response to Clarence's shout, that they were traveling to Franklin Gulch. I'd like to go with you, said Clarence. "Then put your grub here," said the man, "find a spot on the rope and I'll pay you a dollar." The man leered. He thought it was an excellent joke. But it would be easier on Clarence's shoulder to haul rope on his good side than to carry a pack; and he believed, probably wrongly, that the man, Finn was his name, wouldn't allow him to starve. So he threw his things onto the boat. The Indians resisted letting him in. For reasons he could not grasp, they seemed to find his presence insulting. They traveled seven miles without a break. It was hard work. Their feet sank into the muck and the boat moved with the ease of a pregnant cow through quicksand. He laughed when Finn cracked his whip and called them filthy, lazy-asses, purposely refusing to place Clarence apart from the natives.

But in that moment an important shift in Clarence's thinking took place. He was free, because he knew he could not get any lower. And also, there was something else: a knowledge that he did not belong in this deep ravine with these painted men where he had dropped himself. That it would be a sport to climb out. He grunted and sang. After the next break, he took the front end of the rope and wrapped it around his hips. Pulled. Screamed when the rope tautened and squeezed his organs. Pulled. Screamed. The Indians stopped staring at him and began to stare at each other. They said a word, like "shookadi" or "shookdee," which could have only meant "crazy."

3.

The afternoon sun poured over them. The wind finally quieted. The anchor was pulled up, the ship moved, and everyone cheered. They leveled into the dock, and the *Orlantha* was tied to the moorings. The crowd was so thick and intense in its welcome that the Berry party had to put down their heads and run to their waiting carriage. Delaney was more than happy to help, one hand to Clarence's shoulder, the other pushing the admirers back. "Make way! Give him a chance to breathe! Come on people, let the man through!"

Once ensconced in their room on the seventh floor of the Palace Hotel, the sun poured through the big bay window. Alice was amazed to be back on the mainland; amazed to have been transported—in what now felt like a breath's time—from the chilled extremities of the globe to here, the warm core of civilization. The floor was steady under their feet. The chairs did not wobble. The shouts of bellhops climbed the air. Outside, sturdy wheels pulverized the grit on well-placed stone. What country was this? It felt strange, dynamic, powerful, big. It felt like a different America than the one they had left.

In the plush sitting area, coordinated in dark red and gold, Clarence was resuming his conversation with Delaney, still trying to steady himself. He had his back to Alice and Ethel, who sat at the table, starting on all the letters they needed to write.

"A reasonable person would have let their northern excursions end there," Clarence said. "I came home to Selma in early '96 worse off than I'd left. I was dirt poor. I hadn't so much as staked a claim. But here's the trick, kid. Like I told you, I had nothing to lose. And thanks to that, my *will* had altered. I could take risks. I was ambitious again. For instance, that very spring, I had the audacity to ask the prettiest girl in Selma to marry me, and by some miracle of God, she said yes."

"And in a second miracle," said Ethel, not looking up from her work, "she agreed to return with you North for her honeymoon."

"Now we're getting to the summer when Carmack struck?" asked Delaney. "The first big discovery?"

"Exactly right. Ethel and I were in Forty Mile. But I was an idiot. Even though I was on site, I missed staking the best claims on Bonanza. I have my wife to thank that we got away with *Forty-One*." At that, Ethel laughed softly. And Clarence, heartened, said to Delaney, "You can add that to your list of ingredients. Number one, dumb luck. Number two, dogged persistence. Number three, early failure. Number four: marry a girl far smarter than you."

4.

In March of '96, Clarence and Ethel were married, and they rode away from Selma with yellow streamers tied to the back of their carriage. They arrived in Dyea by ship. They joined a group about to head North and traversed the trail with them to what is now Sheep Camp, and then, with picks and axes dug into the snow for handholds, and with Ethel, indomitable Ethel, in heeled boots and a dress, and all the men gaping at her, they hauled themselves three thousand feet into clear sky and over the top of the Chilkoot. They arrived in Forty Mile and made a home together in a drafty, crooked old cabin that had been left behind by a previous resident. The place had no windows, a dirt floor, and a fireplace that wasn't much more than a hole in the ceiling; the only decoration was a pair of broken snowshoes hung on the wall, and the only furniture a lumber platform that Ethel covered with pine boughs and fur to serve as their bed. During that summer, Clarence went out on countless prospecting trips while Ethel worked on the house, but despite their strenuous efforts, the cabin did not rise above its ramshackle state, no matter how Ethel tried shoring up the walls and the chimney, and more importantly, he, Clarence, never came home with any good news to report. By August, they had burned through their wedding money and the little that Clarence had saved working for his father the previous spring. Clarence took a job as the bartender at McPhee's, what was then the only saloon in the camp.

As it so happened, he was behind the bar, on that red-letter night when the infamous George Carmack arrived from the creeks. This was the night that had made history: when a bundled, frozen Carmack burst through the door and announced, "Fellas, it's happened! There is gold on Rabbit Creek, and I have staked a Discovery Claim. If you will all put on your coats and kindly follow me, I will lead you to the place where you may each lay claim to your fortune." Given that one of Carmack's many nicknames was "Lying George," it was no surprise that the response was open derision. They'd stopped laughing when Carmack took a Winchester shotgun shell from his breast pocket and overturned it onto the bar. Bright yellow gold poured out. Clarence would never forget the look of it. The nuggets themselves, oblong and flat, like a pinkie nail, recalled no familiar family of metal. The mood changed. Men who'd been harassing Carmack began to sheepishly gather their winter ware from the hooks. A group of three slipped away. A group of eight.

Clarence had desperately wanted to leave, but a table of Irish holdouts had refused to exit the building, therefore preventing him from closing the bar. One of them had leaned over the counter and said, "We good fellas won't be put into a frenzy by the likes of Carmack, now will we?"

It took till four a.m. before Clarence was able to get away. Back at the cabin, when he told Ethel what had happened, she was horrified. "Oh, Clarence," she cried, "this could be *it*." She'd packed his bag while he sat on the bed with his head in his hands. But he'd been right to panic; he'd waited too long. By the time he'd reached the creek, all the claims near the Discovery claim were taken, and—with the exception of Carmack's two Tagish brothers-in-law, who'd taken claims *Two* and *Three*—all by men he'd seen out of the bar. He'd had to walk up the creek from the Discovery claim past more than thirty familiar faces before he'd reached the next free spot. With an anguished heart, he'd driven his stakes into the mud and taken—as he was sure at the time and what would prove to be true—the almost wholly worthless *Forty-One* Bonanza.

"I should have given up, again," Clarence said, eyes bright now, as he relived it. "How many times can the world tell a man he's rubbish, and he refuse to listen? But I carried on. I slunk back to Forty Mile, recorded my deed for *Forty-One*, and returned to my bartending job. I was so irate with myself I wanted to die. But then," Clarence continued, awestruck by his own history, "another horseshoe turn. I happened to be serving drinks on a second crucial day, weeks later, when an Austrian prospector named Anton Stander trudged into camp and dropped down at the bar."

This Austrian had just staked a promising Discovery claim on a pup creek of Bonanza. But now, Clarence explained, Mr. Anton Stander had found himself in a terrible bind. First of all, he was down to the last of his food. Second of all, he had no camping gear to last him the winter. Third of all, he owned no digging supplies. He'd discovered the gold by tunneling into the creekbanks with rocks and with his bare hands, but to get down low enough to where the real winnings were, you needed better than that. Fourth of all, he had no credit with the Alaska Supply Company, the only place nearby with equipment. He was stuck, as Stander himself confessed to Clarence, downing another drink in a matter of seconds and wiping his filthy, glistening beard. He didn't know what the hell to do with himself, he said, or how to proceed. At this, Clarence had become suddenly alert, like he'd just woken up from a too-long dream. He looked closely at Anton Stander. It was slowly dawning on Clarence that this man was a crazy person; he had that overzealous, gleaming look in the eyes. He was far crazier than Clarence had ever been, and maybe that had been his key to success. For if Clarence had been in Stander's place, what would he have done? With the iron sky closing in? With his stomach twanging for dinner and the food bag down to crumbs? With no promise of any return from the work? He, Clarence, had not even sunk a shaft on *Forty-One* Bonanza, because the claim was not the one he'd thought he deserved. But here, Clarence had thought, was the chance to make up for it. For the amazing thing, as Clarence had explained tremblingly to Stander, leaning over the bar, was that Clarence had a solution to all Stander's problems, and for the damnedest reason too. A year ago, one of his previous mining partners, a man named Yates, had skipped out of the country without paying his debts. Because of their partnership, Clarence had felt some responsibility in the matter and, almost inexplicably, as if to spite Yates for his boorishness, had done good on some of the smaller bills. For this gesture, in a great surprise to Clarence, the Alaska Supply Company had granted him infinite credit. Now, Clarence had said, hardly able to contain his excitement, he was in the position to offer Stander an outfit, a boundless chance at supplies. The catch—the beautiful, life-changing catch—was this: Clarence would trade the food, the tools, as well as a half-share of his *Forty-One* Bonanza, for a half-share of Stander's claims on the pup.

"It was the smartest trade ever made in the Klondike," Clarence told Delaney. "Not counting the early schemes with the Indians." Then he sighed, shaking out his legs, taking stock of the opulent room. "Each time I return home, I wonder, how did I ever make it out of that godforsaken place alive? I take a hard look at my life, and I think, Jesus, it's an absolute miracle. You heard of the Palm Sunday avalanche? Seventy people disappeared in the snow before anyone knew what was happening. We were there. We'd rolled up our tents and packed our supplies. If we'd set out that morning as we'd intended, we would have been buried alive on the Chilkoot—"

He stopped, suddenly stricken, and Ethel, discomfited on his behalf, moved in her chair. "If you don't mind," she said, "I think I'll send down for our supper."

Delaney waited for an invitation, smiled into the silence, then began to gather his things. "I don't suppose I could come back tomorrow? To follow up on some of the details?"

"I'm not some old lady with a diary," answered Clarence. "I can't tell you what I ate for breakfast on the fifth of March."

"Just the same."

"If it means so much to you, kid, how about you write down your questions and slip them under the door. Then I'll do my best to answer them and send my replies to your office."

5.

Finally the door closed on Delaney. And the mood shifted. The gloominess that a stranger's company had pushed away came flooding back from the corners. Now Clarence no longer wanted to talk. He stood at the window looking at the great spread of buildings and the glittering, white-blue ocean beyond. Every inch of the Palace Hotel was designed to give a man like Clarence pleasure, but his pleasure in it had been very brief. Alice watched him, suspicious. They had left the Klondike, they'd arrived in California, but Clarence had not fully escaped, something was holding him there.

His focus roamed to the table with their accumulated mail. He went to it. He tore through paper like the parody of a man searching the snow for a tack.

Ethel broke the silence. "Who wrote?"

"A hundred morons who think I'll help them strike it." He picked out one envelope from the rest. "We also have a letter from Henry."

"You put him into a second category?" Alice quipped.

"Shouldn't you wait till you're married before you start teasing him?"

"Oh, but Henry's different," said Ethel, jumping to her sister's defense. "He likes to be teased. That's part of the reason they make such a match."

They waited while Clarence read. Then, Alice ventured, "He's well, I hope."

"Same as ever." Clarence folded the letter.

"Any news?" Ethel prompted.

"Yes, in fact. The Mounted Police met with him, and with Renoncourt and Pratt. From the witness testimony, they've ruled that I shot Jim accidentally and in self-defense."

"Good!" exclaimed Ethel. "I knew they would, but it's a relief."

"Unfortunately, they won't call off the search for Jane like I asked them to."

"Well, I'm sorry for that," said Ethel. "Her brother dying was punishment enough for stealing."

Alice could feel Clarence's gaze. "I agree," she said. "They should let her alone."

His face twitched but he didn't respond.

The sisters had their meals brought to the room. But Clarence said he wouldn't be able to sleep if he didn't get out, even just to visit the men's grill downstairs. Hours later he returned carrying the smells of smoke and meat and something more piquant; one of the eastern spices that the kitchen was known for. Now he had the late evening mail, and at the top was an unfolded paper dense with script, which he waved at his wife:

"The family wrote. Your letters crossed. Pa's on his way here with Frank and Nellie."

Ethel was shocked. "What on earth for?"

"To welcome the *Orlantha*. What did you write them in Ketchikan?"

"To stay in Selma. I said we'd be home as soon as we had our cash from the mint."

"Oh well."

"That was forward of them," Ethel remarked. "Are your Ma and Cora coming too?"

"No, just the three. I suppose they'll expect a room." Clarence sat down just as Ethel was standing.

"If I wasn't tired already, this does it." Ethel laughed. "I'm going to bed."

Clarence's face clouded with mournfulness. Had Ethel seen it, she would have returned to her spot.

"Hold on." Clarence shook the letter flat. "I didn't tell you what else they wrote. They're scheming ways to spend our money. Frank believes we should get into oil."

"They must be kidding," said Ethel.

"They're not. They leave that to Henry."

"Now I really am exhausted. Don't make me hear more. Good night, my darling," Ethel said. "Good night, Alice, love."

Clarence's gaze chased after his wife, like a small dog at the heels of its owner, then it dropped as the bedroom door closed. He opened the *Chronicle*, which Delaney had left him. He turned the page, grunted. When Poie did that, it was a signal to ask what he was reading. But Clarence, as Alice had learned after months of living with him, did not mean it as a communication. In fact, if you made an inquiry, out of politeness, he was annoyed at the interruption; other times he was surprised that he was not alone in the room.

Clarence put the newspaper down and went to the bar. The bottles clanged, the glass sparkled in the orange lamplight.

"It was nice to hear your stories again," Alice ventured. A neutral comment, for testing his mood.

He quickly countered: "You must be tired of them."

"They sound different each time."

"Why? I only say the facts. I'm not changing anything."

"I meant only, my own life changes. So I hear them differently."

He was cowed. He didn't like his own jumpiness. He lifted the brandy. "Want one?"

Her fingers pinched the air. "Maybe just the teeniest tiniest bit."

"Don't get me in trouble."

He slumped back into the chair, this time looking at her. As she sipped, wincing at the taste, she remembered the lemon juice that a Swiss family, neighbors in Selma, used to squeeze into their eyes. If it burns, they explained, it follows that there must be some medicinal purpose.

Clarence rolled the newspaper into a column and ran it up and down his leg. His mouth turned down.

"It must be hard to do interviews," Alice said. "With Jim on your mind."

No answer.

"I liked Mr. Delaney."

"Did you? I still have that chipper voice in my ear and I don't know how I'll get rid of it."

"Something's bothering you, Clarence." Alice put down her glass. "Not just Jim. Something happened afterward. You were upset all over again on the *Orlantha*."

She wasn't going to mention, yet, the letter he wouldn't let go of. On the boat, she'd thought he might be in trouble with the Mounted Police. But the communication from Henry proved that wasn't the case.

He glared at the wall. As if it were the wall that was talking. He was quiet so long that she thought he wouldn't answer her, and she was already growing resigned to the mystery. Then he said a phrase that chilled her to her core:

"I think I've made a mistake."

6.

For a moment she felt undone by his statement, flipped upside down. She thought she wouldn't be able to bring herself back to the room, but she did.

"Well, if I can help you, I will."

He scoffed. She ignored it, as if it were one of his newspaper sounds.

"You think it's your business?"

"No. I'm only offering to hear you out."

Unhappiness pulled on his face, but that was good, that was movement in the right direction. Better than irritation. He was more private a man than she gave him credit for, maybe. Though maybe not entirely by choice. Because who could Clarence turn to? Not his parents. Not his brothers. Not Ethel. He respected his wife too much to show her this ugliness. He enjoyed too much—as Alice did—the warmth of her good opinion. And yet, her goodness had rendered her useless now. That letter in Clarence's pocket. A white corner jeered at her.

"I'm surprised the information from Henry hasn't put you at ease," Alice said, pushing along. "The officials have excused your actions as self-defense. They've called the shooting an accident."

He took out his pipe. "And yet, as you well know, that cannot be the conclusion."

"Why not?"

"Because there is Jane."

A spasm over Alice's heart. She waited. When she felt she'd waited long enough, she said: "Are you going to tell me more?"

"Do you want to know?"

"Of course." A jaunty, can-do kick. "I doubt anything can surprise me, after the year we've had."

"Jane came to find me after Jim died."

"Jane came to find you after Jim died?"

Alice felt each word. And with the words, the face; the equine length, the doleful eyes. What a fool Clarence was. It had been a matter of days between Jim's dying and their leaving the country. You couldn't let him out of your sight for a second.

"I'm sure she needed money."

Clarence didn't answer.

"Or else she was threatening revenge for Jim's death. I don't blame you if you paid her off. So you gave her, what? Five hundred dollars?" She spoke with a false optimism that was, through deliberate understatement, intended to wound. "What's the loss of even a sum like that, if it bought you peace of mind?"

Again he was quiet. His gaze pooled onto her. She couldn't do it. A yoke snapped, releasing her anger.

"I wish I could go back in time and send her down a fjord on an iceberg. God, Clarence! How did you get mixed up with a woman like that?"

To her surprise, he liked the question. He seemed to think there was something in it; something that could possibly help him now. How *did* he get mixed up with that woman? How does anything happen? The truth, Clarence said, the real truth was that he'd known Jane for years, ever since his first journey North in '95, when he was a bachelor living in Forty Mile. He expected the information to shock—but no, he remembered now—she'd heard this already from Stander. As he spoke, Clarence was growing excited, giddy, almost. Delaney had opened the floodgates. But here, at last, was the story Clarence was desperate to tell.

"It was in the aftermath of that trip with Yates," he said. "After I'd hit my absolute lowest, pulling a boat with forty Indians for that slave driver, Finn. I crawled back to Forty Mile worn down but alive with persistence. The camp was a different place back then. There were not only seventy white men but also a dozen native women. We called the women 'housekeepers,' and they lived with the men who had the best provisions. They probably kept a healthy portion of those fellows alive through the winter too, as they knew how to dry the clothes and make footwear, and other times one of their brothers would show up from out of the trees to act as a guide when the hunting was hard. The thing was, Jane was one of those women. Jane, yes, Jane. The fellow she lived with was a man named Fitzwilliam."

One week, Clarence continued, he ventured out on a prospecting trip with this man Fitzwilliam. Their radical idea was that the failure to strike a rich vein around these parts was a matter of technique. Men had balked at going more than five or six feet down. But bedrock lay at twelve feet. And that was the chest they should be trying to crack. That last afternoon of their journey, they were about twenty miles from town, when they stopped, as usual, tied the dogs, and walked until they'd found a spot to try their luck with a pit. They were down four feet when it happened. Clarence was in the hole; the fire for thawing the earth snuffed under his feet, when Fitzwilliam said, with a languidness that belied the gravity of what he was saying, "It's been an hour since I heard those dogs." For a moment, they both considered it. Each unwilling to break the spell. It seemed possible that if they ignored what might be a fatal occurrence, that they could, by that refusal, erase it.

But at the tent, they faced the worst. Four dogs gone while the remaining two were decimating the tattered canvas. Fitzwilliam caught one dog and fought it. Clarence caught the other dog between his legs and beat it with his closed fists. The dog slid through, disappeared. Clarence was shaking, but Fitzwilliam steadied his anger. No more energy should be spent on punishing animals. They had no food, no shelter, no dogs to haul the sled: they had to get back to Forty Mile before the weather did them in.

At least they had their snowshoes. They buckled them on and started off. Fitzwilliam was more experienced and had to keep stopping to let Clarence catch up. Each time Clarence overtook him, Fitzwilliam said, "Your face is frozen," and Clarence found he could not move his mouth to respond. Along the final stretch, the white waterway to Forty Mile, between rows of scrawny trees, Clarence remembered the feeling of his life slowing down. Vividly he recalled the thought: *if I die it will mean I won't have to keep dragging these snowshoes*. He was almost losing sight of Fitzwilliam when they at last arrived at the familiar, trampled turn in the river. Forty Mile. They did not say a word, but entered the jumble of huts and cabins, and hurled themselves through the door of McPhee's.

"Charivari!" That was the startling shout that had greeted them as they crashed into the warm saloon. A dozen men jumped out of their seats and rushed them like a final blast of wind. "Charivari! Here's Fitzwilliam, here's our boy!"

At first Clarence did not understand. A charivari was a form of harassment. A mob would surround the cabin and bang on the windows and doors of whatever person had broken a sacred rule: failed to share a bounty of meat, for instance, or claimed poverty while hiding provisions. But finally Clarence comprehended. This was the rule that had to do with women. The news was that, while he and Fitzwilliam were gone, a man named Cam Cronister had wooed Jane away from Fitzwilliam's cabin. The other men had been waiting for this, for Fitzwilliam's return, and now they wanted him to throw back his drink, shake out his gloves, and lead the march to reclaim his woman. Fitzwilliam, pink with cold, now pink from attention, agreed to the scheme. A mile ago, he was almost dead, yet one minute inside, and he was thawed out and healthy. Clarence looked at McPhee, trying to get his mouth to form itself around a word, though before he could manage it, McPhee said, quietly: "Clarence, your face is covered in blisters."

"Charivari!" Fitzwilliam yelled, slamming his emptied glass to the table. "Everyone get a pot and a spoon and meet me at Cronister's door!" Clarence touched swollen fingers to the sides of his nostrils, felt delicately along his cheeks. On the left side, there was a crater: hard, coarse, like a slab of dead animal flesh. The room emptied. Ignoring McPhee's protestations, he joined the tail. His boots followed the ruts in the snow. His knees were quivering. What had he done to himself? He felt a rush of tender feeling for his poor and unloved body. Tonight he would cherish it. He would feed it tea and bacon and the last can of peaches. He would build the fire high.

The gang had gathered around Cronister's hut, stealthy, except for the giggling. Fitzwilliam signaled with his fingers, one, two, three! Then, in the freezing quiet: an explosion of life. They banged pots and sang "I Want My Little Baby Home," which was the song they'd agreed on at the saloon. Through the misting snow: a second ruckus. A new group had gathered at the cloudy hunk of ice that served as the window. "Look, look! That's her naked! Look there and you can see her ass!" Five big men broke down the door and reemerged into the frigid air with a raving and half-dressed Cronister mounted high on their shoulders. "To McPhee's!" yelled Fitzwilliam, pointing, and as they passed Clarence, Fitzwilliam yelled at him: "I thought I was raising hell to get her, now I see I am raising hell to be rid of her!"

The party trampled away, leaving Clarence alone. He peered into the cubby of warmth. Then, emboldened, he walked around the outside of the hut and got a full view of her through the still-opened door. Long-limbed. Straight-spine. Her breasts low on her chest and pointed. She was digging under the blanket for what—her clothes—but unhurried, as if she were punishing herself with the cold. Clarence felt something familiar in her expression: the agitation of being put in a place you didn't belong. Like how he was stuck among this horde of cruel and restless men, when he felt in his heart that he was better than all of them.

He felt, at that moment, before he knew her name, that he and Jane were kindred spirits. Both beaten down, both in possession of a secret intelligence. He moved his scarf to say something, but all that came out was a little cloud of arctic nothingness. Jane sensed his presence. Her arm shot out for a fur robe and she wrapped herself in it.

She would have had nowhere to go. So he offered her—in clumsy slurred words—a night's stay in his cabin. Usually he had nothing to do with women. But he was still riding the energy of his own survival, and, in retrospect, it may have been the fact of his frostbitten face that made him brave. If she'd refused, he could have said it was his temporary ugliness that she was rejecting. But as it turned out, she didn't refuse. She swept herself into a standing position and agreed to the plan with all the whimsy and confidence of a fine lady agreeing to lunch. A rabbit snare she packed into a beaded bag along with a stinking sack of dried fish.

The two of them lived together a month. Happy and fine. Fitzwilliam didn't want her and neither did Cronister, and the others found it an unremarkable arrangement. Clarence was poor, and so it was only natural that he should draw from the base of the heap.

7.

Clarence sucked his pipe, breathed smoke onto the gold and maroon wallpaper, making swirls. He had trailed off. If there was more, he seemed content to relive it inside his own head.

"Look at you," said Clarence. "Staring at me with those beady eyes."

"I thought I couldn't be surprised, but I am. I didn't know Jane was like that." Or, Alice thought, that you were like that.

"Because she was good at hiding it. You disliked her so much, you never gave her due credit. You wouldn't have thought her capable turning herself into a civil young lady, after a low life in the camps."

Alice picked up the sewing that Ethel had left draped on the chair: a calico dress with a hem that had been raised for the snow, now half-restored to its original length. Religion works like this, she thought, it preys upon the pleasure of confession. The stitch resumed, a bloodred line. She kept working although she knew she was taking work from Ethel. It didn't matter, wealthy or poor, a person liked something to do with their hands.

"You brought Jane into our home. I don't understand you."

"There's more to the story."

"Nothing can justify insulting my sister like that. It's outrageous."

"I never did wrong by Ethel. I would never risk her well-being to lift Jane up."

"Oh really? Where was Jane the night you caught Jim?"

"Ah." His fingers brushed the furniture. The rise of a threatening grief.

"You're thinking of Jim. But the law called you innocent. I wish you'd be innocent in your own head too."

"You didn't see a bullet blow through Jim's head."

His eyes watered. His fingers moved to his temples, dragging the flesh.

"Did you let Jane get away?" she asked, looking into her lap, while her silver needle darted along its path. "Did you find her in the woods and make a lazy search?"

"So what if I did?"

"Because it emboldened her. It made her brave. If you were willing to help her when Jim was alive, when she was in the midst of robbing you, then what great things would you be willing to do for her now?"

"She's had a hard life."

"Many people have had hard lives. Our own families, God bless them, have had hard lives. The admirable ones don't use it as an excuse for later grabbing whatever they want."

His face was wan. His eyes met her lifting eyes, no doubt as beady as before. Exhaustion, perhaps, was creeping in, because everything about him was soft and round and vulnerable, except his suspicion. His Irish gaze narrowed to crescents. He said, as he had said in the Klondike:

"Just what are you after?"

The lamp flickered and died. They were more intimately connected than two bodies wrapped limb-to-limb in bed. She stood and, taking her time, relit the wick. It was a pretty lamp, with a white china shade and green glass prisms dangling from the rim, which sparkled and danced in the glow.

"I want to know what happened to Jane the night Jim died."

"Ah."

"Did you let her get away or not?"

"Who am I? To do a thing or not to do it."

People with too much money spoke this way, in this injured tone. They liked to pretend they were helpless, that others overestimated the breadth of their control.

"I had feelings for her," Clarence said. "I won't lie about that. I'm not ashamed of being a man. And all that comes with it."

"I'm surprised I didn't pick up on it sooner. Your feelings, I mean." Light, inconsequential sounds, like insect wings, her own small deceptions. "Usually I'm very attuned to the little—I'm not sure what to call them—the little signs between people. Whether they like each other or not. Whether they have a history together or not. So Ethel—"

"She doesn't know. And I trust you won't tell her."

"You know I would never."

"I know." He sucked his pipe. If he wanted to act like this, like friends, like confidants, she was not going to stop it. He was enjoying it, anyway. Every minute he seemed to be daring himself to tell her all. "You and I have that in common," he said. "We'd never risk Ethel's unhappiness. You heard already what I agreed to—regarding you and Henry—making your child our heir. All through that storm coming home, it was the only thing your sister could talk about."

"Lucky I got my chance with Hen. I was sure Jane was going to steal him away from me."

"My brother was never going to marry Jane. That wasn't going to happen." He spoke with disgust; he registered no hypocrisy in his behavior.

She could picture Clarence coming upon Jane in that cabin in Forty Mile. He, half-asleep with death; she, hot, ignoble, seducing.

"You liked her though."

"Like I said. She has attributes every man likes."

"Remember that I'm not yet married."

"Oh, what's this?" he sneered. "You're just a kid now, are you?"

8.

He hadn't expected to see Jane again, Clarence continued. Not after the winter of '95. It seemed important to Clarence that he tell Alice that. When he'd come back in the spring of '96, he went on, his voice hushed and hoarse but determined, he'd had Ethel with him, and the Indian girls would slink away in one dreary clump of brown hair and brown fabric whenever they spotted them coming near. That fall, he and Ethel had built their cabin on Eldorado, and moved out to the creeks. Imagine his shock when one morning he went to Anton Stander's cabin, knocked on the door and yelled for his partner, and when the door flew open: there stood Jane.

"Hello, C.J.," she'd said, with no hesitation, no emotion.

"What the hell are you doing here?"

She'd shrugged and looked askance with infuriating nonchalance.

"You're keeping house in this shack, are you? I should have guessed you'd end up here by your taste in men. First Fitzwilliam, now Stander. You like them broad-shouldered and mean."

"Tony's sick today."

Perhaps she'd meant to explain why she was the one holding a snare, about to go out. Perhaps she'd been spitting lines that Anton Stander had fed her.

"Tell him from me that drinking less whiskey might relieve his symptoms." Briskly, she'd closed the door behind her and walked up the hill. He followed her. She stopped to fix the wire for the snare, and into this gesture he'd read another shrug. "I hope he doesn't let you drink. If I see it, I'll report you both." That same defiant look from when she was naked in Cam Cronister's cabin. This particular provocation of hers: of a woman refusing to be fearful in a situation in which she should be fearful. The temptation was to punch her in the face as a corrective. Instead, he showed restraint, and kicked the snare out of her hands.

Jane rose. Limber as a sapling tree. You could tie her into a knot before she cracked.

"This is Tony's claim."

"No ma'am. You're mistaken there. I own fifty percent of everything I see."

"Oh, is that so?"

"I am here with my wife," Clarence continued. "If you see her out on the claim, you make yourself disappear."

"I don't get to meet her?"

He spoke with full-bodied authority: "Don't make me tell you again."

But his bravado was false. As soon as his back was to Jane, he could feel the collapse within. He'd been miserable, terrified. He didn't care if Jane had ended up with Stander, but he didn't want her on the claim so near Ethel. What if Jane sought out Ethel at the well, at the creek, and whispered some foul and invidious comment into her ear, just for the fun of stirring the pot? And the worst was that, the more he interfered, if he threatened Jane, for instance, more than he already had, it might only rile her up, and hasten disaster. He didn't think Stander knew he had a history with Jane. But if it slipped, if Jane said something incautious, then that was trouble. Stander was a man without sense. He might start an argument over sordid, bachelor matters for all the world to hear, for Clarence's sweet-mannered wife to hear. Ethel, back then, who was as healthy as anyone, strong as an ox and red in the cheeks, as if from the broad strokes of a paintbrush. She'd been the first white woman in the region and all respected her for it: her husband included. Back at the cabin that day, he'd told her in a broken, trembling voice to stay away from the cabin on *Six*, using Stander's dubious reputation as his excuse. But one day as Ethel composed a letter, she had felt him reading over her shoulder and smiled.

"You'll notice I left out mention of the girls," she'd said.

"What girls?"

"The Betty Mae Saloon girls were on the creek today looking for lonely men. They made a wide circle around this house, because they know a wife lives here. Maybe that's why you missed catching sight of them."

What a strange and quiet pride she took, Clarence remembered thinking, in the respect afforded to her by prostitutes. He thought his heart would break from love.

"But I'm worried for them. I believe they doubled back to Anton Stander's place. Won't the squaw get angry with them and scratch out their eyes?"

"You've noticed the squaw?"

"Yes. I thought it must be. Though I've only seen her from a distance."

"Maybe I'll go have a look."

Ethel, shocked: "You can't barge in on a scene like that!"

"Then I'll take a quick walk to the digs and rescue any blind dance-hall girls wandering too close to the creek."

Bright night. The moonlight pooling across the wide smooth snow. The spruce log cabin radiated with life. The window blazed green. It was constructed from five empty bottles lined up in a row; but it seemed otherworldly, like a smudge of aurora borealis brought down onto land. What would the world be without men like Anton Stander? You needed outrageous people like him. They might be hell to live with, worse when they were your neighbor and business partner, but hadn't there been nights he'd slept well, knowing that Stander was in hearing range? That should the dogs start howling, Stander would strut from *Six* to *Four* out of pure, dumb curiosity? And if, on the way, Stander happened upon a Dawson drunk with a knife in his hand, or a raving bear, or a raving, drunk Indian—that Stander would have throttled the man, the animal, without a thought to his own safety or the law?

Clarence reached the cabin and heard the noises of a party inside.

What does a man do with an Indian housekeeper and four prostitutes inside his house? If it weren't for Ethel waiting for him, he admitted he would have liked to go in and see. Figures crossed and re-crossed the small green window. Clarence pointed his gun at the stars just over the roof. He fired, making the girls scream. Again. They shrieked. That was all. He went home to Ethel, believing he'd made his point. In fact, shooting at them had apparently been too subtle a message. Because minutes passed, morning came, and the party raged on.

By mid-June, Clarence had washed his digs on *Four* and *Five* and had two hundred thousand dollars after expenses to travel home with. Though it wasn't yet settled, he was optimistic that Henry could come North to winter on the claim, while he and Ethel recovered for a season in California. The house was packed and the trails were passable. So he'd told his friend Ed Keller, Ed who was now Daisy's husband, and who was still in the country then, to take Ethel ahead to Dawson, and he would meet them there. He himself had a private chore. Stander had left for the mainland too, but his cabin still puffed with smoke in the evenings, and scurrying tracks appeared in the mud.

The roof sagged at its center point, the wood waterlogged and rotten. Clarence kicked open the door. Inside he found the rank of dried fish and beaded mukluks lined up in a corner. Her tolerance for smoke was astounding. The pipe was half-blocked and the air was thick with particles, almost thick enough to knock him back. She rose from where she'd been on the floor, a fur robe enveloping her up to the neck. She was saved from debasement only by her expression, which was one of simple surprise.

She asked him to sit; he did.

He said: "How does Stander treat you? Well?"

She shrugged. It was a motion made small by the voluminous coverings.

"Not well enough to take you traveling."

She made an expression of disgust: as if to make believe that the offer had been there, and she'd refused it.

"I need you to clear out of here," Clarence said. "In a couple of months,

I'll have a bachelor brother wintering on this claim. And our mother would faint dead on the floor if she got wind of an arrangement like this."

From his pocket, he lifted a pouch of pay dirt and tossed it onto the bedstead, where it landed on the outer edge. She walked to him. Stuck out her hand from between her robe and placed it on his arm. Forty Mile rose into being. Like she was performing a spell. She, naked and surrounded by leering men; he, at the open doorway, disfigured and amazed. The pouch tipped and fell. The noise startled them both. He pulled away from her, took three steps, and retrieved it. He placed it into her palm. Her long fingers closed around the material, with the possessiveness of spider legs around a fly.

While he was crossing the threshold, he heard her overturn the pouch and dump the gold-flecked gravel onto the floor. He turned and watched as the hope and the covetousness dropped from her face.

"It isn't enough," she said simply, before he could leave. "You've seen the prices in Dawson."

He thought he'd lose his mind; he was so angry.

"You have some mouth on you, don't you?" he said. "That's what I have to give you. You're welcome."

And apparently, she was capable of reason, because the next day, without a noise or a sign, the woman was gone from the claims.

9.

"Tell me that's the end of it," said Alice.

Clarence shrugged.

"If you were so intent to keep Jane away from Ethel then why did you ever let her back in our lives?"

"I didn't mean to. It all got out of hand."

"You regret it? You really do?"

"Of course I do. Every nice thing I ever did for them, every nice thought I had, came back to bite me. Like how it was stupid hopefulness that made me think it was Frank stealing the gold, instead of Jim. And then what happened? It gave Jim the wrong idea. Because maybe Jim and Jane took it as deliberate on my part, as a sign of my permissiveness. Jim took to believing that I was soft. He stole too much. Then Jane stole Ethel's collection of nuggets, which was the final straw. They got too confident. So once I'd realized it was Jim, even once we'd caught him and arrested him, Jim wasn't properly scared of me, and he went for my gun."

Her voice dropped. "I still don't understand why, after you kicked Jane out of Stander's house, that shouldn't have been the end of it."

"You do know. Because of Jim."

10.

It wasn't his fault, Clarence said. He simply could not get away from them. At first Jane and Jim had not made known their connection. And Clarence never would have dreamed of linking the girl that he knew with the packer he knew. But when they'd landed in Dyea this past spring, Jim had walked out of the shore mist like an apparition and all of that changed.

"Need a packer?"

"Not yet. Not till the Chilkoot."

"Berry?"

His gaze refocused, from the distant nothing to the blazing whites of these eyes: "That's right."

"Don't you remember me? I packed for you over the Chilkoot in '96."

"That's right. You're the fellow named Jim."

"I know you from my sister too."

"Who's your sister?"

"Jane. She said she knew a miner named Berry. I said I knew him too. She said that you would pay me well. She said your claims are some of the best in the Klondike."

"She told you that? Well, isn't that something."

His pipe, which he had thought to smoke on the walk back to the shore, as a little gift to himself after the rough days at sea, made a soft landing into his pocket. What could he do? He couldn't ignore Jim. They needed a packer and it would insult him if now Clarence hired a less qualified fellow.

"What's your rate?" he grumbled.

"Nothing you can't afford."

A stranger in chaps, passing on his way to the boat, patted Jim's shoulder. "Here's a good fellow. A worthless customer. But a good fellow."

"He owns the saloon," Jim explained. "I don't drink."

"I should think you don't. Okay, Jim. I guess this is your lucky day." He handed over the bundle of sugar, light as it was, already feeling defeated. "Where is Jane these days?"

"She has a room in the prospector's town, at the meeting of the two big rivers."

Dawson, he meant. The place of a stomped-down fishing camp, under the watch of incinerated ancestors' graves. That was a sign of defiance, on Jim's part. The Indians didn't like to acknowledge the town's permanence by speaking its name.

11.

The door handle turned and the hinges creaked, startling Clarence, startling Alice. Ethel appeared in her nightgown, looking stunned by the meeting she'd interrupted. She had been alone, just out of sleep, and for that reason, maybe, she was guileless, and all her surprise showed on her face. Only slowly did her feelings sink down to account for the company, and her face readjust to a more sociable expression.

"Look at you. A couple of night owls."

"We woke you," said Clarence, mournfully.

"I was just rolling over. But then I didn't know where I was. I thought, not the cabin. Not the boat. I was confused. And I suppose it was the confusion that woke me."

A retreat was possible now. She could take a sip of water, eat a cookie, and be gone. But she lingered. She teetered in the doorway, her eyes roving the table, the chairs, looking for clues. She sensed something improper between her husband and sister: she could taste it in the air, though for the life of her she couldn't guess what it was.

The family had two connecting apartments. Because Alice was a young woman alone, they left the door wide open between them. At her back, after she'd said her good-nights, she could hear Ethel and Clarence speaking quietly together, and Clarence pouring yet one more drink to take into bed. She turned and was in time to watch a dim golden light switching to black. It was strange to think of her brother-in-law, that he hadn't wanted to be with his wife. He'd rather have kept talking with her.

Her bedroom was like a little jewel box: salmon-colored paper, striped with silver; a compact chandelier on a short chain dangling from a plaster medallion. The bed was puffed up like a cloud. In her bed in Placer County, when she was a little girl, the freezing eddies had swirled through the gaps in the logs and iced her in sleep. In Selma, her bed had one thin pillow and a hard middle that had been worn out for a decade. She felt more at home here. How easy it was to adjust to extravagance.

From a cedar drawer, Alice took her nightgown; let it fall down her body from throat to heels.

She lay down on the bed, awash in thoughts of Jane and Jim. If she were Jane, or not *Jane* the woman but *Jane* the situation, would she have conspired with a brother to pick gold off the claim like that? Yes, yes. It was too easy. In an instant, she could feel herself swooping across the gravel banks, restoring to herself what the others had dared to call *mine*.

A strange way to build a country, this, Alice thought further, turning so that she could see the remaining points of city lights out the window. And that was a problem. England, Ireland, France, Italy, China, and Japan: they had grown up from a seed in their own earth. In Europe, they formed their borders by bumping against one another for a thousand years. True, she had heard of Englishmen and Frenchmen who could not sit down at a table together without showing their teeth. But it was different. Dogs snapping at dogs. A matched pair, those countries, practically in love with each other. Not like this. Here the ghosts walked with the living. They edged between tree trunks and skipped along the banks of good rivers. They held a deck of cards in their teeth, a deck for fortune-telling, these shadows like Jim. It was a problem of birth. A problem in the way that America had built itself up. No easy, concentric rising here, like the measured and ordered birth of a tree. In America, you put out your hand and leveled the land. You took a step, like Johnny Appleseed, and something springy and green grew in the wake. You moved your family fifty miles toward the sunset, and you did it with a plan in your head. You could not countenance those who wanted to stop you. Nor could you mask their blood hatred beneath the scent of fresh sawdust and paint.

It was a common thing now, in the East Coast cities, or so the newspapers told them, to fall over oneself in grief for the Indians. But it was only possible on *that* side of the country—and nearly the whole of Selma felt this way—because the Indians there were already exiled or dead. And even then, it seemed a dubious sentiment, like a person who claims to regret their own birth. The murmurings in California were thick with suspicion when it came, for instance, to the good hearts of New Yorkers and Pennsylvanians. Because to what degree can a person, a country, regret its own origin, before the feeling turns insincere?

12.

The published number from the mint—the gossip was that Clarence Berry had just exchanged five hundred thousand in gold—had done strange things to the clock. Not only had the Berrys arrived from Selma with impossible speed—it had not been a full week since the Bush-Berry's grand return—but the family seemed to have aged backward several years to a vigorous youth. They came thundering down the hallway. "Guess who?" was the taunt at the door. Then Pa Berry burst into the room and shimmied out of his jacket and tossed it over the back of a chair. Given his grin, given his vanity, you could have mistaken him for thirty, if not for the two adult children emerging from around his back.

"Look at you!" cried Nellie at Clarence. "You've tanned up just like a Christmas turkey. Didn't anyone tell you to wear your hat?"

Clarence kissed his sister's cheek. "Careful," he said. "Or I'll return all your nice gifts to the store."

"He's not so bad," said Frank. "You should see some of the lobster faces that pass for human up North. You know," he addressed the silent group scornfully. "Sunburned. Pink and hard."

"Pardon you," said his sister.

Clarence, letting Nellie go, grabbed Frank's shoulder and gave him a squeeze. The last time they'd been together, Clarence had been dismantling Frank's camp and Frank had been yelling that he was no thief. They'd heard through a neighbor that Frank had stayed in the country after the showdown for another several weeks. He'd joined a meandering prospecting group and sunk muddy holes all down Bear Creek before running out of provisions. In Dawson, he'd spent what money he had in saloons, and on the girls who lived on Paradise Alley, behind the main drag, though what details reached Eldorado were mostly kept from Alice's hearing. They knew Frank had left Dawson in mid-September because he'd charged his fare to his brother. From Dyea, he'd traveled to Seattle, then Selma, where he'd broadcasted his high moral character by helping his Ma and Pa on the farm, and likely spent long days nurturing the gift from Clarence of having been falsely accused.

Now the younger brother forced a serious mood. "I owe you an apology, Frank."

"You've already said. I never got to the end of your letter, it was so long."

"Yes, but I want to say it in person too. I don't know how I could accuse my own brother of stealing. I'm ashamed. I hope I can make it up to you one day."

Frank, his indignity flowing back: "I'll never understand how you could point a finger at me when that crooked old Indian was there all the time. It was probably Henry who spoke against me."

"No, I take the blame alone. I was suspicious of everyone."

Frank moved, causing Clarence's hand to drop. "Don't fret. I don't hold a grudge."

"You should save your mea culpa for Ma," Nellie advised. "You were worried Ma would be upset with you for accusing Frank, but it was quite the reverse. We explained to her that Frank was falsely accused. We even showed her your letter. But she only says, I know my son."

Frank swatted the air at his sister, while Pa Berry was discomfited. Pa, an oldest son himself, persisted in his opinion that the firstborn should have the respect of his siblings. A decade ago, Frank indeed had commanded a certain regard. But the positions had shuffled, and not in Frank's favor, which Pa found disturbing.

And it didn't stop there, Alice silently noted. Everyone was trying to gauge where they stood. Words were thrown out like flags into wind. You could gather clues by how far your opinions carried, and in what direction. Where exactly were they absorbed or rebuffed? Or did your own statements return to you, to slap you in the face?

Ethel emerged from the bedroom, her sober expression under a layer of powder.

"Ah," said Pa. "Here's a sight for sore eyes." He took Ethel's hand while she tilted her cheek for a kiss.

"You had us all worried, my dear."

"Thank you. I'm doing quite well now."

"You're looking dandy today."

Ethel laughed. "In this dreadful thing? We've written to Moie to send our wardrobes from Selma. Then Tot and I will go out and spoil ourselves with a fresh dress or two."

"I wish Cora were here," said Pa. "You may take Nellie shopping with you, but Cora would have really enjoyed it." He meant to assert the Berrys over the Bushes, by mentioning his pretty daughter. But Cora was a dull and pious woman whom nobody liked; and it was only Nellie who lost animation and blinked.

"You left Henry in good spirits?" Frank asked Clarence.

"With Henry, is there another option? But yes," answered Clarence, "I did. And with good reason. The cabin's a cozy den. The kitchen is stocked with three thousand pounds of food."

"In a month," said Frank, "he'll crawl into Dawson and tell the whole town how his brother left him to starve."

"How long do you plan to keep him there?" Pa asked.

"He'll take the first steamer out of the country in spring. That will be May, most likely."

"What'll they work, *Three?*" asked Frank.

"Upper *Six*, Lower *Four*, then *Three*."

"You think they can do all that in a winter?"

"No, frankly. But don't you go slipping negative talk like that into a letter to Henry. Hey!" said Clarence, clapping his hands, addressing the group. "Important question. Shall we stay in for lunch or go out? If we go out, here's your warning, you'll have to share me. I can't sit down for a smoke without three fellows toppling over themselves to give me a light."

Ethel, subdued: "In. Please. So Tot and I can join you. We can't go out in our Klondike dresses. You boys can try the Three Muses for supper."

"Good," said Frank. He spoke in such a way as to overcome Clarence. "Because we have sensitive business matters to discuss."

"Now why does that send a bolt of fear through my heart?"

"Listen to him," admonished Pa. "You don't know because you've been away. But all the talk in California has moved from gold to oil. Frank's been meeting with a fellow named Murphy, who we were lucky to get on our side. He's an experienced advisor who knows everything there is to know about oil, and for a reasonable fee can point an investor like you in the right direction. He already has several leases for you to consider. There are two very promising companies—Sunset Oil and a partnership, Jewett and Boggart—which both are getting off the ground as we speak. They like Murphy and they are ready to talk with you."

"Ah yes," Clarence said gently. "You mentioned that in your letter."

"I've been doing some scouting work on my own," said Pa, taking over the room. "Last month I rode out across the desert rim in Kern on a whim. I was in the middle of nowhere, when out of the blue appeared this flock of Basque sheep with their hooves blackened as if by tar. I flagged down the shepherd and asked if he'd mind telling me where it had come from. He was very obliging, very glad for the company. He led me a little way back to a stump, where there was oil seeping from under the ground. I say you mention that to Murphy."

"Well, it does sound interesting." A light and inattentive tone, though too subtle a discourtesy for the detection of Frank and Pa. "Give me a chance to reacclimatize myself to society, then I'll look into it. I have to remember how to hold my fork and knife before I sit down to a meal with fancy fellows like these."

13.

Lunch arrived, rolled in on trays. The room rearranged itself, and Clarence drifted over to stand with the women. Perhaps at one point he really had looked forward to seeing his family. Perhaps he'd thought it would be a welcome distraction. If so, he was rethinking that now. The Berrys took quick stock of the food. Their gazes tallied the cold ham and beef and olives and peppered soft cheese with a smear of plum topping; the mussels submerged in a red wine broth and puffing with steam. Every purchase was a message. How close would the fortune be kept to the breast? Clarence had planned it well: no one could fault the food, and yet he'd left the full extravagance of the Palace kitchen untested. Five good wines but no champagne. Three waiters began making plates. The mood lifted with the final reveal of the lamb, with its trembling, crescent edge of mint jelly.

"I'm telling you, the future's in oil," Frank said, settling down with his food. "You don't want to sit pretty on your laurels and miss this. Like Pa was saying, the question is going to be, who has the foresight to buy up the land? It's like the goldfields all over again. Even the Indians knew about it first. Isn't that funny? That's like the goldfields too. Once when one of the teams was drilling a hole, they hit on a Yokut coffin box, a truly ancient thing. When they forced it open, they found the face of an old man perfectly preserved in an asphaltum coating."

"And what are the present uses?" asked Clarence. "Who are the buyers, besides the Yokuts?"

"The market is just coming into existence," said Frank, now with suspicion. "That's what's so grand. And new uses keep popping up every day. You can use it in place of kerosene. You can put it inside an ink bottle, and I've heard that it writes very fine, and keeps its black color. People are putting it down on the roads. There's a small complication with the oil splattering up, and destroying the wheels and the tops on the carriages. But probably it's only a matter of bringing the oil down to a thicker consistency. As a lubrication, it's simply unmatched. For wheels, machines, anything like that. But the real excitement is the chance to put it in engines. Murphy says he's been hearing whispers among the railroad companies, who've become apprehensive with the poor supply of coal. And then there's the automobiles. You might think they're just a passing fancy, but I'll tell you, these companies are doubling their sales by the day. Everyone who can afford it wants in. People dream of zooming from one place to the next, of piling in behind a steering wheel and racing each other down roadways. Refining the oil in large quantities will be a trick and a half. But as for the profit, look at men like Vanderbilt, Carnegie, and imagine yourself in their place."

"What do you say, C.J.?" Pa demanded. His middle son was sedate, head leaning back, closing his eyes.

"Hold on," Clarence said. "I'm still imagining."

Frank and Pa each recoiled a bit. They were dogs on a leash, attached to an unworthy owner.

"Are you there?" Frank asked. "Or have you fallen asleep?"

"Oh, give me some credit," Clarence said, opening his eyes. "I can listen and think at the same time. But honestly, despite the pretty picture you paint, I'm not sure about this. I thought I was done with the desert. When I look in the mirror today, I see a Klondike sourdough in a fur coat, holding an ice pick."

"And here I assumed you draped sheets over your mirrors, to keep from scaring yourself in the night."

Clarence's glass hit the table askew and splashed. He turned to face

Nellie, who was next to him on the couch, at the same time turning his back on his brother.

"All right, Nellie," Clarence said. "Let's settle this once and for all. You're the only one I trust. Tell me honestly, how do I look?"

For a second Nellie didn't know what to do. Then, with a small twitch of a smile, she started singing under her breath, "Old gray mare she ain't what she used to be, ain't what she used to be . . ."

Clarence clasped his sister's shoulder. He tipped his head backward and laughed.

14.

The confetti welcome was over. It had been almost eight months since Clarence had been with Pa Berry and Nellie in Selma. It was three months since he'd falsely accused Frank of stealing gold from the claims. But he showed no inclination to make up for lost time with his family. Instead—and who would have guessed this, given his previous treatment of her—he wanted to be only with Alice. Alice, it turned out, was indispensable. Alice was the person who understood him best.

In the dead hours between lunch and the pouring of cocktails, he succeeded in maneuvering his blood relations, even his wife, into their rooms. He sought out his sister-in-law the way a young man seeks out his girl. But he didn't want her for her small waist, her pert and pushed-up chest, her nice, dark eyes. All he wanted from her was her ears. A quiet lobby made a ring around the topmost floor. Little chairs scattered across the bright empty balcony. Like secret lovers, she went there on his cue, and he followed her after ten minutes. She was glad to do it. She'd been afraid in the Klondike that she'd pushed too hard, and that she'd been forever repelled. But somehow she had arranged things better than she had even realized at the time. The wall of politeness had collapsed. The violence and accusations and high emotions had cleared the way for this closeness.

A great glass roof rose at sharp angles. A waiter took their order for drinks, and then went seven floors down to fill them.

He should have walked away from Jim, Clarence confessed to her, already breathless, already sweating—his elbows resting on his thighs—when Jim approached him in Dyea. Of course, that was clear to him now. He had taken her, Alice's, point more than he'd ever admitted about Jim saving their lives in Sheep Camp only because his future prospects benefited from a long-term acquaintance. He'd even tried to shake Jim when they got to Dawson, suggesting a lumberyard job, but Jim had been resolute, wanting to work on the claims. He'd given in, and soon Jim had blended in with the workers, causing no trouble, and so Clarence had chosen to forget his worry and move on with his life. The trouble only came later, when they hit that bad stretch, in the aftermath of Ethel's collapse. They were both exhausted then. She, Alice, could remember this low and tumultuous night as well as he did; when she'd promised him a hot pigeon pie then forgotten. Next day, he'd blustered out of the cabin with his pockets low and heavy and knocking his legs, filled with gold nuggets. He hadn't known what the hell he was doing; only that he needed to *hire* someone who would make his life easy again, who would make his wife *well*. A cook, yes. He had in mind his own childhood nurse, an ancient woman with no family who once had boiled a slab of beef with onions and carrots and fed him spoon by spoon and saved him from a dangerous fever. His goal had propelled him nineteen miles through the snow, with his head ducked into the wind, like a bullet in a wide-brimmed hat.

But Clarence's hopeful feelings had died with the journey. When he'd arrived onto Front Street, the noise and hubbub of the place had crushed them. Where to start? With the woman behind the lemon stand, or with the lemons themselves, forty cents a fruit, for their antiseptic properties? Or perhaps he should make first for that laundry sign? To recruit the stalwart lady standing beneath it? A boat had just come in with live chickens, and he thought he'd better quit with the women and go for the birds. He had thought that, once he'd arrived into Dawson, he would know what to do. That the town—so alive, so full—must possess an obvious panacea. The problem was, he was a country boy. He believed too much in cities, and what they could do for him. Come here desperate, though. Come here in need of help. You picked up the thing you've decided to buy—a skinny corked bottle of green-and-purple herbs from the apothecary—you twirled it in your fingers—and you perceived the facade. He became dizzy. Previously united parts disconnected. Horse from yoke. Yoke from cart. Man from woman, their arms in the air, untangling. He blinked and blinked. He wanted to take the overpriced bottle and shatter it on the nearest ledge. He would have, if either the ledge or the bottle had any substantive properties left—if the ground itself were not already crumbling.

Too dark for walking home. A white curl amid the low constellations was all that was left of the moon. Who had tipped her off, he'd never know. Many people knew him by sight, and the remaining populace could have heard it from them. She had converted to a white woman's wardrobe, which was why he did not recognize her during the long approach and had continued on the doomed course until they were suddenly bundled together, outside of Gertie's Saloon, domed by the yellow warmth of a lamp.

"What's all this?"

He flicked her dress, floral print and trimmed with lace.

"I'm married now," said Jane. "To a prospector. He's just bought a half-share on *Twenty-Nine* Bonanza. He's not rich like you, but he makes up for it in other ways." She stared him down. "I heard you're looking for a cook. I worked in a kitchen for eight months. I have a letter from a priest in Sitka that will vouch for my character."

He refused to condone her impertinence by making an answer. He took out his pipe and gnawed it with his back teeth. Men passed around them, shooting rueful looks.

"Come with me," she said, "I have something to show you."

He shouldn't have listened to her, but he wasn't in his right mind. He was lost. He thought that Ethel might die and he was grieving for Ethel. If a voice, any voice, had said, come this way, he would have put one tottering foot in front of the other and followed it.

Up the stairs—little rickety planks that clung to the exterior wall of the building—then through a low doorway originally intended, perhaps, as a window. From the corner of the dark, small room, a wail. She rushed through the shadows, visible only by the haze of the neighbor's lights, and returned with a bundle wrapped up in a blanket. From that thick mass of wool emerged the bright innocent face of a tiny child. Round and soft, with a mop of brown hair on its head.

"I'm sorry for your wife," Jane said, nuzzling the child's cheek with her cheek. "It takes a strong constitution to live on the creeks. Did she lose a pregnancy? The word from Dr. Moorhead was that she's been leaking blood for months."

"I'm not here to gossip about my wife. Can you not afford candles?"

Jane frowned. She turned to the table and fumbled with the match. Then, backlit, she re-presented herself, with the proud smile of a woman who has just changed her hat.

"We don't know," Clarence said slowly. "Moorhead thinks there's an excess of fluid. The body's trying to wash itself out. Maybe from a pregnancy that didn't take, maybe something else."

The answer for some unfathomable reason had made Jane grow only more smug. For Clarence, the need to exit grew strong. He had not felt he was betraying Ethel till now. He had handed over a morsel of his wife's misfortune, and Jane had accepted it like a candy placed on her tongue.

"What a tragedy, if she can't have a child."

"Don't worry yourself over us. I'm the type of man who gets what he wants, one way or another."

Her face enlivened. "And maybe sooner than you thought."

She thrust the creature forward. The forehead creased. The wail resumed.

"Little Horace. You don't need a wife to do it. This is your son."

Hell rose up to meet him—why should it bother waiting for death? It closed around him like a pen. Jane was flushed. Her eyes had grown large with concentration. It overthrew him, the vituperative insinuation. All you remember is the pleasure of being under the sheets in Forty Mile, but I take what men give me, gather it up, and while you are out, thinking of other things, I crouch down, I concentrate, and I mold it into my own treasure.

She was a witch. An evil magician. What else do you call a person who can speak a few words out the side of her mouth and take away all that is good in your life?

Of course, it was the oldest trick. The child was a round parcel of babyish flesh. Too big to belong to *Twenty-Nine,* but too small to belong to him. He told her so.

"You think I'm stupid? That's Anton Stander's child."

"It's yours."

"Quit that."

"I thought you wanted a son."

He'd lost his mind. That was the best he could explain it. He couldn't even recall what he'd said next, though he could hear the echo of his own incensed shouts in his ear. He might have blacked out. Because the next thing he recalled they were backed into the shadowy wall and he was seeing his own large gnarled hand pinching Jane's throat while her neck was being tipped back and her arms were still clutching that infernal child—the tiny boy that was now clinging to his mother for all he was worth. The light was draining out of her. Clarence extracted his hand from her throat and she stumbled. She seemed to be moving more slowly after that, thinking more slowly. She took another fumbling step and leaned into the corner for support. But she remained Jane. She said, lugubriously, from a place almost fully recessed from the light:

"I still need a job."

"What about your husband, the prospector?"

"No one's laid eyes on him in five weeks." She jiggled the fussing child, rocking her hip. "I'm afraid he's prospected himself out of my life."

"Wasn't it enough I hired Jim? The man says he's your brother."

"He is. He's the best brother a person could ask for. He supports me from the wages you pay him. But I can't ask him to do that forever." She waited. Bold, incorrigible. She looked him in the eyes.

"You can't come to the claim. We can't have your child crying and pitching around in our house."

"My grandmother will take him."

Her solution was simple, and simply put. You never imagined people like Jane having a grandmother, or any family at all. It seemed more likely that they'd parted a vertical slit in the atmosphere and stepped into life fully dressed. But Jane produced a stooped old lady in ten minutes flat. From the adjacent apartment too, by the sound of it. A native woman with a spotted, rough face like an old chopping stone. She smiled with decaying teeth and took the child out of Jane's arms—as if her job started that minute.

He felt depleted. Like that time he'd had the measles at seventeen. An ache along the horizontal of his shoulders and also his jaw. He dragged down the flesh beneath his eyes with a finger and thumb: a monster face. His life was one disruption on the heels of the next.

15.

"I was under her power," Clarence admitted to Alice. "I couldn't say no to her. She needed a job and I was looking to fill a job and that was that." He leaned back in his chair. "Or maybe I shouldn't blame it on her. It might be my fault for having a soft spot for the natives up North. I was never that way with the California Indians. But look at my record. I couldn't say no to Jim either. I'm not sorry for striking it rich, but once it happens I suppose a fellow can't help but feel some responsibility for what's been done in the process."

"You told me once you knew nothing about Jane having a child."

"I couldn't have admitted it then. Though what does it matter if she has Stander's bastard?"

"But Stander doesn't own the child. And already, as you described, she's trying to pin the child on you."

"It isn't mine."

"Since when do you know about babies, Clarence? How big or small at what age?"

He grumbled, "I know a thing or two."

Stubbornness—only his exquisite stubbornness—held him aloft. He looked at the wall. His pink mouth sucked the bright warm air. Meanwhile, she held her terror by the reins. Because she was seeing her sister's position in the family collapse. With it, she was seeing her own position in the family collapse. In the gray cold spring, Clarence had ripped up her deed and tossed the white pieces into the rushing, susurrous creek while she'd stood by with all her righteous fury and admonishments lodged in her throat. But since then, she'd worked so hard. Henry had fallen in love with her. Ethel, in her sisterly way, was in love with her. She'd crawled past so many people—past Jim, past Jane, past all of Clarence's pushy blood relations—to arrive at this conference. She couldn't lose it now.

The sun shone through the glass roof like a spotlight. Her underarms were pouring with sweat. No wonder they were alone in this sitting area.

"I was sure that Jane wouldn't talk of her past," Clarence went on. "She needed the work too badly. She wouldn't risk her employment. Anyway, it would have been worse to enrage her. You can't stop a person from spreading a story around once they've decided to do it. But she would use my secretiveness to her advantage. *That* I didn't realize until she was inside the cabin. I could deal with Frank's taunts. I could deal with your own huffing and whining. But the one thing that worried me most of all was Hen. I was afraid that Henry would fall in love with Jane, and that I wouldn't be able to warn him against her, without admitting the past relationship that I was desperate to keep in the past."

"But still," said Alice, "you let her stay on and on."

"The season was short. I thought to myself, let her stay for the summer, then that's the end of it."

"Even while she stole from you."

"I thought—"

"I know, I know. You thought it was Frank."

"Until she was gone. Until she took Ethel's nuggets."

"And yet," Alice said, staying as steady as he, "you tell me that she came to find you on the claim. After Jim died. That you let her. You didn't go to the Mounties."

"You know why."

"Because you feel responsible for Jim."

"How can I, after all the luck I've had, push down people who haven't had any?"

Enough was enough. When Clarence next reached for his drink, on the little glass table between them, she leaned, too, and touched the flesh of his hand with her nails.

"What does she want from you, Clarence? What is that letter you can't put down? That's it, isn't it? What have you promised her?"

He touched his pocket. Indecision spasmed across his face, but it didn't last long.

"Here," he whispered, attempting boldness but unable to keep the shakiness out of his voice. "You're the person who has all the answers. Tell me what to do about this."

She accepted the letter. The paper was soft, from the douses of ocean spray, from rubbing in Clarence's oily fingers for weeks. She knew this writing. She even knew the ink. After what she'd heard, not even the intimate tone, which was immediately felt, surprised her.

Dear Clarence,

I hardly know what I am writing. You say it's not your fault that my brother is dead, but no one forced you to come after us. No one forced you to tie him up and have him arrested when all he wanted was to escape. And even when he'd freed himself you could not let him go. And now my sweet little brother is gone. I hate you for killing him. If God were fair, the gun would have tilted the other way. But no more. If I begin pouring out my feelings here, I could write a thousand pages and it would not be enough.

You made me an offer when we last talked. And now I answer you, yes.

Maybe you think it's irrational that I can hate you and accept your offer at the same time. But when it comes to my son, I owe it to him to be cold and practical. I want Horace to grow up with a family. I would do it myself, but thanks to you I am wanted by the Mounted Police. If they catch me they will tear him away from me and send him God knows where. I have no husband. My grandmother is ailing. Strange to say, I don't have a friend in the world.

But the care of a family, that is my wish for Horace. When I was a child, I was separated from my mother. I told cheery stories about my time in a Christian Mission but in fact it was hell. I tried to run away during my second year there, I wanted to find my mother. They found me in the woods with a broken ankle and made me walk on it four miles back. The boys got even worse beatings and some died and others stopped eating and let themselves die. Once when I went in to clean the boys' bathroom, I found a child about eight years old curled up on the floor. I thought he was sleeping but he was dead. I will do anything to keep Horace away from places like that, even entrusting him to a fool like you.

You begged me on your knees for a chance to redeem yourself. So this is it. I give you your chance. I trust you will take custodianship of Horace and see to his happiness.

With Utmost Sincerity, Jane

Alice looked up. The words were still words; the meaning was still sinking into her flesh.

"When Jane was our cook," Clarence whispered, in a voice hoarse and urgent, "the boy was with Jane's grandmother. But then her grandmother became infirm and couldn't take care of him any longer, and Jane appealed to me for help. In July, without you or Ethel being the wiser, I wrote to the St. Vincent mission in Whitehorse, and I arranged everything to have the grandmother drop him off there. She did it, and I thought the matter was settled. But after Jim died, the first thing Jane did was to rush to Whitehorse to check on her son. She wanted to make sure he was in a good place, in case the Mounted Police hunted her down, and she never again got the chance. But she was devastated by what she found. The boy was wasting away. They hadn't been taking care of him well. It was her absolute nightmare. She took him out of the place on the spot. In Dawson, she put him with a nurse who would look after him till she figured out what to do. Then she came and found me on the claim. She walked up to me in broad daylight, almost in view of the cabin, I'm amazed no one saw it. I'm amazed *you* didn't see it, with your nose always pressed to the window. She was grieving for Jim, and now she'd reached a new level of outrage, on account of her son."

"So you tried to get rid of her?" Alice asked, with no conviction.

"I tried. I said I'd give her enough money so she could put this nurse on a salary or take care of the boy herself, whatever she wanted, but for Jane that wasn't enough. Like she says, she was afraid the Mounted Police would come after her and lock her up or worse. I promised I'd go to the Mounties myself and get her removed from their wanted list. But she didn't believe they would do it—even for me. And as it turns out, she was right. You saw that letter from Henry, how they refuse to call off the search. Anyway, she was crazy with grief. She kept ranting at me that I'd killed the best person in the world, her little brother, the only person who'd ever truly been kind to her. She said that God would punish me. She told me again—you're not going to like this—but she insisted again that Horace was my son. She said I should treat him as a son and give him the opportunities that were the right of a son."

"She dared to do that," Alice said.

"So I asked her," Clarence continued, "if he was with a family, would that appease you?"

"But not—" Alice couldn't bring herself to say it.

"I was never specific." He blinked, nervously moving his hands. "I never promised to do it myself. She might have wanted that. And I admit, I thought, maybe, Ethel—" He cut himself off, then resumed with forced vigor. "Because godalmighty, what are the chances? You can't have a baby, then someone walks up to you and wants to give you a baby."

"But she wasn't really giving him up. Not if she was still insisting that you were the father."

"I knew you'd think it was mad."

"Clarence." She was shocked. "How could you imagine that, for my sister?"

"What did I start out by saying? I told you I'd made a mistake."

Again, the terror. A bright, pulsing globe-large fortune in the name of Clarence Berry. Then, because of Jane and Jane's son, Ethel pushed back from the wealth. And Alice, who depended on Ethel, pushed even further back from that wealth.

"Did you ever imagine," she said, "that once Jane got her pincers into you, she'd let you go by choice?"

"She blames me for Jim. But I swear I did my best for her brother. Never once did I treat him unfairly. What happened to him was an accident, pure and simple." His own words uncoiled in the air, and his eyes seemed to follow them, as if they were a rope he could grasp on to whenever he needed it.

"Your intentions make no difference, Clarence. They don't bring Jim back from the dead. You cannot bring that boy to California. You cannot let Ethel lay eyes on that child. Pretend you didn't receive this. Any communication, even a cold one, will draw Jane closer."

"Then she'll buy the ticket herself, and the nurse and child will arrive on the dock, asking every man and his sister for our address."

He was right. It was too late. If they tried to hide now, Jane would find them. She would force a meeting on her own terms.

"We can put an ad in the paper," he ventured. "Find an interested couple."

"They'll think it's your child. The gossip columns will love it."

"I'll use a fake name."

"Then, once your real name outs, they'll be sure it's your child."

A great crash of self-pity came from Clarence in the form of a sigh. Why was this happening to him, he moaned, why did things like this always happen? No one had paid attention to him when he was poor. Then he got rich and all of a sudden he was responsible for the well-being of half the world's population. People blamed him for making the trek North look too easy. They blamed him for the crowds who'd joined the rush, only to end up sick and poor, and for the two workers who'd died in Hen's care. One reporter had the gall to blame him for the disenfranchisement of the native race. But it wasn't fair. That wasn't *him* at all. In essence, he was just some poor fruit farmer who'd done his best to bring himself up in the world. He'd never gone North with the intention to drag others down. He'd never perceived God's will in a compass direction. Even his own family failed to credit him that. Last Christmas, the tellers had hung a portrait of Christopher Columbus in the Selma bank, and Frank had tapped it with the end of his scarf and said, look, Clarence, they've put up your picture. Yet he was no explorer. Closer to a Massachusetts pilgrim in a humble cap. Obsequious, bartering, bowing, simpering.

"Don't demean them," Alice said finally, once the outburst subsided. "They were more ferocious than you're giving them credit for. They knew a subtle art, those American pilgrims."

"Did they?" he grumbled. "How do you mean?"

"When they wanted to take the Eastern Shore, they took it. They killed anyone trying to stop them. They weren't like us, we vacillating Westerners, who only do a thing halfway."

There were no Indians to bother the Easterners now, for example. No Jims. No Janes. No complications of property. No eyes on the hills, no voices winding through the trees. Walk the streets of Boston, Manhattan Island, or Philadelphia today and it would take a vigorous leap of imagination to reconfigure it into a battleground.

"They are a difficult people," Clarence said. "You can't absorb them into a Christian country."

She assented.

"A bad culture," Clarence continued. He was working hard to convince himself. "I'm glad it's on its way out."

"They put up a fight. They lost. That should be the end of it."

"I suppose that's right."

They meditated on that for a moment, in the Palace Hotel, with the glass table between them and fat droplets of condensation slowly forming on the outside of their drinks. Perhaps, like her, he was seeing the war between the natives and the first Americans, a story they'd known since they were children, from an elevated stance, from a secluded place a little way up a gradient. It was a poor and disjointed way of living that the Indians had. The societies overly small and scattered and incohesive. Their skirmishes never-ending. The aversion to gore completely lacking. Try to explain "chivalry" to an Indian husband and he would have laughed you into the nearest lake. Was that true? Briefly Alice wasn't sure. Because it was also true—wasn't it?—that the Indians must have wondered at those pilgrims. They must have felt, Alice thought, a strong current of surprise at their simpleminded persistence. Because after the mutilations. After the Indian villages burned. After the scalps carved from the wiggling bodies. After the best young men from an Indian clan invited into a house for dinner, then shot. After the pregnant white women stripped and forced to dance before they were sliced. After the cavalry making a circle around a group of three hundred Indians then shooting a hole into each. After the soft skulls of pioneer children bashed against the trees. After all that, how was it—the Indians must have wondered—that our message still fails to get through? How is it that the invaders push on, unresponsive to the point we are trying to make, with such clarity, in the universal language of blood, that we were happy the way we were, and we do not want them here?

A high thin cry interrupted her. The cry of a little boy. Or no. It was the distortion of a noise beyond the triangle roof. A gull, maybe, flying upside down, its clock flipped too, its sharp beak slicing clean through air. She was shaken. Something must be done. This was the steadying command in her head. We must do something.

"What about Daisy and Ed?" Alice said.

Clarence looked up, uncomprehending.

And even she was surprised at herself. One second, she is imagining a blood-washed century. The next second, two insipid, disembodied faces are twirling around in her head, like the bland solution to an arithmetic problem.

"What if," Alice continued, thinking out loud, "Daisy and Ed Keller take Jane's son as their own? They're a young couple. They have money, but they're burning through it fast, and they could always use more." Her youngest sister, Daisy Bush, now Mrs. Ed Keller. A wedding with six roasted chickens, and the whole town in attendance. A new wardrobe. A home by the shore. A diamond ring on Daisy's round, dimpled hand. In their seven-month absence, the dream had come to fruition. "It's better than paying a stranger. A stranger whose motives could become dangerous to you. Keep the child close," Alice said. "Not too close, but close enough. In case Jane tries to cause any problems."

"The Kellers will probably have their own baby soon."

"They might have ten children, for all we know. Like I said, they're young. Or Daisy is. The most important thing is that they're predictable. If you grant them a stipend to keep the child, you'll have their loyalty in the matter for life."

Silence.

"Write to Ed Keller. See what he says."

"You think they'd do it?"

"If you give them support."

Now in the silence, a slow bloom. This was hopefulness come into life. He blinked, he sat up in his chair.

He said, gallantly: "I'll give them a thousand dollars a year."

"A thousand!" She shushed him. Shushed herself. Just when you thought he was reasonable. "How about you start at four hundred?"

16.

"What you should do is get into oil," Frank said.

"If I were you," said Pa Berry, "I'd write immediately to this fellow Murphy."

Whiskey glinted in the air, from bottle to glass, before the open window that let in the late-afternoon light. It was nine days later, and they were still on this point.

Clarence's weight shifted. Alice sat beside Ethel, but her eyes followed Clarence. She could tell, by the slightest flinch of his shoulder, that he had heard his father speak.

"Should I?" said Clarence. A smooth voice against the bang and slice of city noises. "I thought you might want me back in farming."

"Not I! Peaches and grapes were a safe bet a decade ago, but not anymore. You know that, of all people. Look at your eighty acres in Kingsburg."

Clarence faced front, met his father's insult with his whole body. Three years ago, those words would have knocked him to the floor. But look at him now. "I was joking. No one's going back into farming."

"With oil, you stand to double what you put in. I'd say it's worth the risk of investing."

"Easy for you. You didn't break your back for the principal. Fifty dollars isn't just fifty dollars to me. It's a hard afternoon twenty feet down in the arctic mud." Clarence handed Nellie her drink then moved his mouth to show the wrinkly scar. "See here. I even sacrificed my girlish complexion."

"Don't start on that sad story again." Nellie swallowed, loudly; you could practically watch the liquid go down her throat. Big girl, Nellie; healthy and pink. Alice liked her, or at least, liked her more than her own family seemed to. "You might impress all of California," Nellie continued, "but you can't impress your family. It's in the Bible."

"Excuse me," Ethel said. "In the Bible?"

"A prophet is not without honor, save in his own home sweet home."

Clarence scoffed. "If you're quoting Scripture, it's time to quit Cora and make some new friends."

Ethel, murmuring: "Not *quite* quoting."

"Oh, Cora," drawled Nellie. "I love my sister, but she is a god-honest bore."

"You're letting your mouth run," said Frank, with quiet hostility.

Ethel's lips parted then closed. Probably it was best to stay silent. It wasn't her place to defend one sister-in-law to the other. Though perhaps Ethel had been planning to speak in defense of Christianity, which was anyone's right.

Clarence stood behind the couch, his arms across it, making it into a lectern.

"Thank you all for your excellent council. This session is now closed."

Pa bristled. Frank said, "Now, now," in a tone that ineffectually grasped for his old authority. These days, whenever Frank reached for his usual standbys, witty and caustic, he only found bitter.

They were going out tonight and everyone soon dispersed to get dressed. Ethel's and Alice's wardrobes had finally come from Selma, after a wait of nearly two weeks. Ethel's best dress was light blue with silk flowers sweeping across the chest. Alice's was a bouquet of cream-colored fabrics, edged with black velvet. The dresses stood aloft in the bedrooms, a foot off the ground, where they glowed, resplendent in the drench of afternoon light.

Clarence walked into Alice's room without knocking, while her back was turned, as she was tying her bow. He felt no embarrassment, as if she were truly his sister, his mother, his wife. Her neck turned first. Then the rest of her. The thing that was pulling him here was a piece of white paper, a letter, newly arrived and alive in his hand, flapping in air.

"They'll take the boy. Ed and Daisy are happy to do it. They only want me to go up to six hundred, which obviously isn't a problem at all."

17.

Minutes later, the family converged in the hallway. Pa Berry took Ethel's arm. Frank Berry sniffed and scuffled ahead like a lead dog with Nellie determined to keep at his side. And that left Clarence to offer his arm to Alice. She felt triumphant descending those hotel stairs. Clean fabric rustled like paper. The scent of lavender oil trailed from her hair like a wide ribbon, rippling whenever she made a quick movement. Her eyes possessed an extra layer of mystique. Two black lines of a pencil had done it. The whole city was out in the streets. The weather was temperate. It must have been the loveliest night in a month, judging from the public euphoria. The air touching them was like nothing; it neither warmed nor cooled. It was a bath of sky especially drawn for human bodies, with their own particular comforts in mind. As for the rest of the universe? Let it go down on its knees. The twilight sparkled indigo with pink streaks in the west and an early moon. The tan walls of the buildings glowed. To those not here in San Francisco, on their way out to dinner, on the twenty-ninth of October 1898: Alice only felt sorry for them. She herself would not be anywhere else.

A fortune-teller sat at a booth with a sign featuring Chinese letters, while his son played with dice at his feet. Clarence's face was angled back, his chin tipped west, to enjoy the last bright sweeps of the evening.

"I've been thinking," Clarence said, "I should call Delaney back. 'The value of failure' was the wrong angle to take. It should be 'the necessity of ingenuity' or something cheery like that. I can tell him about my steam point, for instance. My little invention. You saw it on the claim. That closed drum of boiling water connected to a rubber hose. It worked wonders on the frozen ground. And I invented that. Me. Just from tinkering. Henry's been telling me for months I should take an afternoon to sit down at a desk, draw up a diagram, and file a patent."

"Absolutely," Alice assented. "Before someone else tries taking credit."

The city hovered at the tail end of a game of musical chairs. People disappeared into buildings, looking for a spot to sit down for dinner. The family walked the sidewalk as if walking a carpeted aisle. Kings and queens, and let it last, let it last. Let it be two hundred years before a new family waltzed in and knocked them off their feet. Let it be an eternity before the country was subsumed and these streets were transformed and teeming with ghoulish strangers, the unborn, with feelings as cold as clay.

Hold on to it, Alice told herself. Enjoy it. For this was not a durable state, in which a person received such love. We better sap it up while we can. There was an expression: to be full of oneself. But wasn't it also necessary to be like that in order to live, with feeling? To breathe like this? To say it is natural, that this heart should flood with blood and pump?

"You spend this long creating yourself as a businessman," Clarence said. "Teaching yourself through a series of successes and errors—the vast majority of which are visible only to yourself—what else can you do but keep on going?"

"I agree with you," Alice said at a clip. "You're on a winning streak. Don't slow down now."

They took several strides. A brass pole slanted from a doorway. An American flag scraped the air over their heads. Bright colors, stiff fabric, washed clean by a day in the sun.

"It's not the cash," he went on. "A stockpile of cash doesn't excite me. A businessman is only the child of the ancient savage. I was bred to fight for every scrap, with my sinew bow and my flint arrow raised in my hands. In my natural state, I am leading a band of fur-clad men through the woods. You see what I'm saying? It's the thrill of momentum I'm after. The hunt. The chase."

He laughed. As he did, he placed his free hand onto hers; it was a gesture that further confirmed their new intimacy. He shared his visions, his joy. He did not realize the danger to himself. How she stood close enough, now, to touch his dreams, and lift them in a pinched grasp, and wrap them taut around one of her fingers.

He drew her in. Into his confidence.

"I can't be angry at Frank and Pa," he said. "They read me right. I'm not going to put the money away, and I won't hand it out either. I'm going to buy more stuff."

9

DAWSON CITY, YUKON

2015

On a dusty road, sipping warmish water from a blue plastic thermos, I was feeling triumphant. We had traveled to Dawson City to reunite a group of people with a portion of a gluttonous fortune that should have been theirs. We were heralding North a reparation for violence, theft, and disrespect that my Bush-Berry ancestors had showed to their ancestors. We were acting in accordance to this modern idea: which said that one culture should not exert itself, to its fullest and most violent capacity, when it meets with a lesser physical force. We were also acting in accordance to a twenty-first-century ethical creed, which said that it was up to the people who had benefited from past violations—and, as in our case, were *still* benefiting—to make material amends. We were doing this in the name of justice, then. In the name of small gestures, as Owen would put it. In the name of morality. Truly, in the name of love.

This is all to say: the intentions were good. Mine. Owen's. My grandfather's.

Only the execution was messy.

OWEN AND I WERE WANDERING down the middle of Seventh Avenue when my phone rang. Of all people, it was my uncle Craig calling, my mother's oldest half brother.

"I don't know if you were expecting to hear from me," he said in greeting. "But something strange has happened and I'm thinking you can help me puzzle it out."

"Okay," I said slowly, while next to me Owen was mouthing, what?

"Can you please explain," Uncle Craig said, "how it happens that I go to my ninety-three-year-old father's house to drop off his heart medication, only to learn he's flown the coop for the Yukon?"

"He didn't tell you about it?" I asked weakly.

"Where are you now?"

"In Dawson City."

"And where's my father?"

"He's here."

"Put him on, please."

"Not *exactly* here. He's taking a walk at the moment." Then, with all the jauntiness I could muster: "I don't know if you've already heard this or not, but he got in touch with that First Nations family he's been talking about, the Lowells. The family who worked for the Berrys during the gold rush."

"I did hear," my uncle answered solemnly. "I talked to his Morgan Stanley office. Apparently Dad's been moving around millions of dollars. They've been worried for months that he might be in the grips of some con. Now we know that's exactly what's happening."

"No, wait. You have it completely mixed up." Desperately, I tried filling my uncle in about the Lowells. I reminded him of the Klondike's colonialist history. The theft of land. The exploitation of labor. The death of the Lowells' ancestor, Jim. I explained how Grandpa had tried offering the Lowells reparations, and how they'd asked Grandpa to donate the money to the Hän Hwëch'in Cultural Center instead.

"Listen, Anna," my uncle finally interrupted. "That's all well and good, but you're talking about ancient history. Meanwhile, I've got accountants and family who are concerned. I've got Sylvia"—Wife Number Six—"wailing into my ear for an hour that my father is in the midst of some kind of delusional episode."

"I'm sorry," I said, "I didn't know everyone had gotten so worried."

"Mike wants to come up there." Mike was my mom and Uncle Craig's younger brother. "And so do I. Kelly"—his wife, a financial advisor—"couldn't find a sitter so we're bringing the kids. We'll sort out the paperwork and do what we can to get him back safely. Maybe we can rent a car and drive him home the two thousand miles or whatever it is. I think it's too risky letting him back on a plane. I'm looking for my own flight right now. By the way, where's my dad staying? I better book us some rooms so we're not sleeping with the bears in the woods."

I tried arguing my point again. I described the Cultural Center, the gallery, but nothing seemed to be getting through to him, and finally, in a cloud of bad feelings, I ended the call. I'd just begun to re-create my uncle Craig's side of the conversation for Owen when the phone rang again in my hand.

This time Mom was calling.

"Sweetheart," she said. "I'm getting a lot of calls from the family and everyone's pretty upset. Did you tell your grandpa he needed to get on a plane in order to give five million dollars to someone you just met in the Yukon?"

OWEN AND I DOUBLED BACK toward Leanne and Winnie's house. In the meantime, I tried to appease my mother, telling her a rushed version of recent events. Though no sooner was I off the phone than I received a string of haughty texts from an older cousin of mine who was in law school. And then, before I could compose a reply, my phone rang again. This time it was my dad. "What are you doing," he said, "getting involved in this mess? What is a trip to the Yukon going to do for your résumé?"

I was miserable. I told Owen, "Everyone's mad at me."

"Look," said Owen, "was it the best idea for your grandfather to ignore his doctor and get on a plane? Probably not. But your family can't criticize what he's doing. If it weren't for the gold rush, he wouldn't have this money. There's really no moral argument to be made against giving a portion back."

"They don't think like that. They think if you get something, you get it. You don't have to be sorry."

After another twenty minutes agonizing over my family's reaction, sipping water, wind chimes jingling over our heads, Leanne emerged from around the corner of Eighth Avenue, looking bashful but happy.

"Pretend I've been here the whole time," she whispered. She added, slightly stunned: "My mom's having fun. I haven't seen her talk this much in ten years."

A few minutes later, the couple came into sight, taking slow steps, locked together in deep conversation.

"Did you have a nice walk?" I called to them, as they came into the yard. They both looked up. They hadn't noticed us watching them.

"The loveliest walk," my grandfather said. "What a gorgeous part of the world."

"I'm glad." Then with resolve, because the mood was high, and it was a shame to bring it down, I explained about the calls, about the family finding out about the Morgan Stanley accounts, and the gathering crowd of relatives who were planning to come here. I was forced to say—unfortunately for the benefit of Leanne and Winnie too—that there was a chance my family would try to stop my grandfather's transfer of funds.

"They can't come to Dawson," my grandfather answered, authoritarian. "Tell them they aren't invited."

"It's too late, I think," I said tentatively, still speaking to everyone. Then, working through the situation out loud, "And I don't want to sound panicky, but I'm starting to wonder, maybe we could get the ball rolling, and, Grandpa, you could make the donation tomorrow morning, before they all arrive."

But my grandfather had stopped listening, he was saying something to Winnie; Leanne, however, despite my understatements, had absorbed the full significance in my words.

"Tomorrow's Saturday," she said. "The gallery's open to visitors, but the office is closed."

"Maybe," I said, doing my best not to sound too interfering, "if it isn't too much trouble, the necessary people could come in on a Saturday?"

Leanne gave me another long look.

"I'm sorry," I said. "My family's a little—unnerved," I explained, searching for the right word, "at so much money changing hands so quickly."

"Oh," said Leanne. "That's not a first around here. We know exactly how *unnerving* that can be."

There was no way to sugarcoat the information, or to keep Leanne and the people connected to the Center from feeling the insult. But still, she agreed to the measure of getting the key players from the Cultural Center together in order to make the transfer.

And truly there was no time to waste. By dinner that evening, my uncle Craig was already on a plane to Anchorage. His wife and two kids had booked less costly seats on a plane that would put them in Fairbanks. Uncle Mike, not to be outdone by his brother, had canceled an important meeting and would be in Dawson City by Saturday lunch. Meanwhile, Wife Number Six, in between calls to her husband and son, had the audacity to try calling me. Her name blared at me twice during dinner before I silenced the phone.

My blood ran hot that night. And with the midnight sun streaming through the window, through the too-thin curtain, I barely slept. I was rattled by the votes of no-confidence that had been leveled in my direction. It was not pleasant to imagine my mother's whole family angry with me, or ready to sit me down at a table, to tell me how I had taken my elderly grandfather by hand and walked him into a trap. When I closed my eyes, I saw them on planes, on ferries, at rental car desks, jamming a key into a slot. *It's called a gold rush,* Owen had said at the Ahwahnee, when I'd bemoaned the role of brute currency in my ancestral stories, *was that your first clue?* But it had started with gold, then kept on going. Even here, a hundred and fifteen years later, my family was rallying together once more and galloping North, when there was money at stake: ready to storm Dawson City again.

EXHAUSTED AND DISORIENTED, OWEN AND I woke up the next morning with just enough time to scrounge up a cup of hot coffee before the meeting at nine. We met Leanne and Winnie in front of the Hän Hwëch'in Cultural Center. My grandfather arrived a minute later, looking highly pleased with himself. Rhett was with him, by contrast, complexion sallow and eyes bloodshot, stooping under the weight of my grandfather's camera. Good, I thought. I hoped he was suffering as much as I was. I wondered if his mother had kept him up all night, whining over lost money, while his phone grew hot on his ear.

We passed through the main gallery—the fur-covered hut, the canoe, the snowshoes, the life-sized photograph of Chief Isaac—and entered into a sparse, windowless office.

Five people stood. Leanne introduced Jack Willis, their accountant, who would handle the transfer of funds. Marjorie Rook, the head of the center. Clinton Hoff, Bo Johnson, and Irene David, three elders in the First Nations community, who had been instrumental to the Center's founding.

My grandfather shook hands all around. He was in his element. "Truly a spectacular museum," he said. "I can't tell you how happy I am to contribute. You'll be able to do a lot with five million dollars. Yes, five. I've bumped it up. Some of that was earmarked for Stanford, but they've got a bigger endowment already than they know what to do with. Your operating budget can't be much, can it? You're going to be comfortable for quite some time if you do your investments right. In fact, before I leave, I'll tell you what I'll do, I'm going to put you in touch with some people in California who will be able to help you along. They can give you a crash course in how to manage a gift like this. I'm sure it's beyond what you're used to."

Owen and I sat down at the conference table too, but we didn't say anything. I couldn't tell exactly what Owen was thinking; as for myself, sipping my coffee, hearing my grandfather talk, I was wilting with shame. I hated the way he showed no humility. How he marched in here and approved of the museum in such a way as to seem to take for granted that the board members had been on pins and needles waiting for this approbation, in order to fully believe in the project they'd spent ten years painstakingly bringing to life.

The only harsh words my grandfather spoke were directed at his stepson. "Make yourself useful," he called to Rhett, who was hovering awkwardly at the end of the table, "put that thing up to your eye and hit the little black button. We call it a camera."

Paperwork spread across the large white table. My phone buzzed—"Uncle Craig"—and I silenced it. Probably he was nearing Dawson. Minutes later, I silenced the buzzing again. Jack Willis pushed a final form across the table for my grandfather's signature: with the wiring number for the accounts.

"And I just want to say," Leanne spoke up, while Jack went to work at his keyboard, "to my mom and to Peter, thank you. Thank you, Peter, for coming here and giving so generously. Thank you to my mom, for deciding that the needs of the group were greater than her own."

"Hear, hear," my grandfather said.

Leanne's gaze shifted. Rhett coughed into his fist. Then, only the noise of typing.

The first attempt at the transfer hadn't gone through.

"Just a hiccup," Jack said, although his expression spoke otherwise. "I better give them a call."

Soon he was on the phone with an accountant in California. My grandfather was getting restless. Everyone was. The small talk about the exhibits trailed off. Even Owen, who usually excelled at this sort of thing, couldn't keep the conversation alive.

Rhett asked directions to the bathroom. He wrestled my grandfather's camera off his neck and dropped it onto the table.

"Is this a recent development?" Jack was asking into the phone, scribbling onto his notepad.

The room was silent. Leanne seemed to shrink inside of her suit. Owen shot a glance at me, with eyebrows up and a look that read as clearly as if he'd spoken the words, *not good*.

"Ah, okay." Before our eyes, Jack Willis was draining of pomp and good feeling. "I understand. This has been in the works for a while."

He ended the call. He looked around at the room like he wished he could be anywhere else.

"We've hit a bit of a snag," he said. "I'm not sure if we'll be able to sort this out or not. But there's a hold on your accounts, Peter."

"What the hell does that mean?" Authority there, but anxiety too.

"It seems," Jack said, wiping a glistening spot on his forehead, "that this spring, someone in your family noticed you moving large sums of money around. I guess the fear was that you were falling victim to some kind of fraud. The accountant I just spoke to says that, according to the papers they have in their office, about three months ago you agreed to grant your family power of attorney over your finances."

"I absolutely did no such thing."

"Did you at any point meet with a man named Randall Larro?"

"He's one of my lawyers," my grandfather said. "We've gone to lunch a few times. He's not my favorite person in this world."

"Okay. Well, that's the lawyer who handled the paperwork. I don't know how closely you read every document you sign your name to. If you feel that your family or your lawyer misled you, then you're going to want to contest this. For now, the bottom line is that you're blocked from independently making any large transfer of funds. I am extremely sorry to say this. But you no longer control these accounts."

10

LOS ANGELES

1903

1.

Sunlight flooded the front room of the three-story house on Ingraham Street. It was a grand house, with a large staircase, wood fretwork in the doorways, and plaster ceilings cast with flowers and vines. There was a modern kitchen, a yellow sitting room, and a dining room with a long table that weighed about eight hundred pounds and could sit sixteen guests. Upstairs were four bedrooms, wide hallways, and an airy parlor with bay windows that she, no longer Alice Bush, now Mrs. Henry Berry, had claimed for herself.

The house was a treasure, and why shouldn't it be? It was gold transmogrified, oil transmogrified. Ingraham itself was a trafficked street at the edge of downtown Los Angeles. Close to restaurants and the theater and with the trolley car stop just around the corner. Five years now since the brothers Berry and sisters Bush had returned from the Klondike, and five years since, despite his initial reluctance, Clarence had acquiesced to the wishes of Pa Berry and Frank and first sat down with that oilman, Murphy. The result was that, thanks to the partnership, Clarence had started his new California career with a bang. He and Ethel had condescended to live in Selma only a matter of months before shedding the nice home they'd rented on Front Street in favor of their current home in Los Angeles. It was important that Clarence open a city office and join the gangs of businessmen who spent their days buying and hiring. They would make big predictions then drive out together to sport around on those crisp inconspicuous surfaces—the ever-expanding oil fields—whenever the spirit moved them. Nellie and Cora had moved to Los Angeles, each with their husbands. Initially, that had left Ethel to enjoy the company of her two sisters-in-law, with her real sister Alice so far out of reach. In late 1899, just after Alice had learned she was pregnant, she'd told her husband that they must move to Los Angeles too, that Selma was too small a host for their future, and—always happy to follow the party—Henry had agreed to it with his usual cheer. Now they had this elegant setup for their little girl, Melba, age three, to grow up in. Clarence and Ethel lived only four blocks away and visited often.

When they could, one should say. When they were not engaged elsewhere.

Alice sat in the upstairs parlor in the weak morning light of this brisk December morning, 1903. Rigid. Alone. Her hand paralyzed over a single page of cream-colored stationery. It was a message—technically an errand for Clarence—that she'd been fretting over for hours, and still had yet to summon to life. The communication must be precisely worded, dispatched quickly, and, most important of all, written in secret. Though none of those things explained why it was taking so long.

You would think that money would make you relaxed. You would think that *ease* would become your natural state. You would think, having crawled up from the filthy American ground, from a drafty shack in the Placer County woods, from a frail, dusty peach farm in Selma, where you mucked the stalls and lived in fear of ruin, from a rough cabin on a Klondike creek where you signified nothing, to here, this place of exquisite comfort, that now your flailing arms would stop, your legs would pause, and your head would turn to soak in the sumptuous view.

So why couldn't she?

Her husband, Henry, often sensed the poor girl's restlessness in her. He would pull her backward into his lap and speak with his warm mouth close to her ear, bemused at her angst: "What do you want? What do you want? Is it not enough that we have a fancy house? And Melba, our sweet sugar dumpling? Is the money still insufficient? Because, I'll tell ya Alice, it's a damned lot more than I ever expected to see in my life." Once he'd added, feeling the tickle of a vague intimation: "Granted, it's not as much money as *some* people have. But ol' C.J. is on track to be the richest man in California. We can't wake up every morning comparing ourselves to *that*."

2.

Clarence and Ethel. Those blurred presences—crossing her mind—roused in Alice a sharp response. At the bright end of the previous century, Clarence and Ethel had already been gold rush celebrities. Now, thanks to their early and daring investments—which had come just at the cusp of this frenzy over automobiles—their wealth and their celebrity had only grown. Their four-story house had two turrets, a grass yard like a monarch's, and a little pool in the back where three elegant stone fish spouted thick arcs of clean water. They kept a butler, two cooks, a housekeeper, and several Irish girls whose greatest pride in the world was to work for the Berrys. Clarence attracted fans like a magnet. Ethel stood sturdy at the center of a whirl of ephemeral, money-flush people. Her best dress was a dusty shade of green. It had puffed sleeves, black embroidery down her chest, and a four-loop windmill bow at her back that showed off her figure by hanging alluringly low. Her "Tales from the Trail" had a new life here, in these houses brimming with fresh, encouraging Los Angeles people. Her eyes shone under bright candelabras. You could often hear her remarking—a sentiment not unlike her husband's—that she couldn't believe the things she had done. In her ears, she wore a pair of unshaped, ragged, raw nuggets. "I once had enough nuggets like these for a necklace," Ethel had mentioned a couple of times, "but my collection was lost in the Yukon." As a lark,

Ethel occasionally clasped around her neck instead, over the gray-green silk and twisting embroidery, a necklace strung with yellowed, half-hollowed bears' teeth, which Clarence had collected during one of his early prospecting trips. Women would saddle up to her. They'd run their fingers over the teeth while remarking that she must be the dandiest, most outrageous woman in all California.

Good for them. Alice enjoyed her brother-in-law and sister's good fortune. She relished watching the name "Berry" grow, not in the least because she sported the designation herself. Though it was also true—and it made her slightly sick whenever she faced this particular fact—that once she had expected more. *More* than this ancillary grace. *More* than presents of stock here and there. *More* than the reputation she'd received with her name. Because once, during their trip home from the Klondike, on a wind-lashed morning in 1898, on the smooth deck of the *Orlantha* and under a vaulting gray sky, Ethel had said: "If you have a child, we'll be able to do something for them. We will make them our heir."

And?

Alice and Henry's daughter was born in 1900. Her name was Melba Ethel Berry.

She had red hair, a twin face to her father's, dimpled fists, and fat little legs that never stopped moving.

Did that not fulfill Alice's end of the deal?

But where an extravagant will, sealed with wax, should be thundering into existence, there were crickets. There were cards and compliments: but not—Alice's heart raced at the thought—an estate.

She sat tense. She was awash in the Klondike today. Maybe that was her problem. The paper under her chin had brought it on: this message she needed to write to a landlord in Chinatown. Jane Lowell—Alice could hardly believe it—would be arriving soon to California and needed a place to stay. It was a visit not born out of pleasure but anger and fear. After years of carefulness, Clarence had let it slip in his private communications with Jane that her son—"Horace" to Jane, "Ed Jr." to the Berrys—was not in fact living with himself and Ethel, but with one of their near relations. Now

Jane, feeling betrayed, had announced to Clarence that she would travel to California and visit her son, no matter that Clarence had explained to her—and this was true—that her son's adoptive parents were dead set against the idea. For the past five years, Ed Jr. was said to be the orphaned boy of an acquaintance of Clarence's. Now, the Kellers had been told a few facts about Jane, how she'd been a cook in the Klondike; though still Henry and Ethel and the rest of the family didn't know anything. A month ago, Clarence, tortured and caught in the middle, had come crawling to his sister-in-law. "Help me," he'd said. "I don't know what to do."

Today Ed Jr. was a regular seven-year-old boy. A boy, like a northern sprite, who had the potential to be molded into anyone's image. In the Klondike, Jane had claimed that Ed Jr. was Clarence's son, and Clarence had said no, that's Anton Stander's son. The mystery might have resolved itself with time, but as it turned out, Ed Jr. looked just like his mother. It seemed to Alice that Clarence did not know how to think of him, or how to measure his worth. Most of the time, Ed Jr. was simply mixed in with the clattering, happy jumble of nieces and nephews. Their own little Melba; Cora's daughter Blanche, age four; Nellie's two little sons, three-year-old Duane and new baby William; Annie's Wanlyn, now a big girl of eight.

"Help me," Clarence had said, and Alice had answered, her voice guiding but forceful, "Leave it to me."

Now her hand dropped the pen. It went instead to cover the lace of her front. She was alone. But not really. Because here was her old friend, dissatisfaction, thumping its muscled wings in her chest.

3.

Below, a spurt of people rounded the corner. The trolley car must have just let off. Today there was a particular person coming to bother her, and soon Alice had spotted her in the crowd: a plump, fair girl of nineteen named Maggie, who also happened to be the special female friend of Anton Stander, and was sent to beg relentlessly on his behalf.

Of course, they were no longer business partners, Anton and Clarence.

In the winter of 1899, Anton had trudged away from his fetid and caving-in cabin and had sold to Clarence his half share of the claims for a round million dollars. He'd taken the payment, moved to Los Angeles, decided on the hotel business and, in three barely constructed would-be luxury buildings that blighted the shoreline, had lost the money that Clarence had paid him. You'd think that this would have nothing to do with Clarence. But Anton didn't see it that way, and had boomeranged back to Clarence to call foul in a transaction that had been closed for a year. Even more baffling, Clarence had declined to laugh in his face. Granted, he didn't fork over the added five hundred thousand that Anton had asked for, but he'd put Anton and Maggie on a monthly allowance and indulged them all their little emergencies, which came up like clockwork.

The doorbell rang. Footsteps from the back of the house, then Nanny bustling down the hall. Melba must be taking her morning nap. Alice hoped the noise wouldn't wake her. Nor the other person—she remembered with a start, she'd almost forgotten—who was asleep. Alice sat still, listening. In the guest room was Alice's twin sister, Annie. She'd arrived last night by train with her daughter Wanlyn, with almost no warning and very scant explanation. She'd sent Wanlyn upstairs to Melba's nursery, eaten a big meal, cried into her tea, declared she wanted no help undressing, and that was all they'd had of the visit so far.

Now there was the heavy noise of two people climbing the stairs. The letter—the three lines to the Chinatown landlord—Alice hastily dropped into a drawer just as the door opened.

"You'll have to be quick today, Maggie." Alice turned as the girl hustled inside. "I have a guest. My twin sister arrived late last night from Chicago. She came to us indisposed. Ill, actually. I was about to check on her when I heard the bell."

"I'll be quick," Maggie said, eyes alight. "It's something very specific I came to tell you. I have news. But I want your opinion." The girl thrust out her hand to show a cheap metal ring. "Mr. Stander proposed, and I said yes."

Alice leaned forward. She took Maggie's soft hand and rocked it slowly left and right, in polite examination. She wondered where this was going. With a strained smile, she asked: "Are you sure you came for an opinion, and not congratulations? It sounds like a settled matter to me."

"The marriage is settled, but the timing's a problem. That's why I need your advice. Mr. Stander is optimistic about the fish canning business, but for now, we have nowhere to live and nothing to marry on. He's telling me that we should go to the altar nevertheless. But I'm not so sure."

"Ah."

An uncomfortable silence. If Ethel were still in charge of these dispensations, the safe would already be open, the money in hand, and the Berrys a thousand dollars poorer than what they'd been during breakfast. From the back of the house, little Melba cried out, and Nanny went thumping down the hall to retrieve her. If Annie wasn't awake before, she would be now.

"Let's see, my dear," Alice said, coming back to herself. "Where did we leave off?" She pulled toward her the red leather book, which recorded the Berrys' most recent charity payments. "We just gave you the usual ten dollars for food and rent, yes? And before that—just a second." She flipped the thick gridded pages. "Goodness, I'd forgotten. We gave Anton one hundred forty-five dollars last fall."

"To pay a debt," Maggie said quickly. "He was sure he'd be shot, if he didn't clear it at once."

"That's right. Now I remember." Was Maggie realizing yet that she'd caught her benefactor at an unlucky hour? Alice felt in a vicious mood, more vicious than usual. "Here's what we'll do," Alice said finally, closing the book. "We will give you and Mr. Stander three hundred dollars. Do you think that will do?"

"Oh yes!" Joy flooded Maggie's face. "I'm sure we can marry on that. I'm sure I speak for Anton when I say we can't thank you enough!"

Maggie tucked her curls behind her ears and glowed. She lost herself for a second: so absorbing were her own emotions and her intensifying sense of herself. She moved her left hand quickly into her lap and the ring, ill-fitting, flew to the joint in her finger, and had to be shoved down into place.

"And you're sure about this? You're sure that this is the husband for you?"

A vigorous nod.

A small key, fished from Alice's dress, opened the safe. A magician's trick, a mind-bending manipulation of cards. Alice put the counted-out bills into Maggie's palm and held them there. Then Alice smiled. Now the fun.

"Well, my dear, I guess you and I should say our goodbyes. Very soon, you'll be a married woman."

"Oh!" Maggie was flustered. She was not accustomed to Mrs. Henry Berry misunderstanding her or making an error. "I didn't mean to imply that we're moving cities. Anton definitely wants to stay in Los Angeles."

"Yes," Alice cooed, "but you'll be living a new life from now on. A married life. It's the beginning of a new story. And the end for you and me. There is one point that Mr. Clarence Berry is firm on," she continued, writing a law out of clear air, "and I tend to agree. We don't like getting in the way of new husbands. You'll soon realize how important it is to Mr. Stander to be the sole head of his family. I understand he's never been much for traditional work. But soon you'll have a baby or two, and the needs of a family will provide an incentive. You wouldn't want us Berrys to get in the way of all that. From now on, we will give your husband the honor of supporting you."

A little bell shrieked in Alice's hand until Nanny arrived with her hair disarranged from its bun and that look in her eyes that said, am I supposed to do everything? She walked Maggie out of the parlor the way one might escort a small girl off the edge of a cliff. The stairway sent creaks through the parlor wall. The front door opened and closed, followed by the click-click of the bolt. Nanny might leave dust in the corners, but you had to say this: she never forgot to draw the locks on the heels of the poor.

Alice turned in her chair, took out the letter again. But no. She was not in the right mind for composing. She could hear Annie next door.

What sounded like sobbing. She walked into the hallway and put her hand around the guestroom doorknob. The sobbing grew louder. She reconsidered her plan and withdrew. Nine years ago, Annie had married William Carswell. Back then, compared to fruit farming, a grocer had really been something, and Annie was heralded to be a lucky girl. But then the gold rush had happened, and made the world spin, and when everyone had opened their eyes, and shook themselves off, it had turned out that Annie and William were in fact the poor branch of the family.

In the kitchen, the air was thick with steam and good smells: fresh bread stuffed with cheese and herbs, egg sandwiches, and a strong-smelling broth. The cook whirled around, Bessie, her face pink and sweating, in the midst of loading a tray.

Alice: "So my twin sister Sleeping Beauty's awake?"

"Enough to ask for lunch."

"Was she dressed?"

"I've told you as much as I know. The shades were drawn and the blanket was up to her nose."

Fourteen hours since Annie had arrived in the house, and already the servants disliked her.

"Let's see this meat."

Alice opened the oven and, with a towel, shimmied the massive pan with the beef.

"You'll drop it," Bessie said, looking down on her with narrowing eyes.

"Quit fussing," said Alice. "I always tell you, I'm stronger than I look."

4.

Alice sent Bessie away and finished preparing the dinner herself, just to have something to do that was pleasant. At ten after seven, Henry arrived at the door, reeking of tobacco; he'd been at his Billiard Parlor, a business he'd founded for the pure fun of it—and you could smell him from down the hall. A yellow, checkered vest, a yellow daisy in his hat: one of his favorite ensembles. Try telling him he looked like a clown, and he'd thank you for the compliment. The year they'd purchased this house the *Los Angeles Herald* had published the headline, "Millionaire Henry Berry Buys Home Here." And ever since, Henry had strived for regular print appearances, which he justified as advertisements for the Billiards. He claimed that his outfits gave a boost—a bit of color, so to speak—to the stories. Now and then a reporter would sketch him meanly, making him seem like a fool. That would put Alice into a rage, though Henry could not have cared less. The niceties of the newspaper articles didn't trouble him, nor did the so-called facts. For instance, they were far from being millionaires. They had a hundred thousand invested at most, and nearly all was thanks to Clarence writing Henry into a few oil deals, as Henry's *Fifty-Eight* Bonanza had never amounted to much. They could never have afforded the move to Los Angeles if not for the no-strings-attached down payment that Clarence had given them. Though even Henry, for all his poor business sense, knew better than to call the newspaper and make a correction. The illusion of wealth, he understood, was often its own advantage, as the world tended to steer money toward people thought to already have it.

"Hello, my queen." Henry kissed her cheek.

She sliced the juicy meat and fed him a morsel with her fingers.

"Oh, that's good. Nice and salty." He smacked his lips. "Any visitors?"

"No one nice. I thought Ethel would stop in. But she must have gotten held up with her shopping."

Briefly, as Alice made their plates, she imagined being forthcoming with Henry, and telling him of the strange chore that had taken over her day. You won't believe who's coming to California, she'd say. But that was impossible. Henry was in the dark about Clarence's arrangement with Jane. Like the Kellers, he thought Ed Jr. was the son of an imagined acquaintance of Clarence's who'd died in the rush. Unlike the Kellers, he didn't know that Ed Jr.'s mother was their former cook.

They carried their plates into the dining room, placed them onto the table. Alice lit a row of wicks in the centerpiece: an artistic masterwork in silver, with galloping horses down the length of each side. Bessie tread quietly into the kitchen to fix the portions for herself, Nanny, Melba, and Annie.

"No Annie, I'm guessing?" asked Henry, sitting down in his usual chair.

"God, no. She's not even dressed. She's been in bed all day crying her eyes out." Alice paused to try the roast, and chewed slowly, finding it passable. Then, "Do you know what she asked me last night? If we knew any divorced women who got married again."

"Divorced?" Henry's fork paused, aloft.

"She's thinking of divorcing William, I guess."

"Jesus. How did you answer her question?"

"I said we knew plenty of women like that. I just couldn't think of their names."

He chortled into his fist as he swallowed. "Can't Ethel take her? They have more room."

"I'm not letting Annie get her claws into Ethel."

"Well, we'll do our best for her then. She does look sick." Henry took a reproving tone. "I hardly recognized her when I picked her up at the station. You think a broken heart can do that?"

"No, but jealousy can." Alice sipped her wine. "I know my twin. She thought, because she was the prettiest of all us girls, that it would be her right to marry best. Instead she only married first."

"Oh, Cooter," he groaned, "I hope you'll be nice."

"I'll be—evenhanded."

"Lovely. It falls to me, then? The cheering up of unhappy sisters?"

"You're dressed for it."

He straightened the yellow vest with a couple sharp tugs. "That, my dear, I am."

Then he was easing over his plate, elbows flapping, the beef and peas sliding every which way. His manners fit the demands of a farmhouse kitchen in Selma, with five rowdy children around a table, a mother who never let go of her best wooden spoon, and a father who took his meal drifting toward the open doorway where the evening light made pretty work of the Sierra Nevada, against a sky of blood orange and dusty blue.

"As long as you're in a cheery mood," Henry said, wiping his mouth with an unfolding napkin, "there's something I've been meaning to tell you."

"What?" Her attention flashed back.

"God, the way you look at me!" He put up his hands. "It's like you suspect me of murder."

"Just tell me, Henry, don't drag it out."

"Okay. Here goes. This week I gave a small loan to a very deserving young man."

She groaned and covered her face.

"Now, Alice."

"How much?"

He swelled with pride. Or was it defiance? "Hold on, before you get upset, you have to hear the whole story."

"Tell me how much. Then I'll listen."

"Twelve hundred."

She groaned.

"But wait, Alice. This was Mr. Edwards, the dentist who took care of me when I needed that tooth out. He came to me in a horrible state. His wife was scheduled for a lifesaving surgery, and on Friday the doctors were refusing to go through with it unless he gave them the money up front." Henry pulled himself up in his chair. "Tell me what I'm supposed to do? A man I consider my friend sprints into my place of business, sweating and practically sobbing into his hands, knowing full well that I have the resources to save the woman he loves from certain death—"

"What kind of surgery was it?"

"I assumed it was private."

"I'll bet it was. Did he tell you how long it would take to pay us back?"

"I could hardly ask at a moment like that. He was desperate."

"There are other desperate people, you know," she said. "There are buckets of them. Walk outside and pick someone off the sidewalk and chances are you'll have a desperate person who's more deserving of your charity."

He yanked his napkin from his neck and threw it beside his plate, making the candle flames tilt. "Now you listen to me, Alice. We are different sorts of people, you and I. You're happy to sit alone in a room all day, but I need to be out in the world. It's part of my business and it's who I am and I won't apologize for having what most of us would call a social conscience."

"Fine," she said.

He retrieved his napkin. He picked up his fork and chased the peas on his plate. "Twelve hundred," he grumbled. "It's not that much. In the scheme of things."

"I said, all right. I'm going to drop it."

"Here's an idea. Maybe you should try making some friends for once."

Her gaze found his across the long table, over the flickering lights.

"But how could we ever afford it?"

LATE THAT NIGHT, THE TABLE cleared, the hallway lamps keyed off, Alice climbed the stairs ahead of her husband. They'd been mad at each other all night, snipping back and forth, but unlike the truly unhappy couples they knew, Annie and William for starters, their fights never lasted. On the landing stood a table with roses. Henry skipped two steps, plucked a single flower, and pointed the flower at her. When she would not even descend the three steps toward him, he stretched his arm and touched the bloom to her chin. He pressed, making the petals bend against her skin, and said, with big eyes, with unflinching sincerity: "Kiss."

Hours later still, in bed, she lay on her side and watched him sleep. She thought, a family with three brothers is not unlike one with four sisters. Each brother must take care during his growing up to distinguish himself: Frank was dashing, Clarence was hardworking, and Henry? Henry must be adored. He shifted. He opened his eyes and saw her looking.

"What'd I do now?"

"Nothing," she murmured. "I was only thinking I loved you."

He woke more. He pretended nonchalance, but you could feel the warmth spreading over him.

"Why shouldn't you love me?" he whispered in a trembling voice. "I give you a house, a beautiful daughter, jewelry, trips, a big family with a Midas touch. I pay the bill without complaining for the best hairdresser the city has ever known. And most important of all," he said, touching her leg, "here I am in the flesh. Handsome as the day is long."

5.

On a chill morning in mid-December, two city workers plodded down the block, tying giant red bows to the streetlamps. Candles lighted the windows. The letter to the Chinatown landlord was long dispatched. Their charge had arrived from the North and was safely established in the apartment, according to the note that Alice had received in reply. Usually Ethel and Clarence hosted Christmas. But not this year. Alice had instructed Ethel: you take Moie and Poie but leave the parties to me. So. Their mantel must have ivy. The doorways must have mistletoe. A statue of Father Christmas in his white fur hood must stand in the foyer. Every flat, capable surface must hold a tray of cookies.

On the twenty-third, the doorbell rang. Alice threw the door open, expecting Ethel, but found herself facing Frank Berry, who'd just days ago arrived from the Klondike. A miniature porcelain head peeked out from under each arm.

"You!" cried Alice. "You should have said you were coming. Henry wanted to put up a 'Welcome Home' banner."

Frank strode inside, eyes flashing, a vicious shape to his lips. "It's crazy out there. Everyone and his mother has gone to the shops." He handed over the dolls. "One for Melba, one for Wanlyn. Can you wrap them for me? I didn't have time."

Nanny and Bessie entered the foyer and practically melted at Frank's feet as he made a grand greeting. In front of the servants, Frank could pretend to be the darling prince recently home from a tour of the continent. Though he understood, if not a second too soon, that in fact he was the prince's dog. Now it was almost two years since Clarence had stationed him on the Klondike claims. He'd worked as overseer for a hundred men. He'd arrived in Los Angeles hardly more than forty-eight hours ago, and according to the whole family, he hadn't stopped whining.

Henry stumbled in: "Well! Look what the cat dragged in!"

"Oh yes, I agree with your estimation," Frank said. "I'm nothing compared to you slick Los Angeles fellows." He tried to tear off his coat, but one of the arms stuck. Meanwhile, Alice sent Bessie to ready a plate of delights, and Nanny to light the parlor fire. "Explain this," continued Frank, righting himself, shoving his coat at Henry. "Because so far, I haven't been able to make sense of it myself. I find the man, Murphy. I go with Pa to survey the land in Kern. I'm the one who had the idea for oil. Just like I had the idea for the Klondike. But here you lot are. And somehow, I'm up a creek in the North."

"You agreed to it," Henry said. "As far as I know, Clarence didn't force you to go."

"Clarence pulled the wool over my eyes."

"Too bad for you."

Frank glowered. Henry left to bring Frank's things to Bessie. As soon as he'd disappeared, Frank's dark eyes fell upon Alice.

"Clarence let it slip that it was your idea to send me North."

"Me?" Her innocent fingers went toward her chest.

But Frank, annoyed by the gesture, grabbed her arm and forced it to her side. It was not quite a playful movement, it was almost crossing a line, and it took her aback.

"Tell the truth," he whispered near her face. "Did you or didn't you tell Clarence I should take the job of overseer?"

"Honestly, Frank, even if I did, what does it matter?" She smiled in such a way as to diminish herself. She was aware of the Father Christmas behind her, how she couldn't take a step backward without knocking into it. "Your brother knows his own mind. He might be sweet to us girls, and lend us his ear, but he doesn't take us seriously."

"You're lying."

Henry returned, and Frank dropped his grip on her arm. From the parlor came a signal from Nanny. Alice turned on a heel and took a long breath while the two men followed her to the back of the house. Nanny had built the fire high; Bessie had left a tray of meat, cheese, olives, and cookies stuck together with jam. Frank fell upon the food and ate from the tray without touching a napkin.

"If it makes you feel any better," said Henry to Frank from the bar, where he was pouring their drinks, "oil is a damned ugly business compared to gold. These poor bastards are out here digging in temperatures that hit a hundred and twenty degrees in the shade. The managers have to tell them fifty times a day to stay away from the natural water, as it's all poisoned with maggots and metal and other foul things. Even so some still succumb to their thirst and make themselves sick. The drinkable water they're carrying in with a four-horse team from miles away, but it's never enough to keep up with demand. And then you have the pits themselves, which are such a sticky mess that often the men work naked. I drove out with Clarence a couple of times and you can see the fellows at lunchtime sitting with newspapers lining their benches, their bodies covered neck down with black tar, and the pages sticking to them like flypaper. It's worse the deeper you go. Clarence wouldn't let me take a closer look at the pits on account of the danger. Once you get down far enough, the fumes grow strong and the light gets weak. The miners have safety lamps, but those are a hazard in themselves. During one of the scouting digs last year, a man opened his lamp to light a cigarette, and the explosion went twenty feet up and incinerated both the man and his partner."

"Tragic," said Frank. "But you look like you're faring okay."

"True, we don't get our hands dirty," Henry said, impenetrable to his brother's attacks. "But the work never stops. Where to buy, how much, and when to sell out. Everyone is out there battling for position. I'll have you know that last month, Tot and I put a great deal of money into a company called Premiere, on Clarence's advice, and we lost every penny. Now we have a company called Vancouver and another called Eldorado, and no one can tell me in plain words how they're doing."

"Both in Kern?"

"Damned if I know."

They were. Alice almost said so, but then thought not to assert herself on so minor a point. Instead, as she accepted her drink from Henry, she instructed her handsome brother-in-law to move to the chair by the fire. "We'd invite you to stay," she added smoothly, as if nothing unpleasant had just minutes ago happened between them, "but we have Annie set up in the guest room."

"That's fine. I've already unpacked my bags at Cora's. God help me. Is your sister here long?"

"Indefinitely. She's talking about divorcing her husband."

"Really? Why?"

"Isn't that the great mystery?"

"Oh, probably not." Frank sneered. "William Carswell, that's his name, isn't it? I thought he had a sly nature when I met him in Selma. He loved to flirt with the girls, the younger the better. Wasn't Annie only sixteen when they married?"

"That's right," Alice said. "But I don't know that we can blame William for this marital drama. Annie was quite content with her husband until Clarence and Ethel started making the national news."

"Still," Frank drawled, briefly distracted from his own misfortune by someone else's. "Divorce. It's quite a step for a little girl like Annie to take."

"Do you think so? It's becoming more common."

"Not among our set. Consider yourself. You'd never up and leave Henry in a fit of pride."

Henry grinned, flushing pink down his neck. Though why should he grin? What was he thinking about? The girls at his club?

"You're right about that." Alice folded her hands. "I would never walk out on my husband. If you're talking about what I think you're talking about, we would stay married and I'd make his life hell."

There, that sobered Henry up. Though Frank was amused, and winked at her. "Speaking of hell," said Frank. "I hear you've taken charge of the ministry for Berry dependents."

"Only to give Ethel a break."

"Too much for her?"

"My sister was a bit too indiscriminate. Even in Clarence's view."

"She was giving it all away, wasn't she?"

Alice touched a finger to her nose.

"But Tot here is doing fine with the job," Henry cut in, as he stood and shuffled behind their chairs to the bar. "You should see this house on a Sunday. The parade of paupers we have traipsing up and down the stairs. And then there's my wife in her sitting room, doling out each person's allowance, with a safe piled with cash like a treasure chest."

"A safe piled with cash?" said Frank. "Maybe you can add me to the list of charity cases."

"Raise the point with Clarence, if you'd like. Others have."

"Like who?" Frank kept his tone casual too. "Name some names, or I won't understand you."

"Take McPhee for instance. We just sent McPhee six hundred dollars."

"McPhee was Clarence's boss at Forty Mile," Henry interrupted. "He supported Clarence when Clarence didn't have a penny—"

"Shut up," said Frank. "I know who he is."

"His bar burned down." Alice said calmly. "Did that news reach the claims? Clarence heard about it and wanted to send him enough funds to rebuild. No questions asked. Like Henry was saying, Clarence has never forgotten how McPhee gave him a job when he needed it most. Or how he showed Clarence paternal concern, that time Clarence came back to camp with a blistered face."

Frank gazed at her. "And?"

"Remember good ol' Charlie? He's on the list. And you'll be interested to hear this one. Anton Stander is being supported by Clarence. He and his fiancée both."

"Did Anton really burn through a million already?"

"And more."

"Clarence must think highly of you. To let you take charge of the money like that."

"Oh, please." Alice waved him off. "This is pennies compared to what he deals in."

"So you say. But I think you're too modest." Behind Frank, the fire danced and popped, though the white parlor, all mirrors and glass, felt cool. "Cora and Nellie have a different read. They think you're an exceptionally clever woman, and that Clarence knows it. They say that when Clarence can't make a decision about whether to buy an oil property or not, he comes to you. Imagine," he said softly. "Two brothers. And his right-hand man is his sister-in-law."

"It's like all things, Frank." Alice lowered her drink. "In a big family, there will always be some jostling. But the important thing is that we shouldn't fight amongst ourselves, not when we should be enjoying this nice life we've all struggled for."

Now the expression Frank wore was a mask. In most cases, Alice thought, it was a mask.

"I just realized," he said, "we forgot to say 'cheers.'" Slowly he extended his arm. He tilted and clinked his glass to hers. "To your wise words," he said. "Merry Christmas."

6.

The gifts stacked high and spilled across the floor, beneath the tinseled boughs of an eight-foot tree. Clarence and Ethel arrived with Moie and Poie, who had traveled from their little white home by the sea in Carpinteria; it was the home Clarence had bought for them during the summer of '99, just like he'd promised Alice he'd do, the afternoon that he'd ripped up her deed. Poie's cane hit a chair leg coming into the room, and Alice caught him by the arm, and loudly kissed his cheek. His retirement had arrived not a moment too soon, as after decades spent in the logging business, then running a farm, his back had given out, and he could not so much as straighten his shoulders. These would have been trying and frustrating years for their parents if their children hadn't come into money. Alice directed Moie to the softest chair. Ethel carried a huge bag of presents wrapped in tissue paper and tied in red ribbon.

"You went overboard," Alice scolded, placing the packages under the tree.

But Ethel only laughed, making Clarence look around, to see what had pleased her: "How can I help it?" she said. "I love you all too much. I couldn't hold back."

The tags were written in code. To Cooter from Tot. To Mimi from Panky. Most were for the children. But there was a set of pots for Cora. A hat and vest for Poie. There was a bracelet for Tot, picked out by Ethel.

The mood was especially bright. Last Monday, the checks had gone out from Eldorado Oil. The results took the form of gold chains, silk enough to dress a family of elephants. For Melba, no less than seven dolls, which she lined up on the back of the couch, as if in testament to what she was worth compared to the average Los Angeles child.

They rode the high mood into lunch, sitting down for a turkey feast in the dining room, where Clarence, as if the Eldorado boom wasn't enough, told them all about the news he'd just had from his advisor of a promising lot for sale in East Kern.

Alice could feel Clarence's attention on her all night. It reminded her of San Francisco, when, like secret lovers, they'd conspired together. His pooling gaze. His attempts to catch her eye. His awareness any time she moved into or out of a room. She almost worried that Ethel or Henry would notice, like the time in San Francisco when Ethel had come out of the bedroom and been surprised to find Clarence and Alice talking lowly together. More recently, Ethel had said, "You're two peas in a pod," about Alice and Clarence, when Clarence had urged Ethel to forfeit the work of dispensing their charity funds and give the job to Alice instead. "He only wants to save you any unpleasantness," Alice had quipped. "And so do I." Though perhaps she'd noticed, before it disappeared, a wrinkle of anxiety in Ethel's smooth face.

Dessert was served, a pyramid mousse with vanilla, strawberry, and a perfect triangle mold of chocolate on top, which all the children claimed as their right. Then the party splintered off to the yard, and Alice drifted alone to the empty parlor with the grand Christmas tree. The gold star at the top—the only gold in the house that was not solid through—shimmered in the light of the fire. Below, the blown glass ornaments of drummer boys and clowns and round-cheeked little girls seemed to stare back at her. She closed the French doors and went to the tree and put her face near the boughs, breathing the deep forest smell.

Behind her, the French doors rattled open. Of course she'd been expecting this. She looked around. His wide back to her, as he restored the doors together with a definitive click.

He turned. His eyes bright, his cheeks flushed from wine. "Have you seen her?"

"No. I'll go tomorrow and bring her a basket of leftovers. If we have leftovers." She added: "This is going to cause a lot of trouble, Clarence. She's come all this way. She's going to want to see her son."

"I've already told her we can't barge in on the family. I wanted to take her right to the wharf and purchase her passage home."

"And she—?"

"She was angry. She says it would take more than the likes of me to force her onto the boat. She has no intention of leaving."

"You backed us all into a corner, the moment you gave Jane the impression that you and Ethel would be raising the boy."

"It was a terrible time," he defended himself. "We were both in grief over Jim. I was grasping at anything I could to assuage it."

"Well, I'll do my best to assuage her now."

"Good."

"There's nothing to do but wait her out."

"You think so?"

"Yes. Let her make a fuss and stomp her feet and hate us while we stand by. We'll be nice, of course. No one wants a big confrontation. God forbid one day the bell rings, and there she stands at your door. But later,

Clarence, once her feelings have tempered, we'll buy her a passage North, and she'll go."

Clarence stared, nodded, and apparently feeling that the matter was settled, he reached for the door.

"Wait." Alice stepped forward and touched his arm, which froze him where he stood. "Before you go. I'm curious to hear more about this new Kern property you mentioned at dinner. Do you really believe it's going to jump?"

Clarence hesitated. Then, deciding this really was a straightforward question of business, made a slow nod. "I've seen the seepings and I've heard it from three men whose opinion I trust. If you want a one hundred percent guarantee that you won't lose your investment, I can't give you that."

"No, that's fine. I think I'd like my family to have a stake in it."

"Your husband is invited to put in as much capital as he may choose."

"I meant something else." Her voice was tranquil, but she was picking each word with exquisite care. "I always believed," Alice said, "you had in mind doing something for Melba. And today, when you mentioned Kern, I thought to myself—maybe Clarence will see an opportunity here."

"I'll happily pay for Melba's school when the time comes. But on the matter of a big purchase like Kern—"

"It's not so big, though, is it? Compared to ideas you've had in the past?"

She stood very still. He seemed to sense the shift in the air. Since Melba was born, she had three or four times touched a finger onto this subject. Always a firm, deliberate touch.

"You made a promise to me once," she continued. "You said my child would be your heir. It's quite a generous thing. I don't deny that. It's also a thing a person doesn't forget."

"We didn't realize back then," he said with a heavy exhaustion, "Ethel and I, before all the children were here, how difficult it would be to raise one niece or nephew over the rest."

"You've mentioned that before. But is that it? Truly? There isn't some other impediment?"

"Of course not. What else would there be?" Then, when she was quiet, when she wouldn't speak the names Jane or Ed Jr., he added, adamant, "Henry isn't upset with me."

"Henry lives in the moment. He doesn't understand what's at stake. Don't pretend you're unfamiliar with his nature, you know him as well as I do."

Now Clarence considered her with large blue eyes. Beneath his breaths—labored after a meal washed down with red wine—you could almost hear the grind of gears: the great noisy opera that was Clarence Berry producing a complex thought. He was unnerved. But she had every right to bully him in this sisterly way. She'd followed him to the Klondike and back. She'd sat with him how many countless nights, consoling him, counseling him.

"Clarence," she said, now in a voice as smooth as the new silks hung over a chair. "I'll let you know about my visit with Jane. And I'm sorry, I didn't mean to quarrel. Let's go join the others, they sound so jolly."

7.

A twenty-minute trolley ride delivered Alice from Ingraham Street to downtown. The driver gave her a quick look as she hopped off the step, which seemed to say: if you're sure. The store signs were marked in foreign print, though not one that was entirely new to her. Their home in Placer County had been on the same side of the river as the Chinese camps, and she and Ethel had used to visit them. One dark night, the winter they'd almost starved, Alice had stumbled from home and down the dreary, snowy, moonlit bank desperate for something to eat. The workers had brought her into their tent, and a man with a kind expression had fed her from his bowl. They'd sent her home with a bag of rice, which their whole family had then lived on for more than a month. In May, the *Los Angeles Herald* had run an article arguing that Los Angeles should follow the example of San Francisco and force the blot on the city known as Chinatown to some outlying and isolated district. Alice had announced that she was opposed to it; and she'd encouraged every political person whom she crossed paths with in Clarence's house to reject the idea.

Now she entered the building—into a viscous scent of stew—and climbed four zigzag flights of stairs. She repeated to herself this steadying thought: it is only Jane, only our old servant, our hired ex-cook.

A humble door opened into the cave. And here she was. She stood upon a floor smooth and bare as stone. Her hair was slicked to her skull, and her eyes jumped out. She was jaundiced from traveling and the bad meals on the boat. But beautiful, stately. Somehow it was easier to see that in Los Angeles. More beautiful, Alice thought, than I'll ever be. Jane stared back. As if she, too, needed a moment to take this in.

"You really are in California. I had to see it to believe it," Alice said finally, closing the door. "Merry Christmas. I've brought you some treats. I'd eat the turkey today, if I were you. The rest should keep into the weekend."

Under the weight of the basket, the table rocked. On either side was a spindle-legged chair.

Jane walked over. She lifted the cloth. "What day is it?"

"The twenty-sixth."

"Christmas came and went and I didn't notice."

"Traveling can do that. Sea travel especially. You lose track of the calendar."

"I thought you'd invite me over for dinner."

"For Christmas?"

The two windows were northward facing. What light there was came by way of reflection. She couldn't stop staring at Jane; her way of carrying herself, her clothes, her expression; after months of living closely together, it was like no time had passed. Now Jane opened the basket, found the meat. Now she ripped the heel from the bread. But like their first days in the Klondike, when Alice had given her Ethel's apron, there were no compliments, no thanks, no grace.

"When will I see my son?"

"I believe Clarence explained the problem. The husband and wife strongly object to the idea. They fear it would rattle your son. And Clarence feels we should honor their wishes."

"I don't care what they wish."

"If I understand the situation correctly," Alice continued smoothly. "You wanted a safe place for Horace. You couldn't keep him, not with the Mounted Police chasing after you. The schools were no good, so you wanted him to live with Clarence and Ethel. I understand you're upset that the arrangements were slightly changed—from Clarence's household to a different household. But I assure you, you have done what you set out to do. Your son is with an excellent family. He lives just outside the city. He rides horses and picks berries and drives his parents mad. Isn't that how a boy should be?"

Their eyes met. Once they had hated each other in the North, now they hated each other here. There was almost something triumphant in it: the irrelevance of two thousand miles when it came to the nature of their dislike.

"I brought something I think you'll enjoy," Alice said finally. It was a peace offering. The center portion of a letter Daisy had written some months back, describing Ed Jr.'s prowess with a racquet, which Alice had extracted with scissors last night at her desk. But this was another mistake.

"They really have named him Ed," Jane said. "I hate that name. Every Ed I ever met was a rascal. Why couldn't they have kept it Horace? My father's name." She pushed on her eyes with finger and thumb, as if to block Alice out. "When can I see him?"

"Haven't I just said?" Alice's surprise was earnest.

"Then send Clarence here."

"Clarence sent me."

"He tells you everything, does he?" Jane's gaze held her still. "Then you know my son is heir to his estate."

"You're insulting my sister. Don't ever say that again."

Jane stared on, then, as if some crucial dam had broken within her: "I can't stand it. I want to be done with this."

"Done with what, Jane?"

"You. For starters." A wave of heat filled the room. "I trusted Clarence to love Horace. I knew him before he was rich, and I understood him to be a superior, even-tempered man. After Jim died, Clarence said he was grieving for Jim. Did he tell you how, right before he left the country, we spoke on the claim? He got down on his knees, on the wet gravel, and kissed my hand and begged for forgiveness. He said he'd never forgive himself for what happened to Jim. He begged to be in my service, and I accepted his help. I shouldn't have done that."

Jane, as if briefly consumed by the memory, ran a hand down the length of her face, her neck. When she spoke next, she wasn't speaking to Alice.

"The things I've done make no sense. When I was a child, my life went wrong, and I haven't been able to get a hold on it since. When the prospectors came into Forty Mile, everything went ugly again. I don't know how I got here. There's a tightness," the hand spread over the throat, "it hurts when I swallow. I walk in circles, I sleep, but I don't know what I'm doing. Yesterday I stood at that window and wondered why I don't jump out."

"When people make flip comments about killing themselves," Alice said slowly, with care, "they often mean 'I want an escape from my present situation and I don't know how to do it.' I admire you, Jane, I really do. Having done this great journey myself, in reverse, I know it's exhausting. But just because you're here now, don't think that pride obliges you to stay. Now." She stood. "The apartment. I do apologize for this. This is slightly more rugged than what I was expecting."

"I suppose you have a cozy place."

"We have a fine little house that's perfect for us."

"You and your husband."

"Yes. And our daughter."

"I gave you a fight for Henry." Jane waited, braced for a cutting response.

"You did. Between you and me, I'll say that you did."

"And we were both paid employees."

"You want me to say 'we're the same,' but I don't disagree. The day you stepped into the Klondike cabin, I identified a kindred spirit. A woman whom the world had told 'you're nothing' but would not consent to be nothing. I remember the story you told about being taken away from your mother. I'm sorry for that. I had a difficult girlhood too. For my first ten years of life, I lived in the Placer County woods in a shack by Canyon Creek. We nearly starved. My father was in the logging business, but he made almost no money at all. I was just thinking about it, on my walk over here."

"Don't compare your past to mine."

"No? You don't think that people like us, who've been hungry and hurt, spend the rest of our lives running away from the feeling?"

"The things that happened to me are worse than the story I told you."

The shadows moved; beyond the windows, above the tall sides of the buildings, the clouds must have shifted. Jane took out a pin and pulled back a long wisp of hair that had fallen over her ear.

"There's one thing I do want to know from you," Jane said, her voice changing slightly to a more formal tone. "You'll think it's strange but here it is."

"All right."

"It's something Clarence told me the night Jim died, which I haven't been able to puzzle out. That night the men found our lean-to, I was hiding in the trees. But Clarence knew I must be close and came looking for me. I was scared but I did let him find me—"

"I knew it," spat Alice. "I had a feeling he let you get away that night."

"We only had a minute together," Jane continued, not heeding her, "but there was something that he was desperate to tell me. He gripped my arm and whispered into my ear—and here's the strange part—he told me, 'Spend Ethel's nuggets.' *Spend Ethel's nuggets.* Isn't that odd? I didn't have time to ask what he meant. We broke apart a second later, and I had to run to keep from being discovered. I didn't think much about it. Maybe he mistakenly believed that I'd received some gift from your sister. But then he told me the same thing again. The day before you left the Klondike, the day I came to find him on the claim, when he got down on his knees in the gravel and swore to me that he'd watch over Horace. 'At least you can spend Ethel's nuggets,' he told me. I said I didn't know what he meant. He thought I was playing a part. And, again, we couldn't keep talking. The workers were coming out of their tents and I needed to run. But after that I thought and thought about it, trying to work out his meaning. The only thing I could think of was that brown velvet pouch, your sister's collection, which she'd taken out during the party to show to your cousins. Clarence must have thought I'd stolen them. But I hadn't taken your sister's nuggets. I'd left the cabin that night with nothing more than the pay I was owed."

The blood in Alice's body, defying gravity, rushed to her face. Her heart beat with such force that she thought it might kill her. "Of course you stole the nuggets," she said. "Who else would have done it?"

But Jane's eyes were alive at Alice's distress.

"Let me see Horace."

"No."

"Do you want to know one of the last things I ever said to my brother?" Jane said. A body rising, revived from the low place it had been only minutes ago. "I told him, 'you should have let the Berrys die in that avalanche.'" The words were a hot lick onto flesh. "Oh that he had."

8.

On December 28, Clarence stomped into Alice's parlor and tossed across her desk several stock certificates. They were thick, very pale yellow, and bordered with a richly detailed lattice design. The Kern shares in Melba Berry's name, with Henry custodian. A little triumph. Alice looked up slowly, no matter that she was humming with anticipation.

"Does Henry know?"

"Yes. He was at the office with me this morning. He was surprised. He couldn't imagine what had brought on such a gift."

"Well, I hope he was pleased. We're so grateful, Clarence, for all that you do for us."

He grunted in response. She dropped her pen and picked up the certificates. Her fingers moved the papers, checking the numbers.

"And Jane?" Clarence asked.

"Despondent. But she'll survive."

"What can we do?"

"I honestly don't know. I've never encountered a person less adaptable to city life."

"Do you think we can convince her to go sooner rather than later?"

"Maybe with your special powers of persuasion."

He understood. "A thousand?"

"Clarence, dear. Jane claims that her son is heir to your entire estate. A polite thousand isn't going to do it."

Her gaze slid swiftly across him, but his expression was blank. The palm fronds brushed the house. He was weighing options. It was difficult for him.

"I'll have to see her, won't I?"

"If you do, you'll be playing into her hand. She's looking for a chance to have it out with you in some dramatic way. She tolerates me. But you're the person she wants. We cannot give in to her histrionics."

"Is it so bad?"

"Oh, yes. She was threatening suicide while I was there."

"Jesus. Really? What did you say?"

"Very nearly nothing. Why?" Alice raised her eyes. "What would you have said?"

In the week that followed, the East Kern property stayed flat at a dollar and twenty cents a share. Then, on January 10, a drill hit a latent, roiling vein. Without warning, a black torrent shot one hundred feet into the sky, and the value exploded.

They christened it the Sunrise Gusher. It poured oil into a reservoir at a rate of five hundred barrels an hour and showed no signs of slowing down.

Spectators drove out from Los Angeles. Alice and Henry borrowed Clarence's car and went to take a look for themselves.

If Hen, before, had felt the sting of his brother and wife cutting a deal for his daughter, without involving him in the proceedings, he was over it now.

They parked in a row with the other tourists. Not too close to the gusher, because sometimes the wind blew and sent oil droplets flying into the cars, which ruined the leather. One black raindrop did happen to land on Alice's dress. She didn't even bother to rub it away.

"I like it," she yelled to Hen through the gusts, "it's the mark of cash."

The gift had gone to Melba not a moment too soon. Upon their return to the city, Alice made an inquiry downtown and discovered that Melba's portion was now worth ninety thousand.

"So now do you have what you want?" Henry asked.

She pressed against him, kissed his lips. "It's a start."

9.

The next day, Alice roamed the house, cleaning in places where Nanny had missed. She considered the furniture and imagined improvements. She took a hard look at the art on the walls and wondered if they shouldn't buy higher. She paused in the nursery, where the soft covers, fringed with lace, were tossed about on the two little beds. She went to the window and spotted the cousins, Melba and Wanlyn, who were taking their morning exercise on the green square of grass in the yard. Annie was outside too. Sitting on a bench in the shade. Waiting for someone—not Alice—to notice her and feel sorry for her. Thank God Alice had never told Annie about that sweltering day in Selma when Henry had poured his heart out, confessing his love for her twin, that awkward wretched moment when Alice had been forced to tell him: I'm sorry, I think Annie likes William Carswell. If Annie had been allowed that sweet gumdrop of information, she would have been sucking at it every day, showing it off between her teeth. On the other hand—and Alice was grateful for this—she didn't fret over Henry. True she didn't like the girls at his club. But in essential matters like this one, her husband was gallant. If Alice were to remind him of that conversation under the cypress tree, so many years ago now, he would insist that she must be mistaken. It simply didn't add up, he'd protest, when he'd been in love with Alice forever.

Now the cousins shrieked and ran and ducked. Most people would have been helplessly drawn to Wanlyn, the beauty, but she, Alice, was the mother of the other girl, and just as helplessly her mother's eyes followed her. The white, lively dress beat against Melba's pale legs. A plump, freckled child, her daughter, with bright orange hair and large teeth. After three years, Alice had finally stopped waiting for her own face to appear. The wind blew. The cousins merged. Now the joyous shrieks were piercing. Wanlyn had a kite that she was dragging around like a tortured pet and she was preventing Melba from taking a turn. Melba's claws came out. She bit, and Wanlyn screamed and clawed and bit in return, and Annie was compelled to jump out of her seat to break the children apart. But then, look. Melba was her mother's girl after all. Because once the limbs and hats and ribbons and skirts had parted, Alice could see that now it was only Wanlyn crying, and little Melba triumphant, smug as can be, clutching the kite.

10.

In celebration of the New Year, Clarence bought each household a fraction of a new property in the McKittrick district, then he hired three cars to take them out to the desert to see it. They brought champagne and cold sandwiches and laid everything out on a picnic blanket under the shade of three umbrellas. The land was empty yet, except for a team half a mile away marking the spots for digging. There was some talk about walking over to say hello, but Clarence ultimately decided against it. He was a real businessman now. He couldn't have told you the names of the people who worked for him: he didn't know them by sight, and he felt no deep obligation to greet them. They sang "For He's a Jolly Good Fellow," while Clarence, not insisting they stop, stood and stepped out from under the umbrella and christened the scorching earth with a douse from his glass.

"You're quite the wonder," Alice called to her brother-in-law when the song was done, "I'd love to know what blow to the head you took at twenty-nine. Ever since then, you haven't known how to fail."

After lunch, the sisters walked arm in arm in wide circles around their picnic place. In the Klondike, the rocky earth under their shoes had rumbled with gold. Here, the soft, blond earth, as far as the eye could see, rumbled with oil.

The following week, Premiere was down, but Eldorado Oil was soaring. Soon Clarence bought up more property in Bakersfield and divided it evenly among his brothers. He put a portion in Ethel's own name, though with the caveat that a gift a thousand times its value wouldn't do his wife justice. He gifted Moie and Poie a percentage: with dividends that swiftly tripled their income. Out of sheer generosity he brought Daisy and Ed Keller into a promising deal he was making with Strummer, one of the big ones. But Melba's Kern property was still doing best of all. The wells were deep and consistent. The checks arrived with the steady movement of the steel barrels crossing the desert. The roar of car engines, which tore through the house, and used to irk Alice and make her feel cut off from what the country was becoming, because she was afraid of cars and found comfort in the clops and whinnies of horses, now that very noise evoked in her a pride so visceral it was almost lewd. Cars weren't so bad, she supposed, when your stock holdings were tied to them.

Henry said that life was grand. He came home for lunch one day towing Clarence and Ethel, whom he'd picked up in town, and sporting a flushed face and a bad case of the giggles. He plopped into a chair beside pale sour-faced Annie and relayed convoluted plans to buy the San Francisco Seals, the baseball team, and wondered if Clarence would front him the cash. "Forget oil a minute," he told Clarence, banging his fist, "for once, let's do something fun."

Alice steered the talk to safer waters, away from frivolous favors that might use up a wealthy brother's goodwill. It is up to me, she thought, turning away to fuss with the tea things, to do anything right in this family. She thought, readying her expression to face them again; if I ever get Melba her once-promised estate, it will be in spite of every person I know.

11

DAWSON CITY, YUKON

2015

My grandfather was outraged, scandalized. Nine people watched helplessly as a stream of curses poured from his mouth. Who had done this to him? Who would dare? Meanwhile, my heart raced, my face became hot. They'd lied to me. Uncle Craig, my own mother. Had they really held all of this back while they were on the phone with me yesterday? Had they really let my grandfather humiliate himself? Did they not understand that they were also acting rudely toward the people of the Cultural Center, who had not asked to be a part of this mess?

This morning, I'd thought my grandfather would die having never learned to check his very large ego. But his ego was crumbling now, and it was horrible. He had seemed younger stepping off the plane yesterday, now he looked his age. He was aghast. He was ashamed to see his gesture fail.

"I'll be right back," I whispered to Owen.

In the circular gallery, under the crossed nineteenth-century snowshoes, I took out my phone. With clumsy fingers, I composed a group text to Uncle Craig, Uncle Mike, Aunt Kelly, and my mother.

Did you get a power of attorney over Grandpa's accounts? Because his donation won't go through.

Aunt Kelly and Uncle Mike didn't reply, which made sense, as they were probably either driving or flying right now. But within thirty seconds, Uncle Craig and my mother had both written back. They had no idea what I was talking about.

My mother: *Can you explain a little more about what's going on, please?*

Uncle Craig: *I tried calling you. Where's my dad? I'm at the Dawson City Museum.*

Then a text from Owen: *It's not happening. Everyone's leaving. Where are you? I'll meet you out front.*

OUTSIDE, THE BRIGHT SUN AND the spray of the river were invigorating after the stale air indoors. About thirty feet away, in front of the row of restaurants, I spotted Rhett on his phone. He saw me too, but didn't acknowledge me. He turned away with a lumbering gait I'd come to know well. Suddenly I couldn't believe I'd suspected my aunt and uncles and mother.

The glass doors whooshed open and my grandfather and Owen stepped out of the building.

"Uncle Craig's here," I said, turning and showing my phone. "He's at the Dawson City Museum right now."

"He did this, didn't he?" my grandfather growled. "Golly, when I get my hands on him—"

"I don't think it was him," I said, testing the idea for myself.

"Like hell it wasn't."

"I'm pretty sure, Grandpa. I'm beginning to think it was Rhett."

"Rhett?" my grandfather cried. "That man can't put two and two together."

Instead of arguing, I said we better go meet Uncle Craig. And soon we were up the steps and inside the Dawson City Museum, a tribute to the glory days of the '98 Rush. Past the cardboard display of Clarence Berry with his steam point contraption. Past the artifacts—a rusty kettle, a stained leather satchel. We found Uncle Craig alone on a bench, in a small, dark alcove, watching a film of black-and-white, stringed-together photographs from the height of the gold rush. Destitute, wan, and startled faces looked out from the screen.

"There you are," Uncle Craig said, lifting his cowboy hat from the bench and standing stiffly, tearing himself away from the film. "Amazing place, right? I've always wanted to come here. Though not quite the circumstances I'd imagined." He grasped his father's shoulder. "How ya feeling, Pops? I brought those pills for your heart. You can't go disappearing on me like that."

My grandfather said: "I don't need you chasing after me."

But before the ill feeling between father and son could intensify, I explained to Uncle Craig what had taken place in the conference room. My grandfather listened without reacting; he accepted the pillbox from his son and slipped it into his pocket.

By the time I'd finished talking, pointing my accusing finger at Rhett, my grandfather was merely bewildered, and it was Uncle Craig who had taken the job of being irate.

"What does that moron think he's trying to pull?" Then, "He used Dad's plans for this donation as his big opportunity. He's always wanted to shift the whole estate onto Sylvia."

My grandfather, reflexively, out the side of his mouth, defended his wife. But Uncle Craig was too far gone. He was a peaceful, laconic, even phlegmatic man most of the time. But offend his honor, offend his father's honor, endanger his financial legacy, and he'd light up with rage.

"Come on, Owen," he said, with a vigorous pat to my husband's back. "Let's give this jerk what he's asking for. We'll stop by the hotel and see if Mike's rolled into town. Then it will be three to one."

Owen, who'd mostly kept to the sidelines of this conversation, was startled.

"Right. We should definitely make it clear that we're planning to legally challenge—"

"Forget the courts. I'm ready to send this guy to the moon."

WHEN WE REACHED THE DOWNTOWN HOTEL, there was no sign of our other family members, but there, inside the Sourdough Saloon, was Rhett. The blinds were half-drawn and the bar impressed upon the eye as a great assemblage of glass bottles and mirrors. Rhett stood at the center of some kind of ruckus. He was on his feet in front of his chair, raising his drink and bellowing "cheers" to the room. A dark lump sat at the base of his glass, and I realized that Rhett was about to attempt the famous Sourtoe Cocktail, which last night had so excited him.

We crossed the threshold just in time to see him pitch the shot to his lips, with the toe sliding to kiss his mouth. Two men at the bar hooted their applause and the bartender whistled. Rhett, triumphant, lips glistening, slammed the glass down beside a full pitcher of beer. He wiped his face with the back of his hand. As he did, he caught sight of us. Far from being ashamed, he was pleased, and seemed emboldened by the fact that he had acted in such a way as to shepherd us here.

"You caught me at my finest hour," he called. "I've just become a member of the Sourtoe Cocktail Club."

He wasn't lying. The smiling middle-aged bartender in a leather vest brought him a certificate, which he said Rhett could take home and hang up on the wall.

"I've got a bone to pick with you, Rhett," said Uncle Craig, pushing his way through the tables.

I'd just taken a step to follow him when I felt a touch to my back. "Your grandpa," Owen said, urgently, near my ear. I turned. My grandfather was lowering himself into one of the captain's chairs. He took out a handkerchief and wiped his face. I rushed to the bar for water, and, with Owen also urging him, insisted he take a sip.

Then I left Owen tending to my grandfather and joined Uncle Craig, who was arguing with Rhett in front of three elderly couples and two middle-aged men at the bar.

"Just say what you did," I said to Rhett. "We've figured out most of it."

"My mom was granted power of attorney three months ago." Rhett grinned. Not at me, but at Uncle Craig, whom he'd identified as his equal and his adversary. "She noticed he was up to something—something involving a woman—and she assumed it was probably predatory. Good for her, she got their lawyer involved right away. Peter can't do anything with his money without my mom signing off on it."

"We'll get it removed," Uncle Craig said.

"Good luck doing that before it's too late."

"What the hell does that mean?"

"Look at him," Rhett flicked his chin at my grandfather. "He's got one foot in the grave."

It was a cruel thing to say. From across the room, my grandfather heard it, and felt the full effect. He could pontificate on his own death, he could joke about it, mourn it, but the rule was that the rest of us never did. In fact we were meant to pretend that his dying was impossible, preposterous, as I'd done during our dinner at the Ahwahnee. Now my grandfather was startled that his own stepson would speak about him this way. He flushed and, showing none of his usual self-assurance, wilted under the words. Uncle Craig could not bear it. He loved his father. He picked up the pitcher of beer, knocking over the shot glass with the desiccated toe in the process, and flung the tidal wave of gleaming bronze liquid into Rhett's face. Rhett let out a gleeful shout. He relished the chance to be violent. He picked up one of the barstools, and used it to shove my uncle Craig against the wall, pinning him under the mounted, broad-antlered head of a moose.

The situation was bad. Uncle Craig was not a young man. He was over sixty. He couldn't push Rhett away, and the effort played out like the echo of a bad movie fight, performed by actors too soft and slow for the roles. Still, my uncle, against the pressure of the barstool, was truly in pain. His face swelled, his mouth opened, he was gasping for breath.

My grandfather struggled to stand, to help his son, but I went to him and pushed him down without looking at him, my hand pressing his shoulder and holding him there.

The bartender was willfully distracted, rescuing the shriveled toe from the carpet and dropping it into a mason jar with what looked like coarse salt. A couple in their eighties gaped at us with their straws in their mouths. A man in a red flannel shirt wore an expression of startled bemusement. "Back off!" I yelled at Rhett. But it seemed hopeless, and as if the room was against us, silently rooting for their Sourtoe hero.

Then there was a motion beside me and in smooth, determined steps, Owen was striding across the room. His long, bare arm drew back, like a spring being loaded. Then it hurtled forward and smacked into the side of Rhett's face.

Compared to my uncle, Rhett was young and strong, but he was neither of these things when compared to my twenty-eight-year-old husband.

Blood splattered from Rhett's nose, then down his hand, which was trying to stop the flow. He took two staggering steps, nearly falling to the floor, before clumsily regaining his balance. Uncle Craig was freed, holding his ribs and gasping.

"Jesus Christ," Rhett said. He pulled himself upright. He seemed, for a tortured second, to consider hitting Owen back. Then he thought the better of it. "Fuck you people," he said, then stomped away, his hand cupping his smeared, gushing nose.

Meanwhile, Owen stood at the center of the room, looking bewildered. He was cradling his own hand, stretching the fingers, staring at them as if they might not belong to him.

"I can't believe I punched someone," he said. "I haven't hit anyone since I was five."

He was happy, abashed. Then his eyes moved and as they did, his expression changed. At the same moment, what Owen saw, I felt; as my open hand had remained during all of this on my grandfather's shoulder. But where I'd been restraining him, against the pressure of his trying to stand, I now felt a release. His body wilted under my touch. When I turned, it was to look into my grandfather's blue watery eyes, which were bright with fear and surprise. His hands, as if holding something delicate, beautiful, invisible, between them, were crossed together over his heart.

12

LOS ANGELES

1904

1.

Deterioration—a slow eroding of walls, of furniture, of spirit—had taken place in Jane's apartment. Like the worst days in the Klondike cabin when the heaviness of Ethel's illness had fallen over them all, here the stench of a chamber pot mingled with the stench of puckering fruits. Grapefruit and pears, by the look of the bruised globes that were melting into the counter. The air was thick. Alice would have liked to be breathing elsewhere. But her own machinations had put her here. Elbows out, hands on hips. Hair pulled back in that style: flat across her skull and balled at the nape of her neck. Poke a finger into it and the strands would probably crackle like hay. "I will see Horace." The keeper said Jane would not. "I will speak to Clarence." The keeper said, better if not. "I've told you a hundred times," the keeper continued, dropping Bessie's basket onto the table. "The best thing you can do for your son—and I understand this is hard—is to leave him at peace."

Here Jane rounded on Alice. She was a formidable woman, svelte but with shoulders and hips that put her on scale with the Bush sisters, who in their womanhood had never been slight.

"Listen to how you talk. But if you were in my shoes, you'd act just like me."

What did she mean? Today, Alice had arrived determined not to be bullied by Jane. And yet despite her resolve, she was jumpy. Did Jane mean, you are a mother, and would also claim the right to intervene in your child's life? Or was this a sharper observation? As in: *you, too, have positioned a child in order to make a grab for Clarence's money.*

"Happily," Alice said, straining to sound composed, "I am not in your shoes. You and I were thrown together in the Klondike. We shared a similar standing. We still moved in the circle of youth. But then true adulthood sets in, and the differences of situation, of standing, begin to show. They were there before, under the surface. But now they show."

"You're an evil woman."

"We live in worlds of our own making," Alice answered at a clip. "That's all I'll say in my defense. Evil hearts see evil. They're attuned to it because it's their own nature and it's what they're familiar with."

"My son is Clarence's only child."

"Your son is Anton Stander's child. Show us a little respect." She was shouting. She shouldn't let Jane push her to this. Outside, the trolley rang. People called to each other as they crowded on board. She had told Henry, it's an afternoon of errands for me. "You're raving," she said, quietly now.

"How do I know you haven't killed my son, like you killed Jim?"

"Dear God, Jane, what a thing to say." Her laughter broke the stagnant air. "All right, why don't we slow down a bit? Let's you and I agree on some points. You're not a thief. Not really. Jim wasn't a thief. Not really. And Clarence is not a murderer. Not really. What happened in the Klondike was a catastrophe. Every single one of us would like to go back and change it."

"What will you do, if one day Clarence decides to own my son?"

"Oh, please."

"You'll hang yourself from rafters in your great, big house before you suffer the humiliation of Horace being raised above you and your daughter."

2.

At home, Chopin beat against the enclosure. Henry reclined in their softest chair, eyes closed, his hand swirling a glass nearly emptied. Not drifting, quite. Because when the piano music reached another thunderous climax—and Wanlyn did the dramatic parts well, she knew how to throw her shoulders into them—Henry smacked his lips, drinking the music down through his gullet.

Alice dropped her purse. Shakily, she untied the scarf at her neck. In the noise of her niece's performance, her mind was wandering over mountains and oceans to faraway places. She wondered what instruments Jane's people played, and who they would count as their finest composers. If one day Alice dared to ask Jane that question, Jane would understand the insinuation, and would twist it into a new comparison to fit her own measures of worth. And yet, Alice thought, what was so spectacular about one culture subsuming another? It was a process as old as civilization. As old as England and older. As old as Jerusalem, Persia, Mesopotamia, the Aztecs, the Ancient Egyptians. As old as all the peoples that had crashed together and changed through time, without leaving a record, not as much as one coarse mark etched into stone.

The music was doing uncomfortable things to her heart. Moving it. In the gallop of chords she saw horses, buffalo, trains, all crossing the prairie, heads pointed west. She thought, it was inevitable that Europeans took over the continent. She thought, if a country is flourishing, it can't be wrong. No forest ever sprang up from sand. There must be something biological in the soil. When Melba was born, she came out in a bubble of blood. Mother's blood. That's life. It has a cannibalistic streak to it. Never to be outgrown. You take off your shoes and walk across the floor, across the grass, and you feel energized because you are walking over wet graves stacked in layers, and you are sucking their thick juice up through your soles.

A final chord. Fingers arced, tensed, and still, the pedal depressed. Then the child rotated on the bench and looked at them with slight surprise. She had not heard her aunt come in. Her smile was only a small elevation, but it was proud. Already, Wanlyn played for herself. An adult response had begun to mean less to her.

Henry opened his eyes. "Lovely, dear."

And Alice concurred. Because it was the truth, and she was not above admitting the truth. "Lovely."

3.

Monday: they reinvested a slice of money from the Kern lease.

Wednesday: Vancouver jumped and they let go of twenty percent, at a profit that had Henry whistling.

Thursday: The clouds like blurs in a marble vase, the long palm fronds brushing the house.

"If we aren't careful," Henry said, "we'll soon be as rich as the Carnegies."

"You're getting a little ahead of yourself, darling," Alice said. But she touched her cheek. She was smiling too.

Then, just as they were pouring champagne, Clarence's car came screeching up to the house, without Clarence inside it. It came to a rocking halt at the curb.

Alice was first to the door. "Is somebody hurt?"

"No, ma'am," answered the driver, his face full of sunlight and sweat. "But Mr. Berry says that Mrs. Berry is asking to see you."

4.

At the black iron gate, Clarence was waiting. There was no danger, he answered her swiftly, as Alice jumped from the car. There was nothing physically wrong. It was only the old anguish of Ethel's: the wound reopened by new information.

This morning, Clarence explained, Ethel had been to a new doctor, a venerated leader in the field of female health. And this doctor's expert opinion was that—judging from Ethel's medical history—the root of her long-standing illness was an early pregnancy that had, in '98, rooted outside of the womb. There was a name for it, a tubal pregnancy. It was a rare occurrence and very dangerous. What happened was that the fertilized egg implanted too early, inside the narrow passageway that connected the place of eggs, instead of getting all the way down to the womb. Then, once a fetus began to grow, it strained the confines of the tube, and eventually ruptured it, often causing the woman to bleed to death. There had indeed been a rupture in Ethel, Clarence told Alice, now blinking and blinking. And a serious one, as the doctor guessed that Ethel had gone a staggering fifteen weeks into a pregnancy, about as far as this condition can go. It had ended that day Ethel had collapsed on the claim, pouring blood, and they'd thought she would die. In her case, she was lucky, the bleeding had stopped on its own, and the ensuing infection had cleared. Though the aftereffect had remained of a damaged inside. In the five years since that terrible day on the claim, though they'd visited countless other doctors, there had never been even the hint of a pregnancy.

"I blame myself," Clarence continued, anguished. "There is a surgery to prevent scarring. But it must be done right away. Five years later is out of the question. I should never have let her travel that summer. I thought it was her appendix," he said. "I never imagined—"

Clarence left Alice at the entrance of the parlor, then drifted, a wandering soul, down the hall. Alice took a breath and turned the knob. Pressed against the arm of the cream-colored couch, her dress disarrayed, sat Ethel. Her hands huddled on top of her thighs.

"Did Clarence tell you?"

"Yes." Alice softly shut the doors.

"So I was pregnant. Once."

Pride lifted the words, which was confusing. What did Ethel want? Only pity? Or pity and congratulations both? She hesitated, and Ethel noticed the hesitation, and was abashed. Alice crossed the room and wrapped herself around her sister.

"I feel so stupid," Ethel said. A sob burst from her, cracking the dignity of her tranquil round face. "I thought I was at peace with my life. But now I see I must still have been hoping. Because I feel the loss again. Do you think I can mourn something I never had?"

"Yes." Alice stroked her sister's hair.

"But I'm afraid, Tot. I don't think I'll ever feel happy again. I've been slapped down. I know it doesn't look that way from the outside. It sounds absurd. But I can tell you, life has slapped me down. The tiniest things make me miserable. I don't have the courage to open the windows." Their heads turned, the curtains mint green. "A bird built its nest in the eaves," Ethel explained. "You can see it from the porch, to the left. We hear the little cheep cheeps all morning. Do you know how that feels? A bird can have babies and I can't."

"You'll be okay, Ethel. You're the strongest person I know."

"Strong doesn't help when all you want is a child."

Alice touched Ethel's cheek, beloved cheek, smudging a tear; she thought her heart would break for her sister.

"Come stay at my house," she said. "Get a change of scene and let me take care of you."

"You have Annie already."

"I'll send her to Nellie."

"Don't. I don't want a fuss. It's too humiliating. Please don't say a word to the girls."

"I never would."

"One thing the doctor said was worst of all," Ethel continued. "He said that, perhaps, if I'd sought treatment immediately, if, for instance, I'd been in Seattle instead of the Klondike when the tube ruptured, a good surgeon might have been able to save my womb."

"Clarence said."

"So you understand?" She was anguished. "Remember in the hotel in

Seattle when you told me to stay back and forget the trip North, I refused you. I said it was the apex of my youth. My adventure. But now I see that I paid for that big adventure with what could have been the rest of my life. My own little babies who will never exist."

Ethel dropped her face and sobbed. All barriers melted: and Ethel, her most inner and vulnerable self, left exposed. Frantically Alice kissed her head, her arm. But it was only after several minutes that Ethel at last was quiet, depleted. She'd been awake all night, nervous for the appointment. Now she needed to sleep. From a little box, she took a morphine pill—just like the ones they'd had in the Klondike—swallowed it and stretched out across the couch. The minutes passed, and finally Ethel was really asleep. Very slowly, Alice slipped away, leaving her sister with her cheek on her hands, on the arm of the sofa.

With the latch depressed, with only a quiet bump of the wood, Alice closed the doors behind her. A light down the hall, in the kitchen. She went to it and found Clarence; huddled away in a chair in the corner. His face, bright in the shadow, was bald with feeling but also withdrawn. "Thank you for coming," he said, and she answered softly, "You don't have to thank me, we're family." It was like Seattle. There were some things, Alice observed, he simply could not face. He was tender in the wrong moments. Solicitous in the wrong moments. Never when he was needed most, and toward those who deserved it.

5.

After Ethel, Alice had no stomach for Jane. She brought Jane's basket of food only as far as her door.

At home, too, she was anxious. She sensed the presence of an upheaval. Pieces hovering, at eye level, waiting to fall.

In the meantime, young Maggie returned. Bold. Shameless. She was now, as promised, the wife of Anton Stander. But she picked up her begging where she'd left off, forgetting Alice's big goodbye.

Each day Alice sat by, shining with anger. At Maggie. No. Who? At

Clarence. Because, if it were up to him, he would leave her to deal with Anton and Maggie forever.

And Jane. They were stuck here. Clarence didn't know what to do to make her give up and go home, but he expected Alice to feed her, speak to her, keep her calm in the meantime. Jane had been in Los Angeles four weeks already when Clarence told Alice to extend the lease to March. The one decision in months that he had made on his own. Alice went to tell Jane. But that was a mistake: to go there when angry. Jane, outraged, mirroring Alice's reproach and abuse without pause.

Then Alice was home again. Alone in a parlor, drenched by the sun. And Maggie was standing next to her chair, telling her how she and Anton were on the verge of homelessness, ruin.

This time, Alice raised a hand to stop her speech. She said, through her exhaustion, "No handouts, Maggie. Nothing more for free. But listen. I have a job for you."

The next week, Maggie went to Jane's apartment with a basket of food prepared by Bessie. It was a secret mission. Maggie was at liberty to tell no one, excepting of course her husband, who inevitably would be privy to all.

When Alice informed Clarence what she had done, he was distressed. But Alice answered, ruthless, "It's Anton who fathered Ed Jr. It's you who funds him. At least let his wife take some work off my hands."

6.

Now, the first Tuesday of February, Maggie was on her way here: prancing around the corner, inside the crowd that had just come off the trolley. A new dress, for once. Aquamarine, trimmed with navy, with a shimmering, oyster-gray sash at the waist. The fabric was loose, and it puffed behind her as she skipped across the street, laughing at herself, laughing at the coaches and drivers, who stopped to wave her through. The girl at least had that figured out about life, blue was really her color.

Now she darted and leapt onto the sidewalk, punching down her hat with one hand. The bell rang. The steps, shadowing Nanny's up the stairs, were loud and self-important. The door swung open and struck the wall, grazing the antique chair that had this morning arrived from the dealer.

"She thinks you've killed her child."

Alice turned. "What did you say?"

"I told her it's mad. I said, sweet Jesus, Miss Jane, where do you think you are? This is Los Angeles. As in, a big American city. As in, civilization. Last I checked we don't go around killing schoolboys. But she's an impossible woman. Do you know what she called me, for arguing with her?" Dropping her voice: "A little bitch."

Maggie sat down. Pleased with herself. More so than usual.

"I don't think you pay me enough," she continued, "to deal with a person like that. Fifty dollars a week would be more suitable."

Alice stared on, slightly dazed. She went to the safe. The bills scraped as she counted them into a pile. "Here's fifty dollars. A tip for the indignities you endured today. But don't expect this next week."

"Anton will be upset."

"Anton. Anton."

"We can't live on what you pay us."

"Has it ever occurred to Mr. Stander to supplement this income with that thing called a job?"

Maggie's lips flared. "Jane doesn't like you, you know."

"Unfortunately Jane and I never took to each other. I'm not sure how much of the story you've heard, but Jane's brother, a packer named Jim, was caught during the height of the rush stealing gold from Clarence's claim. He was very tragically killed while trying to make a run for it. It was an awful thing for us. Clarence had known Jim for several years and had trusted him completely. And as you can imagine, Jane was grief-stricken after the accident. She hasn't been the same since."

Maggie was silent. She didn't know this. Which gave Alice heart.

"Jane was in on the thefts," Alice continued, "I'm sorry to say. Though of course you can't fault a woman to the same degree, after being led astray by her brother. And sadly for Jane I'm sure her own involvement made her grief worse."

Maggie's expression wavered. Rotating, Alice picked up a pen. She began to make out an envelope. But Maggie said, "We really need fifty dollars a week."

Alice, licking her finger, took a new page of stationery from the top of the pile.

"It isn't fair. Anton discovered gold on Eldorado, and now he has nothing. It isn't fair that Clarence is so filthy rich."

Now Alice dropped the pen. She laughed her loud, poor girl's laugh. "You don't know how many people agree with you, Maggie. So many that it makes my head spin."

7.

At first, just after the doctor's diagnosis, Ethel and Clarence had walked lowly through the world. Ethel lingered behind the curtains and iron fence of her home. She could not bear to go shopping or sit down to a family dinner. Then, with the passage of time—and ever resilient—the woman who had survived poverty in Placer County, who had kept house for her Moie and Poie, who had survived two journeys North, began to feel out her footing, and grow sturdy again.

It would remain a loss. Not to have a child when one had wanted a child. But in a strange way, Clarence and Ethel seemed today—in a way they hadn't before—completely grown up. The diagnosis was definitive. Their past and their future resolved into focus. Ethel stood firm on the earth. She was thirty now. She was a Christian and she would dwell on her blessings, and she would cherish this life God had given her and make it whole.

And what a life. Alice watched from a distance as every day the Berrys' wealth and reputation rose, and at such a pace that it showed no signs of pausing, certainly not for long enough to allow on board the likes of her.

Clarence was making plans to build a second house, this one nearer the oil fields.

The *Los Angeles Herald* printed a handsome sketch of Mr. and Mrs.

Clarence Berry, after another of Clarence's acquisitions, that took up half a page.

You couldn't sit down with Clarence and Ethel for an hour alone in their garden, without some visitor barging in on his way home from the city, wanting to make his regards.

Cora stopped by Alice's house with her daughter Blanche on her way back from a ladies' church tea downtown. "Ethel came with us," Cora said, "she couldn't stop marveling at Blanche's good manners." Another day, Nellie mentioned to Alice that her older boy, Duane, had walked with Ethel to Clarence's office. He liked to sit on his uncle's knee, Nellie said, and draw pictures on his slate while Clarence attended to business. Annie and Wanlyn visited Ethel on weekends, so that Wanlyn might play Ethel's Steinway piano.

Just when Alice thought, *we're forgotten,* an invitation arrived for Melba. Clarence and Ethel wanted Melba and Nanny to join them on a two-week trip to Laguna Beach. The offer was accepted with grace, and with expectations. Alice kissed Melba's cheek. She whispered into her child's sweet little ear, cupping her face, "You're going to have fun. You're going to see the beach with your aunt and uncle."

But then the house without Melba was quiet. Too quiet. Henry, doting, moved a photograph from the mantel to Alice's desk. In this one, Melba, not quite two, was on the chaise lounge, her fat cheeks pushed up by her fat baby fists. Alice stared so deeply into the image that Bessie cooed, passing behind her, "Careful, or you'll fall in." Her baby, though. Perhaps the fact that Alice would only have one made her feel everything stronger. When Melba was born, she had dragged too much of her mother with her and, like Ethel, Alice had bled. She remembered the sopping red sheets, and Bessie and Nanny rolling them up, staining their fingernails. For seven weeks afterward, while a wet nurse tended the infant, Alice had lain half-conscious in bed, her body straining to make more of itself. When she'd finally stumbled free of that bedroom, and returned to her life, she'd done so knowing that she could never go back to that place. Another delivery would empty her out, leave her a pallid, drained corpse on the bed. Henry knew it, and had adjusted his needs to the facts.

Of all things, in this quiet and lonely house, Alice's thoughts turned to Jane.

She was like Alice. She was a mother who'd been, in a much more permanent way, cleaved from her child.

Ed Jr. A boy with a fixed, aloof expression—intelligent and headstrong, like the Lowells. Tall, healthy, and well taken care of. He'd been loved by a family, which is exactly what Jane had wanted.

A new thought took shape within Alice: Why hide?

Daisy and Ed Keller didn't want their son meeting Jane.

But since when did people take orders from Daisy and Ed? Alice thought. Since when do I?

We've been too mean, Alice thought with a jolt. At the expense of being strategic. Melba is at the beach. Clarence and Ethel adore her. My aim is nearly met. Don't shatter a perfect thing, she told herself, with malevolence.

Later, in the black night, Alice was in the same state of mind, though now the thoughts were large and chaotic. A stack of pots crashed down in the kitchen and she'd jolted awake. She thought it was Jane, a person who—thanks to the Berrys—had neither son nor brother nor fortune nor city to lose. She could see Jane: standing before the open window, swinging her arms, demanding directions to Alice Berry's room.

By morning, she was foggy and dull, but she had made a decision. She wrote to Jane:

I was wrong to keep you from your son. I will explain to his adoptive parents the necessity of a meeting.

She touched her cheek. Her face was hot. She knew why. It was the feeling of knowing she'd made a mistake. Jesus, she wondered, what have I done? If someone separated me from Melba, I would knock down men, women, children in order to grab her back. How did I not see the danger before?

8.

The trio arrived home happy and tan. The couple in love with Melba, and Melba in love with them. Alice snatched Melba up to her chest and held her cheek to cheek; she didn't let her down when she squirmed, and eventually Melba gave in, collapsing against her; this was the violent right of a mother. As for Melba's future, that was a mother's prerogative too. And here was the culmination of the journey that had begun in Selma in 1897, when Alice, hysterical, sword at her throat, had received her sister's explosive announcement of gold. Or maybe further back than that. To a time of blustery winds and candlelight in the Placer County woods, when as a starving child her own burgeoning mind had formed itself around the resolution: I will not die, I will fight against the cold, and I will live with a vengeance.

The next week, the doorbell rang when it wasn't expected, and Clarence and Ethel tumbled into the foyer, aglow. They bumped down the hallway like people who'd spent the morning saddled up to a bar. In fact they'd come straight from their lawyer's.

In the parlor, Clarence swung his briefcase onto the table and sprung the latch. He said, "Now here's something you'll want to see." He gave the bundle first to Henry, several sheets of watermarked paper. Henry read them. His eyes clouded.

"Are you sure about this, C.J.?"

"It's been in the works for weeks. No, years. Now show your wife." The gentle instructions of a king: obeyed in kind.

Alice accepted the papers. The document bore today's date. A little way down, past the general language of probate, the searing pronouncement.

Melba Berry would take the place of Clarence and Ethel's child. Her blood would be as if it had come from Clarence and Ethel. Melba would be their heir.

Alice read it and read it again.

"Well, Tot," Ethel said. "What do you think?"

"I'm overwhelmed," she answered truthfully. Then: "You told me once that you didn't want to place one niece or nephew over the others."

Clarence said, "We reconsidered."

"And you don't mind she's a girl?"

There was perhaps the slightest waver. But then Clarence answered, sure of himself, "As Ethel said at the beach, what has God been trying to tell us, by giving us Melba? She is the descendant of both our families. We can't get closer to a daughter than that."

Instead of speaking, Ethel joined Alice on the sofa. She put an arm around her, holding her close. No one else did this, held her with this female warmth. Even in their childhood, Moie had never been one for rocking her daughters, while Ethel had been a sweet little mother. "I needed time to come to terms with, you understand, with my own situation. I suppose I needed to hear once and for all that I would not bear a child. But you had Melba. You extended our family, and you have no idea how happy that makes me. I love her so much, Alice. We both do. She's everything in a daughter that Clarence and I could have imagined. She even looks like us," Ethel laughed through her tears, "if you don't mind me saying that."

"Remember coming home from the Klondike? I promised I'd share."

"And will you?"

"With all my heart."

Henry said, "This calls for a drink."

He left to search for a worthy bottle. He was nervous. The facts were too new; he needed time for their light to sink into his bones. When he left the room, a quiet fell over them.

"Speak, Alice," said Clarence. "It isn't like you to sit there with your mouth hanging open."

"Thank you." She laughed. "What can I say? Melba's a very lucky girl."

"She's a wonderful girl," said Ethel. "If we'd had a child, I truly believe she would have been just like her."

As the sisters pressed close, tears touched down on Ethel's cheek.

"Look at this," said Henry, returning with the champagne, pausing at the back of his brother's chair. "Pretty as a picture. I swear to God, I've never seen two more beautiful women in all my life."

9.

So why not be happy forever? Why not dance down the street, clicking her heels?

Because nervousness was there. Worse when Maggie burst into Alice's parlor the very next day and dropped into Alice's hands a letter from Anton.

> *Last I went to Clarence for a loan, he said go to you. Now Maggie tells me you're sending us back to Clarence. I don't appreciate getting the runaround.*

What had she been thinking in letting Maggie meet Jane? Alice's vision blurred. A bird's shadow whooshed over the desk, startling her to the back of her chair.

The nervousness was there the next day when, making good on her latest letter to Jane, Alice ordered a car and went to visit Ed Keller and Daisy at their home on the outskirts of the city, about a half-mile east of Clarence and Ethel. On the back porch, she accepted a plate of soft, half-rotten strawberries. Far away in the yard, Ed Jr. played with a bat and ball that he pitched to himself. Alice spoke artfully. This was delicate work. And made harder due to the fact that, after six years of marriage, Daisy and Ed had not had their own baby, and so valued Ed Jr. much more than they probably otherwise would have. It was strange, Alice often thought: how none of the Bush girls had inherited their mother's fecundity, though on the other hand, one could never tell the whole. In the case of the Kellers, for instance, it could be Ed who was the problem. It was even possible that he'd known of a problem before marrying Daisy, which would explain why

Ed Keller had given his adopted son his name, instead of saving it for some future boy of his own.

Alice said many things during the visit with Daisy and Ed, all which precisely followed the same line: how Ed Jr. briefly meeting his mother would benefit them, the Kellers. He was the age for it. The timing, she said, could not be more propitious. He would learn to feel gratitude for his parents, his school, his opportunities, for the parents he loved.

In that one afternoon, slowly but steadily, the Kellers came around to her way of thinking. They were straightforward, regular people. They eventually believed anyone who claimed to see the world as they did: which is to say, with themselves at the center.

10.

Alice sent Jane a letter naming the hour and telling her what to expect.

And Clarence? Surprisingly, this part was easy. He'd only needed permission. He'd wanted Jane to get her way all along. His single worry: "Ethel?"

"I told Daisy and Ed that Ethel must never know. They're fine with that. They're proud to have a secret with you."

"She'd get the wrong idea."

"That's what I think too."

They were in the yard. An old almond tree, which predated the house, sprawled over their heads. A little ways away, the three stone fish of the fountain poured taut streams of water from their open mouths into the glistening pool.

"When we started this, only Ed and Daisy were in on it." He was anxious, accusing. "Then you brought in Maggie, so Stander found out. The circle is getting awfully large."

"It stops here."

A breeze blew again and the leaves twirled, and the shadows percolated over the grass.

"There's something else we should talk about," Alice said, with less confidence. "I want to know what you think about the idea of keeping your will quiet for now. I'm worried for Melba. What the response will be from all our brothers and sisters."

"You can't have your cake and eat it too."

"Can't I?" Alice said weakly.

"Well, I already mentioned something to Frank. And Ma and Pa know."

"Do they? Already?"

"What's the matter? You keep rubbing your neck."

Alice dropped her hand.

"That's what you used to do on the claims when you were nervous," he said. "You used to be scared of me."

"You're right," she said. "I used to be afraid of you. Now I'm afraid of something else. I hardly know what." She laughed, striking a high, clear note. "Maybe I'm losing my nerve."

11.

Seven days was almost too long to wait. But finally the morning arrived. Alice met Daisy and Ed Jr. in downtown Los Angeles. On the way over, Alice had been thinking of Jane. Now she could only think of Ed Jr., and what they were doing to him. They had told Ed Jr. that his mother was dead. Now they'd told him, matter-of-factly, in truth she's alive, and here in Los Angeles, waiting to see him. They met at the corner of Spring and Fourth and crossed the road together under a thick web of cables. They stayed under the awnings when they could, as the sun today was uncovered and hot. Two trollies, a car and four carriages got into a scramble outside the Hotel Florence, and several of the pink-cheeked drivers hopped out to shout at each other. It was crowded everywhere. There was dust and noise from the construction of a new municipal building scheduled to open next year. They walked widely around the lot until a new spurt of horses and automobiles compelled them back to the sidewalk. At the next corner, they left Daisy off at Milton's Clothier, and she parted from them without kissing Ed Jr. goodbye.

Walking toward Chinatown then, through narrower streets, Ed Jr. scuffed his boots. When he spotted a stick, he picked it up, and ran it along the side of a building.

How to prepare him?

"This will be a happy day for your mother," Alice chirped. "She's waited for this moment for years."

The boy's expression revealed an undertone of alarm. They reached the building, and Ed Jr. gave the crumbling tan exterior a quick, worried glance. He was used to nicer places. He climbed the stairs like Wanlyn did, as if he were climbing a mountain. Then the door swung open and Alice found herself greeted by a woman transformed. Her hair, her clothing, but more, the life in her eyes. Jane reached out. She gripped her son by the shoulders. She said how handsome he was. Then, tentatively, she drew him into a deep embrace, squeezing her eyes shut, tilting her face to his, mouthing a prayer.

Inside, on the table between the spindle-legged chairs, there was bread, apples, cheese, and sliced meat on a platter.

And Ed Jr.? When Alice said, give a kiss to your mother, he did not protest. It was a deep relief. For once she was sure that she'd done the right thing. She even thought, of herself, watching woman and boy: What would it have been like, to have a son?

Alice said she'd come back in three hours. She wandered around Chinatown, touching piles of brightly colored fabrics, looking into crates of green vegetables then looking away, vaguely aware that people were staring. She imagined Jane stuffing clothing into a satchel, and Ed Jr. on the lookout for her. If they ran away, it would be hard on the Kellers. But maybe Clarence could find them a different child.

At the prearranged time, Alice returned to Jane's building. Ed Jr. was at the table. The lunch eaten, a toy in his hands. It was a rough brown bear cut from wood. When he saw his aunt looking, he angled it out of her sight, keeping it private.

Alice kept waiting for the explosion, but it never happened. The parting, though Jane cried, was a matter of a few simple words. A promise, from Jane, to see her son soon.

As aunt and nephew made their way through the city, Alice's eyes were stuck on Ed Jr. Perhaps he had impressed Jane, with his good looks and the breadth of his learning. His shirt and trousers were the finest that money could buy. At least you could rely on Daisy for that.

"How was it?" Alice asked.

"Fine," he said. "She said she'll come again in the fall for my birthday."

"Well, my goodness. That's news to me, but I don't see why it can't be arranged."

Alice dropped Ed Jr. off at the Kellers. Daisy was already home from her shopping, and she drew Ed Jr. jealously into their house, and declined to ask Alice in for a drink. Then, feeling energized—feeling the best she had in months—Alice thought she'd try calling on Clarence.

See how well it went, she would say, *see how there's nothing to worry about, when you hand over arrangements to me.*

She made the trip in good time. She felt in love with her life. It was completely bizarre to remember how anxious she'd been just hours ago.

The house glowed orange in the warmth of late day; the trees casting pretty shadows against the exterior.

Then she noticed two people. Coming down the stone walkway were Anton and Maggie.

As they passed Alice at the cusp of the property, Anton glared murderously at her; and Maggie, hanging on her husband's arm, smirked as she said, "Good afternoon."

A chill. If Anton was bold, if Maggie was smug, that couldn't be good for her. Alice pushed through the black iron gate.

The door to the house was open. Just inside, in the shadowy foyer, stood Ethel, her face gray and stricken and her white dress making her look like a ghost.

12.

"They came to ask Clarence for money," said Ethel. Her voice high and strained. "Clarence is downtown at his office, but I invited them in."

"Did you?" asked Alice. "You needn't have."

The gate swung closed, the latch not quite catching, while Alice stepped down the flagstone walk. At the base of the white steps, she looked up, but Ethel did not move aside to indicate that she should continue.

"They told me Jane's in Los Angeles."

Alice said nothing.

"They told me that you and Clarence arranged it. She's been here since Christmas, and Maggie's been helping. Anton says Ed Jr. is really Jane's son."

"Let me explain—"

"Clarence told me that Ed Jr. was the orphaned son of a miner. An acquaintance of his, from Forty Mile, whose wife had died. He never said Jane."

"Let me tell you the reason."

"If there's no wife and no miner, then who is the father?"

"Anton Stander is his father." Into that statement, Alice poured all conviction.

But Ethel shook her head. She started to cry. "I don't believe you."

"You have to."

"Does Clarence love her?"

"Love Jane? God, no." She was emphatic. Instinct told her to fly up the steps, though the stronger fear of Ethel recoiling prevented her. "Ethel, please. If you believe nothing else, believe this. Clarence loves you and only you. He wanted to help Jane, but only out of guilt for what happened to Jim."

"I don't know who to listen to." When Ethel uncovered her eyes, the gray gaze was cool. "Maggie told me things I can hardly believe. It has to do with something I haven't thought about in a year. My little collection of nuggets. The velvet brown pouch. Clarence always said that was the final straw. He decided to chase after Jane and Jim when he saw it was missing. But Clarence never found those nuggets. They weren't in the lean-to with the other gold. Maggie says that Jane swears on her life she didn't take them. She admits that she and Jim took the other gold, the gold from outside, but not the velvet bag. Tell me, Alice, why would Jane deny this one accusation? My nuggets were the things of least value that went missing that summer. But if I believe her denial, if it wasn't Jane, then the question becomes, who took my collection of nuggets? It was only Clarence, Henry, me, and you in the cabin that night."

"Who did—" The world tilted. Alice gripped the steps, the house, with her gaze; she felt dizzy; she needed to keep her thoughts upright. "Who did they say?" The Klondike, the frenzy, the flashes of yellow cash in gravel, the face of Jane, the face of Jim. It was vivacious, the truth, and the details were arranging themselves into a new story that she couldn't control.

"According to Maggie," Ethel said, her voice sharp over the flagstones, "Jane says it was you."

"Ethel, I can explain that too."

"Yes?"

"Clarence was putting us all in danger. Jim had stolen from us twice. That's proven. Clarence was refusing to call the Mounted Police."

"What are you saying?"

I could drop to my knees, Alice thought hazily. I could do it now. And beg for forgiveness.

"I had Henry to think of. Our neighbors."

"You did take the nuggets? Is that what you're saying?"

"Only to help."

"My God, Alice." Ethel was astonished. "A man died."

"I realize that."

"And where are my nuggets now?"

"At the bottom of the Pacific."

They did not speak. Ethel, in ghostly white lace, in the shadowy foyer.

Her round face pale as the moon; this darling, good sister. The door open, but Alice would not be walking into the house.

"I've known you all your life," Ethel said. "I held you in my arms on the day you were born, and I've loved you since that moment. My sweet little sister. When you were tiny and sick, I remember thinking that I would die of grief if you died. Do you know I've never let Clarence say a word against you? I told him once—this was the night Jim died, when Clarence was so furious with you—I said, I'll defend my sister to the death. I've been wrong, Alice."

"No." Her thoughts rebelled. Though without hope of restoring the world to the shape she liked. The Alice who'd lived inside Ethel's head was disappearing. She, the Alice standing here, of cracked expression and wrinkled conscience, against her will, was stepping in to replace her.

Ethel, leaning just slightly into the house: "I don't understand you at all."

13.

In the week that followed, Alice spent long hours in the pool of sun at her desk. Sometimes she sat for twenty minutes without moving a finger. She walked to Ethel's house. She waited in the foyer. But the maid said that Mrs. Berry couldn't come down.

One day, Clarence stopped in to settle some business matters with Henry, and she asked, in a moment they were alone together: "Are you still planning to keep Melba's standing?"

And Clarence answered, surprised: "Why wouldn't I?"

True, he blamed her for their keeping Jane away from Ed Jr., and for involving Maggie, which had resulted in the one thing he had yearned to avoid: Ethel learning about his secret history with Jane and her son. He was angry with her. Whatever intimacy had once existed between them, Alice knew she would not regain it. And yet, by this slightly baffled response alone—"Why wouldn't I?"—Alice was sure that he didn't know of the nuggets.

A different day, Henry said, "Why didn't you tell me Jane had come to Los Angeles?"

Finally, Henry also knew all. But he didn't care much; he seemed to read the years of secrecy as the silly result of his overcontrolling brother and his idiosyncratic wife. He was only afraid he looked rude, for not calling on an old acquaintance. He wondered if he and Alice could have Jane to the house. "Think of the crew from the Billiards," he said. "They would absolutely relish the chance to sit down to a four-course dinner with a genuine girl from the Klondike."

He didn't think it was a great revelation that Ed Jr. was really Jane's son.

"The Kellers have done a handsome job with him, haven't they? Little rascal that he is. And Jane must be pleased, too, with the results. The Kellers raise him, and our dear Jane is free to do as she likes. That probably suits her nature best. Very clever arrangement. Who came up with the scheme?"

In the hot spring, as her lease came to its end, Jane declared that she was ready to return to the North. Once the purchasing of the boat ticket would have fallen to Alice, to her secretarial duties. Now the job was the province of Frank Berry, who, after steadfastly refusing to return to the claims, and with Alice withdrawn, had realized his earthly dreams and stepped into the role of Clarence's right-hand man. By luck he happened to be in their house that morning. He'd come to visit, of all people, with Annie, who now was rapturous, floating from the attention. When Frank picked up his hat and cane, needing to catch the next trolley down to the docks, Alice asked to go with him.

"Why not, old girl? You look like you could do for some sun."

He had her measure. He didn't know the details, but he knew that Ethel had some quarrel with her. He could not pity her for it. Not after what had been done for her daughter. Since the writing of that will, among all the emotions that might be leveled at her in the family—barring some unspeakable tragedy—pity would never again be among them.

The docks were crowded. A persistent wind pulled at their hats. The line shuffled forward until they arrived at the window. There was passage available for March 8 on the *Equine*. But then the teller said, "Only one? And a lady? I think I have something earlier."

"Go on," said Alice, when Frank hesitated. "Cheaper and sooner, you can't beat that."

She caught sight of her own reflection in the glass. She looked worn down and embittered, like one of the old sailors milling around at her back.

The teller looked up. "One ticket for the *Silver Dollar*. It departs from this dock on March 6."

14.

Who was she? After Jane's grand departure, Alice's life felt strangely flat.

She tried to busy herself with the house, with Melba. She liked sitting snug in a chair with Melba and unpacking her best sewing basket: spools of lace, coat fasteners, ladies' buttons wrapped in silks that matched evening dresses, sequins, gems that had once ornamented a shoe, which Melba might now take for herself, to make into a brooch for her dolls.

Poppies bloomed in the yard. The birds made a racket outside her window.

Annie sang to herself as she moved through the house. Despite William Carswell's reluctance, it seemed that with pressure from the Berry family, the divorce would go through. It wasn't really fair to William. Officially, Annie was claiming abandonment, though there was good evidence that William had never done worse than long surveying trips for expanding his grocery. In any case, there was no stopping Annie now. Yesterday, she and Frank had been whispering together, and Frank had made a big show of kissing her hand. You could almost hear a faint ringing in the distance; the wedding bells of some hazy, hot church they'd all be squeezing into next year.

ON MARCH 10, THE MORNING paper arrived. It sat folded on the hall table for two hours before, walking by, Alice chanced to unroll it. The picture was of a tall boat, moored at the dock.

The *Silver Dollar* had gone down the previous night in a squall off the coast of British Columbia. It was thought to have sunk very quickly, and without much done by the crew. As of this writing, there were only twelve survivors, most of them deckhands, and none of name. The manifest had numbered three hundred and twenty. Except for the twelve, who'd reached shore on a lifeboat, all were presumed to be drowned.

WITH THE FORCE OF DYNAMITE, Alice burst from the house, gripping the paper. She could only think of finding Clarence. If there was a mistake, or other news, he might know.

She had just reached the block as Clarence emerged from the large doors of his office building, cigar in hand. When he spotted Alice, he shook free of his colleagues.

"The *Silver Dollar,*" he said thickly.

"You saw."

"Yes, and I'm distraught. We bought her the ticket."

"You think she's dead."

"The paper says as much."

"There were twelve survivors." The words a sob. "I don't know what to think. We need to find out if she lived."

"The article said, none of name."

"Clarence. Jane is not of name."

"Well, that's true now, isn't it?" Briefly, he was stunned. He stumbled, until his clumsy feet found a new platform from which to speak. "I suppose, if she's alive, we'll find out pretty soon. She'll send us a telegram."

At first Alice thought that Clarence was right, but then she felt the pull of the truth. "I actually don't think she will." A raucous group of men, taking an early lunch, passed them by, giving them breadth. "Jane was on the manifest," she said, the thought still forming. "The ticket was in her name. If she survived, if she was on that lifeboat, she'll take the opportunity to be marked as dead by the Mounted Police. That was the one thing you could never do for her, Clarence. You could never clear her name with the Mounties. She gave up her son, it scared her that much."

For some seconds, Clarence did not speak, then he shook his head. "The way you think. It amazes me."

"I need to know if she's alive or dead."

"Why do you need to know, Alice? Excuse me, but I never suspected you and Jane of being friends. I'm sorry to tell you this," he said. "But you're raving. Why can't you leave poor ol' Jane alone?"

Why? Why couldn't she?

It was true. And she was horrified. Was her mind so narrow? Did she only know how to scurry? Like when Clarence had said, in San Francisco, speaking of his Klondike fortune, "I'm going to buy more stuff." Was it possible that she, too, only knew this one game?

"Listen. It's awful and there's no getting around that. But what can be done? Go home. Try to be tranquil."

"Tranquil?" She lowered herself to a stone ledge that ran alongside the building. She stuck out her legs, her pale leather boots. Even her boots looked odd. "I'm afraid I don't know how to be that."

"Then you know what I'll do?" Clarence said. "I'll have Ethel pick you up in the car. She's out of her mind over Jane. When I left her this morning, she was doubled over in a kitchen chair, crying her heart out."

"Was she?"

"Of course. She was Jane's employer after all."

"They hardly spent a minute together."

"That's not true. Jane used to bring Ethel her tea every morning. Now you listen to me, Alice," he continued, turning appraising eyes on her. "I know it's been a hard stretch for you sisters, and I don't understand it, but enough is enough. You've stopped having your chats and outings like you used to, and I think you both are the worse for it." Clarence patted her leg. "You didn't forget this weekend's Ethel's birthday, did you? You two better find a way to make up."

15.

Alice walked home, her boots catching on every misaligned stone. Her thoughts were in the boat. Jane in a low cabin on the *Silver Dollar*. A tiny compartment. A frail bunkmate sobbing that she could not swim. The water rising. Jane clawing the bed, the walls. Jane sucking for air, one last gasp, before the water enveloped her and met in a lapping and fatal seal with the ceiling.

She touched her own throat, feeling the want. A carriage careened around the corner, its polished black side passing an inch from her face. A yell from the driver gliding away from her, "Lady, watch out!"

Then, stumbling clear of the street, Alice saw something else. Jane alert. Shooting up from the depths of her cabin. Fighting her way down a narrow corridor and pushing other passengers back. Jane throwing herself into the throng of rowdy mutineers, who are loosening a set of ropes, unwilling to go down with the ship. Jane in a lifeboat. The wind and rain beating her face. Jane tumbling onto the bank, her boots gone, her stomach and chest slapping the earth, digging her elbows into the land, dragging herself forward, clutching the grass to heave herself free of the ocean, her wide, joyous mouth kissing the mud.

She imagined Jane in a dry room. Wrapped in a thick wool blanket.

What Alice wanted to do was to pick up a blanket and throw it over Jane. But the minutes crawled on in this infinite day. And still, the facts of the day, and Jane, were stronger.

At home, Henry was bouncing Melba high on his knees. Bessie and Nanny were cleaning pots in the kitchen. They did not know. The newspaper with its outrageous headline had flown out of the house with her.

"This is the way the lady rides, *trit-trot, trit-trot*."

Alice stepped into the foyer. It was possible this life was not her life. Or rather, that this was not the life she should be living. That her mind had, at some early and vulnerable moment, been poisoned, and grown from that point forward in this grotesque and distorted form.

In the house, they saw her. Melba slid from Henry's lap.

"Here," Henry said, patting his daughter's bottom, "go bother your mother."

Melba ran screaming at her, caught her skirts, clawed at them, then, receiving no reaction, continued on to Wanlyn, who was on the third stair, lacing her boots.

A problem: Alice lifted the blanket to throw it over Jane and the blanket grew to the size of the house, to the size of the sky, and covered them all. And here was Henry, winking at her. And here was Ethel, with Alice's heart in her hands. Here was Jane, both alive and dead, voluptuous within the shadow, as intimate as one more sister, her arms spread in a welcome embrace.

"Alice?" Henry said. "What's the matter?"

She didn't answer. She heard a car rumbling up to the curb.

She went to the door and saw that it was the Berry car, with a blurred, stiff, feminine form on the back bench. Clarence really had sent Ethel to her.

"I want to go for a ride," Wanlyn exclaimed.

Melba, jostling forward, "And me!"

"Shush," said Alice, with a malice that abruptly silenced the children. "You're both staying here."

She flew off the step and down the walk. She opened the car door without waiting for the driver to get out and do it. She sang "Happy early birthday to you" in a straining falsetto until Ethel, her expression steadfast, admonished her for being bawdy and blushed.

"Where to?" the driver asked, pulling free from the house.

"To the ocean," Alice said, glancing nervously at her sister. "We could both do with a hearty dose of clean air."

In Los Angeles, a person could move with speed. They were racing along new streets, past restaurants, a bank, the skeletal beginnings of buildings, all blessed by the day's searing sun. Ethel was in a gray dress. Her collar taut at her neck. The flower brooch at her bosom, ruby and amethyst, slicing and parceling light.

"You heard about the *Silver Dollar*?" Alice asked.

"Of course."

"And?"

"And what? It's a tragedy."

Ethel's hands curled over her purse, eyes ahead. She was only here because Clarence had forced her to come.

Alice reached out, terrified of an outright rejection, but took her sister's hand in hers.

"So much wrong has happened between us, darling," Alice said quietly. "But I want to set it right. I ask your forgiveness."

Silence. Then Ethel said, "How dare you ask me for anything."

The words were filled with plain dislike. And Alice was startled.

Ethel continued: "Of course I have my own regrets. There was jealousy, for whatever might have happened between Jane and Clarence. I've had bitter thoughts. But I'm embarrassed of them. We were so cruel to Jane."

"Not really," said Alice. "I object to that. We were doing our best. She didn't make it easy."

"Alice, do you hear yourself?" Ethel turned to her, finally, and her face was flushed. "You have everything, and still you're dissatisfied. You sit here begrudging a small kindness to a woman who's dead."

"You're right. I'm sorry."

"Don't try to pretend." Briefly Ethel closed her eyes; she seemed to be collecting her strength. Then: "When I heard Jane's ship went down, do you want to know what I thought? It's an ugly, ludicrous idea that struck me."

"Go on."

"I'm almost afraid to tell you this, but my thought was, it was Alice. *Alice* sank the ship. I know it's insane, but that's where my mind went."

Too much. Too crushing. Forget Jane. What Alice longed to do was to force time to double back to how they'd been before. When Ethel sent the telegram to Selma and plucked Alice from the scorched yellow and weed-strewn farm and named her as the person who must travel along at her side. Or else to the time when Ethel had needed her, the mother of Melba, to bring her joy.

"I can't sink ships."

"I said it was silly."

"But you love me." Alice's hand reached for Ethel's again. "You have to. My life will only make sense if you do. Monster or no, I am your sister. We've been through so much together. Imagine if we could have seen a glimpse of this life when we were girls. We never would have believed it."

The engine roared, straining over the bumps. In a span of minutes, the city had given way to poppies and lupines bright on the hills. Then the car rose with the road. It traced over the earth that for a millennium forward, if not forever, would be called California.

"You have to love me," Alice said, leaning closer to Ethel, relentless, like everything in her life had taught her to be.

She squeezed her sister's hand, almost smiling now, no matter Ethel's efforts to pull away.

"Look in my eyes. You cannot help but love me."

They reached the hill's crest. Alice speaking. Ethel facing ahead.

A wide swath of ocean appeared beneath the swath of sky. While at their backs, like something cinched to their necks, was the whole of their country.

13

DAWSON CITY, YUKON

2015

My grandfather was an old man who was cheated out of his money. You couldn't feel too sorry for him. First of all, it happened when he was ninety-three, past the age when he could fully feel the effect. Second of all, it was money that had been earned through cheats in the first place. The wealth had dropped into his hands, gifted to him by his own mother and grandparents and great-uncle and -aunt. Except for his five years of Naval service and his dabbling involvement with the family business, he hadn't held down a conventional job in his life. What right did he or any one of his children or grandchildren have to say that the money belonged to them? And where is the profit, in being angry about it?

He was not doing well. He was on the floor. And then, amid the chaos, Uncle Mike, Aunt Kelly, and my two little cousins, Craig and Kelly's kids, a boy and a girl in neon-green baseball hats, had the bad timing to arrive into the doorway of the Sourdough Saloon at this terrible moment. Grandpa was on his back, gasping and afraid, with a balled-up jacket under his head. A nurse, the only medical worker in town, was kneeling on the floor beside him, talking rapidly into her phone, arranging to have him airlifted from Dawson.

Once everyone had fully absorbed the emergency taking place in front of our eyes, Uncle Mike pushed forward and knelt at his father's shoulder and launched into a heated exchange with his brother, over who would board the plane with their father to Anchorage. It ended up being Uncle Craig, the oldest, who would not back down; to the point that, even after the matter was settled, he kept repeating to all who'd lend an ear, red in the face and overwrought (and still undone, I was sure, by his humiliating interaction with Rhett, who by this point was nowhere to be found) that his father was not leaving Dawson City without him.

Within the hour, I was standing on a dirt road with Owen as the silver plane, with my grandfather and Uncle Craig and two medical technicians inside it, whisked upward and was swallowed into the massive sky, like a needle disappearing into a blue fold of fabric. It hit me only then that I hadn't really said goodbye to my grandfather, that the logistics of getting him out had kept all sentiment at bay, though now, in the sudden quiet, I felt a heavy shock, and grief rising into my throat.

My uncle, aunt, cousins, Owen, and I passed the rest of that day and the next very awkwardly. We saw the show at Diamond Tooth Gerties. We brought my cousins around town, indulging their whims: visiting the Jack London cabin, the Robert Service cabin, feeding them fried salmon, French fries, and moose tracks ice cream for lunch.

I had texted Leanne what had happened, and she wanted updates. When I told her the news from Uncle Craig, that Grandpa was hospitalized, in the ICU, and certainly would not be returning here, and also that Owen and I would be imminently heading back to Los Angeles, she asked us to come to her house as soon as we could.

The screen door banged open, and there was Leanne, pushing the dogs back with her legs. She worried aloud that all the activity from the last several days had caused my grandfather too much anxiety.

"Rhett was the one who upset him," I said, as Owen and I followed her to the back of the house. I filled her in about the power of attorney, about the fight at the bar between Rhett and my uncle.

We joined Winnie at the kitchen table, and Leanne served iced tea and caprese sandwiches, though it was all I could do to force down a few bites. After a short while, Leanne disappeared into the other room, and reemerged holding a small, cardboard box.

"If it's not too much right now, I have a few family treasures I thought you should see. I had them ready for when Peter arrived. But with all the chaos over the money, I never got the chance." She lifted a small frame from the box and passed it to Owen and me. "I can't remember the last time I'd looked at this."

It was a black-and-white photograph of Jane. She stood on a dock, leaning against a pier. She was alone. Her hat was crisp. Her dress bright against the expanse of rippling ocean behind her. Her expression was happy and lively, if a little bit wavering, a little bit stunned.

"Remember this one, Mom?" Leanne said.

Winnie squinted as I handed over the photograph. She brought it close to her eyes.

"Oh, yes," Winnie said, smiling. "Of course I do. My grandmother used to carry this picture around in her purse. She'd just survived a shipwreck when this was taken. She used to tell people she had to keep taking it out and checking it, to prove to herself she was alive."

"Wait. Was that in 1904?" My thoughts were cutting to something in Alice's letters.

"I think it was."

"I read about that shipwreck!" I took the photograph back from Winnie and gazed again with even deeper interest. "Alice mentioned it. The *Silver Dollar.* The Berrys didn't know if Jane had survived or not."

"She survived," Leanne answered, with satisfaction. "She was one of only a handful of people who made it to shore. The deckhands tried to keep her from getting into the lifeboat, but she fought them off for all she was worth. At one point while they were rowing to land, one of the men felt the bump of her wallet, and ripped her dress down, trying to get it.

Can you believe that? In the middle of this storm, when they didn't know if they'd live or die, one of these men tried to rob her." Leanne shook her head in disbelief. "As soon as she felt the boat brushing against the reeds, she jumped out. She waded to the shore alone in the dark. Half swimming, half walking. She lay down on the bank until morning, catching her breath. She said it was an experience that changed her forever. After she survived that, she said that she wasn't afraid of anything. Speaking of which." Leanne brought out a second photograph. "Here. This is the only photograph that exists of my grandfather and his mother together."

In the picture, Jane had her arm slung around the shoulders of a young man. It was Winnie's father: Ed Jr. For me, it was a surprising image, one that leapt past the history I knew from the Berry journals and letters.

"When did Ed Jr. come North to live with his mom?" I asked.

"A couple years after the shipwreck. His adopted parents had enrolled him in a boarding school in Washington State. The Collins School. Very prestigious. Lots of rich people went there."

"So he liked it?" Owen asked.

"He never put a foot in the building," Winnie corrected. "Jane met him on the steps outside. They just walked away."

For a second, no one spoke. As for myself, I was imagining Jane and Ed Jr., mother and son, together on a long incline of pale steps in the sun, taking hands, turning their backs on the tall school and the throngs of students and desks and teachers inside: walking into a different life.

"He loved his mother," Leanne said, reading my thoughts. "But you know. Life was hard on my grandfather. He was very intelligent, a very gifted engineering mind. He knew he would have done well at that school and begun a career. He probably could have asked Clarence for help when he was older, but he was too proud."

"Do you think the Berrys would have helped him?" I asked, half-attentive, still gazing into the photograph.

"Maybe," Leanne said. "According to Jane, Clarence was Ed's biological father."

My eyes flew to Leanne's. She seemed to both anticipate and take satisfaction in my surprise. "*Your* family," she added, "never believed that."

"I've seen hints in Alice's papers," I answered swiftly. "Of course she hated the idea. She was afraid of anything that could threaten her daughter's estate."

"My father used to say of the Berrys," Winnie cut in. "That's the family that robbed us twice. First by putting stakes in our land. Second by casting me off."

Gently, I put down the photograph. Exhilaration was building in me—a defiance against I didn't know what. "Let's prove it," I said. I lifted my bare forearm: ready to proffer my blood. "We can order a couple of those DNA tests. We'll have the results in a month."

Winnie looked at her daughter. Owen and I did too. I was eager. I thought Leanne would agree to it, though a second later I saw a boldness—a defiance different from mine—growing within her too.

"A month from now is just about a hundred and fifteen years too late," Leanne said. "What can it do for Jane and my grandfather now? What can it do for Jim?"

"But for us," I said. "Wouldn't it be interesting to know—"

"No. Your grandfather is interested in rewriting his family story, giving it a nice coda. But the more I think about it, the less I agree with what he was trying to do. I don't like people using their wealth to put a new gloss on the past. One that's best of all for themselves."

Then startlingly, Leanne's expression, which had been grave, relaxed. She leaned back in her seat and looked at her mother, and a communication passed between them—a joke—which Owen and I were not invited to join. What Leanne said next were not the last words of that afternoon, though they are the ones that stuck with me long after:

"Listen to me, I'm still talking about the Berry money. But according to our own accountant, there isn't money available. In 1898, your family stormed North and dug a fortune out of our land. You come back to Dawson City in 2015, and in a matter of—what has it been, four days?—it's starting to look like that whole gold rush fortune is gone."

14

CALIFORNIA

2015

As for my grandfather, teetering at the brink of existence, insentient to these conversations, he did not want to die. Ninety-three or not, of any use to the human world or not, deserving or not. But in defiance of his wishes, he was losing power, like a character in an early video game, becoming transparent in front of everyone's eyes.

My mother flew across the country to meet him. She found him in his hospital bed, gaunt and immobile, with a tube delivering a thin stream of oxygen into his nose. Several weeks into that stay, he went in for a procedure to drain an excess of fluid from around his heart. It was supposed to be the first in a series of interventions to make him more comfortable. "He put up a hand to say goodbye," my mother said on the phone, one Tuesday in August, more stunned than aggrieved. "They rolled him through the doors, and he never came out." No one had asked his permission. No one had asked him to sign the paperwork and agree to the contract. The way science is headed, maybe even in such a desperate circumstance, the rich will be able to buy their way out of death: although, for better or worse, we aren't there yet.

Wife Number Six and Rhett were in Anchorage also. They weren't inside the hospital when my grandfather died, but they arrived soon after, and said their goodbyes to his body and collected his watch, valued in the mid-five-figures. It was only a taste of things to come. Wife Number Six and her sons had already been using the power of attorney to its fullest effect. During the time that my grandfather was hospitalized, accounts disappeared, properties that everyone assumed had been jointly owned ended up in the names of Rhett and his brother. The power of attorney did not grant Wife Number Six the liberty to rewrite her husband's will. But because of certain loopholes, for instance, directing that the Berry Oil stock would be split among his biological children, but without stipulating the numbers, the mother and sons had simply sold the stock off in large batches, until there was almost nothing left to dispense.

Whether or not this was legal, whether his signature was fraudulently obtained, is currently the subject of an ongoing lawsuit, brought against my grandfather's widow by the united group of his six biological children. If my side of the family wins, one boon among many will be that my grandfather's last act, his donation to the Cultural Center, will be allowed to proceed. Though whether there'll be anything left of my grandfather's ravaged estate, once it's been invoiced by the lawyers on both sides, is every day becoming increasingly doubtful.

All of which is connected to the fact that, in August, when the bill for my semester's tuition appeared on my student account, it stopped the air in my throat. My lifeline—my grandfather's financial backing—was gone. All of a sudden the bill was what it always had been: exorbitant, criminal. It threatened to crush the future that meant everything to me. Owen helped me while I worked through the numbers, though with the weariness of a person who has for years lived in the trenches of this particular war. Eventually I did what everyone does: I put in my application for a massive loan, the first of many, to cover my tuition and living expenses.

That was a bad moment for me, and it took until the autumn months before I could reflect again on that swift and disastrous trip to the Klondike in a calmer state of mind. I did my best to let go of what could have been, and what I could have done differently. As time went on, too, I was able again to think of my grandfather, just as himself, in ways unrelated to the fortune he'd lost. In fact I noticed it had become the case that, whenever my grandfather's face came into my head, it was with the grand and luxurious backdrop of the Ahwahnee Hotel. So much so that, when my check from the estate arrived in the mail in October, a hair over ten thousand dollars, a tremendously modest sum compared to what it could have been, I announced to Owen that—after our own penitent donation to the Hän Hwëch'in Cultural Center—I wanted to blow at least five hundred dollars on a one-night stay in Yosemite, in a final tribute to my grandfather.

Owen was against it. He thought it was not only unwise, but depressing, and it wasn't until we were walking into the lobby, with its dark, stately furniture and grand lodge-style architecture, and, for a flickering instant, my eyes jumped to the entranceway of the gift store, as if expecting my grandfather to stride into view, his arms loaded with presents for us, that I realized Owen had anticipated, correctly, what I hadn't wanted to see.

Grief choked me. Peter Bailey had been by no measure a perfect person. But he'd been mine, my grandfather. And I was sad he was gone. Owen and I dressed up for dinner, Owen in his best suit, which he'd worn at our wedding, I in a dress and heels and makeup to rearrange the palette of a face that had been, after a day in the car, flushed and streaked by the sun.

In the large, opulent dining room, we ordered dutifully from the menu, intimidated by the prices, although I'd earlier insisted to Owen that we should get what we wanted, the money no object. I felt in the company of ghosts. People like the Ahwahneechee, but also the people who'd been here two thousand years ago, maybe seven or eight thousand years ago, people who had walked and slept and foraged food and raised children and stood on this spot looking up at the stars.

When the check arrived, in its large leather pouch, Owen and I let it sit for a second, perhaps expecting a vaporous hand, with godly credit, to swoop down from between the dark chandeliers and whisk it away.

This time, when we left the dining room, we walked to the cozy bar together: with its giant hearth and large crackling fire, and a collection of self-satisfied patrons lounging deep into the couches. The last time we were here, my grandfather had sat on one of these barstools with Owen. It seemed impossible. Impossible, even, that my life had overlapped with his life, a person so old-fashioned that he'd thought it inappropriate for a young woman to have a drink at a bar after dinner.

"In the best-case scenario," I said to Owen, as we accepted our glasses, and with the black night framed by the window beside us, the low hoots of an owl reverberating beneath the noises of the inside, "you and I are still doing this in fifty years. Happy, healthy, sitting together in a warm, beautiful room with a beautiful landscape outside the window."

"Cheers," Owen said, clinking my drink.

"We'll be old," I said. "And that's if we're lucky."

"Didn't I tell you the good news?" Owen said, lowering his glass to the glossy bar. "You and I are going to be the exception to nature. We're going to live to be a hundred and ten, but without looking or feeling a day over thirty."

THAT NIGHT, I BARELY SLEPT. When the alarm went off at seven, I felt tired, disoriented, though I struggled to hide it. After breakfast, I peeked into the gift store again, still feeling the ghost of my grandfather there. I told Owen I wanted to look for a second. Here was the rack of postcards, the Native American pottery I remembered so well. Also: the homeware, drums, dream catchers, Kachina dolls, T-shirts, turquoise and silver jewelry behind locked glass panels.

"You want something?" Owen asked, walking up from behind me, glancing up from his phone.

I was running my hand along a wool blanket, arranged to show off bold colors and patterns.

"It's nice. We don't have anything like that."

But I drew back my touch. "No," I said. My head felt heavy. My thoughts were rolling back to reality. The cell phone bill starred in my inbox; the coming months of our lease.

Beside the cashier's desk was a stack of free hiking maps on a plexiglass stand. I grabbed one as we were walking out. I joked to Owen, waving it at him:

"This is perfect. This will be my souvenir."

The map actually proved very useful. There was an ongoing study site in the park, having to do with the removal of invasive plant species, which didn't seem too hard to get to. We exited into the mild weather, the morning light, the air that was thick with the sounds of birds. I flipped the map over. On the back was a list of rules for visitors. I said, forcing a spirited tone:

"They have guidelines for how to behave at the park. Should I read them?"

"Sure," Owen said, squinting into the sun, adjusting the straps of his backpack.

"A lot of people could set their life by these," I said. "And be the better for it."

We crossed the hotel lawn and started on the trail that would lead us, in addition to the study site on invasive flora, past a crystal-clear waterfall that, judging from the online reviews, was well worth the trek.

"The first guideline," I said, "is 'Plan Ahead.' Map out your trip in advance and pack what essentials you'll need for the journey."

"Check," he said, patting his backpack.

"'Leave a Light Footprint,'" I read next. "'Limit the waste you create. Don't take anything with you. Take only pictures. Every flower, plant, and every rock should be left in its place. You are not at liberty to disrupt it for your personal enjoyment.'"

Owen nodded, with what I suspected, from his shining eyes, the curl of his mouth, was a put-on solemnity.

"The next," I continued, in a lightly warning tone, "is 'Knowledge Is Power. Your safety and the safety of others depends on your being well-informed.'"

"Got it," said Owen, grinning. "I hope."

"Now here's the last one," I said, glaring at him. "It's the most important, so pay attention. If only the whole world could agree. If only this simple thing weren't so difficult."

"Okay. Let's hear it."

"The last guideline for visitors is, 'Always be Considerate.'"

"Right," Owen said, "unfortunately, we have trouble with that one."

He laughed as he took a big step, and a round, yellow warbler leapt from the trail, straight into the branches over our heads. He laughed again, and this time I joined him, folding the map and tucking it into my back pocket.

We walked for miles that day. Not only to the study site and the review-approved waterfall, which cooled us inside its tall cloud of mist, but also along circuitous routes, to places and sites that we hadn't deliberately planned for. The grooved cliffs. The sky striped with long white clouds. A vast and extremely flat pool of water. The green upon green of swaying and rotating leaves and lush pine needles like a maze for the eyes. It was possible to feel time's largeness here, and also the present that seemed tactile and alive in its own animal way. Here it is, I thought, taking the moment in. There it was.

ACKNOWLEDGMENTS

During the writing of this book, I relied on countless sources. To list each one would be too much, but I owe particular gratitude to the memoir written by Alice Bush, *The Bushes and the Berrys*, as well as to Pierre Berton's *Klondike: The Last Great Gold Rush, 1896–1899*. As for the other archives that informed these pages—everything from the maps at the Geography and Map Reading Room at the Library of Congress to the family stories recorded online by Joy Isaac and her relatives—my thanks to those who believe in the unceasing work of recording the past.

For a greater understanding of the history of the Bush-Berry family in California, I am indebted to Chris Goode, Betsy Lumbye, and Randy McFarland. Randy is almost single-handedly responsible for preserving the Berry family letters, and his work in documenting Selma's first decades made the place vivid to me from the start. My gratitude to the Fulbright Foundation, which funded my travel to the Yukon when this novel was in its earliest stages. During my time there, I was lucky to meet many curators of history and cultural memory at the Dawson City Museum and the Dänojà Zho Cultural Center. Both institutions were essential to my understanding and fascination with the region, and compelling to me in their own right.

More recently, I am immensely grateful for the generous guidance and insightful reads of Glenda Bolt and Fran Morberg-Green, both of the Dänojà Zho Cultural Center. Thank you for sharing your knowledge, for allowing me to ask questions, and for creating and granting me use of the name Hän Hwëch'in Cultural Center, which I hope in these pages reflects the excellence of the original. While this book only looks with an outsider's perspective at the immense history of the First Nations peoples in the Yukon, I hope that these glimpses show the damage done by the influx of prospectors during the gold rush, and do justice to the vibrancy and historical work being done by so many people today.

I am enormously thankful for the creative, talented people I have the honor to work with at Union Literary and William Morrow, especially: Sally Wofford-Girand, Molly Mittelbach, Emily Fisher, Kaitlin Harri, Ariana Sinclair, Nancy Singer, Ploy Siripant, and Taylor Turkington. Thank you to Virginia Norey for diving into long-ago geographies and creating a map that makes it all clear. To the readers and supporters of my early drafts, Ben Thompson, Alicia Oltuski, Lindsey Palmer, Anne Stameshkin, Celeste Ng, and Marissa Perry, I am lucky, always, to have you as my brilliant friends.

Thank you to Jenni Ferrari-Adler, who knew what this novel was about before I hardly knew myself, accompanied me on the long road to making this book, swore we would make it, and put a hand to my back when the walking was steep. Thank you to Liz Stein for swooping into this book at a critical moment, setting sharp eyes upon this story, asking the right questions, and pointing the way through obstacles of my own making. Every page is better for having been in her hands, and I am so grateful.

The Bushes, the Berrys, Jane, and many others did not give me permission to borrow from their lives. They were all extraordinary people, and I am thankful for the imprints that they left upon the historical record. I hope they would condone what I have done here: I rewrote their lives as fictions, but every word chases their essences.

Thank you to my grandfather, Peter Bennett, who was my bridge to the past during the thirty-three years that our lives overlapped. When he was in his nineties, he sat down with me for a series of interviews. Not only did his retelling of family stories shed light on bygone eras, but his way of talking and telling a tale were also the best time capsules that a writer can ask for. He inspired the character of Peter here, though his circumstances and his personal life were different. He lived a long life and to his credit, even in his later years, did his best to keep growing up.

All my thanks again to my parents, Gregory Djanikian and Alysa Bennett, and to my in-laws Howie and Joan Sandick, and to Zach Djanikian, my brother and friend. Thank you to Jesse Blatt, whose conversation and company I so deeply miss. Thank you to Phil, my first reader always and from the very beginning; who is with me on every adventure and makes the adventure a joy. Elaina and Nathaniel remind me every day of the mystery and value of each individual life, and why I work to capture in words even a wisp of those landscapes.

ABOUT THE AUTHOR

Ariel Djanikian holds an MFA in fiction from the University of Michigan and is the author of *The Office of Mercy*. Her work has been published in *Tin House, The Paris Review, The Rumpus, The Millions,* and elsewhere. She has received a Fulbright and a Hopwood, among other awards. She teaches at Georgetown University and lives near Washington, DC, with her family.